Buzz Kill

Also by Jeff Jacobson

Sleep Tight
Growth

Buzz Kill

Jeff Jacobson

LYRICAL UNDERGROUND
Kensington Publishing Corp.
www.kensingtonbooks.com

LYRICAL UNDERGROUND BOOKS are published by

Kensington Publishing Corp.
119 West 40th Street
New York, NY 10018

All Kensington titles, imprints, and distributed lines are available at special quantity discounts for bulk purchases for sales promotion, premiums, fund-raising, educational, or institutional use.

Special book excerpts or customized printings can also be created to fit specific needs. For details, write or phone the office of the Kensington Sales Manager: Kensington Publishing Corp., 119 West 40th Street, New York, NY 10018. Attn. Sales Department. Phone: 1-800-221-2647.

Lyrical Underground and Lyrical Underground logo Reg. US Pat. & TM Off.

First Electronic Edition: September 2022
ISBN: 978-1-60183-494-2 (ebook)

First Print Edition: September 2022
ISBN: 978-1-60183-495-9

Printed in the United States of America

"I own that I cannot see as plainly as others do, and as I should wish to do, evidence of design and beneficence on all sides of us. There seems to me too much misery in the world. I cannot persuade myself that a beneficent and omnipotent God would have designedly created the Ichneumonidae with the express intention of their feeding within the living bodies of caterpillars, or that a cat should play with mice."
—Charles Darwin, in a letter to American Naturalist Asa Gray, 1860

"Fuck you."
—Every wasp, ever

PROLOGUE

John Anderson was scared. Scared of a lot of things. Scared of a million things, really.

But mostly scared something was seriously wrong with his son.

Of course something was wrong with him. There was absolutely no doubt of that. John was just scared that whatever it was, it was something the doctors back home couldn't fix. John had seen what had happened, and it wasn't anything natural.

It was… unholy.

He had seen the abomination crawling over the infant. Had seen that awful stinger thing or whatever, poised and quivering, and the sudden strike. Had heard his son's awful, piercing scream, then the abrupt silence.

Despite everything, all the death, all the horror from the village, the desperate flight along the road of mud through the endless jungle to the city of Tegucigalpa, God's will had shown through, and his son was alive.

Baby Matthew was sleeping, but he was alive.

At first, there had been an uneasy relief. Their baby was only sleeping. That's all. He was still breathing. Then, the discovery they could not wake him up. No matter how much they screamed, pleaded, or even   God help them—slapped him.

He would not open his eyes.

That's when John made the decision to seek medical help back home.

* * * *

And here in the Honduras's Toncontín International Airport, John was also scared the stone-faced customs officials would notice. That he would clearly see that something was wrong with the Andersons' baby. That the official would discover their treachery, and then he would put them all in some sort of wretched, third world quarantine.

Or even worse, the officials would think that he and his wife, Shelley, were trying to trick them. That these emissaries of Christ were trying to smuggle drugs inside of their baby somehow, trying to sneak something back to the States.

This idea of being persecuted for his faith, it was ridiculous. He knew that. But fear didn't listen to reason.

The customs line edged forward. John resisted the urge to shift the baby carrier to his left hand and tried not to think about how the History Channel had ranked the Toncontín the second most dangerous airport in the world. He forced himself to breathe slowly, inhale through his nose, exhale through the mouth. This only made the aromas of the airport worse.

All around them, bodies seethed and roiled as if they were all one giant organism, reeking of sweat, fresh pineapples, sweet Honduras peppers, and fried iguana. John knew it was not their fault. In fact, it was precisely this ignorance of the one true Lord, this unclean state of being, this chaos, all of it, which had drawn Shelley and John to the vast wildness of the Mosquitia jungle to share the joy of Christ's saving graces with the pagan tribes who still hid from the enlightened twentieth century.

John was also scared his wife was losing her mind.

Shelley couldn't stand still. She kept rocking, back and forth, repeating, "God is peace, God is love," in a kind of singsong, breathless chant, constantly fingering the crucifix at her neck. "God is peace," on the inhale, "God is love," on the exhale.

The Anderson family had been sent to seek out the Cáceres, a small tribe in a remote, mountainous region. The location not simply difficult to reach, but more or less impossible without a guide and definitely impossible to reach during the rainy season. While most had never actually seen anyone from the tribe, many had heard grim stories and knew enough to never seek them out. When rumors of the tribe reached the desk of Reverend William "Big Willie" Johnson, the inaccessibility was irresistible. He knew the video footage and photos would be the crown jewel in his distinguished decades of service to the Lord. He blessed the mission with the deep resources of his megachurch, the Kingdom of Faith Christian Center, arming John with professional-grade video cameras, modern pharmaceuticals, freeze-dried food, a very large bribe for a guide, and fifty English Bibles. A tad expensive, but a small investment in what he hoped would be next summer's lucrative fundraising Cornerstones from Christ campaign.

John and Shelley also saw their missionary work as not only an investment in their future, as they hoped to settle into a comfortable life within their church back home, but as their true calling in spreading the word of God, the message of Christ's sacrifice to the darkest corners of the globe. They'd been missionaries in Guatemala, Papua New Guinea, Tanzania. And now, Honduras.

Except this time, they brought their newborn son. For their last mission. But God had not protected him.

Although, as John was quick to reason with himself, God's protection was absolutely not demonstrated in any way that he could understand. The old cliché was true. No one could deny that God and his universe spun in mysterious ways. This outlook of John's, his Job-like optimism, his resourcefulness, his relentless cheerfulness, his spirit, his talent in capturing the poor, unwashed indigenous people on video, all of it had been recognized and rewarded within his church.

And yet, for a man who had perhaps never truly felt the insidious cancer of self-doubt, John found himself under attack from a growing panic that he was defying God by taking his son back to Alabama and trusting him in the medical care of his homeland. In all his twenty-nine years, he had never, ever doubted his Lord.

He just prayed that the official would let them pass.

Because beneath all that fear, buried deep beneath the surface panic as they moved slowly through the line at customs, on their way back home—back to their church, their sanctuary of serenity, their oasis of comfortable predictability, where nothing truly awful happened, where nature was kept in check, barricaded safely behind concrete and stout fences—John was scared that his faith wouldn't be enough to save their son.

He was scared their God had abandoned them.

* * * *

The customs official barely glanced at Matthew.

John was now scared his son was no longer breathing. He hadn't looked at him in the last few minutes stretching up to the customs official as the line slowly unspooled, passengers either passing along into terminal 1 or being sent back for additional travel documents. He'd been worried that checking on his baby would seem neurotic, too nervous.

John wondered if he could see contempt in the official's blank eyes. Their trip to Honduras had been neither business nor pleasure. How do you explain spiritual fulfillment to a bureaucratic cog in a soulless—Catholic at best, perhaps pagan at worst—government? How do you explain the call for evangelical Christians to spread the word of the Gospel? How do you explain the hunger of the very soul to share the joy of Christ?

Shelley had stopped mumbling her prayer and grew still, except for breathing in hitched and ragged sniffles in the stilted cadence of the chant.

The customs official, a small man with deep vertical lines crinkling his lips into a permanent sour outlook on life, glanced wordlessly at the missionaries and their baby. He rolled his stamp between the first and second fingers of his right hand like an angry cigarette. He waited for John to say something.

John gave his most benevolent smile. His wife stopped rubbing her necklace and looked down at her other hand tracing the cover of the baby carrier. Their son lay quietly inside.

Asleep.

The customs official waited until John's eyes crept back up and made contact. The small, dark man waited an eternity, then stamped their three passports in six rolling movements, smacking the ink in sudden barking gestures that made John flinch. It reminded him of the hideous, nearly obscene spasms of the horror in the middle of the jungle.

The customs official slapped the passports down, waved them through.

John nodded his thanks, took the baby carrier from his wife, and they walked through the airport and thirty minutes later, they climbed aboard Céntrico flight number 87, a nonstop flight from Tegucigalpa to Miami. There, the Andersons would hop into a church van, and be delivered home.

* * * *

They'd been in the air fifteen minutes when the captain turned off the seat belt sign. John swallowed, tried not to vomit. He couldn't put off examining his son any longer. He jerked the baby carrier out of the seat between him and his wife and headed for the bathroom. Shelley's eyes never left the window, blankly staring at nothing as the edges of Tegucigalpa were swallowed by unforgiving jungle. The shock of the last eighteen hours was hitting her hard.

John found himself wishing that Shelley would just give up, and simply trust in Xanax or Valium instead of merely Jesus. He was worried that the

old adage about the Lord not giving you more than you can carry was…
misguided.

If not absolutely wrong.

* * * *

The light in the airplane restroom was severely inadequate. At least it was enough that he could see that young Matthew was still breathing. Thank God on His eternal throne for small favors. John lifted his son out of the carrier and laid him on the foldout diaper-changing table.

Matthew reacted to the cold, stiff plastic by clenching a pudgy left fist and breathing faster. For a moment, he looked like any other infant, caught in the stages between waking and alert. His head rolled absentmindedly back and forth; he whined deep in his chest.

John unsnapped the cotton one-piece outfit. Once white with cheerful steam trains chugging around, it was now stained with sweat and dust and blood. Shelley would never have allowed him to remain in such filthy clothing, but she hadn't touched him in hours. John pulled the fabric off his son and recoiled at the distended, swollen belly. The skin across his abdomen was stretched taut like a drum.

John peeled open the diaper and checked.

Nothing. The diaper was clean.

This was not like his son. This was not normal.

Matthew fussed and cried more than any other baby John had every encountered. He soiled his diaper eleven, twelve times a day. His fragile sleep could be disrupted by a cough, a whisper, a sideways look. John hadn't slept for more than three solid hours since his son's birth. His patience was beginning to fray around the edges, like an old flag in unrelenting winds. He ran his fingers through his receding blond hair and looked everywhere but at his reflection in the foggy mirror.

Matthew's fists shook. His legs were still.

John got hold of himself, recrossed the diaper, and sealed the right side against Matthew's left hip. His practical and frugal upbringing held fast. No point in wasting a diaper if it wasn't necessary.

The air rushing past the fuselage sounded unnaturally loud.

Matthew's tongue protruded from blue lips; his arms fell to his sides. His head rolled back as his backbone shook, arched.

John heard a tiny pop inside the rib cage.

Then another. And another.

Matthew's chest expanded, as if he was taking a deep, gasping breath, but it never stopped. The infant's torso continued to inflate; a wave had unfurled under the skin, burbling from under the thin ribs and swelling across the stomach, stretching the diaper to the point of ripping open the sticky fastening.

John's first instinctive thought was to fly into action at the inevitable assault of gas and diarrhea, to frantically look for paper towels, water, anything to handle the excrement sure to erupt any moment now.

This time, though, Matthew's legs lay limp, not at all like every other time when his gastrointestinal system would evacuate his bowels with a force fit for the devil. Those times, he'd kick and holler, expel every last millimeter of watery excrement, and it would all be over in ten, fifteen seconds.

Now, his son's eyes remained closed.

Matthew's back arched and his head rolled listlessly back and forth; the angle of his head tilted in a horrible, painful position. Both fists clenched and unclenched. His toes, with their nails perhaps a tad too long, curled as well. But the legs remained still, paralyzed.

The bubbling continued, distending the skin of his stomach and chest, like a water balloon unevenly filled with marinara sauce. Matthew's ribs splintered into a dozen fragments in sudden snaps, crackles, and pops, yanking John back to an unpleasant memory of a long-ago picnic where his cousins had demolished three entire fried chickens inside of ten minutes.

A shrill, tortured gasp escaped out of the infant. His lips stretched tight over a cluster of eight-month-old baby teeth. Then his head lolled back in a collapsing surrender, giving up all at once, and the rest of his body went limp.

John took a step backward, God help him, right into the door.

Some kind of insect crawled out of Matthew's throat, up over his tongue, squirming through dry, slack lips. It quivered, flinging blood and mucus. The segmented body was nearly two inches long, fantastically slender, coated in a dark, slick liquid; it marched across Matthew's soft face and glared out at the world through a distinctly hairless head, marked by two large blank eyes with three tiny, alien orbs in between, and a formidable set of mandibles. Translucent wings rose from the slim body, fluttered, then quivered with a speed beyond the range of human seeing.

The fast, high-pitched sound absurdly reminded John of a kitten's purring. It carried a vicious weapon and looked exactly like a miniature version of the ungodly things back at the village. At the other end of the creature, a stinger the size of a twenty-gauge needle curved over Matthew's closed eyelid.

Clearly a big wasp, it crouched over the infant's forehead, watching John. A scream locked itself in John's throat.

Lightning bolts of blue veins erupted across Matthew's stomach. With a sound of a boot crushing a watermelon, his torso burst open in a volcanic eruption of wasps, spitting from within the tight flesh like seeds through overripe fruit pulp. Blood and viscera hit the walls, the ceiling, the father.

John's legs gave out as the realization of this wet explosion hit him like a claw hammer between his eyes, slamming his consciousness into a stupefied shock. By the time his ass hit the floor, his only coherent thought, a plea that this wasn't real, that he'd ingested some sort of pagan drug, fluttered through his dimming mind. He collapsed against the toilet and blinked at the blood in his eyes.

Thirty, forty, maybe even fifty wasps crawled out of Matthew's ruptured insides like meth-addled worms. They seemed in overdrive, unable to control their bodies, twitching and spasming, flexing their wings, filling the air with blood and a sour amniotic fluid.

John's red flecked eyes filled with dreamy awe as he gazed up at the blood-spattered walls and his son's twisted feet jutting from the changing table. Perhaps it was God's mercy that he couldn't see the rest of Matthew. Perhaps all of this was some kind of test, something like Abraham faced.

The creatures of red and black floated drunkenly around the tight restroom in looping flights, testing their wings. They clung to one another, mating, fluttering through the air like spinning maple tree seeds. Gravity eventually brought these clusters of whirring wings and exoskeletons, still wet and flexible, down to land gently on the floor, the changing table, the toilet, and John's body. Although aware of the weight and movements of the hundreds of pinpricks, he didn't flinch. He couldn't. Shock had paralyzed him.

After a moment of frantic coupling, the wasps separated and explored, bumping against the walls and ceiling as if testing the limits of their new world. Within seconds, they descended over Matthew and swarmed over the infant's corpse, sometimes so thick it was impossible to see flesh underneath.

John flung one last prayer into the universe, begging for blissful ignorance of what was happening with the wasps, but it was too late. He already knew with a sick certainty that the wasps had returned to what was left of his son's body to feed.

Finally, the scream unlocked itself from John's throat.

The wasps rose again, this time finding warmer flesh.

* * * *

Most airline bathrooms have a secret door handle, even if locked from the inside. If you have to open the door in a hurry, simply slide the plastic RESTROOM sign across its housing and push the button hidden underneath. This will unlock the door. Flight attendants know this; too many children had locked themselves inside.

Forty-three minutes and thirty-seven seconds into flight number 87, after hearing the horrifying screams and that strange buzzing, they opened the door.

CHAPTER 1 ·

Andy didn't expect the prison bus seats to be this comfortable. The Army didn't go out of its way to make things comfortable. Especially for men such as Andrew Shaw. Sure, he'd had to wear shackles the whole time, with both his wrists and ankles cuffed and connected by a chain, but his legs hadn't gone numb and his back wasn't sore.

That was about the extent of the Army's hospitality.

Just before dawn, twelve prisoners had been shuffled to the back half of the bus, two to each seat. That might work fine for third graders, but it didn't make a whole lot of sense to Andy, like the brass in charge were trying to shove a dozen eggs into half the carton. Two MPs waited and watched from behind bars at the back of the bus. They carried sidearms and .12-gauge shotguns. Two more were up front, along with Second Lieutenant Thompkins.

They drove south the rest of the morning.

It got boring real fast.

Mostly, Andy tried to be content looking out the window through the tiny gaps in wire almost as thick as his little finger. It would be a long time before he would have a chance to watch the world outside. Perhaps the worst part was that it looked like the outside world wasn't much more than gas stations, fast food, and strip malls.

Fucking Florida.

At least he was halfway comfortable. For a while, anyway. Until the sun came up. Now, even though it was only midmorning, the real problem was the heat.

The bus didn't have air-conditioning. Or at least nobody'd turned it on. And they sure as shit weren't jumping to open the windows, as thick steel mesh covered all of them; the glass was bulletproof. And it might as well have been a goddamn cast-iron oven. Already the sun had baked the inside near 110 degrees. And as the day wore on, the temperature, outside and inside, kept climbing.

It smelled like roadkill at high noon.

Andy couldn't understand how people could think straight not just in the heat, but in this humidity. His skin felt more like a sponge than anything. Sweat oozed from everywhere. It stung when it slid across the scrapes the handcuffs had made on his wrists; it wormed down his back and collected in his ass crack.

A different seatmate might have helped a whole lot. This guy was black and huge. He was built like the sculptor had used rough black coal and somewhere inside that coal was still on fire. When the man had stepped aboard at the beginning of the ride, the bus had squealed like a surprised goat. Even the guards didn't want to get too close.

Maybe they put him in a seat with Andy because Andy was a little guy.

But Andy was a little guy with a shorter temper.

The giant next to him radiated heat, as if the rest of the coal was catching. They pretended to ignore each other.

Andy hadn't decided if the guy was an asshole or not yet.

The man's race didn't matter a whole lot to Andy. Andy didn't like most people he met. He'd been around everybody the Army had to offer, black guys from both the inner cities and suburbs, scowling Puerto Ricans, resolute Mexicans, defiant Hmong refugees, and of course, good old desperate white trash. Color made no difference. Like any job anywhere, some folks you work with are assholes, some are okay. Even decent sometimes.

Nevertheless, they all had one thing in common: They were all poor.

In their minds, the military was supposed to provide a way out of the cycle of poverty. Choices were limited to men in their situation. Forget college. Deal drugs, steal shit, or drink yourself to death working at a job where your name was on your protective gear uniform. Jail, addiction, or a dirt nap. Not much fun or future in that. The military claimed to offer a clean, honest way to live. Put in a few years, sit back and collect the rest of your life. Too late, they found out it wasn't much different than any other job. The Army was nothing but bureaucracy, red tape, tiny tyrants, and always, always their old, intimate, and dearest friend, violence.

* * * *

The bus stopped and Andy tried to get a sense of whether or not they'd arrived at the prison yet. It might have been a prison, with all the high fences and security, but it looked more like they were driving onto some kind of air base, maybe even a civilian airport. Andy didn't know a damn thing about Florida anyway. All he knew was that they were somewhere down near Miami. Not that he could see the ocean. Perhaps it was for the best. He wasn't sure he wanted to see the beaches, the ocean, the bikinis.

The bus lurched through a series of checkpoints, passing booths and sliding gates with so much razor wire sprouting wildly from the top it almost looked like unruly pubic hair. Andy tried not to think about sex. Down that path lay madness.

The bus rolled out onto an empty airstrip and stopped at the far end.

Second Lieutenant Thompkins stood and addressed the prisoners. "There will be no speaking. Eyes on the floor. I make eye contact with you, I will make you hurt. I see you making eye contact with anybody else, I will make you hurt. If this is understood, give a nod while you stare at your knees. If not, I will make you hurt."

Andy looked at the floor along with everybody else.

Second Lieutenant Thompkins stood at attention at the front of the bus and never slouched, never leaned against anything, never even shifted his feet. The minutes crawled past, dying of dehydration.

Andy blinked sweat out of his eyes.

This fucking heat.

All of a sudden, he'd had enough. They arrested people who left dogs in cars in weather like this. His temper, stunted and frayed at the best of times, was gone.

He looked up, yelled, "Hey, you think you can turn on the AC? Or at least open a goddamn window?"

Something crashed into the back of his skull, bouncing his forehead off the seat in front of him. The MP behind him, Haylock, had slipped his shotgun through the bars and jabbed him with the unforgiving end of the steel barrel. The prick didn't even have the decency to reverse the shotgun and use the rubber-covered butt. Andy felt a warm trickle pool in his hair and drip down the back of his neck. It wasn't sweat.

Second Lieutenant Thompkins shook his head, saying, "Let me try to explain the situation in terms you can figure out." He zeroed in on Andy. "Speak, and I will stomp your ass and piss in your face."

Andy sat back and was quiet, but it didn't sit right. It was too much, overdone; the second lieutenant was going out of his way to be a hard-ass. Dumbshit didn't understand that it was always a hell of a lot scarier not to say a damn thing. Andy wondered if the second lieutenant was nervous. Andy remembered guys like that, players that couldn't shut up before football games, or later in basic training, soldiers as they were about to embark on exercises with live rounds.

What the hell did this guy have to be nervous about?

CHAPTER 2

When the phone rang, Jen debated whether she should actually answer or just let it go to Dr. Fletcher's voice mail. Technically, she was supposed to answer the calls, take messages, and all the rest of the bullshit that came with being Dr. Fletcher's intern/assistant/slave. Morning light filled Dr. Fletcher's cluttered office and Jen had to squint to see the phone.

The caller ID read *blocked*.

She was in a rotten mood, and the anonymous ringing phone didn't help.

She knew damn well she'd been blaming her mood on everything but the real reasons: the stupid malfunctioning printer, the slow elevator, the way parts would bounce out of her car whenever she hit Chicago's monster potholes, and the inevitable realization slowly creeping up on her that academia was nothing more than a self-perpetuating circle jerk. She knew all this, and understood it was her brain's way of blowing off steam while it avoided the true cause of her irritation.

Dr. Fletcher was going on an expedition to Peru and he wasn't taking her.

She had no idea why.

Or maybe she did have an idea, but just didn't like it.

Dr. Fletcher had a reputation. To everybody outside the University of Chicago and the Field Museum, he was a genuine rock 'n' roll scientist, a brilliant entomologist, a man who had discovered over a dozen new insects, a preeminent researcher, and a Hymenoptera expert.

Not for the first time, Jen couldn't help but wonder if it was just a coincidence that the word *hymen* was contained in that particular classification's order.

Dr. Fletcher had another reputation, an open secret within the inner circles of the labs and classrooms. If you knew the right people, or if you'd spent nearly any time at all with the esteemed doctor, you'd know that Dr. Fletcher was a hedonistic, slow-motion tornado with a fondness for fame, tequila, and ambitious coed grad students.

As an ambitious coed grad student herself, Jen wasn't sure how she felt about that.

Maybe that's what bothered her.

She couldn't decide if she was more insulted about this openly secret reputation, or the fact that he'd never tried to ask her out for drinks after work. He'd never tried anything, not even "accidentally" brushing up against her, like so many of her female peers. Notorious for inviting his grad student assistants on expeditions, getting them drunk on whatever local hooch was available, encouraging them to "Experiment! Seize life!" then talking himself into their sleeping bags inside the Field Museum's tents.

Jen hadn't been invited. Why not?

It certainly wasn't her mind. Then again, maybe it was. She suspected she already knew more about the symbiotic relationship between wasps and polydnaviruses than the good doctor himself, but she would never admit such a thing out loud, even if her doctorate thesis would.

Then it had to be her attitude. Sure, she could always use more makeup, and instead of her usual T-shirt and bulky cargo shorts, she could instead wear too-short khaki shorts, tight T-shirts, and maybe try to flirt with him, but the thought made her nauseous. If that's what it took to secure a grant, forget it. She would never be the type of scientist that could bury her principles in the quest for immortality in the form of scientific discovery.

That left simply her looks. And that made her depressed.

In her better moods, she saw herself as being trim, smart, with a guilty love of puns.

But in her worst moods, she saw herself as being tiny, flat-chested, and she suspected that somehow worst of all in Dr. Fletcher's eyes, her parents were from Kaohsiung, Taiwan. Short of plastic surgery, which repulsed her on a primeval level, there was nothing she could do.

Of course, the thing was, she didn't even like Dr. Fletcher. He was a shallow, egotistical asshole, but it still somehow bothered her that he hadn't even tried to molest her. Instead of including her on the next expedition, he put her behind a desk to deal with his paperwork.

The phone stopped ringing. Whoever was on the other end didn't leave a message.

* * * *

Five minutes later, the phone rang again, vibrating everything in Dr. Fletcher's office, textbooks, diagrams, and specimens. Forget lunch; she still had a hell of a lot of work ahead of her today, at least five hours of recordings to make after observing subjects in the Field Museum labs, then a drive a few miles south along Chicago's Lake Shore Drive, tortuous in heavy traffic, for more recordings at the university. So much for any chance of a social life.

God knew where Dr. Fletcher was. Probably sleeping. He haunted a dusty couch in some forgotten small room upstairs, full of outdated maps. The man was fond of his siestas, claimed he'd gotten into the habit during his many expeditions to South America, and they helped him think more clearly. Jen figured it was mostly for sleeping off hangovers so he'd have more energy and stamina for his nights.

She brushed her bangs out of her eyes; her hair was long on top and cut severely short on the sides and back and she idly thought maybe she should bleach and dye it a bright pink. Maybe that would get the good doctor's attention. She gave in and answered the phone out of more of an ingrained sense of obligation than anything. "Dr. Fletcher's office."

"May I speak with Dr. Fletcher, please?"

The voice on the end spoke with so little inflection she wasn't sure if it was from a human or computer at first. She dutifully said, "He's not here at the moment. May I take a message?"

"Who is this?"

Over the years, Jen had dealt with enough professors and scientists who had as much familiarity of basic manners as a housefly soaked in human excrement on a birthday cake, so she took the blunt question in stride.

"My name is Jen Huang. I am Dr. Fletcher's assistant." *Assistant* sounded better than *intern*. And anything sounded better than *grad student*.

"What's your Social Security number, Ms. Huang?"

Jen laughed. "If you think I'm dumb enough to give out my Social Security number over the phone, Mr....?"

"One moment. Is it 83-692-4433?"

Jen forced another laugh. Didn't know what to say.

"It is, isn't it?" When Jen couldn't form a response in time, the voice took her silence as a yes. "Trust your instincts, Ms. Huang. It is a matter of national security that we speak with Dr. Fletcher."

"If you have my information, I'm sure you know Dr. Fletcher's cell number."

"He turned it off six hours ago."

"You probably know his address, then."

"He is not home. Based on our latest intel, he is somewhere in the building. We do not have time for this nonsense. Get him. Immediately. A car is on the way."

Jen found her balance, inhaled through her nose. She focused, exhaled, and even though she didn't like being bullied, she somehow knew this wasn't a scam. "I can pass a message along, if that would help."

"That would help tremendously. I am not exaggerating, Ms. Huang, when I say that this is an urgent matter of life and death."

"Is there a number where he can reach you?" Jen asked.

He rattled off a sixteen-digit number.

Jen jotted it down. "I will see if I can find him. I'm sure he'll call you as soon as possible."

"I certainly hope so." The phone clicked in Jen's ear.

CHAPTER 3

A couple of Humvees roared up and flanked the prison bus. A dark SUV with darker windows followed and parked off to the side. A dozen soldiers wearing full armor and enough weapons to kick-start a civil war jumped out of the Humvees and formed a rough perimeter. Nobody got out of the SUV. Andy didn't blame whoever was inside; it probably had air-conditioning.

For a while, nobody moved. The driver never shut off the bus, but they could hear jets taking off and landing in another part of the airport.

"Shitfire," somebody whispered from the seat across the aisle. "You were right, complainin' about the heat. I woulda spoke up, but those good ole boys popped you in the head, so you know what I'm talking about."

Andy didn't answer.

The prisoner across the aisle sighed in satisfaction. "Damn straight," he said in a stage whisper. After four hours, the guards knew this particular prisoner couldn't help himself. Clearly his mind was broken so they ignored him most of the time. "Shitfire, it's hot."

Andy risked a quick glance.

Mr. Talkative was next to the window. He leaned forward and looked past the two prisoners between them. Weak chin, feral eyes. One of his ears was misshapen, as if a drunk uncle had tried to twist it off a long time ago. "Folks call me Squirrel."

"I bet they do," Andy said.

"I liked to crawl under houses when I was a kid," he said, as if that explained everything.

Next to Squirrel, in the aisle seat, was a Hispanic man with a permanent half smile, as if his very existence amused the hell out of him. The smile was not reflected in the man's eyes and Andy doubted that he was the only one on the bus who had killed somebody. His orange jumpsuit had a series of numbers and the name, J. Ramirez, stamped on it.

A small, thumping shadow passed over the formation.

Everybody outside snapped to attention.

A bulky black chopper settled a ways off. Like the bus driver, the pilot didn't kill the engine. Andy just hoped if they were all waiting on some high-ranking cocksucker, he'd make his speech and get the hell on with it. Andy was sick of the bus. He wasn't exactly in a hurry to get into his cell, but goddammit, enough of this heat was enough.

The MPs on the bus tensed as if they were on camera and Andy heard the dry snaps of the little safety buttons just behind the trigger guards being flicked off. The soldiers outside, all suited up and prepped for war, brought their M4s to their shoulders. Maybe it wasn't some official military or political prick on that helicopter.

Whoever it was sure as hell had everybody's undivided attention.

Nobody was really paying a whole lot of notice to the prisoners, and the possibility of taking advantage of this, maybe elbowing a guard behind him in the throat and grabbing a shotgun, flitted across Andy's mind. Just as quickly, he dismissed the thought. There was nowhere to run, and it mostly sounded like a good way to get himself shot.

A couple of guys in suits finally climbed out of the SUV and waited as the chopper's fuselage split open and stairs lowered to the tarmac. Two soldiers in dark camouflage fatigues were the first to emerge. The chopper was big enough and the blades split the air far enough over their heads that they didn't bother crouching; they bristled with advanced automatic rifles, helmets, goggles, thick vests, fingerless gloves, black kneepads, knives, at least two handguns apiece, the whole nine yards. They wore dull gray bandannas over their faces.

Andy'd been in the Army nearly seven months and he'd never seen badasses like this. If these dudes weren't Special Forces, he'd eat his own boot.

The badasses met the guys in suits and while those cool machine guns weren't entirely up and ready to rock and roll, the barrels weren't exactly pointed at the ground either. There was a short conference and the suits presented some papers. One of the soldiers examined them, then tucked the folder away under his bulletproof vest.

They came for the bus. The doors slapped open and the Special Forces soldiers exploded up the stairs. The MPs in back were too nervous to feel outclassed. The soldiers swept through the bus and one of them mumbled something into their throat mike.

A man in a black hood and handcuffs stepped out of the chopper. Two more Special Forces boys followed, one holding the base of the hood at the back of the prisoner's head and the other a semiautomatic pistol, held loose, slightly away from the body, aimed at the base of the prisoner's spine. They started down the stairs, slow.

He didn't think much of the prisoner at first. Beyond the black hood, Andy couldn't see anything special. The guy wore the same shapeless orange jumpsuit as the rest of them. Same shackles too. And he was blind as a bat. When he stepped off the stairs onto the tarmac, he stood still for a moment, ever so slightly cocking his covered head, like an experienced dog listening for creeping pheasants.

Leaving two soldiers on board the bus, the rest took up positions around the vehicle with their backs to the transfer, keeping watch on the rest of the airport.

"Move out," the guy with the pistol said.

The prisoner nodded and shuffled forward. He got close enough that Andy could see the black canvas bag expand and contract as the man breathed easily. If the prisoner knew that he couldn't pick his nose without ten, fifteen trigger-happy soldiers opening fire, he didn't give it away. He might have been strolling across the street for an ice cream cone.

Despite himself, Andy had to admit that shit was pretty cool.

They propelled the man through the bus doorway. Once on board, the prisoner moved carefully, feeling about at the bus seats. The two badasses slammed him into a seat near the front.

The prisoner sat still for a moment, then reached out with both hands and explored the seat around him. He rolled his head around, getting comfortable, then settled into his seat for what looked like a nap.

Nobody else moved. Nobody else, frankly, looked like they knew what to do.

The guy in charge, whose insignia only identified him as Hobson, dropped into the seat behind the prisoner and gave a nod to Thompkins, who snapped his fingers at the driver. The bus pulled into a tight circle and headed back in the direction the way they'd come, while the second soldier stationed himself across the aisle from the prisoner.

The guys in suits climbed back into their dark SUV, but it never moved.

This time, the gates were open and waiting, like they couldn't wait to get rid of the prisoners. The bus roared through without slowing down and headed north.

Andy caught the rest of the men on the bus glancing at each other.

Squirrel looked like he was gonna meet a celebrity and casually brought his cupped, handcuffed hands to his mouth to check his breath. He couldn't resist the presence of anticipated royalty and elbowed his seatmate, nodding at the hooded prisoner.

The handsome prisoner shrugged.

Andy never played poker because he couldn't control his expressions. Watching this government circus, he knew his own face was full of curiosity. He risked a glance up at his own seatmate.

The big guy kept his eyes on the ceiling, arms crossed; he didn't look like he gave a damn one way or another.

* * * *

Miami traffic jams are like ants getting caught in honey.

Two hours in, even the badasses were getting bored.

Andy found out later the prisoner's name was Carver.

And he was more badass than anybody.

CHAPTER 4

Dr. Fletcher was not happy to see Jen. He sat up on his favorite couch, squinting and running his fingers through his long hair that grew mostly around his ears and the back of his neck. He'd been experimenting with different shades of brown. He was smart enough to know that he was too old to pull off any shade of black, and he'd even started leaving the temples and sideburns gray, going for the esteemed professor look.

He sat up and scratched his balls before Jen could turn away and asked, "I—what—Do you know what time it is, Ms. Huang?"

"Yes I do. Two-twenty-six in the afternoon, Dr. Fletcher."

"Yes, so, exactly my point…" The doctor trailed off about his point.

"Dr. Fletcher…" Jen met his eyes. "Someone called. Someone important. I think it would be a very good idea if you called them back."

Dr. Fletcher managed, "So you took a message, then?"

"Yes. They want you to call them as soon as possible."

"Yes, well, remind me in the morning. Would you happen to have any aspirin?"

"Dr. Fletcher, I got the distinct impression they needed you to call them as soon as possible. As in, now."

Dr. Fletcher knew he couldn't talk his way out of it. "Fine. Give me the number," like it was Jen's fault. She handed him the Post-it note and he looked at it for a moment as if he was unsure of what to do with it.

Jen smiled and didn't offer to help.

Thoroughly irritated, Dr. Fletcher finally located his phone, turned it on, and dialed. He started to speak was cut off even before he could get out his name. He listened for a few seconds, then said, "This is highly irregular. Do you have any—" He went quiet again, still playing the part of the confused guest of honor whose speech had been interrupted with an engagement announcement.

He kept trying to speak. "I see. Still, I have no—" He was quiet for about thirty seconds and his face grew even more pale. He tried to swallow as he put down the phone. "Ah, it appears that something… I don't even know what I'm allowed to say." He spoke quickly to get it over with. "Something bad has happened somewhere and our skills and knowledge are required. I'm told your dissertation has gotten some attention. Gather whatever you may need for the next twenty-four hours. We're both supposed to be outside in five minutes."

The thing was, Jen hadn't actually published her thesis yet, let alone given it to Dr. Fletcher. The knowledge that somebody had been inside her computer kept her moving quickly and her mouth shut. Even Dr. Fletcher seemed to have lost whatever fight he had been trying to summon. He grew silent and sullen, crunching three dry aspirin and pulling on a pair of round sunglasses as if trying to prove he was too cool for this government bullshit.

A pair of sheriff's deputies politely hustled Jen and Dr. Fletcher down the vast southern steps of the Field Museum to a waiting Cook County cruiser. Jen couldn't help it and paused for a moment as a warm appreciation for her city flared inside of her. It was still mid-July, and while memories of a vicious winter still lingered, nobody had had a chance to get sick of the heat yet. The bright sun was still high in a sky dotted with a few wisps of clouds, and gentle breezes swept in from the lake like the soft, contented exhales of a resting giant.

Then the deputy had a hand on her shoulder, telling her to watch her head as he eased her into the back seat. He slammed the door and the driver pulled away immediately. The officer in the passenger seat hit the lights and sirens and they tore out onto Lake Shore Drive.

The driver put his foot on the floor and kept it there.

* * * *

The deputies marched them straight into the TSA checkpoint at the Chicago Executive Airport; apparently, even those summoned by the government for some kind of emergency weren't immune to FAA regulations. As she took off her shoes, Jen's attention was drawn to CNN on the televisions in the terminal. There must be some law somewhere, another FAA rule, that all TVs in airports must broadcast headline news and nothing else.

She caught some of the crawling text at the bottom of the screens. *CÉNTRICO FLIGHT #87 JETLINER MISSING. DISAPPEARED WEST OF FLORIDA COAST—GULF OF MEXICO.* Jen's instinctive reaction was a disquieting sadness for those poor people on the flight and all the families waiting for them. The second thought, quick on the heels of the first, was that this wasn't the kind of news one wanted to see plastered all over every TV in an airport terminal.

The third was a question.

She couldn't help wondering if this was somehow connected to the government emergency. A Learjet was gassed and ready for them; the pilot headed for the runway and took off as soon as Jen and Dr. Fletcher were aboard.

* * * *

A pair of men waited for them on the tarmac and identified themselves as special agents of the FBI. Jen barely had time to register the humidity before they helped her and Dr. Fletcher into a Crown Vic. They drove fast, swerving in and out of traffic, but this time there was no lights, no siren.

The agents were either unwilling to share any information or were telling the truth that they knew as much as the two scientists in the back seat. All they could confirm was that it did indeed have something to do with the plane crash. Dr. Fletcher chewed on some more aspirin and pouted. The cheese and crackers they'd eaten on the flight weren't sitting well in Jen's stomach and weaving through northbound traffic on Interstate 75 at eighty miles an hour didn't help.

She didn't even try to ask any more questions when they approached a huge stadium and jerked to a stop amidst art-deco fake trees in front of the BB&T Center. The entire area buzzed with activity. Military equipment and soldiers scurried around the parking lot. The FBI guys opened the car doors and indicated the waiting soldiers flanking one of the northern entrances.

Inside was wonderfully air-conditioned, downright cold.

Another security check point. Jen and Dr. Fletcher surrendered their laptops and cell phones. Jen put on a canvas necklace with several color-coded badges, including a copy of her driver's license. They stepped through the metal detectors into the arena's main concourse, where organized chaos reigned.

Soldiers jogged through in long lines, rifles out. Men in Carhartt coveralls unspooled yards, perhaps miles of cables. Along with Jen and

Dr. Fletcher, about twenty or thirty more confused-looking people were shepherded upstairs into a plush team meeting room.

The dark room was curiously quiet. Jen was used to academia's high ceilings, wooden chairs on wooden floors, notebooks, various talismans on a long wooden table. Echoes of screeching chair legs on ancient wood floors and quiet, droning voices. Questionable lighting that depended mostly on the sun.

There were no windows here. The lighting was pristine. Soundproof walls.

Two guarded doorways.

A large screen filled with images from CNN dominated one end of the room. The carpet was thick, the walls somehow soft, adorned with Florida Panthers logos. The polished table, more than large enough to sit all forty players, including coaches, was now filled with laptops, chairs full of haggard people murmuring to each other with clenched jaws and darting eyes. Most of the room knew something bad had happened and were frantically talking around it. Two serious men stood close to each other at the front of the room. They talked in muted tones, almost into each other's shoulder in a practiced manner of men used to discreetly discussing state secrets without being recorded.

The TV sound was audible, but there must have been hidden speakers, because it didn't drown out any of the other discussions around the table. Now CNN had their computer-generated maps out, and experts shouted at each about the area where the plane might have hit the ocean. Every expert tried to get in, "possibly at least nine hundred miles an hour," at least once.

Jen and Dr. Fletcher's group joined others on the far wall, standing room only.

The main double doors were closed and locked.

CNN's audio went mute, but the video feed continued.

One of the men at the front stepped forward and slapped a black folder stuffed with printouts on the table. "If I could have your attention, please." Fifties. Not military. Gray hair. Long-sleeved eggshell shirt buttoned all the way up to the last button. Jeans. Sport jacket. Slim black tie, like he'd been at a country wedding before stepping in front of the drawn faces.

"First of all, I must apologize to those of you who have yet to be properly briefed, and thank you for taking the time to be with us today. My name is Bill Schultz, executive director of the FBI, and along with Stan Albers, chief of operations of Homeland Security." He nodded at the other serious man. Albers was a short, gaunt man who looked like he'd swallowed a few dozen fishhooks on purpose.

"We are the joint leaders of this task force, for the moment at least. It should go without saying that everything within this arena is classified, and I know we can count on your cooperation. Officially, this task force does not exist and this meeting never happened. At least, not yet. I will try to catch everyone up on the latest confirmed data, but at the same time, we must move fast, so we can get to the real reason we're here."

He tapped his folder. "At ten fifty-two this morning, Céntrico flight number eighty-seven crashed into the waters nine miles off the western Florida coast. All three hundred and forty souls are presumed dead."

Silent video images of the Gulf of Mexico filled the wall of flat panels behind him. Off to the sides, the other TVs continued to broadcast FOX and CNN, their screens full of grim, earnest anchors nodding somberly, as if they'd heard Schultz. The footage switched to a live shot of the Miami International Airport, full of anxious relatives.

"We can, however," Schultz paused to survey the room, "confirm the death of three hundred and thirty-six passengers. The release of this information is being delayed to the media for the time being. It will remain that way until some hard decisions have been made. To do that, we need your help."

He turned and gestured at the screen. "Flight eighty-seven crashed in approximately one hundred and fifty feet of water, two miles off Florida's west coast. The wreckage was located within the hour of impact and recovery efforts began immediately."

The video went black for a moment, then switched to an out-of-focus underwater shot, with a time stamp and date at the bottom. Up at the top in no-nonsense, bold red lettering, in case anybody was confused, was a single word: *CLASSIFIED.*

At first, Jen wasn't sure what she was seeing. Underwater, with no clear up or down, all she could make out was a string of unidentifiable pale shapes floating from left to right, like a string of cooked rice. Then the camera straightened and focused, and with a cold, tight squeeze around her heart, she realized she was watching a line of body bags, attached to some sort of pulley system and guided by divers, being hauled from the inky green darkness far below up to the surface.

Schultz said, "Very little of what you are watching is SOP. This crash would have been only met with a normal emergency response, but some of the communication between the captain and the tower was highly irregular, suggesting nothing of a mechanical malfunction, or even a terrorist incident. Shortly after impact, Homeland Security made the decision to get involved and took over from the FAA." He chewed on his lower lip, unsure how to present the next round of information. "The captain, from our initial research, was more than competent, highly experienced. No record of substance abuse. No indication of psychological impairment. Stable. Married for twenty-two years. Three kids. Nothing whatsoever out of the ordinary."

He knocked on the table. "This had every sign of a possible attack."

Now the video showed the side of the plane, as it had landed sideways, crumpled and torn, rising out of the blackness of the bottom of the ocean like an exposed bone. More divers laboriously pulled body bags from a gash in the side. Swirling yellow light glowed from within, spilling out of the row of windows.

Schultz took a sip of coffee. "During his request for assistance, certain words can be recognized among the... panic. The captain himself used this phrase at least twice." He opened the folder and pulled out a report. He read directly from the paper so slowly each word became its own sentence. "*Wasps. Loose. In. Cabin.*" He took off his glasses. "This operation began under the strong possibility that a weaponized hallucinogen may have been released inside the aircraft. This is why many of you in the pharmaceutical fields were called. Fortunately, the primary structural integrity of the fuselage was maintained during impact, and the second responders were able to recover the aircraft's black box."

Now the camera slithered into the broken plane, gliding through a green cloud of pretzel wrappers, empty soda cans, in-flight magazines the consistency of tissue paper, and a few shoes. Rows of sideways seats hung above, mirroring the rows below. The bottom, left side of the plane, was covered in scattered laptops and cell phones.

It looked as if the bodies had been hauled away and for that, Jen was glad. Neither her nor her stomach needed to see any swollen, waterlogged corpses.

"Upon closer examination of the crash site, however," Shultz said, "We shifted our focus from chemical warfare to a more... biological threat."

The camera zoomed in on a darker, red and black object. The thing was long, thin, and flexible, rippling as it gently floated from side to side in the current, held in place between two seats. At first, Jen thought it must be some plastic bags tied together, or maybe—God help her— part of some poor soul's mutilated internal organs.

Then she saw the wings.

Torn and ragged, to be sure. But they still held that unique petal shape, shot through with veins like lightning. Dr. Fletcher clapped a hand over his mouth when he saw the narrow skull tapering down to a horrid set of mandibles, the alien, protruding eyes that gave the face a sinister appearance, the torn antennae of an obvious wasp.

Close-up, with flickering pixels, it was impossible to tell the size. Schultz let the image sink into the room. "We are now actively investigating the possibility that the captain may have been describing an actual event." The video blinked out and the lights in the room brightened. Jen hadn't realized the lights had been dimmed and tried not to be impressed again with the luxury of a professional sports team arena.

Shultz surveyed the room. "So. You entomologists can now understand why you were invited." The doors behind opened and a surgical table was wheeled inside. A white sheet covered the table. "The primary focus of our investigation has shifted."

Schultz pulled the sheet back, revealing a dead wasp almost two inches long. He looked out across those standing behind the table. "Dr. Fletcher, I believe? University of Chicago. I'm particularly interested in anything you notice about this specimen. Any additional information is vital."

Dr. Fletcher absorbed this request like he was hard of hearing. "I'm sorry?"

"I've heard you're the one to talk to about this," Schultz said.

Jen saw Dr. Fletcher's slack-jawed expression of incomprehension harden into a cold assessment of the situation, picturing himself on the edge of one of those fabled moments that could either make or break a career. He said, "Well, yes. It might possibly be Hymenoptera."

Jen found herself wishing he wouldn't use that term.

Dr. Fletcher surreptitiously grabbed her by the wrist and gave her a quick tug along to the front of the table. "Based on the video evidence," Fletcher told the room, hesitantly, like he was trying to put a sentence together for the first time, but gathering momentum, "and this partially destroyed specimen, my initial opinion is that this appears to be a highly specialized species."

Nobody said anything. Smart enough to grab the spotlight, Dr. Fletcher seized a pair of surgical tongs and pointed out the wasp's obvious characteristics. "Head. Thorax. Abdomen."

Jen felt like she was in sixth grade biology.

Dr. Fletcher, however, enjoyed his moment in the sun. "Notice the legs. Not curled underneath the body like bees." He grew quiet for a few moments, getting a better look at the creature. "The size is... quite large, but not impossible," Dr. Fletcher said finally.

"Yes," Shultz said and didn't even bother keeping the scorn out of his voice. "We'd worked that much out." He leaned on the table to emphasize his point. "We need to know what it is, where it came from, and what happened on that plane."

Dr. Fletcher bit the inside of his cheek in concentration. "How many specimens have you found?"

"In one piece? Thirteen. Parts of at least; seven, eight more."

"There is undoubtedly more."

"How many?"

"I cannot say."

"Why not?"

"This is a male, for one thing. I would need to examine any female specimens. And I need some sort of halfway accurate ratio, males to females. The social structure of any wasp species will tell you almost everything about its life. Most are solitary. But if you found thirteen intact specimens… " He grew quiet.

The stinger reminded Jen of a long, slender malevolent hummingbird's beak. The creature fascinated her. The body was jet-black, with red symmetrical starburst squiggles down the center of its back. Like many species of wasps, the colors were a brilliant contrast, a striking *fuck off* warning from Mother Nature. With the Rorschach inkblots of blood on an almost pearlescent black, this wasp looked like a goddamn flying black widow.

"Doc?" Schultz asked. "We know this is some kind of wasp. What we need is more information about these things, and we need it five minutes ago."

"There are over a hundred thousand different species around the world," Dr. Fletcher said in an apologetic tone. "Undoubtedly thousands more undiscovered. In fact, two brand new species were discovered in the Ugandan jungle just a few months ago."

A sudden buzz in the silence made everybody flinch, as if the dead wasp had somehow reawakened. That primordial fear of being stung, ingrained since childhood, was back with a vengeance.

It was Albers's cell phone. He answered, then said, "Dr. Fletcher, I'm sorry to interrupt."

To Schultz he said, "They're ready and waiting downstairs."

Shultz gathered his folder and nodded at Dr. Fletcher and Jen. "A mobile lab has been set up downstairs. Personnel are starting dissections as we speak. We'd like you to join them."

* * * *

Jen and the rest of the scientists followed Schultz and Albers as they marched through private corridors, through another series of doors, and finally out into the sudden noise and controlled chaos in the public concourses. Lines of soldiers jogged past. Jeeps roared through the concourses and the drivers pounded on the horns in urgent, steady rhythms.

They turned down a utility corridor under the stands and stopped at a row of tables full of latex gloves, surgical masks, eye protection, and rubber boots. After forming a shuffling line, everybody donned the protective gear and squeezed past a Zamboni into a large holding room that funneled into the tunnel where equipment and hockey players could enter the rink.

A group of exhausted officials and doctors stood around a line of trauma stretchers. A dozen body bags covered the stretchers. Most were open, revealing the pale flesh inside. Salt water dripped from the bags. Technicians in purple scrubs and eye protection bent over the bodies and held the cameras only inches from the cold flesh. Flashes popped. Off to the side, large monitors were stacked over two MRI scanners. The body of an older woman was being prepped to slide into one of the large machines. It appeared that she would be the first to be scanned.

Beyond the makeshift morgue was the cavernous sports arena. Jen could see a path of ice, but something obscured the rest of the hockey rink's surface. Something white and crumpled. For a brief, disorienting second, the rink almost looked like the top of a billowy, amorphous cloud. She faltered as the sickening realization hit her that these were the airline dead; she was looking at hundreds of translucent white plastic body bags. The military had brought them here to one of the few places near the crash with the ability to store this many bodies at a low temperature.

Jen found she could not look away. While it was one thing to read about the death toll on the scrolling news feed at the bottom of headline news, or even hear it described as Schultz had done, it was quite another to see the hockey rink overflowing with the dead, the bags sometimes stacked three or four high. The sheer enormity of all that death could not be rationalized or dismissed. The lines of a poem from the cold war echoed through her head, something about fifteen million body bags.

One of the doctors stepped forward and said, "Good morning. I'm Dr. Polderman, lead pathologist for the southeastern CBRN response team. I'm afraid that the clock is ticking, and we had no time to prepare any negative pressure autopsy suites. These twelve cadavers were chosen at random. In addition to the obvious large local reactions on the face, thorax, and hands present on every body, we also noticed something interesting on these four." He gestured at the four body bags at the end and lifted a heavy gray leg. The flesh behind the ankles had been savagely shredded. "It would appear, from the bite marks correlating with large sets of mandibles, the attackers concentrated their efforts on severing the Achilles tendon."

Dr. Polderman lowered the foot carefully and went over to the MRI. "Cursory examination has revealed unusual puncture wounds that extend well into the hypodermis. These larger perforations are generally concentrated on the torsos." He indicated with a laser pointer at the old woman positioned on one of the MRI patient tables.

Jen forced herself to methodically focus, to observe with objective, dispassionate eyes. Before today, she'd seen a grand total of two dead bodies in her life, both at open casket funerals. This woman was not posed as if serenely sleeping in her finest dress. This woman was naked; her clothes had been cut off. Her flesh was gray and mottled as if bruised. Her rib cage had been shattered. Black welts the size of quarters ran across one side of her face and down her neck. The other side of her head had been flattened, crushing her eye socket. Her thin breasts spilled onto her arms. One foot had been twisted into a perverse angle.

The machine hummed and the table slid the corpse smoothly inside the MRI. Jen was relieved; she didn't want to have to look at the woman any longer. Everyone watched the monitors as the images appeared, displaying the soft tissue in slow, measured increments, one monochromatic strip at a time.

A gaggle of voices rose above the noise from the pandemonium on the concourse.

"Is that—are those tumors?"

"There's too many."

"What is all that?"

"Damage from the impact?"

"It has to be tumors."

"That's—there's too many."

"Why's it blurry? Something... something's moving in there."

Jen couldn't make out anything recognizable on the monitors. She could have been looking at a computer reproduction of a clump of old lasagna for all she knew. Dr. Fletcher didn't have a clue either, but pretended he could read the MRI results. "Interesting," he murmured, stroking his goatee.

Dr. Polderman told an assistant, "We need an ultrasound down here, now." Then, to the technicians, "Get her out of there so we can take a look."

As the woman slid back out of the MRI, a soldier ran down the slight ramp from the rink and yelled, "Sirs! You need to see this. We've got movement out here."

* * * *

Everybody headed out onto the ice. Jen's rubber boots slid around as if coated in oil, but she decided she'd rather fall and break her nose before she grabbed Dr. Fletcher for support. He wasn't doing so well himself, lurching and slipping along. More than a couple of times he'd stepped on body bags to regain his footing.

The game lights were on, making every detail jump out with an unnatural clarity, as if lit from a hundred white suns. The wrinkles in the crumpled white bags. The gouged surface of the ice. The way some of the body bags stretched out at strange angles. It had been only about twenty hours or so since the crash, and Jen realized rigor mortis had frozen the bodies into the positions they had been flung inside the plane. The silhouettes of the stiff forms inside looked like dubious gas station chicken skewers behind grimy glass.

The soldier led Schultz and Albers and the rest to a lone bag at the far end of the ice. Soldiers had pulled all of the surrounding bags away, leaving a bare patch. Jen and the others followed, forming a small semicircle at the edge of the clearing.

The bag lay perfectly still.

The first soldier said, "Wait for it."

Schultz and Albers saw the movement immediately. Everyone could see it. The bag appeared to be… breathing. The plastic billowed out in random places along the length, slow at first, trembling back down and resting for several seconds before fluttering up again in a different spot. A faint thrumming vibration accompanied the movements.

Schultz got within three feet and cautiously got down on his hands and knees. He pulled out a small flashlight with a blinding beam and aimed it at the bag. The light bounced off the white plastic and everyone squinted. He handed it to Albers. "Get it from that side. See if any light shines through. Maybe we can get a silhouette of what's happening in there."

Jen glanced up at Dr. Fletcher. His eyes met hers. The twisting sliver of fear started to spread inside of Jen. She said quietly, "If those puncture wounds were from an ovipositor…"

Dr. Fletcher looked like he might be sick.

Albers put the flashlight on the ice on the other side of the bag. Schultz tilted his head and said, "No. I can't make anything out. Let's get this one on the table, see what's inside."

Jen elbowed Dr. Fletcher. He gulped for air, raised a quivering hand, and said, "Uh, I think we should first discuss the strong possibility the corpse in this bag may be, ah, contaminated. If these wasps are parasitoid... then some of these bodies may be hosts."

"You're saying that's more of those goddamn wasps in there?" Shultz asked while Albers said at the same time, "The remains were brought up from the ocean, two hundred feet down. Nothing survives that."

"You are correct, of course. Any wasps in the cabin certainly perished." Dr. Fletcher pointed at the bag. "Nevertheless, parasitoid wasps lay eggs either *on* their hosts... or *inside*. This body may have been... inseminated. It's possible the larva may have survived, protected inside the body. Even if the host is dead, theoretically, depending on the species, I suppose the larvae can still gorge themselves on the surrounding tissue."

"They've hatched." This time, Schulz wasn't asking a question.

No one spoke, instead contemplating the implications.

"This isn't the only host. The old woman," Jen blurted, as the fear spread inside in lightning flashes, crystalizing a realization about the corpse still on the MRI. "Get her in a body bag now. Trap the wasps inside."

A soldier sprinted back to the entrance, yelling, "Seal those bags!" He disappeared inside. "Zip 'em up!" A few seconds crawled past. A moment later, he reappeared and yelled back at them, "All clear."

"Quick thinking, Miss Huang," said Dr. Polderman. "Well done."

Jen tried not to blush.

The bag swelled up again and this time there came a curious sound, almost like someone stepping on a handful of Rice Krispies. Albers brought the flashlight beam over the expanded part of the bag and froze. "*Daaaaammmmmmnnn.*"

They all got closer for a better look. Jen swallowed. Seven or eight stingers had popped through the plastic. More followed.

"They can't..." Albers trailed off.

The stingers, nearly half an inch long and gleaming black, withdrew and were replaced by a flurry of commotion at the hole. "They're chewing at it. My guess is that it's the males. The females made the initial breach," Dr. Fletcher said.

"They can't chew through that plastic," Albers finished.

"They can't?" Schultz asked Dr. Fletcher.

"I have no idea," Dr. Fletcher said, edging toward the path back to the tunnel. "I don't know if I need to stick around to find out, though."

"Perhaps prudence would be the wisest choice in this situation," Schultz said to Albers. Albers nodded and pointed upwards, swinging his finger in a circle, letting the soldiers know it was time to wrap it up and evacuate. The first wasp head wriggled through the plastic. It was still slimy after crawling out of the corpse. The skull was hairless. Black and red exoskeleton. Blank, dead eyes. Jen couldn't help but feel as though it was looking directly at her.

"Time to go," Schultz said. Jen discovered that while they were focused on the lone bag in the middle of the clearing, the other bags were swelling now as well. More tiny pops, more and more, until the entire rink was alive in a liquid snapping, crackling, and popping symphony.

"Move!" Shultz yelled. "Go! Go!"

Jen immediately slipped and landed on her ass. Schultz hauled her up and they scurried along the trail as it snaked its way through the body bags. She wasn't the only one to fall. Dr. Polderman's feet went sideways and he landed hard on several of the bags.

He cried out and jerked away, holding his arm. Jen saw tiny dots of blood blooming through the white cloth of his lab coat and the latex glove on his palm. The pain hit him immediately. "Oh fuck, oh fuck, it *hurts!*"

The other people ahead of him did not look back. They hustled toward the tunnel.

Dr. Polderman stumbled after them.

Jen and Dr. Fletcher followed him, the last of the civilian scientists and doctors. Albers had pulled out a small pistol. Jen couldn't think of a reason why. There was nothing to aim at; it was impossible to kill the wasps by shooting at them.

All around them, the bags were moving, erupting with black needles like wriggling albino cactuses. The bright white bags were now spattered with fine specks of black clots of blood and the air suddenly bloomed with wasps.

The wasps rose, forming a slow, disorganized cloud that roiled over the rink. They weren't moving tightly, like a tornado; this was more like a young hurricane that hadn't been named yet.

The cloud changed, the wasps somehow compressing their mass inside the cloud, and small clumps formed, spinning slowly as they drifted down. Little by little, these clumps dispersed into clusters of wasps that further broke apart into couples; the male and females copulated in a frenzy of thrusts, frantic tiny movements of the males, mimicking the females' impregnation thrusts into prey, only faster.

After twenty or thirty seconds of enthusiastic sex, the wasps apparently plumb wore themselves out and drifted gently down to Earth through the horde fucking around them. They landed on the body bags, a mess of tangled limbs and wings, momentarily stunned, leaving the arena looking like black and red cherry blossoms from hell had fallen over speckled snow.

But only for the length of a heavy, resigned sigh. And for just a moment, the arena was still and quiet as the grave. Then the wasps rose into the air and went on the hunt.

CHAPTER 5

The bus hadn't moved up the expressway, not one inch, in at least fifteen minutes. They could see smoke up ahead from an accident, just this side of an overpass. It looked like it involved at least five cars. The cops had shown up ten minutes ago; the fire trucks and ambulances a couple minutes later.

Off to the left was nothing but the queasy green of the Everglades Wildlife Management Area that stretched endlessly to the horizon. East, there had been nothing but pink subdivisions for too many long miles. Now the pink townhomes were gone, swallowed up by another gigantic parking lot. It surrounded a vast white building, vaguely beetle-like in structure.

Andy had no idea that he was looking at a professional sports arena. He didn't give two shits about professional sports. He liked amateur bull riding, mostly. And backyard wrasslin'. Even if you knew damn well that behind-the-scenes stories and rivalries were made up, you drink enough beer, smoke enough weed, the spectacle was better than any expensive movie. At least the blood and broken teeth were real, not cheating special effects. He couldn't wipe the sweat out of his eyes with his shoulders anymore. The jumpsuit was coated in some chemical that repelled water, so it just smeared the salt back onto his eyeballs. He twisted, glaring up at the guard behind him. "I'm writing to my congressman about this. And I'm going to start with you." He read the guard's uniform. "Haylock? I'm putting your name in the email, first goddamn line."

Haylock ignored Andy. He wasn't looking too happy in the heat either.

"You in a hurry to get to your cell?" Squirrel asked, leaning forward to see Andy. "Say goodbye to all this sunshine?"

Andy didn't have a chance to figure out if Squirrel was being sarcastic or if he was serious because a fire truck rolled out of the smoke up ahead, siren shrieking, and came barreling back down the grassy median that split twelve lanes of the Sawgrass Expressway. At least a dozen firefighters clung to the sides, some on top with all the hoses. Red lights filled the bus as the truck passed.

Something was wrong. It didn't feel right. This wasn't just a few firefighters going for a ride on their way to somebody's suburban backyard to mop up a malfunctioning BBQ propane tank spill. This was something else. Something serious. And the speed; the truck was hitting at least fifty miles per hour by the time it passed the bus.

They weren't supposed to drive that fast *away* from a fire.

Hobson, the Special Forces officer, was speaking in low murmurs into his phone, a heavy, blocky thing with a stubby antenna. "Quebec Victor Charlie, I have a ten-twenty-six in progress. Requesting a visual." He checked his watch. "Copy that." He hung up, told the other soldiers, "Two minutes."

A scream. Somewhere up ahead.

Second Lieutenant Thompkins hunched over in the front and surveyed the trucks and cars and chaos surrounding the bus. He said, "Okay, men. We've got ourselves a situation here. Our job is simple. Control and contain the passengers on this bus. I don't want no heroes. You see any shenanigans, you shoot to kill. I mean that."

"Shut the fuck up," Hobson said without anger. "I'm on the phone." Second Lieutenant Thompkins wasn't sure if he should respond to that or not.

Gunfire cracked from the accident scene.

The effect was immediate. Most of the cars on the outside lanes peeled off, turning around on the paved shoulder. Others spun onto the median and followed the fire truck south. Drivers in cars in the middle lane began to panic and smash into the vehicles in front and behind in an effort to get clear. People began emerging from their autos to confront other drivers and try to gain a sense of what was happening. Horns and shouting rose along the expressway.

The Toyota Corolla two cars up from the bus suddenly decided to pull out, but found there wasn't enough room. Whoever was driving said *fuck it* and simply put the engine in reverse and hit the gas. The rear bumper crashed into the Lexus between it and the bus with a crunch, hard enough to knock the Lexus back into the bus.

The bus driver called back to Hobson. "Ah, what's the plan here? Things are getting tense outside."

The Lexus's driver, an old guy with long gray hair and black compression socks, got out, shaking his head in disbelief, as the Corolla found enough space and whipped a U-turn. The old guy yelled "What's your problem, asshole?"

Neither one of them saw the man run out of the smoke.

"Fuck you," screamed the Corolla's driver, a harried-looking Asian man with five older relatives in the car yelling directions and recriminations at him.

"Hold on," Hobson said. He murmured into his phone again.

"Fuck *me*?" The geezer went back to his Lexus and pulled a revolver out of the trunk.

"Fuck *you*, asshole," and squeezed a couple rounds off. If he hit anything, he didn't know it.

The running man got closer. He hadn't moved faster than a reluctant shuffle in at least a couple decades, but that wasn't slowing him down. His beer belly was quite impressive, even by Florida standards. It bounced and swung back and forth out of his open pink Hawaiian shirt of dancing women in hulas and exploding volcanoes. He had a New England Patriots logo tattooed on his forearm. He wore camouflage golf shorts and one flip-flop. His face was the color of a baboon's ass.

His single bare foot slapped on pavement like a steak onto a cold grill. He was screaming like his dyed hair was on fire.

He wasn't the only one. Other people followed, abandoning their cars, either running up through the stopped traffic or following the tracks of the fire truck. More gunfire.

A police car came shooting away from the accident, heading south on the median, but yawed to the west and smashed into the gridlocked traffic there. No one got out. The windshield was full of holes. A crowd gathered.

The guy in the pink Hawaiian shirt crashed into the old Lexus driver and they both tumbled to the pavement. But then Andy saw the floating shadows following. The black shapes, just vicious squiggles in the harsh sunlight, seemed to float on dust motes suspended in the gossamer heat of a Florida afternoon. They looked almost like tiny balloons, something made by a vindictive child's birthday clown who liked to twist his black and red balloons into something uncomfortable and menacing. They could have been attached to the tourist's legs by lengths of thread, floating serenely along in his wake.

"Fuck are those?" Squirrel asked.

"Toys?" the handsome prisoner suggested. He had introduced himself as "Juan Angel," that with a Spanish-accented hard G, "Benedicto Ramirez."

For some reason, Squirrel had focused on the name *Angel* and couldn't get his head around that. "Angle?" he kept asking. Now, Squirrel was skeptical. "I don't think they're toys."

"Toys. You know, little plastic robots that fly? Little helicopters?"

"RCs, man? Remote control? Who's flying 'em?"

Andy was glad he hadn't mentioned balloons.

The fat guy untangled himself from the Lexus driver and kept running. The old guy took one look at the shadows and jumped back into his car, locking the door for some reason. They moved slow, bumping gently against the car as if they were nearsighted.

"Birds? Grasshoppers?" Ramirez suggested. Then, more confident: "Birds."

More of the floating creatures descended out of the sky. Hundreds. Then thousands, until the sun resembled a congealing scab. Many settled on swimming pools to the east and disappeared into the Everglades to the west. Some followed people running through the cars at a distance, like it was a game. Everybody else stayed squarely in their cars, watching terrified as the insects landed on the windows and explored the edges of the glass with a disquieting concentration. Some landed on the bus windows, crawling over the wires. It became very clear these were not birds.

"Holy fucking Jesus. You ever seen wasps like that?" Squirrel asked, truly awed.

"It's them murder hornets. I saw 'em on the news," Ramirez said.

Andy noticed that Carver, the prisoner in the dark hood, had lifted his head, cocking it slightly, again a curious movement, as if he was finding a better position for echo locating. Although his movements were slow and muted, there was a certain wildness in the way he moved. It made Andy pay attention. Dude looked ready to explode. Andy wanted to be ready for anything, so he shut out the world outside, all the chaos on the expressway, and confined his full attention to the inside of the bus.

CHAPTER 6

They'd almost made it to the stairwell in a backstage corridor when Dr. Polderman collapsed. His hand looked gangrenous, the wet kind, where the skin splits and weeps a foul mix of bad blood, rotting plasma, and dissolving tissue. The putrefaction was spreading; his arm had swollen until it had filled the sleeve of his lab coat and now the sour liquid was seeping through the once white fabric.

Little thought had been given to where they were all running, just a mad dash to get as far away as fast as possible. Some hadn't gotten out of the arena in time. They went down thrashing as hundreds of wasps went for bare skin and crawled under collars, up into shirts and pant legs. Jen and Dr. Fletcher found themselves following Shultz and Albers in a group of about seven or eight others.

Once off the ice, they staggered into the tunnel and broke into flailing sprints. The soldiers trapped inside opened up, blasting impotently at the wasps. The only real damage was to the expensive OLED displays.

Dr. Fletcher lagged, gasping for air. Despite her reluctance to touch him, she grabbed his sleeve and pulled him along. "I—can't—breathe," he panted.

"I don't care. Run!" Jen yelled.

More soldiers ran toward the shooting and Jen felt a sharp stab of shame. She was fleeing while others were trying to save lives. Shultz pushed her and Dr. Fletcher along with rough hands before she could think clearly. He kept the group moving, calling out quick directions when necessary.

They'd reached the back of the arena, in a large corridor that gave large vehicles and cargo access to the center, when Dr. Polderman crumbled. Shultz knelt over him. The group's headlong rush faltered. They stopped for a couple seconds, hands on their hips, catching their breath in a semicircle while Schultz knelt over him.

Dr. Fletcher had to use one hand on his knee, one hand on the wall to steady him as he gagged, trying to breathe and throw up at the same time. Jen curled her hand into a tiny fist and pounded on his back, possibly harder than necessary.

Albers waved his hand frantically and made a hissing sound like he was quietly trying to scare a cat off a desk.

Dr. Polderman struggled to his feet, using his left hand to push off the floor. "Please, please help, me." His eyes were wide and terrified. Schultz took him by the crook of his good arm and pulled him up. He took two wobbling steps before his knees gave out again. He slipped out of Schultz's grasp and landed on his right side and screamed. The cry echoed through the girders and along the curving concourse full of abandoned equipment.

Several wasps now floated at the end of the corridor like malevolent jellyfish.

"Quiet," Albers said out of the corner of this mouth.

Dr. Polderman either wasn't listening or couldn't hear him. He groaned and managed to rise to one hand and knees. His right arm hung limp and dead. "Oh God, oh please. Please!" Schultz pulled at his armpit and belt. Albers grabbed the belt on the other side, but bumped Dr. Polderman's swollen arm, prompting a fresh shriek.

More wasps appeared. Dozens now.

Albers met Schultz's eyes. Albers shook his head. Together, they gently lowered Dr. Polderman back to the floor. By this point, a dark, viscous liquid was seeping from his nose and eyes. Even his ears. Bubbles of the substance popped and leaked out of the side of his mouth. He protested and begged, sounding like he was gargling with oatmeal. "Please, please just wait. I can make it. Oh God, don't leave me here."

Twenty to thirty wasps cruised down the corridor.

"We'll be back to get you," Albers promised.

Dr. Polderman didn't believe him and began to cry. Black tears filled his eyes.

Everybody began to edge away, to the stairwell doors.

"No big movements. They'll see it," Jen warned. "Don't panic."

Albers couldn't listen. He drew his pistol again and rested it on his hip, finger on the trigger.

Several wasps landed on Dr. Polderman, crawling up his quivering legs to his torso. More landed on his head and started chewing on his cheeks and lips. He gave one last good howl, spraying clotted gore all over the wasps. The rest floated up near the ceiling, bobbing back and forth on invisible, lazy currents, waiting for more prey to reveal itself.

"Put that away," Schultz said through gritted teeth.

"It makes me feel better," Albers said.

No one else moved, barely even breathed, until a heavyset radiologist from the Mayo Clinic couldn't take it anymore and bolted. He was nearest the doors to the stairs and couldn't resist twisting the handle, shoving the doors open and dashing up the stairs like his ass was on fire. Most of the group followed him, clogging the doors, giving wasps time to streak after them, wings sounding like a rock polisher working on empty .22 shells.

Like the radiologist, Albers couldn't help himself. At least he moved in slow-motion, smart enough to know Jen had spoken the truth. He started for the doors, creeping along the concrete floor. He brought the pistol up, slower than a watch's second hand, aiming at a couple of slow-moving wasps that drifted closer and closer.

A third wasp came from nowhere landed on the barrel, lightly, like a dragonfly alighting upon a brackish part of the creek, just to snatch a quick sip of water and escape before a predator could strike.

Albers flinched.

He fired, punching a hole in the ceiling. The wasp recoiled, folding its wings over its body as the blast of gunfire rippled through the corridor. It rode the wave, then attacked. Albers was turning to run when it landed on his forehead and thrust its stinger into his eye. Albers involuntarily twitched and squeezed the trigger again. The time, as the bullet exploded out of the pistol at that precise angle, it burrowed through the lean muscle of Shultz's jaw and popped out the other side, blowing Shultz's ear off.

Albers's head snapped back. His scream came out as a gargled yelp, and he spun blindly into the wall, screaming and thrashing as he went down. The wasp yanked its stinger out of Albers's eye and rose, wings thrumming. Blood and pink eyeball viscera dripped from its stinger.

More wasps pounced.

Schultz's mutilated mouth fell open, hanging from one tenacious jawbone as he staggered back against a maintenance door and went down.

Everybody broke in all directions, some trying to go forward into the doors upstairs, some back down the corridor to the ice. Dr. Fletcher kicked Shultz out of the way, grabbed Jen's arm, and pulled her into the maintenance closet. The door closed with a soft *snick*. They heard wasps bump the door in light, exploratory whispers.

"We're safe, we're safe," Dr. Fletcher said, heaving the words out between great gulps of air. Jen realized she could see light from below, between the door and the carpet. They took a few more deep breaths, hands over their mouths, muffling the sound. The dim light flickered; shadows broke the narrow beam into pieces as several wasps crawled under the door.

CHAPTER 7

The wasps disappeared from the expressway. It happened fast. Together, acting on some undetectable cue, they all flew off at once and were swallowed up by the sky.

For a few minutes, nobody moved, just waited to make sure the monstrous insects weren't hiding somehow. When it became apparent that the wasps had well and truly disappeared, a palpable sense of relief settled over the frozen traffic. People opened their doors cautiously, stuck their heads out to get a look around. Others settled for peering through the windows, staying inside where it was safe. As far as anyone could tell, the pale blue sky was empty. They couldn't even see birds. This feeling that they'd been spared from some awful disaster grew. A couple of heartfelt "holy shits" echoed up and down the lines of cars. Even some nervous laughter could be heard.

Hobson looked at his phone curiously, hit a few buttons, put it back up to his ear. After listening a couple seconds, he shook his head and called up front. "What's the situation?"

The soldier up front, Carradine, shrugged. "They're gone." Hobson put his head back up against the window, trying to see straight up. "Where?"

Carradine shrugged again, then tilted his head at the door in a question.

Hobson nodded. "Something's going on. We've lost contact with command for the moment." He told Carradine, "Go see what's up," then leaned forward and gently pressed his semiauto against Carver's head. "You know what this is, don't you? You sit tight, hear? I'm just as happy to deliver a corpse."

Andy heard Carver's voice, faint from under the bag. "Anything I can do to help... sir."

The driver opened the door and the soldier up front went down the stairs. He shielded his eyes against the sun and didn't go far. Looked up and down the line of cars, noting other drivers who were also getting completely out of their vehicles to look around. Someone shouted a question at him. He ignored it and wandered around to the front of the bus. He got down on his hands and knees, checking under cars.

Then a sound like a distant wave crashing into rocks. The sound grew, like approaching thunder, rising in volume until the ground itself seemed to shake. It was the wasps, streaking out of the sky like black hail. Although they did not understand glass, only the movement and smell and vibration of prey on the other side, they targeted windshields and back windows, splattering themselves into instant death. They slammed into the glass with such a fury and suddenness it reignited the panic along the expressway. The impacts left fissures and craters, and when the next four or five wasps struck the cracking windows, it created holes large enough for the rest to crawl inside.

Most of the people outside of their cars were taken down almost instantaneously. They had no cover, no protection. Diving back into cars only gave the wasps another opportunity to get inside. Caught out in the open, between the baking pavement and sizzling metal of the cars, humans didn't stand a chance. The wasps swarmed over the shrieking, running crowd, cunning enough to target the fastest and strongest people first. Even as the person would slap at the air in frantic but ultimately useless motions, seven or eight of the smaller wasps would cling to the head, thrusting their stingers into the neck, the cheeks, the eyes. Another four or five would attack the back of the ankles, severing the tendons. With their prey hobbled, crumbling to the ground in screaming seizures, the wasps went in search of new warm flesh.

Carradine didn't even have time to pull his pistol out of its holster, not that it would have helped. Wasps streaked out of the sky and struck him so hard they knocked him off his feet. He spun, arms flung wide, and crashed into the Lexus. The old man inside was still trying to find *drive* when more wasps burst into the vehicle and viciously attacked his face and neck.

The wasps assaulted the prison bus in the same fashion, smashing into the windows to get at the men inside with endless kamikaze enthusiasm. The sound was incredible, as if a tornado was flinging gravel at the bus. The glass cracked under the assault, but it was bulletproof and had been reinforced with thick wire, so it held.

Second Lieutenant Thompkins yelled at the driver, "Go! Get the hell out of here!"

"Hold up," Hobson said. "We have certain responsibilities here. I'm waiting on further orders."

"Your man's dead out there," Second Lieutenant Thompkins blurted. "Maybe we should wait for orders... somewhere else."

"We need to leave. Now," the driver agreed.

Andy saw Carver shift again. The movement was nearly imperceptible and if he wasn't watching close, he'd have missed it. The movement told him to get ready. Andy's universe grew smaller and he willed himself to ignore the chaos and screaming outside. He became intensely aware of only two people, Carver and Haylock. If things got worse outside, it wouldn't take much to break out of the bus in all the noise and confusion and slip away into the emptiness of the Everglades. If he survived the wasps, he could survive out there. Easy. Well, probably. He'd bury himself in mud for a day and wait for the boats and search parties and dogs to skip past. The authorities would have their hands full with all the wasps anyway. Hell, didn't rich folks pay good money to get covered in mud?

Andy made a decision. If a shattered eardrum was the price to pay for escape, so be it. He tensed and said, "I believe my rights are being violated. This is unsafe, hazardous conditions." Everybody ignored him except for Squirrel. Andy raised his voice. "The safety of my physical well-being is at serious risk. This is all going in the fucking letter."

Haylock stuck the shotgun through the bars and jabbed the back of Andy's skull with the sharp barrel again. "Shut the fuck up." This was what Andy had been hoping for.

Someone screamed and pounded on the bus door in a desperate attempt to escape the slaughter. It caught everyone's attention, at least for the briefest moment.

Almost everyone.

* * * *

When Carver moved, so did Andy.

Carver exploded backwards, twisting his body until his hips hit the top of the seat, and looping his cuffed hands over Hobson's head, then pulled back, slamming the man's head off the bar on his seat. His pistol spun away. Using the man's head and the back of the seat, Carver kicked out with both feet, connecting with another Special Forces soldier, Davillo, across the aisle.

Andy drove his legs down and bashed himself into the bars, pinning Haylock's shotgun between his right ear and shoulder. At the same instant, he grabbed the end of the barrel and slammed it into the bus wall, careful to keep his hand and head out of the blast range just in case. Even if it wasn't too smart, most guys like Haylock kept the breech open because they just loved that particular sound of intimidation, jacking a fresh round into a pump shotgun. Even beyond that, Andy was betting that the MP, being a professional cop, was at the very least keeping his finger off the trigger, holding it instead alongside the trigger guard.

Haylock was not a professional.

Andy yanked on the barrel, trapping Haylock's finger inside the trigger guard. Andy twisted the shotgun. The sound of both knuckles cracking was lost in the deafening roar of the chaos outside. But Haylock's shriek got everyone's attention. At least he'd been smart enough to keep the breech empty, so at least Andy didn't have to deal with a shattered eardrum. He twisted and viciously slammed the rubber butt into Haylock's chest, tearing the man's right nipple halfway off.

Meanwhile, Carver was using Hobson's head as leverage as he kicked out and wrapped his leg manacles around Davillo's shoulder. He rolled his hips, cracking the soldier's forehead into the metal edge with the crunch of a hard-boiled egg.

Ramirez leaped out of his seat, looped his cuffs over an MP's head and jerked backwards, slamming the man's head off the window a few times.

Carver ripped his hood off. He had wild eyes above a full beard.

The big guy next to Andy had managed to get his fingers through the bars, getting hold of the second guard's collar. His right hand fumbled for the shotgun, but the guard had dropped it and was clawing at the giant with both hands.

The MP in front went for his pistol.

But Carver was faster.

He snatched the pistol out of Hobson's shoulder holster and squeezed off two rounds with the fluidity and grace of an eagle snatching a salmon. The first went through the MP's foot. The second punched through the CB radio. Plastic shrapnel burst into the air.

Second Lieutenant Thompkins was still crouched, unsure if he was up for a gunfight, using the MP in the aisle as a shield. That man had just lost a couple of toes and was now howling on the floor, leaving Thompkins wide open downrange. He scrabbled for his own pistol, seeing both of the Special Forces soldiers fighting to stay conscious. Before his pistol could even break free from its holster, his eyes flicked up and he saw that Carver was already holding a steady bead straight at his head.

"Don't make me," Carver said.

Second Lieutenant Thompkins saw the score, laid his pistol on the floor, and slid it down to Carver's feet. The only one left up front was the driver, and he was busy trying to pluck a big plastic splinter out of his eye to give a damn about anything else.

Carver turned and faced the rest of the bus. Ramirez had released the other MP by now, so Carver grabbed Hobson by the hair and jerked him upright. The bridge of Hobson's nose had been split, and blood ran into fluttering eyelids over white eyeballs. Carver pressed his pistol against the man's skull and gave everybody a meaningful look.

The MPs were helpless and pathetic; they couldn't stop their eyes flitting back and forth from the psycho with a gun to the wasps and pandemonium outside.

"Understand this," Carver said. "You can walk off this bus or be carried out."

The second MP in the back slowly slid his shotgun out to the giant.

Andy was still pissed about the jab on his noggin' earlier, with the goddamn barrel, no less, and decided Haylock wasn't taking the situation seriously enough. So he reversed the shotgun and popped Haylock in the teeth with the muzzle. Blood spilled out of the MP's mouth as he tried not to whimper. "Go ahead, move again," Andy said.

Nobody had much fight left after that.

"You," Carver pointed at Andy. "I like you. Swap uniforms with Mr. Sleepyhead here."

He shook the spec-op officer's head by the hair.

Carver unzipped his own orange jumpsuit. "That goes for the rest of you. Gentlemen in orange, get those cuffs off. Make yourselves look all official. Pigs, you get in those jumpsuits instead. See how it feels. Then you sit your bad selves down and this time, boys, make sure all these Captain America wannabes are handcuffed to the seat. Hate to have another mutiny. Twice in one day would not look good in the report."

He nodded at the giant. "What's your name, soldier?"

"House. Cause…" He lifted his heels slightly and the top of his head hit the ceiling.

"Well, House, you ain't gonna fit in none of these boys' clothes, so I want you back there, acting like any other prisoner on this bus. But you're gonna keep an eye on things, you and that scattergun."

Andy had the opposite problem. He had to roll up the MP uniform's pants cuffs and shirtsleeves and cinch the belt tight just to be able to move. The hat kept slipping down over his face, but the sunglasses helped hold it in place. Carver pointed at Ramirez. "You drive stick?"

Ramirez nodded.

"Put on the driver's uniform and get set up there. We're leaving."

Ramirez put on the uniform and sat down behind the wheel, strapped himself in, and got used to the dashboard. He nodded at Carter.

By then, everybody had more or less swapped clothes. There wasn't enough to go around, so those that took pants wore their undershirts, while the rest took the MPs' shirts over the jumpsuits and put on the helmets. Law enforcement personnel were handcuffed, and this time the original prisoners ran the chains through the loops on the back of the seats.

A dozen prisoners, now armed and halfway disguised, waited for orders. There was no discussion to be had. Carver had taken control over the entire bus, MPs and inmates, quick as snapping his fingers.

CHAPTER 8

When shadows appeared in the light under the door, Jen quickly shrugged out of her cashmere sweater, stretched it the width of the door, and let it float gently down to the gap between the door and the concrete. The wispy material settled just as the wasps' heads were emerging, draping itself over them with the grace and weightlessness of a spiderweb. The wasps gave the fabric a few exploratory nudges and bites, but ultimately decided it was nothing. They withdrew and Jen jammed it tighter under the door with the side of her shoe. The sweater remained inert, proving dense enough to stop any more explorations from the wasps.

The closet light was controlled by a motion detector and after thirty seconds, it vanished, leaving the two in near total darkness. The two of them fought to control their breathing. After a while, Dr. Fletcher waved his arms to reactivate the light and turned to the shelves. Amidst all the mops and buckets, boxes of latex gloves, stacks of toilet paper and paper towels, he found a can of WD-40. That went on the floor between his shoes. He dug deeper and found a can of Raid.

"I'm not sure that will be enough," Jen whispered.

Dr. Fletcher gave her a sick smile and pulled a plastic lighter out of his pocket instead.

"Any get close, and they'll wish they hadn't."

Jen whispered, "Don't kill any unless we have to. Might bring others." They waited another ten minutes before they eased open the door slightly and another ten before opening it enough to slip out.

Dr. Fletcher and Jen could either head left, away from the center to the huge rolling doors, presumably leading outside, but Jen didn't think they could get the rolling doors open quietly enough without attracting any wasps.

They certainly couldn't go to the right, back toward the staging area off the ice. God only knew what the area around the MRI scanners looked like now. Even within the corridor itself, the bodies of Albers and Schultz and the other doctors and scientists were strewn across the concrete. No wasps could be seen, but they both heard a faint thrumming, seemingly coming from the center of the structure.

These wasps were big enough that you could actually hear their beating wings as they fluttered through the air. Jen realized with a start that she had solid information, something that could help, instead of the general overwhelming awfulness. It almost made her happy, knowing that she would have a warning if wasps got close.

Dr. Fletcher was already heading for the stairway doors. There was really nowhere else to go. He turned and urged Jen along by waving his hands, both of them trying to move lightly enough so their footsteps on bare concrete wouldn't echo. Dr. Fletcher held up the can of Raid and his lighter while Jen carefully twisted the handle and inched the door open. They both remembered how wasps had followed the heavyset radiologist into the stairwell.

The stairwell was empty, except the bodies. The dead radiologist had made it the farthest, and he had only reached the next landing. No wasps could be seen or heard.

Dr. Fletcher said quietly, "Small consolation. These have been used for food. Not hosts."

* * * *

Deciding to try for the conference room, where there was a phone and the probable location of any survivors left in the building, they continued to creep up the stairwell for three more floors. Jen flattened herself against the wall and pressed her face against the edge of the doorframe. Dr. Fletcher eased the door open. She saw the familiar plush carpet of the executive suites. "I think we're close to the conference room. Can't see any wasps," Jen said, barely more than breathing the words. "Not from here, anyway."

Dr. Fletcher gradually opened the door until Jen could twist her head around the doorframe. The corridor was empty. Back on familiar ground, Dr. Fletcher slipped the can of Raid and the lighter into his jacket. He had regained some color back in his face and cleaned most of the vomit off his chin. He took Jen's hand in a tight, clammy squeeze and pulled her along.

For a moment, Jen instinctively submitted. She thought about it for a half second and yanked her hand back. Why he thought she needed help mystified her. Like she couldn't figure it out herself. Maybe old habits died hard. Then, more depressingly familiar, was the recurring thought that maybe she should have let herself be passively pulled to safety.

Dr. Fletcher didn't slow down until the corridor ended in a T-junction. No wasps in either direction. He knew where to go and strode purposefully down to the big double doors and put his ear up to the wood. He gave the door a quick shove to see if he could rouse anything inside.

Jen hung back, ready to run in case any wasps burst out of the conference room.

All remained quiet, so Dr. Fletcher opened the left-side door and stepped into a sudden cloud of pepper spray.

"Oh shit!" someone exclaimed and Dr. Fletcher was pulled inside. Jen heard harsh whispering. "We thought it was wasps! Oh damn. Sorry. My bad."

Jen caught the door and slipped inside, screwing her eyes and mouth shut as she passed through the cloud of pepper spray. She blindly shut it behind her, wanting to close it before the smell brought any wasps to investigate.

Dr. Fletcher was on his knees, making a steady, droning cry of pain from deep in his throat, like a reluctant patient getting a tooth drilled. A man in medical scrubs was pouring bottled water over his face. The woman who sprayed him hovered nearby, alternately shushing Dr. Fletcher and whispering she was sorry.

About two dozen more people were gathered near the podium at the far end of the table, where Shultz and Albers had made their presentation earlier. The top FEMA guy was on the landline. It looked like everyone else was prepared to run deeper into the inner offices if necessary. The survivors ranged from wide-eyed young soldiers clutching their AR-15s to various technicians to lesser FEMA officials to two cleaning women. Their gray plastic rolling garbage bins had been shoved into a corner.

"Two additional survivors just arrived," the FEMA guy told the phone.

Jen saw the TVs.

Images of disaster and chaos and death took her breath away. It was overwhelming, too much to take in, to make any sense of the footage at first. Every single TV was tuned to live coverage of the mindless cataclysm the wasps had created, much from news helicopters. Chyrons screamed *MIAMI HORROR* and *TERROR IN SOUTH FLORIDA*. Anchors, looking ill-prepared and shaken, stumbled and stuttered as they inanely tried to describe scenes of the rapidly unfolding emergency. Most spent more time listening to their earpieces than delivering any kind of coherent message.

Jen saw people running, traffic jammed everywhere as citizens tried evacuating at the same time; car accidents, quick shots of bodies, some bloody, some not. She recognized the BB&T Center from the aerial shots, and the destruction surrounding it left her feeling hollow and helpless. The parking lot looked like the floor of a playroom after a rampaging toddler had tossed Matchbox vehicles all over the place. The helicopters were close enough to make out the bodies strewn across the lot, most of which were clustered around the front of the Center.

"What kind of wasp can open a fucking door handle?" Dr. Fletcher asked no one in particular.

"I said I was sorry," the woman said. "Now be quiet."

"Susan." the FEMA guy said, pointing to the phone and to his lips.

"Don't you shush me, goddammit. You're the one that tried to blind me," Dr. Fletcher shot back.

"Stop whining," Gary, the male nurse, said. "You'll live. More than most of the people downstairs can say."

Dr. Fletcher knew he didn't have much of an argument for that, so he kept his mouth shut.

Chopper 4/CBS Miami dropped from around 1,500 feet and settled around 500 feet, hovering over the parking lot. The camera zoomed in on the shattered glass of the front of the building, and Jen clapped a hand to her mouth in horror as she saw the heap of bodies jammed in the doorways. The shot steadied and grew clear until the camera could distinguish wasps crawling over the awkwardly splayed corpses.

Other stations picked up the feed until at least half the TVs displayed the same footage. Some of the anchors tried to explain the presence of the wasps, but most could only mutter empty commentary like "...this truly disturbing footage..." or "...almost too ghastly to comprehend..." or "...waiting to receive word if these creatures, are indeed, the infamous murder hornets." They always ended with some variation of "...If you are anywhere in the Sunrise area, leave immediately. We have word that refugee centers are currently being set up in the towns nearby and as soon as we receive more information we'll put it on the air."

A news chyron from FOX asked, *MURDER HORNETS TERROR STRIKE?*

Jen shook her head without realizing it. She didn't think they were hornets, for one thing. Even though hornets, for the most part, grew larger than wasps, she knew that only species of wasps impregnated living hosts with their young and could not think of any parasitic hornets. However, if they were wasps, she couldn't deny that these would be the largest wasps in the world by far. And murder? Insects killed to defend themselves or for food. That was simple survival. Murder was too emotional.

The close-up of the bodies was yanked sideways as chopper 4 wobbled and started climbing, fast. A blip of the reporter screaming came over the live newscast before an engineer back in the TV studio realized his mistake and killed the audio. The rest of the TVs switched over to shots from the news choppers that looked down on their stricken brethren. Chopper 4 began to spin and three long seconds later, it whirled into the traffic just beyond the overpass and exploded across the southbound lanes of the Sawgrass Expressway.

CHAPTER 9

Carver propped an automatic assault rifle on his hip and grinned at everybody. "Okay, men," he said, nailing second lieutenant's slight needling whine. "We've got ourselves a situation here. Our job is simple. Control and contain the passengers on this bus. Now, I don't want no heroes. You see any shenanigans, you shoot to kill. I mean that."

A news chopper spun wildly overhead and exploded in the southbound lanes, sending flaming wreckage across the expressway. "Time to go," Carver told Ramirez.

Ramirez laid on the horn and popped the clutch. He lurched the bus to the right, threatening a tiny Smart car that had been inching forward, trying to sneak up the expressway. He spun the wheel back the other way and yanked the gearshift into reverse, looked to back up until he could turn around. Carver touched his arm, lightly, shaking his head. "No. I'm pondering, in situations of great panic such as this, if pilgrims such as us shall find salvation by plunging into the abyss." His eyes looked to the east.

Nobody quite knew what that meant.

"There," Carver said, pointing up ahead and to the right at the off-ramp that led under the Sawgrass Expressway toll sensors and eventually turned east a half mile down.

Ramirez hit the gas, pushed the Lexus out of the way, and bumped an abandoned Subaru to pull out onto the shoulder. The bus was the only vehicle headed toward the smoke.

Andy held onto a bar as the bus yawed and swayed back and forth as Ramirez swerved wildly around other empty cars. He said, "These bugs. They gotta be coming out of the Everglades, right? You want to head out there?"

Carver shook his head. "Not unless we have to. Running through swamps won't help us. What we need is civilization. There's a whole shitload of activity over there, see it?" He pointed at the BB&T Center off to their right. Indeed, at least a dozen helicopters hovered amidst the plumes of black smoke. As he spoke, the distant boom of heavy gunfire and more explosions erupted from the Center. If anything, the wasps were even thicker in that direction. "Let's lose ourselves in there."

The bus rolled onto the Pat Salerno Drive exit ramp, passing so many palm trees it was almost a goddamn cliché. The first entrance to the BB&T Center's parking lot came up on their right and Carver nodded. They swung into the parking lot at nearly twenty-five miles an hour and came upon two Humvees blocking the road. The bus slowed and stopped. One Humvee was on fire. It all looked to be the remnants of a checkpoint, with four or five Jeeps forming a single lane. The Humvee windshields were full of holes and soldiers were scattered across the pavement like last winter's crumpled leaves. Wasps hovered above the bodies like clotted ground fog.

It was a mistake to stop.

They attacked from all sides. Tiny, dense grenades of pure hatred smashed into windows. Glass exploded into the bus, but the wire mesh held. Carver slapped Ramirez's shoulder and yelled in his ear, "If you're going through hell, don't fucking stop."

Ramirez shifted from *drive* into *low*, then hit the gas. It made the bus jump, crushing the bodies of soldiers as it surged ahead and plowed through the two Humvees. The sound of skulls under the tires would haunt Andy, but not right now. That aural memory went into its own safe-deposit box, locked away until he had a chance to breathe. He'd been through enough trauma to know the cycle, and that gave him an edge. It allowed him to focus on the simple task of survival.

Clear of the soldiers' bodies, Ramirez shifted back into *drive* and picked up speed. Some wasps clung to the sides of the bus, still fighting to get inside, but the majority left to join the dark cloud swarming over the BB&T Center. A straight route was impossible, not only because of the tangle of emergency vehicles, but the palm trees. Ramirez tried an indirect course and followed the four-lane access road that ran along the western edge of the lot.

The cracks in the shattered windows made it difficult to see, but details came into focus as they grew closer. Along with all the eighteen-wheelers and the emergency vehicles like police cruisers, the many, many ambulances and fire trucks, there were also black SUVs and luxury sedans with diplomatic plates scattered across the lot. Many of the vehicles' doors were open, as if the wasps had attacked immediately.

The men on the bus got a better look at the dead. Out in the open, bodies lay face down, arms and legs splayed out in unnatural angles, brought down while running away. Some had died trying to crawl out of their car or truck and were now draped upside down, heads swollen and purple. Others had tried to hide under the SUVs.

The bus reached a fork in the road, and down the left fork the front entrance was now an open, burning wound. The explosions had flung flaming debris across half the parking lot. They could also see that the flying nightmares were emerging from the arena itself. An unholy fountain twisted upward for several hundred feet before flattening out, spitting wasps in all directions as they sought fresh prey in the business and homes surrounding the Center. Most ignored the bus.

But not all.

Carver was pointing to the right fork that continued south and appeared to curl around the back of the arena, saying, "Let's circle—" As he spoke, a black flock peeled off from the mass migration above and swooped down. Andy couldn't tell if it was a few hundred or a few thousand. When the wasps hit, the impacts sounded as if the bus had flown through a load of buckshot.

Ramirez hit the gas and made the bus jump. Wasps fluttered, then dove back at the bus with a vengeance. The mesh wire continued to hold. When they reached thirty miles an hour, he eased up until he spotted a few wasps floating in the road ahead. He stomped on the gas again, making the bus roar at a slow-moving wasp. The impact left even more craters of crushed glass on the right side of the windshield and raised a cheer inside.

Ramirez took his foot off the gas entirely, letting their momentum carry them forward in relative silence. He didn't want to bring any more attention to the bus than necessary. At least, not any more. Eventually, as before, most of the wasps, if not all, gave up and went in search of easier flesh.

Something caught Andy's eye.

People. And they were still alive.

CHAPTER 10

"If I can have your attention," Lawrence Murphy, the FEMA guy, stood and loudly addressed the table, "I'm on the phone with the agency that is organizing our rescue operation right now." He adjusted his thick framed glasses. "We have been instructed to remain sheltering in place and will be escorted to the nearest hospital as soon as they wipe out this—this pestilence. It is safe in here. After all, those things can't go through walls yet." He gave a weak chuckle but no one else even smiled.

"Have you considered the possibility that one of the solutions our government no doubt is currently considering is bombing the living shit out of this place?" Dr. Fletcher said.

Murphy covered the phone's mouthpiece as if he was embarrassed and didn't want the other end to hear Dr. Fletcher's question. "No. That will not happen." Murphy shook his head in emphasis. "Not with... Americans trapped," and as if he couldn't help himself, his eyes flickered to the cleaning women.

They glared right back. One was them was a fierce little Hispanic woman. Her name tag read Rosie. Her partner was Lauren. Lauren was young and black with close-cropped bleached hair. Her nails, somewhat short due to the demands of her job, were still rocking brilliant shades of neon and no small amount of glitter.

"They are taking control of the situation and we will be rescued as soon as possible."

Murphy limped to a finish.

"I have no doubt they're taking control. Wonder how soon is 'as soon as possible.' And just curious, have you talked with anyone else? Outside

DHS? Wonder if they told anybody else we're all in here," Dr. Fletcher asked no one in particular.

Murphy said, "Why would I want them to call anyone else?" He was loud and patronizing. "I've been on the phone with the chair of the House Committee of Emergency Response and he passed me to General Granger. At this very moment, I'm being transferred to officials on the ground in charge of the operation." His voice grew strident and he drew himself up as he shook the phone at Dr. Fletcher and the rest of the group. Jen thought he was acting like he had a full-blown panic attack blooming inside, but was determined to force it down by sheer force of will. "Don't you understand? This is the United States federal government. They are in charge and they will take care of this situation."

The outburst left everyone a little stunned and quiet.

Murphy straightened even further when the phone beeped and said into it, "Yes, sir. Yes, sir. Most definitely, sir." He looked up at everyone seated around the table and said, "I'm going to put Captain Lewis on speaker for all of us. It's on here somewhere...Aha!" He found the right button. "Can you hear me?"

"Am I on speaker now?" a voice asked. He sounded rushed and out of breath.

"Yes, sir," Murphy said. "Everyone, say hello."

A few people said *hi* to be weirdly polite and Dr. Fletcher said, "I think he gets it."

"Okay, yeah. I'm Captain Lewis and I'm calling from inside the Dade County Mobile Command Center. Folks, we are about to engage in the first phase of the assault. Hold tight now, things are gonna get loud and bumpy."

"Wait, what? I don't—" Dr. Fletcher stopped speaking when the room rumbled. They felt the thump, the impression of a tremendous wallop somewhere downstairs. They all turned back to the TVs and watched as the front of the BB&T Center burst into black smoke.

"And those bugs are toast. Goddamn! Look at that!" Captain Lewis's voice got distant, and it was clear he was talking to someone else. "Huh. Suckers can fly when they're on fire." Then back to the phone, "Hang tight, folks, looks like we're gonna have to... ah, extend phase one." Apparently, they could still see wasps flying in the smoke. Another series of explosions.

A pause, while everybody waited for the images to clear. "Here we go! Phase two has begun." On the TVs, Jen could now see seven or eight Humvees hauling ass through the lot, smashing through many of the smaller cars and jeeps. They roared up to the entrance and distant crackles of automatic weapons could be heard. Soldiers jumped out of the Humvees and rushed into the smoke and wreckage. More gunfire.

"You folks hang tight. You'll be out in a jiffy. We... ah, we gonna—uh-oh." Captain Lewis was talking to someone else again. "No! What the hell? Oh, fuck shit fuck. Get 'em out of there!" Back to the phone, "Uh, folks, I'm gonna have to call you back."

The phone clicked.

"Maybe it's not such a bad idea that we think up a way out of here as a plan B," Jen said in a low voice. "We can stay here for now, but if... anything else happens, we can find a way out."

The group nodded and murmured in consensus, agitating Murphy. "We've been told to stay put," he argued. "Those are orders." He didn't elaborate why civilians would be forced to follow military orders, but Jen supposed it had something to do with the state of emergency and all that. "They're on their way," Murphy said. "Soon as they blow these things back to hell."

"That's not what it looked like. It looked like they got their ass handed to 'em," Dr. Fletcher said. "How long you think before they decide to use bigger bombs?"

Jen reached for her phone with the idea of going to the BB&T Center home page for some kind of map of the place. Then she remembered that her cell phone was still at the security checkpoint downstairs, along with everyone else's. "Rosie. Lauren," she said. "Are there any freight elevators, back hallways for staff, anything like that on this level? We should find another way out, some way that doesn't take us through the main concourse."

Lauren said, "They don't give us keys to anything bigger 'n a bathroom."

"This is all unnecessary and frankly, I think it's a waste of time," Murphy pointed out. He knew he'd lost all his power within the group and fretted over it.

Most ignored him as a second news chopper began to spin and tried to climb to safety. But it was too late. The wasps had breached the cockpit. Still, it climbed until it was almost straight up and down, then it finally pirouetted on its tail rotors, twisting and falling toward a subdivision to the south, where it crumpled into a pink roof and erupted into flames.

"Look, all I know is that it's almost certain death out there," Dr. Fletcher said, pointing at the TVs. "And it's certain death if we stay in here. *Almost* is still better than *absolutely fucking guaranteed* certain death. Or worse. If they don't kill you to eat you, they use you as an incubator. And once the babies have eaten most of you from the inside out, only then do you get to die."

The FEMA guy made a show of putting his finger in his ear and turning away while surreptitiously jabbing the *redial* button. Susan shushed everyone with a series of sounds like the raspy trills of a tiny bird.

Lauren pointed at the burning wreckage filling the TVs. "My car's way out in lot G. Right out over there, where the employees gotta park. Them things fly just as fast as you can run. You got yourself an invisibility cloak?"

"Yes. How will you hide?" Rosie asked.

Dr. Fletcher snapped his fingers and pointed at the ladies' cleaning bins. "Turn those suckers over you and crawl out."

Lauren and Rosie glanced at each other. He was too stupid to deserve pity. "Fantastic," Lauren said in a voice so flat and cold you could ice-skate on it. "Good thing we got—" she made a show of counting everyone in the room—"thirteen, no, fourteen parked out in the hall."

Jen went through the room, peering under the table, opening cabinets and drawers. Inside the podium she found a dizzying array of cables for every make and model of what looked like every computer since 1967. Twenty or so remote controls. Two laptops. Cases of batteries. And three twenty-five-foot extension cords. She gave a silent shout-out to whoever didn't let money get in the way of being prepared when they put this place together, pulling out the extension cords and putting them on the table. Two were still brand-new. She opened those and holding onto each end, she spun the cords down the table. Stepping back a few feet, she dragged the cords with her, pulling and straightening the cords as they unrolled from their coils. She tied the ends together, then began lightly twisting the cords into one large cord. Every two to three feet, she tied a fat knot. "Just in case," she said. Others saw what she was doing and stepped up, feeding her the cords.

Susan looked at the knotted extension cords and said, "What are you doing?"

"It's a kind of ladder," Jen said, untwisting the cords between two knots. "You can put your feet in here."

"I can't climb that." Susan looked at the group for support. "I can't."

"Very clever," Murphy said, looking over the knotted extension cords. "But you'll see. Any minute you will hear a knock at the door."

"Try not to Mace 'em, Susan," Dr. Fletcher said.

"It was pepper spray!"

Rosie asked, "You hear that? Shhhhh."

"Are you kidding me?" Susan was pissed and wasn't shy about shaking her finger at Rosie and Dr. Fletcher. "Don't you dare shush me. You have no right. No right. We're all under a lot of stress here."

"Shhhhhh!" Rosie said again, patting the air in front of her as if to tamper Susan's indignant yelps. Jen heard something, like a bare wire striking metal in an irregular rhythm. It had a lazy rhythm with no apparent purpose.

"Wait. Shhhh!" Gary said. "I hear something too."

Jen listened harder in the silence. Still nothing. Still no special telltale buzz of their wings. Or at least, she couldn't discern it from whatever it was she could hear. It had grown louder, filling the room in furtive whispers. Everyone could hear it now.

Jen tied knots as fast as she could.

Dr. Fletcher snapped his fingers and blurted, "They're in the air vents." Panic rippled through the room, picking up steam as it spread. He shook his head at Murphy. "It's because those stupid motherfuckers bombed the building and drove the wasps into the upper floors."

Murphy opened his mouth like he wanted to curse Dr. Fletcher out, but couldn't find the words.

"We gotta go," Dr. Fletcher said, looping the braided extension cords around his left arm, jerking the ends out of Jen's hands. "Now." Only three others followed immediately. Out of the rest of the survivors, two or three were with Murphy until the wheels came off, but the rest, about six or seven, were torn. They were scared to death and had no idea whether their best course for survival lay with Murphy or Dr. Fletcher.

"Just close them!" Murphy said. "We can keep that foul abomination out. Just close the vents!"

"How do we close them?" Gary asked Rosie and Lauren.

The women shrugged. "Never had to," Lauren said.

"I don't give a good goddamn if or when you can close 'em," Dr. Fletcher said, gathering his things and heading to the door. "They'll get in here. You can't stop them." He stopped, his hands on the handle. He looked back at Rosie and Lauren.

Rosie was tugging on her coworker's arm, trying to get Lauren to leave with Dr. Fletcher's group. "Balcony. To the left, look for the glass door. Right?"

Rosie nodded, looked one last time into Lauren's eyes, and dropped the younger woman's wrist and walked across the room to join Dr. Fletcher, Jen, Gary, and Susan. She turned her back on Lauren and said, "I'll show you."

Dr. Fletcher opened the conference room door and held it for Rosie.

It was unclear if Murphy was more upset at the blatant disregard for authority with a mutinous group about to walk out, or the fact that he'd been betrayed by what he thought of as his closest, most trusted advisor: Susan. She'd chosen to follow Dr. Fletcher, and was now even trying to use

Gary as a shield so she'd get out of the room as quickly as possible. Murphy was so furious that real emotions split his political facade, triggering a hateful sneer.

Jen addressed the rest of the group. "Please. Come with us. You will not survive in here. He's wrong."

Everybody flinched when the sounds coming through the vents grew teeth and the noise scraped through air; still lazy, but relentless in its insistence. Lauren took one hesitant step toward Rosie, who was clutching Jen for support, catching her breath before the dash to safety. Rosie nodded in encouragement. Lauren took another step. She was still ten yards from her friend when the wasps burst into the room.

CHAPTER 11

Andy pointed.

There, dangling down the side of the arena was a line of people, climbing down some kind of tangled rope or something. One man with long hair in jeans and a sports jacket, was the first one down. Soon as he hit the ground, he sprinted for the bus, leaving his companions behind without hesitation. Next was a red-haired woman who shuffled along in a tight skirt and bare feet. More followed.

Ramirez took his foot off the gas. "What's the word, boss?"

"Fuck 'em," one of the other prisoners said. This was Magnus. Without much of a chin, his face had a yawning, full moon effect, round and white; all the features were slightly off-center, as if they'd been tossed there by a disgruntled pizza maker.

Most of the prisoners agreed, but quieted when Carver shook his head. "We got ourselves a tail up there somewhere, keeping an eye on us. These poor bastards might just prove useful."

The survivors ran to the bus through the smaller parking lot behind the Center, mostly ringed with luxury four-door GTs. Mercedes. Jaguar. Audi. Their frantic movements left wakes in the drifting smoke.

Wasps followed these ripples.

Carver yanked the handle and the first survivors fell inside. "Thank God you're alive," he yelled and pulled the professor dude and woman in the conservative suit aboard before they got a close look at anything and decided to take their chances outside.

Andy watched three more sprint through the cars, some guy in scrubs, a cute little Asian girl, and an elderly woman in a maintenance uniform. Someone else appeared up on the balcony. This was a young black woman, dressed like the older lady, moving too fast. She dove over the railing, scrabbling to grab the tangled cords as she fell. She managed to slide her fist through a loose cluster of wires at the last second. As the rest of her body plummeted toward the pavement, the closest knot jerked shut around her left wrist at the precise wrong angle, and the brutal jerk popped the carpel bones right out of her wrist. The sudden, blinding pain, combined with the sudden lack of resistance, allowed her hand to slip free, and she fell fifty feet until cracking headfirst into a dumpster and flopping to the cement.

The old lady heard the impact, turned, and screamed. This caught the girl's attention and she turned back as well to pull at the lady's arm.

Andy bolted out of the bus with his new pump-action shotgun as a torrent of wasps cascaded over the balcony. The doctor or nurse was at the bus now, watching the sky with wide eyes. Carver yanked him inside, then followed Andy out with his own shotgun. "Sure about this?"

Andy blasted a wasp at random about twenty feet up. Even though he misjudged the lead time just slightly, the effect was both immediate and beautiful. The lead shot tore through the wasp, leaving a viciously shredded husk behind, as most of the wet insides exploded into a fine, damp mist behind the corpse.

The women raced for the bus.

Carver fired. He got lucky with the wasps' erratic, looping method of flying and vaporized one that was getting too close to the running women. The wasps were roughly the same size and shape of hummingbirds, and a direct hit left nothing bigger than specks of tissue fluttering in the shock wave.

More wasps rained down.

In less time than it takes to blink, both men pumped fresh shells into the breeches and fired again.

The women reached them just as the wasps began to attack en masse. Carver and Andy blew through five shots apiece in less than three seconds. Wasp guts filled the air. The young woman pushed the older one through the door first.

Carver dropped his empty shotgun and drew the pistol and kept firing without losing a beat. He backed against them as the old lady slipped and fell. Someone grabbed her from inside. Andy had both hands on the young woman's tiny waist and was about to shove when a wasp appeared right next to him. It latched onto her ear and drew back the stinger to plunge into her neck.

Without thinking, Andy grabbed the surprisingly fragile creature, squeezing until it popped in his fist. It spasmed crazily, and the slimy viscera allowed it to squirm slightly out of his grasp. The wicked, curved stinger twitched and stabbed him right between the two knuckles of his ring and pinkie fingers. The stinger scraped bone. Andy went blind with rage and punched the side of the bus with the wasp so hard he left a dent. The lower abdomen of the wasp was now no longer attached to the thorax, but it still shivered and jerked, hanging from the stinger stuck deep into Andy's ligaments. He hit the bus again. And again. Ragged chunks of the wasp slid wetly from the cracks in his fist and dripped to the pavement.

Andy went to punch the bus again, but something was happening to his balance. And vision. The pain hadn't quite hit him yet, but it was coming, racing up his arm like a freight train. He felt the girl's hands on his as everything turned weird shades of green and gravity started to pull him sideways. He collapsed into bright, sizzling numbness as shock wrapped itself mercifully around his mind and turned everything off for a while.

CHAPTER 12

The first thing to hit Jen when she climbed on the bus was the smell. The odors had weight and substance; they ripped her attention away from Andy's hand. The sheer amount of sharp acidity of sweat alone in the air was enough to bring tears to her eyes. It almost was enough to obliterate the other smells, smells more gastrointestinal in nature that threatened to make her gag.

The second thing was that they'd made a serious mistake. It didn't take a genius to see the convicts had taken over. At least ten greasy men had taken up positions in the front half of the bus. Even Susan had figured it out. But Jen was too numb to care at that point. Death had been breathing down her neck for so long that her adrenaline was depleted, leaving nothing beyond seeping exhaustion. So instead, she focused on Andy. Of course, she didn't know his name yet. Somehow, she suspected it probably wasn't *HAYLOCK*, as the badge on his ill-fitting MP uniform claimed.

The cracking sounds of the wasps hitting the windows tapered off and eventually stopped completely, as if they had learned.

Jen took off her sweater, ripped it in half, and tied one piece as tight as she could around his palm. She settled him in the aisle, with his head on her lap. Gary was in the seat to her left, holding Andy's wounded hand high, away from the heart. Rosie and Susan shared the row ahead.

Dr. Fletcher was across the aisle, sharing his seat with a guy wearing a guard's pants and dirty T-shirt. The guy gave Dr. Fletcher a furtive smile every now and again.

The guards were spaced along the bus, keeping an eye both outside and on their new passengers. Some guy with a thin-lipped, casual grin drove, while the scary one who acted like a sadistic game show host stood up front and watched everything and everyone with an eerie calm. The prisoners sat stone-faced and bloody in the seats in the back.

The stinger had popped free fairly easily, despite being wedged in the ligaments of Andy's knuckles, leaving a nasty hole the diameter of a spaghetti strand. It bled surprisingly little. Venom darkened the bulging veins in his hand. His fingers grew rigid and wouldn't uncurl.

"It's swelling and hot," Gary said, shaking his head.

"That's what she said," Squirrel piped in.

Gary used his thumb to push on Andy's upper palm, trying to squeeze venom out of the back. Clear plasma peppered with black flecks ran across his hand and down his arm.

"It's spreading." He looked up at the leader, a man they would come to know as William Alexander Carver. "This man needs immediate medical care."

"Don't we all?" Carver grinned down at him.

Jen heard this in a distant way, as if she was listening to the conversation in another room down the hall. She couldn't help but feel that she was personally responsible for this man who had saved her. So she scraped and shoved the dregs of her adrenaline into a laser of concentration on Andy. Her mind whirled through the endless variations of the intricate properties of venom, measuring against it everything she knew so far, including the fate of poor Dr. Polderman. Some patterns she recognized, such as the paralyzing effect of the venom, but much of what she'd witnessed had flown in the face of all known characteristics of any wasps, anywhere. This species was obviously parasitic, yet every parasitic wasp she'd ever read about lived in a near total solitary existence, and this particular creature hunted in swarms like colonies. And when she factored in the absolutely gigantic nature of this wasp, the implications of the existence of the species itself threatened to overwhelm her.

Jen made a calculated guess that it had been a male wasp that stung Andy. Males were generally smaller, and from their behavior, she theorized they acted more like hunters for the females, immobilizing the host so the females could inject their larvae, as well as bringing down prey for food. But the male venom did not kill. At least, not outright. The wasps' survival depended on their young feeding on living tissue.

That meant that Andy had a chance. As she looked at him, she blinked and realized with horror that she was blushing. Something about him, the stubble on his sharp jaw, his obvious lean body, how he'd grabbed the wasp without hesitating. It was that something, a feeling that she'd never experienced before, the knowledge that someone could be so quick to sacrifice themselves for her, a total stranger. Abruptly, like realizing you're surprisingly ravenous, she recognized her increasing primal attraction for this man.

Jen stiffened her spine and shut that particular train of thought right down, mortified at herself. Still, the warm, comforting feeling in the pit of her stomach remained.

* * * *

In the same distant way Jen had heard the conversations around her, she was vaguely aware the bus was now moving, lurching through the debris-strewn parking lot. Her attention—purely professional, thank you very much—remained on Andy. Specifically, his hand. Even the plasma had dried up, as if his hand was like a sponge drying in the breeze. She'd only seen wasps going for the head or torso, and sometimes on the legs and upper arms. The stinger in Andy's hand had been stabbed not in deep tissue, but instead the densely packed network of bones and ligaments between his knuckles. She had no idea how the venom would contaminate his nervous system. If the wasps had evolved to primarily inject the venom into thick muscles or organs, using the soft tissue to dilute the toxin before it reached the heart, this meant that a higher concentration of the venom could be about to course through Andy's body, if it wasn't already.

"I don't know what's in the venom, but if too much hits his heart, it might kill him, instead of just paralyzing him," She told Gary. After a moment's hesitation, she twisted the remaining half of her sweater into a tight band, then wrapped it once around Andy's wrist and pulled it as tight as she could, nearly cutting off the circulation. She looped it again, maintaining the tension, then snapped her fingers so boldly at the closest new guard it surprised her more than the convict pretending to be an MP.

She pointed at the small flashlight clipped to one of the black straps.

Magnus glanced at Carver for guidance. She'd never gamble, not for real, but she'd lay down at least a hundred bucks this guy had a Confederate flag tattoo on his shoulder. Carver told him, "Assist our passenger, Magnus. She's helping us, remember."

Jen had him hold the flashlight flat against the back of Andy's hand, then tied her sweater around the metal shaft, enough so the material had a solid grip. She twisted the flashlight, spinning it clockwise across his wrist, cranking the fabric tight. Magnus winced. Gary shook his head. "He'll lose the hand."

Jen said, "I'll back it off later, if I can," and cut the circulation off to Andy's hand completely. She tied the remaining ends of the sweater into a delicate bow to hold the flashlight tight and gazed down at his slack face. "Better his hand than his life."

* * * *

Carver pointed something out to the driver and the bus veered to the right. Andy's head lolled in Jen's lap and she cradled him, sliding her right hand down to rest her index finger on his carotid artery. His heart could stop at any second.

"Look, I don't want to sound ungrateful or anything." Dr. Fletcher went up on one knee on the seat. "But, uh, what's the plan?"

"Settle down, Grandpa," Magnus said.

"Don't be rude," Carver said absentmindedly as he pointed again, concentrating on the world beyond the windshield riddled with impact craters and wasp guts. He eventually turned to Dr. Fletcher, saying, "The plan, such as it is, is for us to seek temporary shelter in yonder shopping establishment. With any luck, there's multistory parking somewhere close. We'll get ourselves out of the sun for a while and perhaps seek alternative transportation. I trust that meets with your approval?"

The bus rolled across 136th Avenue, leaving the BB&T Center behind. For the most part, the avenue was nearly empty, with only a few cars scattered up and down the six lanes. Most had shattered windows. A few were wrapped around unyielding palm trees, oozing steam. A short drive took them past several retaining ponds, complete with fountains. Two rows of smaller palm trees divided right and left lanes. The left lanes were clogged with a line of cars, all full of the dead and crawling with wasps. Ramirez took it slow and as they emerged from the trees, a huge mall loomed and a tasteful sign proclaimed *Sawgrass Mills*.

"Alternative transportation?" Dr. Fletcher asked. He tried hard to be casual, but Jen heard the hesitancy in his voice.

"Can we get him to a hospital?" Jen asked. "Please?"

"He's still alive?" Carver appeared genuinely interested.

Jen nodded.

"Good for him. Tough little bastard."

"Hey, boss?" Ramirez called back to Carver. "The only parking I'm seeing is your basic flat lot. No multistory parking." It was true. The lot stretched out forever, yet another lake of asphalt that spread out over at least a dozen acres.

"Built with the arrogance that land stretches out forever." Carver shook his head. "Let's get to the other side of this monstrosity, see if we can't find an appropriate ride. Something perhaps less conspicuous."

The bus rolled around the northern perimeter of Sawgrass Circle. The lot and the mall almost looked normal, if you ignored the smoke that filled the horizon to the west and south. Jen felt the sun slide from her face and circle around behind the bus, leaving a large, blissful shadow behind. Andy remained limp. But his pulse remained steady.

Carver rummaged around in the pack he'd tossed the phones and a few pistols. He pulled out a Glock, set it aside, tried a few phones. He found one he liked and held it up. "Whose phone is this?"

No one answered.

"I will get a thumbprint of every motherfucker on this bus and when your thumb tells us all the truth, I will shoot the person to your immediate left for shits and giggles, then cut your thumb off to make sure I've made my point."

Carradine raised his hand. His nose had been broken by Carver's kick and only now was the bleeding slowing down. Carver walked it over to him. Carradine knew better than to try anything so he unlocked the phone and handed it back over.

Carver consulted the phone, then typed something. When he passed over Jen and Andy on his way up front, she could see that he'd brought up Google Earth. Ramirez brought the bus closer to the mall and slowed.

Jen raised up to her knees, just enough to see if everything looked as normal as it did from at the back of the lot. It didn't. Chili's was on fire and looked empty. The Outback Steakhouse's windows were full of holes and she saw bodies littering the sidewalk. Clusters of people, families mostly, lay where they had fallen. Some had made it as far as the parking lot.

The remaining wasps appeared to keep busy, scuttling over and around the clumps of bodies. Some zoomed away or back, while others floated around, seemingly at random. No pattern could be discerned. A few of the bodies grew bloodier by the minute as the wasps fed. It looked as if those were the only people truly dead. The rest, even though wasps crawled all over them, were left relatively unmolested and intact.

They had to be at least a half mile from the BB&T Center. The fact that the wasps had spread this far didn't surprise her. Many normal wasps covered even bigger areas in search of food and God only knew how large of a territory these would claim.

Carver told Ramirez, "There's a delivery road or alley or something behind that lululemon over there. Let's see if we can't cut through this mall." Jen settled back to the floor when Ramirez drove over several people she hoped were dead on the way down the access road. She didn't need to see any more and tried to ignore the occasional soft bump as they crept along for a while. Soon enough, though, she had to look as the bus hissed to a halt.

A tangle of smashed cars clogged the access road between a Saks OFF 5th and a Coach outlet. It looked like everybody had tried to leave at once, creating a wreckage yard full of smashed windows and steaming radiators. Ramirez coasted up to the jagged barricade and had to stop. The bus would either have to smash its way through the blockage or reverse back the way they came in.

Carver eyeballed the vehicles on the other side. The road widened into an employee parking lot that shared space with loading docks for the larger stores. At least seven or eight cars had been parked in a row along the Saks wall. Several 18-wheelers had potential. A UPS truck was even closer. "Possibilities, possibilities." He grew quiet and peered out of their own smashed windows and tried to spot their helicopter followers.

* * * *

Carver rested his elbows on the seats and squatted by Andy's legs. "He still breathing?"

Jen wanted to say that Andy needed a ventilator, at the least; wanted to say that he needed a transfusion, wanted to say that she needed to take him away from all this, but couldn't get anything out. She managed a nod instead.

He gave Jen a warm smile. "Keep him with us."

Again, Jen only nodded.

Carver stood. "Rest of you, a bit further, all the way to the back, if you please." His eyes had gone cold and soulless, as if he'd left any humanity he'd had with Jen and Andy. Rosie was the only one to stand. "I'm afraid this includes you as well," he told Dr. Fletcher and Susan.

"Uh, I gotta help your buddy here," the nurse said.

"That's very kind of you," Carver said, "but this lovely young lady has already filled that position. You, sir, are needed in the back with the rest of... the unexpected guests we've accumulated."

Dr. Fletcher, Susan and Gary reluctantly stepped over Andy and Jen and joined the MPs and soldiers.

Sensing a massacre, a panicked second lieutenant blurted, "You're a liar!"

Carver stepped back, offended. "How dare you, sir. I am many things. Many bad things, true. But I am also a man of my word and I give you this promise. I will never lie to you." He waved the Glock. "Everybody in the back, except you, good sir. I have no doubt everyone is quite relieved now that you've volunteered your services."

The second lieutenant chewed on the insides of his cheeks for a while until he gave up and joined the convicts at the front.

"See that UPS truck, over by those trucks? I have no doubt the key's still in the ignition. Door's open. See the driver? Brown shirt, there. He made it all of maybe ten feet."

"Okay..." Long pause. The second lieutenant swallowed painfully. "And?"

"I promise you," Carver said, "you have my full permission to step off this bus without a bullet in your head. I cannot make the same promise if you remain aboard."

"And then?"

"You'll bring that vehicle back over to the other side of this traffic jam here and I won't have to shoot anybody else in the head. Your best chance would be to get to that UPS truck, but that's up to you. Godspeed."

Ramirez slapped the door open as Carver grabbed Second Lieutenant Thompkins by the back of his stiff collar and his belt and threw him down the stairs. Thompkins rolled out of the bus like a broken Slinky. Ramirez shut the door.

Everybody watched as Thompkins gathered himself and struck out for the brown truck. So far, no wasps. He kept low, and Carver approved. "Good. Make yourself less of a target." Second Lieutenant Thompkins picked his way through surprisingly few bodies. Most, if not all, were very dead with obvious fatal wounds, splayed out on the pavement and shards of glass in pools of blood that formed their own retention ponds in the uneven surface of the access road. He went for the safety of the massive wall and Carver shook his head. "Not where I'd go. No room to maneuver."

Second Lieutenant Thompkins flattened himself against the Saks building and shuffled to his right, easing on down the beige wall. This new path brought him closer to the row of cars. He got close and hesitated.

"Let this be a lesson, boys and girls," Carver told the bus. "One way or another. You watch, see what he picks. I told him to go for the UPS truck, and why. It's farther, but worth it. Driver made a run for it. Left the keys. Might even be still running."

He crossed his arms and settled in, thoughtful. "But those cars? They're trouble. See how they've been parked all neat in an obedient row? It's all deliberate. Not somebody in a panic. They took their keys."

A shrieking car alarm exploded from one of the cars as the second lieutenant tried to open the driver's door. "One," Carver counted. "Two." Thompkins bolted down the row and was actually dumb enough to go for the last car. More alarms. "Three. F—" Wasps boiled over the roofs like heat lightning and rushed him, going for his face and his ankles. He tumbled to the ground in a thick cloud of wasps.

Carver turned back to the rest of the bus. He sighed. "Alas, our second lieutenant Thompkins chose door number two, and well, that was the tiger." Carver smiled. "To be honest, I was just curious how far he'd get. Who else is ready for some fresh air?"

* * * *

The wasps cruised between the buildings for a while and everybody waited, taking care to be as silent as possible. Every so often, a few wasps would slow down and drift close to investigate the bus. They must have not liked the smell of the hundreds of their dead brethren smeared across the windows, because they rarely stayed long.

As she waited, Jen had an irrational, secretly joyful moment when she realized she didn't have her cell phone and it wasn't her fault. Her parents could not find fault in her radio silence. And Andy? He wasn't her fault either. She was saving her own life by saving his. This reassured her until her parents spoke up in the back of her mind. She was surprised they'd been quiet this long. As usual, they scolded her for putting herself in danger simply because she wanted to impress Dr. Fletcher. It wasn't so much their exact words, but the tone was clear. And that was enough. Her parents made it obvious how disappointed they were in their daughter, since she was obviously not thinking of herself or them, and placing this stranger, this failure of a man who brought nothing but shame and misery upon his family, how she was selfishly prioritizing his survival over the safety of herself, their only daughter.

In the outside world, her mother and father owned several dry-cleaning businesses back in the Detroit suburbs. They were nowhere near as harsh as the voices in her head, yet still could be masters of manipulation in startling displays of passive-aggressiveness when they felt it necessary. Jen knew why these voices had targeted Andy. Her parents treated every single man she encountered as a potential husband and father to grandchildren, and Andy could not be furthest from their approval. Especially since she had reacted with such a delicious ache.

Eventually, Carver stood and said, "I'd like to thank our second volunteer, the professor! Again, I'm sure everybody appreciates it." He started soft applause.

Jen refused to turn around. Did he mean Dr. Fletcher? He must have, even though Dr. Fletcher nor anyone else had actually given their names. *Maybe he means me*, she thought, and her stomach turned queasily.

"Yes, you," Carver said, staring at Dr. Fletcher. He laughed. "If you're not a professor somewhere, I'll eat his jockstrap." He nodded at Squirrel, who was clearly honored.

"I'm an entomologist, actually," Dr. Fletcher snapped.

"Of course you are. Who signs your paycheck?"

Dr. Fletcher wasn't sure how angry or scared he should be. "You want me to run over there, maybe find something that starts, and what, drive it back over here? No disrespect, but *I'll* eat his goddamn jockstrap if I can beat anybody on this bus in the hundred-yard dash. Why not one of these guys, the experts?" He indicated the soldiers and ignored the hard looks. "They signed on for this shit."

"Can't trust 'em. I doubt any of them would come back, even if it meant the deaths of every single one of you. They'd run off to notify the authorities. Not really their fault. Training. But you, you have no room in your conscience for being responsible for the deaths of anyone. You'll bring that UPS truck back, won't you." There was no hint of a questioning lilt at the end of the sentence.

"I don't want to die," Dr. Fletcher said.

"Most people don't," Carver said. "You will, though, in about five seconds if you don't get your ivory tower ass over here."

"Boss, we got company," Ramirez said, glancing at the big convex side mirror.

A thick gray Brink's armored truck crept around the curve behind them and came up to within twenty yards of the bus. It parked diagonally in the middle of the access street.

"Well now." Carver bent over and peered through the back windows. "Looks like someone was kind enough to bring us some truly impressive new wheels."

The armored truck's headlights began to flash, a mixture of short flickers, longer beams, and random pauses. "Morse fucking code. This can't be good. Magnus. Take this down. Dot, dot, dash, dot. Space. Dash, dot, dot..." He continued and Magnus kept track by using the knife he'd found in the tactical vest to carve into the bus seat.

After a while, Magnus said, "What the hell does that spell? A-L-G-I—"

"Algiers. 2007. You can stop now, Magnus. I got the message."

Ramirez said, "What the hell is it?" He was getting antsy, looking like he was ready to stomp on the gas and smash through the cars in the road. "It's an introduction of sorts. If it's who I think it is, we're fucked."

"Who is he?"

"Calls himself Haaga. Don't know if that's his real name or not, but he's the coldest motherfucker I've ever met in my life. Trust me, you don't want him on your bad side."

"CIA? DOD?"

Carver shook his head. "He works in the rarefied air above anything so petty as a department or official position. He's the guy they go to for permission. Not the other way around."

"We got hostages."

"You're not listening. Why do you think he decided to send this particular message? Back in 2007, in Algiers, guess who gave us the go-ahead to vaporize a building to kill three suspects, even though they had taken over a cafeteria full of people? He won't blink at taking out a bus full of convicts and a few hostages."

"Fuck 'em. We got guns," Ramirez said.

"Guns don't mean a whole lot of doodily-squat when this bastard's got enough juice to call in a drone strike with one phone call. No. Fighting our way out is a no-go. He wants something, otherwise we'd either be dead or ignored. Probably dead. Let's go see what the old slippery fucker has to say." He racked a round into the Glock's chamber. "Can't hurt, though, to remind him who's in here. Ms. Huang, will you be so kind as to join me on a short perambulation outside."

Jen froze, not knowing how he knew her name, until she looked down to see she'd forgotten about her FEMA necklace.

"Your boy here'll be fine." Carver held out his hand to help her up. "You'll be back at his side in no time at all."

Of course, there was no choice but to obey. She slid back and gently laid Andy's head on the floor. Then Carver had her by the hand and was pulling her outside, which felt almost cool as a slight breeze whispered along the access road. Carver didn't wrap his left arm around her throat and push her along, gun at her temple like some bad TV cop show. Instead, he walked slightly close and to her left, keeping the Glock out of sight behind her back.

They kept their eyes on the sky. When they reached the back of the bus, he put his left hand softly on her shoulder and stopped her. They didn't have to wait long. They heard a door swing open on the other side of the truck, and a second later, a man appeared around the front of the truck. Tall. Thin. Dark suit. Her first impression that he was some kind of undertaker.

Carver nudged Jen forward until both sides met in the middle of the access road between the armored truck and the bus. "Haaga."

"Carver," Haaga said and that ended formalities.

Jen wasn't sure who was scarier. She guessed Haaga was somewhere in his early sixties, but it was impossible to tell for sure. He looked to have been whittled out of fragments of steel from someone in a hurry, nothing but sharp angles inside a bespoke suit so black it might have been a black hole, a portal to another dimension. Crisp white collar. Slim black tie. A thorny shock of blinding white hair halfway encircled a tan skull. His jutting nose accentuated the gauntness of his face. His eyes had an unnatural awareness that seemed to look right through all your intimate secrets. He had a casual, disinterested way of listening, as if whatever you were saying meant little to nothing. With his nose, shrewd eyes, ringed skull, and obvious menace, Jen's overall impression was of some cunning, vicious bird of prey that wasn't above feeding on carrion if necessary.

"Been a while," he said finally.

"What do you want?" Carver cut to the chase. "This how you've been spending your golden years? Keeping an eye on prisoner transports?"

Haaga gave a smile that dropped the temperature at least ten degrees and lit a cigarette. He took his time before answering. "Depends on the prisoners. Every once in a while somebody special has to go somewhere, and if they're truly remarkable, then it's my job to make sure there aren't any… complications."

"I'm not special. None of us are."

"Don't sell yourself short, Carver. You and I both know exactly what you are."

"So why go to all the trouble to come here in person?"

Haaga used the cigarette to vaguely indicate the larger world beyond the access road. "Well, current events have thrown a rather large monkey wrench into said plans. Events that, truthfully, take priority over you and anybody else in that bus. However, we have one loose thread to tie off. You and this bus. One way or another. Therefore, you have a choice. Listening?"

"I'm listening to *me* about to tell *you* to go fuck yourself."

"Up to you. You can release all the hostages immediately and consent to going back under lock and key, at least for the moment."

"Or I can tell you to go fuck yourself."

"Then get back on the bus. You'll have maybe ten seconds to give each other high fives and after that, I can guarantee that bus will be nothing but a big goddamn hole in the ground. There won't be enough of you left to fill a sandwich baggie."

"What if I've got a third option?" Carver said, showing Haaga the Glock. "I'll shoot you and we fight our way out."

"Is that supposed to make me piss my pants? You should know me better. But hey, if you think that'll give you leverage, then by all means, knock yourself out. No. There's only two options. Besides, I don't think a gunfight is in anybody's best interests. No need to involve the new local wildlife. Don't get the wrong idea. I'm not your savior. I'm not your brother-in-arms. I'm not your pal. I'd just as soon snap you out of the living, but you and your new friends may be useful."

"Useful, huh. Heard that before. How?"

"Don't exactly know yet. Depends how current events continue to unfold. You have no idea, do you, that you've gone… viral, as the kids say. News choppers were right on top of you when you 'saved' those five people, providing a live video feed to the whole wide world." Despite being stuck between two obvious killers, Jen's thoughts went again to her parents. They must have seen the footage. Her heart broke when she thought of them clutching each other in front of the TV.

Carver spit. "That'll teach me to help anybody. No good deed goes unpunished."

"Must admit, I didn't expect it. As for punishment? It's in your hands. Certain parties agreed with my suggestion that keeping you alive for the time being might be perhaps more… beneficial than not."

"Do we get a shiny new medal pinned to our spiffy uniforms?"

"Only if you ask nice."

Several quiet seconds passed. "They watching us now?"

Haaga gave a short bark that may have been laughter.

Carver regarded the pale blue sky for several more quiet seconds and thrust his middle finger at the heavens.

Haaga exhaled smoke out of his nose in twin streams. "I have no doubt they are duly shocked and appalled." His voice was so dry you could have scratched a wooden match to life from the sound waves alone.

"Never could get used to the taste of a shit sandwich. You?"

Haaga shrugged. "Life is shit. Time for you to put on your big-boy pants and belly up to the bar. As the kids say."

"And all this?" Carver asked, meaning the wasps.

"I have a feeling this clusterfuck is just getting started."

"First chance I get, I'm taking out as many of you fuckers as I can."

CHAPTER 13

Pain awoke Andy. It took a long time.

He stretched out from a deep and dark and silent place toward light and sound. On the cusp of consciousness, full of confusion and fear, he flashed to the morning when he'd woken up between the wall and the end of the couch at his buddy's parents' basement, Fireball whiskey soaked into his jeans and bong water in his ear. He had managed to crawl outside and vomit on the porch. He laid there so long he'd gotten sunburned. He'd always believed that would be the crowning hangover of his entire life. Nothing would ever be able to even compare.

This was worse. Everything ached; his entire body was infected with dull, throbbing misery. He had a sneaking suspicion someone had cracked open his head, stirred his brains once or twice with a rusty spoon, then stapled the top of his skull on backwards. He couldn't open his eyes; they were crusted shut or something. Maybe that was a good thing. Every once in a while, a crackling line of molten lava sizzled up his left arm, all the way from the tips of the fingers on his left hand up to his shoulder. He sucked in air through clenched teeth, and realized it wasn't enough. His lungs felt full of cobwebs and he could picture the droplets of oxygen caught in the web, sparkling as though he was seeing dew at sunrise. He tried pulling air through his nose and at last, he felt the blooming relief of sweet, sweet oxygen. As sensation returned and grew throughout his body, everything seemed to hurt whether he moved or not. He tore his eyes open and couldn't make out much at first beyond a few blobs of light seemingly coming from behind him.

Gradually things grew crisper, cleaner. He was lying in a hospital bed, but he didn't think he was in a hospital. A needle in his right arm ran up to a bag of clear liquid. Other machines kept their eyes and ears on him, snaking various wires and tubes to his chest, finger, and his forehead, as they measured his heartbeat, oxygen levels, and the like. He realized he could breathe better through his nose because of the oxygen tube.

Andy couldn't make out a whole lot of detail of the room. The only lights came from his electric caretakers and a soft lamp next to a door off to his right. As his eyes got used to being open and halfway useful, he made out an accordion-style room divider midway down the room, now collapsed against the right wall. Bookshelves swam into shape. A whiteboard. A round, industrial clock read 1:32. Andy had no idea if that was AM or PM. Stacks of small plastic chairs. A flat-screen TV, now quiet and dull. Posters. Children's artwork. A preschool classroom?

No windows, though. He rolled his head ever so slowly and gingerly to the right, but it still felt like he was twisting the vertebrae in his neck into a running table saw. Then he understood. Giant letters made of tiny crosses and purple flowers marched across the wall, proclaiming *BLESSED ARE THE CHILDREN.*

He was in a goddamn Sunday school.

He'd gone to church fairly regularly for about five months when he was eight. It had been almost a second home for a while there, because his mom would use the church as a free babysitter for him and his brothers and sisters while she pretended to attend the AA meetings.

Looking back, he was surprised it lasted as long as it did. Eventually, though, the church had enough of seven hellion children contaminating their place of worship with filth and disrespect and when their mom showed up drunk for the third time, the entire family was escorted to the parking lot and told the church would pray for them.

Gradually, images and moments floated back to him from the more immediate past. The bus. Second Lieutenant Dipshit. Carver. The wasps. Then that amazingly cute girl and how he'd be damned if he let any motherfucking wasp touch her. After that, not so much.

His right hand was handcuffed to the bed. That was expected and almost comforting. His left arm was elevated for some reason, up on a stool. It looked like he had a white cast or something that encased his arm nearly to the elbow. From his vantage point, he couldn't see beyond his wrist. His hand hurt like hell, though. He'd feel that jolt of agony spark in his fingers and bolt up his arm to explode in his shoulder once in a while. The stool had been attached to the bed with two zip ties. Three more locked the cast in place on a stool's armrest. His thinking was slow and sluggish, to be sure, but this arrangement still felt a little unorthodox. Unprofessional. Malpractice territory.

The door opened. The man who came in wore a stained white medical coat, glasses that made his eyes look uncomfortably large and distorted, and an expression that said he'd rather piss his own pants than help anyone, especially a patient. "Oh," he said, his voice flat and bored. "You're awake." He scratched out something on his clipboard and came over to Andy, irritable and so tired he couldn't stop yawning.

Andy tried to groan, to make a sound, any kind of sound.

The man clicked a penlight and burned out Andy's pupils for a bit. He clucked his tongue and pulled Andy's jaw down, took a look inside. He spent a while poking around Andy's left hand, sending those bolts of fiery agony up Andy's arm. He yawned. "Well, champ. I don't know what they put in that dog chow they feed you dumb pricks, but your oxygen levels have stabilized and your fever is down. You might just make it. That would make you one of the few I've heard about that survived a sting. Congratulations." He didn't sound enthusiastic. He sounded like he was being forced to read insurance actuary statistics out loud and might fall asleep any second.

Andy tried to swallow. It locked up midway through and refused to move. He coughed it back into the back of his throat and snorted air. His eyes lazily followed the man that he still wasn't sure was a real doctor or not.

The man pulled a walkie-talkie out of his lab coat. Clicked and said, "This is Dr. Kauer. The bed in room four-twenty is still occupied. Indefinite time frame."

"Reason?" crackled the radio.

"The occupant is now conscious."

"State again?"

"He's looking at me."

"Copy."

Andy breathed out, "water...drink..."

"Yeah, I'll bet you are." Dr. Kauer crossed the room to a small kitchenette in the far corner and poked around in the half-fridge. He brought an apple juice box over to Andy and popped the top with the straw, held it to Andy's mouth. "Didn't think you were ever going to wake up. Just about moved you out yesterday, but your pals raised a fuss when they heard. I'm sure they'll be pleased."

The juice was so sweet it made Andy's teeth hurt. It tasted glorious, but after a short few seconds, the doctor pulled it away. "That's plenty for the time being. We're... uh, a little short-staffed around here, and I'd rather not have to clean up your vomit."

"Where..."

"Not my job to fill you in, champ. Fact is, I'm not supposed to tell you a damn thing." Another bolt of lightning flashed up his arm and Andy winced. Dr. Kauer yawned and rubbed his eyes. "We'll increase your pain meds." He scribbled something on the clipboard and left, saying, "Try and rest. Somebody'll be in shortly with something that will make you feel better. Might be me, though I hope not."

* * * *

A medic in camo fatigues stopped in later and injected clear liquid into his IV's secondary line. The meds hit damn hard, and he knew nothing more until he felt a cool washcloth on his forehead. It had to have been hours later as well, according to his empty stomach and how he felt so thirsty. The first thing he searched out was the clock: 2:47. Again, no idea if it was AM or PM. The cool, slightly rough tickling of damp fabric across his skin popped his eyes open.

The washcloth disappeared.

Squirrel loomed over him and smiled. The smile made things worse, as regular dentist appointments weren't a high priority. "Shitfire. Heard you were about dead." His breath smelled of sour cream and onion potato chips.

Andy decided to see the glass half full. At least his sense of smell still worked.

"We been taking turns checking on you," Squirrel said. He pulled a preschool chair off a stack and sat next to the bed. "Goddamn, tougher than genuine leather, yessir." He spoke softly as if he didn't want anyone in the corridor to hear.

Andy managed, "What—how'd we get here?"

"What happened is we got caught up by our short and curlies." Squirrel scratched at his mangled ear. "Carver said this old fucker that he used to work for was keeping an eye on the bus. They's been watching us the whole time. Saw it all."

"Wasps?"

"Murder hornets! Them bugs, they'll kill you faster than death on a cracker. Nobody tells us a damn thing, 'course, but Carver's been listening, says things aren't going well for Miami, or Florida in general, no sir. Murder hornets one, humans zero. Can't stop 'em for shit."

"...hostages..."

Squirrel giggled and used his tongue to suck something nutritious from a triangle-shaped gap in his teeth. "Well, turns out your girl's name is Jen… Shit. I can't remember. Some kinda chink name. Anyway, last time I saw your girl she was helping the old fart with the ponytail into an ambulance. She was all good and breathing."

"Where are we?"

"We ain't far from what they're calling ground zero. Maybe ten, twelve klicks."

"Why keep us… here?"

"Your guess is good as mine. Carver says his old boss is hanging onto us. Don't know why."

"Church?" Andy tried to indicate the room.

Squirrel grinned proudly like his kid had just won a spelling bee. "We's locked up in the basement of the biggest church I ever seen." His voice dropped an octave as he pretended to be God. Or at least Moses by way of Charlton Heston. "The Calvary Chapel." He shook his head a little in disbelief. "Shitfire, this congregation, they got more people than my hometown."

"Escape?"

"We're working on it. You rest up, cause when the time comes, Carver says you're coming with us."

"Okay." Suddenly, a tidal wave of exhaustion washed over him, driven by the medicine. The chemicals in Andy's bloodstream didn't give a damn about much of anything then. They needed Andy to sleep, to stop fighting. He said "Okay," one more time before he fell off a dark cliff. As he slipped into the blackness, he thought he heard Squirrel say, "Sorry about your hand, man."

* * * *

Something yanked Andy out of his sleep. He didn't know if it was a sound, a light, pain, or even some kind of smell. He lay still a moment, tasting fear like some soft, tiny mammal, wondering if something with sharp teeth lurked out in the gloom. The room was still dark. The clock clicked, marking another minute gone, but his eyes couldn't focus enough to see the actual time. Then he realized someone else was in the room.

He tensed, curling his hands into fists, tensing every muscle he could muster, ready for an attack. His confused, chaotic mind tried to remember if there was anything nearby he could grab and use as a weapon.

"At ease, soldier." Carver's voice came from somewhere behind his head. "Couldn't help yourself. Went and got yourself well and truly fubar."

"You oughta see the other guy," Andy croaked.

Carver chuckled and slid into sight on Andy's left. "I have no doubt. How do you feel?" The man's beard stuck out like the rest of his hair, like it had been rinsed in antifreeze while he'd stuck his tongue in a light socket. It wouldn't have surprised Andy if smoke still rose from the scraggly black hair.

"Like I got hit by a truck."

"I am genuinely impressed with your fortitude. Your death has been declared more than a few times. Yet here you still breathe."

Andy tried to think of something cool to say. His mind didn't cooperate, though, and all he could manage was a lame, "Uh-huh."

Carver held the chart up in the dim blue and white lights of the machines and consulted the clipboard. He listed off the latest vital statistics, his tone somehow astonished and dispassionate at the same time. "I believe you, as the saying goes, are comprised primarily of gristle and gumption. I will ask you again. How do you feel?"

Andy was too tired for games. "What d'ya want, man?"

"I want to know if you can hold your own when we escape. Can you move fast?"

"You're goddamn right I can move fast." Andy had no idea if he could even walk, let alone move fast. He didn't think he'd even been out of bed in at least a day, probably two. The bedpans were a testament to that. His eager dedication was more than just a yearning for freedom, though. It was an overriding desire to not let Carter down, to live up to the man's high expectations. If Andy could impress a bona fide baddass like Carter, then his life had meaning.

His will, his spirit, was tough enough to be noticed and therefore meant something.

He struggled to sit up to prove himself. Each contraction of his abs, every muscle that struggled to even twitch, sent bolts of sizzling lightning shrieking through his joints. Beads of sweat popped out of his pale forehead. Still, he fought through the agony as he bent his body to his will. It wasn't enough. The zip ties holding onto the cast on his left arm and the handcuffs locking his right arm to the bed made any significant movement impossible.

Carver patted his shoulder and eased him back to the rubber-coated mattress, saying, "I believe you." He produced a scalpel from somewhere and sliced through the zip ties, freeing his left arm. Andy didn't move it; he was afraid if it got jostled that might bring the pain back.

The scalpel disappeared and a twisted shard of metal took its place. He leaned over and inserted it into the handcuffs, and a few quiet clicks later, Andy discovered he could reach up with his right hand and scratch his nose, which had been itching like a motherfucker.

Carver folded the bed's safety bars down, opening the right side. He turned his hands over, palms up, in a gesture that invited Andy to take hold. Andy swallowed his pride and did just that; he took Carver's procured hand, twisted his body until his legs were dangling over the edge and he was sitting upright under his own power. He was too busy adjusting all the wires that connected him to the various machines and didn't notice how Carver's right hand slid up to support Andy's elbow instead of taking his left hand.

Andy scooted forward, an inch at a time, as the thin mattress protested with sad squeaking sounds. Carver moved to Andy's left, sliding his right hand up to Andy's armpit while his right hand cupped Andy's elbow and lifted. Using Carver's support, along with his right hand, Andy stretched out his feet until he could feel the floor. His heartbeat audibly increased. Slowly, he left the safety of the bed and stood, wobbling for a moment on his own two feet.

Carver gradually pulled his own hands away, leaving Andy to stand by himself.

"Told ya I can move fast," Andy said, just before his knees collapsed. He fell forward and instinctively threw his arms out to block his fall as he dragged all the instruments down with him. When he hit the floor, a blast of agony shredded his meager understanding of pain and stopped his heart cold for a split second, ricocheting through his entire body, especially his left side. His face smacked into the vinyl tiles and he couldn't breathe. This was a pain that he didn't know could even exist. It blotted out everything and that was all he knew for a while. It left him gasping and weeping, sprawled across the floor on his back, hugging his arms to his chest, until a thought pierced the torment. He realized something felt... wrong.

Then he saw his left hand was gone.

* * * *

At first, it didn't seem real. He raised his left arm in disbelief. A magic trick? The meds must have fucked his head right up, that's all. The pain was so intense that it was causing hallucinations. Something was wrong with his brain, not his arm. There was no way any of this was real, it was that simple. He could feel his left fingers tingling, for God's sake. How could he possibly feel any kind of sensation if his hand wasn't attached anymore? Nothing made sense.

Carver returned the IV and the rest of the equipment to their upright positions, silencing all the alarms as he said, "God bless the graveyard shift." He eased himself down next to Andy and leaned against the bed, scratched at his wiry beard, muttering a half-remembered verse. "And if thy right hand offend thee, cut it off, and cast it from thee... something-something, and not that thy whole body should be cast into hell."

Andy didn't hear him. His excuses were running dry and he couldn't pretend any longer. His hand was gone. And he no idea how to cope. How could this happen? He wasn't supposed to lose his own goddamn hand, like he'd absentmindedly misplaced it, left it on a bench at the mall or something. This wasn't how his life was supposed to work out.

Granted, Andy never really had any substantial goals or dreams or even a solid plan for his life. Escaping the grim, claustrophobic existence in his mother's small hometown was as far as he got. The only way that seemed to show any kind of promise to get out was to join the military. None of it had worked out. All it accomplished was to push him deeper into shit.

He'd become a cripple. A freak. Something that couldn't take care of itself. He started to shake and seemed unaware that tears had filled his eyes and trickled down his temples.

Carver dragged the young man into his lap. The movement was much like when Jen had cradled him on the bus. With astonishing gentleness, Carver touched the tip of his middle finger to Andy's forehead, just above and between the eyes. The skin-to-skin contact was so brief it may not have happened. He did it again.

Andy blinked. Another tap. And another.

Carver kept it up, slow at first, then settling into a hypnotic beat that matched his own measured heartbeat.

Andy closed his eyes, flushing tears down his cheeks. The shaking dropped to a couple spasms every minute or so. His own heartbeat slowed.

"Easy, son. Easy." Carver's voice was warm syrup. He kept tapping his middle finger, but he'd withdrawn so much that the skin-to-skin contact was broken and only psychic waves remained. "You're not the first one I've held while they looked for their missing pieces. Most went out like that, still looking. You're alive, though. Ride it out. You're just catching up to what your body's known for a few days. Let your body tell you what you need. Trust what it's telling you."

"I still feel my fingers."

"You're smelling burnt popcorn. Leftover sparks from broken nerve endings. You'll adjust."

"No. I won't. I been awake long enough to know. I'm done."

"Done, how?"

"I'm done with all this, everything. Can't fucking walk. Can't do shit."

"Ah."

"I can't tie my own fucking boots."

"Stop feeling sorry for yourself. You'll figure it out. Think you're the first guy ever lost a hand?"

"It doesn't matter. No family worth a shit. I wish the fucking wasp—"

"Murder hornet."

"I wish the fucking thing had just killed me. Be easier."

"Sometimes death is easier, true. Sometimes, not so much."

"Don't psycho-super-soldier-fortune-cookie bullshit me. Gonna get some painkillers and check out of this fucking world."

Carver was quiet for a while. "A decision such as this should not be made in haste. Think on it. I will return tomorrow. If you still feel the same, then I will assist you myself."

"How?"

Carver lifted Andy into the bed. "It'll be quick and painless, that I promise." He relocked the handcuffs around Andy's right wrist and arranged the stump back up on the raised stool. He looked down at Andy. "If you do not see me in, oh, twelve hours from now, and you haven't changed your mind, you can swallow this." He held up a single tiny capsule. It didn't look much different than any number of over-the-counter pills.

Andy looked at it suspiciously.

"I know. Doesn't seem very powerful, does it? Trust me. You'll drift off to sleep and won't feel anything. No more pain." He made sure Andy was watching when he hid the pill under the mattress, just enough to be out of sight, but Andy could still reach it with his handcuffed right hand. "All I ask is that you wait. If this is what you truly want, then escape will be waiting for you. You only have to swallow it. I will try to be back to administer the final solution, but again, if I'm not here by the deadline, then it is your decision and yours alone, if you wish to end things."

"I can tell you right now, that's what I want."

"Do you promise to wait?" Carver asked.

Andy was silent for a while before saying, "Okay."

* * * *

He didn't sleep. He lay in the dark, watching the pulse of his heartbeat and the clock. He wanted it done before he got cold feet and talked himself out of it, but he'd given Carver his word. Part of him knew he should be trying to talk himself out of this decision as he lay there, marking time and suffering under the onslaught of never-ending waves filled with misery. He waited for this last, lone dissent to give up and be quiet. As the night crawled past, he got tired of waiting and went looking, eventually cornering this sole surviving plea for life and demanded to know why he shouldn't be able to end all of this as soon as possible. And when Andy pinned this last shred of defiance down and stared it in the eye, the hope within this thought withered and died, whimpering, "I got nothing."

It was decided.

Perversely, when that particular hope was extinguished, the hole filled with new hopes, albeit much smaller. He hoped Carver's pill contained some kind of morphine or some other equally heavy-duty painkiller, cause if you had to check out, you might as well go out higher'n a kite. He hoped it would be fast. He hoped he didn't piss or shit his pants after.

The rest of the day passed in numbing slow-motion. He watched the clock and listened to the machines dutifully recording the mundane operations of his body's last day. He had hoped to see the sun one more time, but it wasn't in the cards. He refused to answer any of Dr. Kauer's questions.

Andy stared at his stump and the clock and nothing else. Dr. Kauer noted this new decline on his chart and told the two medics to jolt Andy's system with a blast of vitamins and antibiotics. He said that he'd stop by tomorrow and they'd continue to monitor his vitals. Eventually, though, Dr. Kauer grew tired of the silent treatment and shrugged before leaving without saying anything. The medics finished and fled as well.

Andy watched the clock.

* * * *

Two AM came and went. Andy started to sweat. He reached down with his right hand, straining, straining, further and further, until his fingers found the single naked capsule and rolled it into a position where he could pinch it between his forefinger and middle finger. He paused, taking a long, even breath, willing himself to slow down. If he dropped the pill on the floor, life would be nothing but suffering. So he took his time, breathing shallow. He brought it up to his hip and rested. His heart was hammering, threatening to explode. At least the capsule was nestled safely between his thumb and forefinger, waiting patiently for one last signal to his right hand.

He lasted twenty-seven minutes.

The final push came from the realization that he'd end up some kind of lab rat, with doctors and scientists and politicians sucking his blood out, pint by pint. He'd seen pictures of vivisections and was damned if he'd allow that to happen. The images of screaming animals being sliced open and examined exploded behind his eyes and fueled the incredible task of sitting up so he could reach his handcuffed right hand with his mouth. The top half of the hospital bed had been left at an almost 45-degree angle and that helped. Still, the pain was utter and total. It was necessary. It kept him alive and fighting, even if all he could manage for several seconds at a time was to simply not fall back. This agony was worth the ability to decide his own fate.

His dry tongue was still moist enough to latch onto the capsule and draw it back into his mouth. It took almost a full minute of scraping spit together before he could swallow, squeezing the capsule down into his stomach acid. The constant burning of rage flared up inside and made him slam his head into the bed's bars in impotent fury a few times. It passed.

He felt better.

Best he'd felt since he'd woken up, actually. It was done now, and there was nothing else to be done. No decisions to be made. Nothing. In this, he found peace.

When the classroom door opened, he was ready for Carver to see him off to the land of the dead. He was ready for the goddamn Angel of Death.

He wasn't ready for Jen.

CHAPTER 14

Jen had promised herself that she would maintain her composure regardless of Andy's condition. That resolve lasted until she opened the door to the Sunday school classroom and saw him in the hospital bed. In the harsh fluorescents from the hall, he looked ten years older. His skin had the pallid color of white asparagus that had never seen the sun. His lips were dry and cracked. His eyes were three-day old hard-boiled eggs, half-submerged in coal slush. She'd never seen anyone that desperate, that hungry to drag himself across life's final threshold. He had the false bravado of a man willing to slip Death a date-rape drug, just so he could fuck the Reaper and get it over with as fast as possible.

Before she stepped inside and let the door shut behind her, Jen realized she'd seriously miscalculated…everything. For example, she'd never even considered any kind of possibility where Andy might want to kill himself. He might even want help. She faltered, not knowing how she would react if he asked.

She tried to take refuge in her hypothetical scenarios. There was one where Andy gave her an aw-shucks grin and said *don't worry* about his missing hand. It only hurt when he laughed. One where Andy asked her for money. Not for him, for his family. One where Andy wept and told her that he felt more human than before. He'd been to the other side and brought back wisdom and grace. One where Andy told her it hurt, but it was okay and gave a quick kiss on the lips as a reward. That one was her favorite.

But not suicide.

A sudden fury gathered in her heart, aimed squarely at herself. *You stupid, naive little child.* She had no idea. No idea at all.

* * * *

The need to see Andy first popped up when a bunch of men in suits and combat fatigues had hustled her and the rest of the survivors off the bus. They'd been pushed into the back of an ambulance in the midst of the chaos that came to be known as the first wave. She'd grabbed Dr. Fletcher's hand as he rolled around on a stretcher while the ambulance tore out of there, but all she could see was Andy. His sweat lingered on her hands and forearms.

The ambulance followed a line of dozens of other ambulances and emergency vehicles transporting survivors from near the BB&T Center and Sawgrass Mills. The procession flowed east along Broward Boulevard, a single tight current within a slower, sluggish river, as they weaved in and out of near-standstill traffic. Everyone within a five-square-mile area had been ordered to evacuate and most of the population couldn't flee fast enough after witnessing the wasps' carnage on the news.

They passed under Florida's Turnpike and turned south, bouncing up and over the curb onto a fairway of the Fort Lauderdale Country Club. While the rest of the ambulances followed a golf cart path south, Jen and Dr. Fletcher's peeled off and sped east, straight to the clubhouse. When Jen got out she saw over two dozen Quonset huts being constructed on the spotless green links. The entire country club had been hastily designated a temporary FEMA emergency operations center.

National Guard soldiers flooded the grounds. The main dining room had been transformed into a huge fusion center, collecting any and all information concerning the savage attack. This data was processed, analyzed, and ultimately presented in an overall concept of operations, from which a series of memorandums of understanding were issued to all agencies involved. Jen couldn't understand how all of the seemingly frantic and chaotic movement could coalesce into meaningful and actionable procedures and strategies. Somehow, though, she felt reassured, as if good ol' human ingenuity would prevail. They were, after all, the dominant species on the planet. She thought she saw the wraithlike figure of Haaga at one point, but he was swallowed up in a flurry of activity, washed away in soldiers and equipment.

They were escorted to a room in the lower level. It had been converted into temporary examining rooms, cut into screening sections by hospital screens. A couple of no-nonsense medics took their blood pressure, pulse, oxygen levels, measured how fast their eyes could dilate, and used flashlights to peer down their throats. They told Jen to strip. She did, down to her bra and panties. Her clothes were secured in sterile containers. The medics clicked their flashlights on and went over her flesh with far more concentration than Jen had ever wanted focused on her skin. They noted and recorded every blemish, scar, and irregularity on her entire body. It was nothing personal, but… still.

When it was over, one of them wordlessly held out a plastic sack, hermetically sealed. Inside was a green and blue hospital gown.

"No," she said and refused to take the package.

The medic continued to hold it out, still not saying anything.

Jen crossed her arms, both in defiance and to cover her breasts. She'd decided she wasn't going to say anything until the medic did.

After a full thirty seconds, the medic gave in. "I know. It sucks. Your clothes are to be sent to the lab. Orders."

"Then give me something else to wear. Something not totally embarrassing."

"I don't have time to go shopping for every refugee processed at this center."

"Then I'll go out there like this, and I'll make sure I mention your name—" she peered at his name tag—"Jose Juarez, as loud as I can. And I can get very loud. Just try it."

Juarez glowered at her for a while, but eventually caved. He left and his partner, Xavier, smirked and ducked through the curtain keeping Jen and Dr. Fletcher separate. Jen heard Xavier say to Dr. Fletcher, "Put this on."

"No."

"Excuse me?"

"I'm not deaf. I distinctly heard my assistant"—Jen's heart leapt at his assignation of her—"tell your amigo no. *No*. All right? You get me something else to wear."

"You get this or you go out there naked. I don't care. I will make sure, however, that everyone knows it was your choice, and yours alone, to parade around in your birthday suit."

"Goddamnit." Dr. Fletcher sounded ready to break. This was yet one more indignation in a day full of life-or-death situations and he'd had enough. "This is ageism, racism, sexism, ableism, all fucking rolled into one fascist command."

Xavier was silent for a moment as he took the accusation to heart. "I guess it is," he said finally and Jen was impressed she couldn't hear a hint of sarcasm. Dr. Fletcher had been so primed to attack Xavier's denial that the admission left him blinking and speechless for a few moments.

Finally, Dr. Fletcher grabbed the crinkling plastic and said, "Fine, fucking fine." As he changed on the other side of the screen, she sat in her underwear, almost cold in the aggressively air-conditioned country club, wondering what would happen if she was pushed out of her tent, if she had to go out into all the soldiers bare like this.

Juarez reappeared and said, "You will not remember where you got this," and handed her a stained, wrinkled jumpsuit from some nurse's closet. It was so perfect she could almost kiss him, and right on the heels of the gushing gratitude an image of Andy bubbled up, where he grinned at her with the pulped wasp crushed in his fist. Lost in the vision, she actually took a step forward, stepping in too close, almost as if she wanted to kiss Juarez, but in her head it was Andy.

She caught herself as she tilted her head up at Juarez and while he was confused as hell, it seemed like the polite thing to do, so he bent his own head to kiss her back. She jerked back, startling him.

"I'm sorry," they both said at the same time. He tossed the jumpsuit at her and fled.

Jen was mortified. What was wrong with her? *Get a grip, girl.* Maybe the shock of the day was hitting her harder than she realized. She stepped into the jumpsuit, zipping it all the way up to her neck, and left her little examination cubicle to wait for Dr. Fletcher. When he appeared, he was not pleased to see her in a nurse's uniform instead of a skimpy hospital gown like him.

* * * *

Another soldier with a clipboard and earpiece steered them to a cluster of corporate offices. Yet again, Jen was directed into one office while Dr. Fletcher was escorted into another. The desk had been pushed against one wall, while a video camera had been set up on a tripod in the far corner. It was aimed at a couple of old-fashioned, very comfortable looking armchairs. Two men in dark suits shook her hand and immediately implored her to sit and relax in one of the leather chairs. They introduced themselves as Agents Ortiz and Papillion of the FBI and offered her bottled water and a protein bar.

Her stomach growled and she realized she hadn't eaten in over seven or eight hours. She said, "Oh my God, thank you, thank you, thank you," and tore into the protein bar, and followed it by swallowing half of the water.

Agent Ortiz grabbed three more bars from the desk along with a couple more plastic bottles of water and put them on the thick leather arm. He leaned back and folded his hands over his slight paunch. "I can't imagine what you have been through. Soon as we're done here, I promise you rest and a quick phone call to your loved ones to reassure them of your safety." He leaned forward and peered at his laptop. "I have no doubt your... parents are worried sick." His voice was gentle and his eyes were kind. "This is just a formality. We need a preliminary short statement before we can release you to speak with a psychologist who specializes in PTSD. She will arrange for your phone call, then show you to your bunk."

"The main thing to remember is that you're safe now," Agent Papillion said behind the camera, letting her know he was about to hit record. He had a kind of Cajun accent, like a redneck French. "It may take a few hours for the shock to wear off. Just between you and me, your psych officer will offer you a mood stabilizer. I highly recommend you take it." He waited for her to finish chewing and asked, "Okay. Ready?"

Jen nodded.

Agent Ortiz gave the date and time, and explained how he and Agent Papillion were assisting an emergency DHS operation by debriefing individual survivors of the murder hornet invasion. "We are here with Miss Jen Huang, who's had one hell of a bad day."

Jen gave a low snort of laughter that nearly shook loose tears.

"Miss Huang, all we need is you to state your name and tell us what happened today, starting with your arrival at the BB and T Center. Take all the time you need."

That morning felt like five years ago. She found she couldn't manage a straight, chronological recount. It was too much, and whether she was in shock or just exhausted, she bounced around the past nine hours like a child with ADD and too much Cap'n Crunch. The agents were patient and reassuring, and when Jen spoke of Andy her eyes glinted and the edges of her lips curled into flashes of small smiles as she recounted how he had sacrificed himself.

She realized then that she needed to back up and explain how they had climbed down from the center to the parking lot and ended up on the bus. "We found enough extension cords..."

"Oh, yes. The extension cords. Quick thinking, Miss Huang. Respect." Agent Papillion used his right fist to lightly punch his left open palm, then clasped them together and bowed.

"Indeed. We've all seen your escape," Agent Ortiz said.

Jen was confused.

Agent Ortiz turned his laptop and filled the screen with a shot from a news helicopter, clearly showing Jen, Dr. Fletcher, and the rest climbing down from the balcony. She winced when Lauren fell and hit the dumpster. She saw the bus, the two men who jumped out, using shotguns to blast anything that came close, and then recognized Andy as one of them. The other one was the scary prisoner. She clasped a hand to her mouth as she watched herself run toward the bus with the others, while the two prisoners protected them with a genuinely impressive display of firepower and prowess with .12-gauge pump shotguns.

Then she vanished inside the bus and the camera followed as it crossed a hellscape of bodies and burning vehicles, all the way to the mall. She looked up. "I had no idea…"

Agent Ortiz nodded. "They're keeping your names secret, of course, but it's only a matter of time. This isn't even the only footage. There's four or five shots from other choppers online."

He spread his hands, both in apology and admiration. "You're famous. Or will be soon enough."

Jen felt like she'd swallowed salmon sashimi gone bad. "My parents…" She trailed off. If they had seen the footage, then words could not capture the full extent of the vast array of emotions her parents would be going through. "I have to call them!"

Both agents nodded, Ortiz saying, "Of course, of course." He put a thick folder on the desk. Post-it notes and markers stuck out like an angry cactus. "Soon as you sign this metric shit ton of NDAs." He shrugged. "National security."

* * * *

Dr. Fletcher was waiting for her. Despite how the hospital gown contrasted sharply with his pale, hairy legs, he couldn't stop pacing around the corridor in his paper slippers. He was fucking thrilled. "Did you see it? Did you? Holy fucking Jesus, Batman. We. Are. Famous. Do you know what this means? Papers. Lectures. Tours. Oh, God. Books." He took a deep breath, speaking with deep reverence. "Reality television."

Forget tomorrow; Jen could only think about five minutes ahead. The thought of life after today was laughable and ridiculously distant. She nodded, more out of muscle memory than anything, reverting to her instinctive obedience. The only thing she could focus on was finding a phone to call her parents and soon enough found a table with banks of landline telephones. The rest of the phones were in use, held by men and women alternately shouting into their phones or scribbling furious notes. Jen realized she didn't know her parents' number by heart. She'd never had to worry about it, because it had always been *MOM & DAD* on her phone. After a couple seconds, though, she nailed it down in her head and dialed. She wasn't sure if her father would answer or not. He was far too polite to telemarketers and would avoid them if possible by simply not answering the phone if he saw the call wasn't from someone already in his contacts. This time, though, her father answered, no doubt waiting for anyone to call with news of his daughter. Her mother joined her father in crying and admonishing her for being in the middle of such a disaster to begin with. Jen talked her parents off the ledge and assured them she was safe and would be returning home as soon as possible.

The woman next to her happened to catch this last promise and snorted in derision. "If you're still here, then they've got plans for you. You're not going anywhere."

* * * *

Those who had no immediate responsibilities gathered in the cocktail lounge. Jen took a glass of white wine and settled on a stool next to Dr. Fletcher. He'd brazenly plucked a bottle of sixteen-year-old Lagavulin from behind the bar. The lounge looked west, overlooking much of the course. Night was settling slowly over the Sunshine State, darkening from burnt orange to bruise purple, until finally allowing the pinpricks of stars to appear.

No one was looking outside. All attention was glued to the TVs. The walls weren't covered with them; that would be tacky. After all, this wasn't some cheap sports bar where any slob could park his ample ass. This was a country club, and they weren't savages. There was even some talk from the older members that TVs had no place in the club at all. Cooler heads had prevailed, understanding a basic need to watch football, baseball, basketball, golfing (of course), and occasionally NASCAR, unless it was a Sunday. No one would admit to enjoying the roar of engines screaming around a staggeringly unimaginative oval, but the races always drew boisterous crowds pretending not to pay any attention.

This evening, all five TVs were broadcasting all murder hornets, all the time. The avalanche of images and sounds reignited too many painful moments of the day and she had to look at her glass of wine. Her gorge threatened to rise and Jen tried to remember what the caseworker had suggested. Inhale through the nose. Touch something solid and pull strength from its immovability. Exhale, slow and deep from your mouth. Inhale through the nose. Find a sound, something slow and regular, independent from anything troublesome, and focus solely on that.

Exhale, slow and deep.

She flattened her palm on the smooth wood of the bar and listened for a slow, monotonous sound. There was nothing beyond the cacophony of voices, both in person and digital. She said to hell with it and finished her wine in three long gulps. It didn't do much for her stomach and she knew she was taking a hell of a chance. Odds were, her stomach would revolt before the wine got upstairs to ease her mind. This time, though, it worked. So she followed it by grabbing the bottle of Lagavulin out of Dr. Fletcher's hand and taking a healthy swig.

A bemused Dr. Fletcher watched as the wonderfully smooth magic potion burned its way down her throat and illuminated her tummy in the soft, buttery light of a harvest full moon. She could hear her parents sternly reminding her that alcohol was strictly forbidden because she had already taken a couple of sedatives. As the scotch's wonderfully soothing energy spread throughout her bones, she patiently explained to her parents that after the day she'd survived, her liver could damn well take a long walk off a short pier.

* * * *

The crop dusters came in low over the Everglades National Park at dusk.

Four planes, silhouetted against the setting sun, piloted by madmen who delighted in going *under* power lines. They swept over the BB&T Center less than twenty feet from each other and the ground, spitting a viscous cloud that enveloped not only the center but most of the parking lot. They held that formation for a few more seconds, then each peeled off in their own direction.

The cocktail lounge erupted in cheering and applause.

Dr. Fletcher said loudly, hoping somebody from the press would hear and want an interview, "I bet they gotta be using some kind of prallethrin, cyhalothrin, and maybe phenothrin." He'd raided the lost and found bin of the country club and was now dressed like a lecherous yacht captain. "Wasps won't know what hit 'em. I'll demand at least a hundred specimens. And they damn well better charter us another private jet home. Let 'em try flying me coach after this shit."

On TV, someone from DHS was explaining that the insecticide was a combination of pyrethroids and pyrethrins. He'd clearly never been on a camera in his life and spoke very quickly, as if he was afraid of getting cut off. The anchors had run through all the adjectives in their arsenal and were more than happy to let him talk. He stumbled to a finish, saying, "These chemicals are in all your basic insecticides sold in stores across the entire USA, so you've got nothing to worry about."

"Told ya," Dr. Fletcher told the bar.

"I'm not getting my hopes up," Jen said. She took another sip of the scotch and hissed in harsh pleasure through her teeth. "Neither one of us has ever seen anything like this. You know damn well parasitoids are solitary; not these guys. This species hasn't behaved like any recorded Hymenoptera. I'm not taking anything for granted."

Dr. Fletcher dismissed this with an airy wave. "Neurotoxin is neurotoxin. It doesn't give a damn whether the organism follows known behaviors or not."

Jen didn't say anything as the crop dusters regrouped over the glades and settled into their positions for another run at the BB&T Center. The image was so stunning that it gave most of the anchors a chance to stop talking. For several seconds, anyway. The optics were custom-made for maximum impact as the lights in the parking lot had recognized the fading sun and were now flickering into brilliant life, revealing wasps, thousands of wasps, wasps everywhere.

The news choppers caught everything, even though they'd learned their lesson and now stayed well back, no closer than a mile and a half. The telephoto lenses were clear enough to zero in on single wasps. None of them were moving. The anchors started getting cautiously optimistic, but Jen and Dr. Fletcher were sitting forward now, looking to make out as many details as they could. Jen said, "That doesn't look right." They could now see that the wasps had wrapped their wings over them like a shroud. They remained motionless.

The cheering in the cocktail lounge grew louder as the planes drew closer for the second approach.

Until wasps erupted out of bushes along the Sawgrass Expressway like tornadoes in reverse, reaching up to the planes in great swarms as if the Earth herself had spit these clouds of pure rage at the poison-filled machines in the sky. That quieted the crowd down to a single, impotent, "No!"

The far left plane dove abruptly into the retention pond. The other planes violently altered course in rapid succession, but too late. Two veered sideways into McMansions, and the last pulled straight up before tumbling backwards into the parking lot. The insecticide was flammable and all exploded in spectacular fashion.

* * * *

Jen couldn't sleep. She suspected shock. Or inebriation.

She couldn't hold any position for more than fifteen, twenty seconds. She'd have to adjust her body into something tolerable, anything so she could drift off. Soon, though, the feeling would creep up again, and she finally gave up and crawled off the top bunk. Dr. Fletcher had fallen asleep with his mouth open on the bottom one.

She shook him awake. "Where are they keeping the prisoners?"

"I never did that—I don't—what?"

"From the bus. Where did they go? I saw you, when that scary guy was talking to you."

"Which scary guy?" He ground his knuckles into his eye sockets. "The prisoner one or the government one?"

"Government one."

Dr. Fletcher blinked several times. "He was saying that so far, he'd beat the one-hour margin and was still alive"—meaning Andy—"putting me on notice, I guess, that I might be called if anything turned up in the boy's blood."

"Where?"

"Where what?"

"Where is he? Where are they keeping him?"

"Some big church, north of here. It's two AM. That boy's most likely dead. You saw those bodies on the bus. You know what happened."

"What big church?"

"Saint Jesus of the Holy Fire Cavalry or something." He sat up. "Ah, fuck. You're thinking about him, aren't you? Forget it. Forget him. Bad idea. Bad, bad all around. As in not good."

Jen was already zipping her jumpsuit to the very top and heading for the exit. In bunks around them, more VIP refugees huddled and looked for rest. Dr. Fletcher shook his head and barked a very loud, "Goddammit!" The outburst got him a few hard looks. He fumbled for his new shoes and tried to put them on in the half light. He yelled at Jen's diminishing figure, "Oh, for fuck's sake, hang on. You won't get two fucking feet. Let me fucking help you."

"Language," someone shushed. "This is still a country club and decorum will be followed."

"Of course. My bad. Heaven forbid anyone says a naughty word when thousands of people are dead."

"You don't know that."

Dr. Fletcher found his yachting cap. "I hope you're right."

* * * *

All he had to do was mention Haaga's name and they were allowed inside. Dr. Fletcher was all primed and pumped with a big story about needing a sample of the boy's blood. He'd scrounged around and found a medic's bag and wanted to claim that he might just be able to save the entire world. Almost disappointingly, the guards at the gate gave them zero trouble and even escorted Jen and Dr. Fletcher through the sprawling church campus, down into the subbasements under the main auditorium.

Not only did the arena-sized auditorium and expansive grounds provide shelter and meeting places for refugees and government officials, two vast subbasements had been constructed under an already impressive basement. The first level held emergency dormitories, various storerooms and workrooms, kitchens, maintenance, and a dry-cleaning service for all the robes and costumes.

The bottom level had been designed and built with several possible future expansions in mind, primarily as a faith-based rehab center. It was no secret within the Florida Calvary community that they wanted the Calvary Chapel to one day rival the impressive resources of a sister facility, the Calvary Healing Center in Phoenix, Arizona. Many agreed this was a long shot, that they had neither budget nor the resources for a luxury spa/rehabilitory business—*ahem*, church charity. The West Cypress Creek location worried that they couldn't even compete with the supposedly brutal Lord's Compass Center in Kentucky. Rumors swirled that they weren't shy about using fire hoses on their clients, especially if the men showed the slightest inkling of homosexual behavior.

Still, most of the Fort Lauderdale chapter were realistic. They agreed that while they'd like to be able to start to encroach on the "pray the gay away" territory firmly established by the America Family and Freedom Council, they knew they were too late to the party. Too many big fish had been caught. So they focused instead on offering an evangelical solution to their flocks' opioid addictions, even though their marketing department outlawed the term *addiction* and encouraged using *Satan's clenched fist* instead.

While Dr. Fletcher kept the guards occupied in the hall, demanding signatures, Jen slipped inside Andy's room.

And realized how wrong she'd been.

* * * *

Andy broke into shaky laughter. "I was expecting somebody else."

"Oh, I'm sorry… I can come back?"

That question elicited more soft giggling from Andy and Jen felt her very soul wither in shame. She thought, *This is a disaster.* Three seconds in, and she'd already made their reunion more awkward than she thought possible.

She decided she had nothing left to lose, so instead of a question, she tried a statement.

"Ah, hello, Mr. Shaw. I'm Jen Huang. You… you saved my life."

Then he went and shocked the hell out of her by sitting up and swinging his legs over the side of the bed, as if he'd been practicing all day "Wow. I didn't know it was gonna be like this." He fixed her with a stare and tried to bring her image into focus. "I don't even know if you're real." This appeared to blow his mind and he started giggling again.

That made Jen laugh right along with him before she could stop herself. She flung her hand up to cover her open, smiling mouth and froze. What if he thought she was laughing *at* him, not *with* him? Instinctively, she moved closer and reached out, touching his knee. She'd held his head while he was near death and this time, skin-to-skin contact with him was electric.

He *did* look better. Tousled bed hair, blank-eyed stare, and sloppy grin. His arms bulged with muscle. His legs were even better. Her professional resolve faltered. She looked down again and found herself fixated on his calf muscles.

"Hey, did you make it out okay?" He was happy, ecstatic even.

"Yes, yes, of course. Because of you. You—you saved me."

He nodded, as if she'd stated something so obvious it wasn't worth acknowledging. He rolled his shoulders and held his arms up. He gazed at his one remaining hand for a while and snorted, "Am I dead?" trying to hold gut-busting laughter in check, as if that was the funniest, raunchiest joke he'd ever heard, but he was in Sunday school and had to hide it.

"No, no. You're not dead." Jen didn't know what to say, where to look. The classroom had suddenly gotten warm. "Thank goodness," she rushed to add, and couldn't help noticing how his hospital gown was riding up past a well-defined thigh.

"Bummer about my hand." He regarded how his arm ended in a bandaged nub. Shrugged.

"Ah, well. What're ya gonna do?"

"That is…" Jen had no idea how to end that sentence. Instead, without thinking, she stepped in until their legs were touching and took his head once again in her hands and kissed him long and slow. Later, it occurred to her that it would have been cool to have said, "Let me thank you the only way I know how," or something like that. But the moment had passed. Actually, they were way past that particular moment and on to something far beyond. His arms and chest and lips were suddenly just *there*, and she couldn't believe how flat-out hungry she felt, and she was straddling him on the bed before she knew what happened. His gown slid up and her jumpsuit got unzipped. From there, everything got blurry. She had one distinct moment imprinted within her, when she breathed in the sweat on his neck while he wrapped his right arm around her waist and pushed her down, thrusting into her at the same time. After that, there was nothing more than a wave of sensations, dreamlike and wonderful.

* * * *

Jen had just found her lost shoe when the door opened a few inches and Dr. Fletcher said, "Ah, is the patient awake, yet?"

"Yes, yes, the patient, Mr. Andrew Shaw, is doing… quite well, all things considered,"

Jen said, running a quick hand through her hair and across her face.

For his part, Andy lay in bed with a perfectly stupid grin on his face.

"Excellent," Dr. Fletcher said as he came into the room. The guards waited in the hall. "We can add your name to the terribly short list of survivors." He made a few check marks on his clipboard and clasped it in front of him. "Well done, young man."

Jen was sure that compliment meant something else.

Andy grinned vacantly.

A voice came from behind them. "I am most gladdened to hear the news, brother traveler." The scary prisoner was in the doorway. The guards were gone.

Jen felt light-headed; too much had happened in too short a time. Again. She was still catching up.

Carver came over to the bed, nodding hello at Dr. Fletcher and winking at Jen. He tilted his head and said to Andy, "How ya feelin, bud?"

"I'm not dead, am I?"

"Not yet."

CHAPTER 15

They came to get Andy around dawn the next day, just after the Department of Homeland Security ordered the Air Force to bomb the living shit out of the BB&T Center.

He'd been sound asleep; it was the first truly restful sleep he'd had in over a week and was none too thrilled about being disturbed. The two medics didn't care. Despite Andy whining like some lazy teenager who didn't want to get up for high school, they hauled him out of the hospital bed and dropped him into a waiting wheelchair without hesitation. They were not gentle.

Andy had figured out, all on his own, that Carver's medicine wasn't a suicide capsule, but more of a wickedly effectively painkiller and mood enhancer all in one glorious and simple mode of delivery. The only thing that Andy really cared about, if he was honest with himself, was getting hold of more of Carver's magic happy pills.

That, and seeing Jen again.

They wheeled him out of the Sunday school classroom, down a quiet hallway, and into a waiting elevator. This took them up to the ground floor, where they pushed him down more empty corridors until finally into a relatively small side chapel. The place fit maybe fifty worshippers, but was mostly empty this morning. The only people in the pews were the six surviving convicts from the bus. Five of them sat in the front pew, all wearing both wrist and ankle chains. Double strands of twisted bicycle flex cable had been strung through all of the restraints, making sure nobody wandered off.

Three soldiers stood against the far wall, standing guard, expressions blank. Again, no way they were just regular National Guard. They wore full-on combat gear and carried several rifles and pistols apiece; they looked more like the Special Forces team that had escorted Carver off the chopper. Every single one looked like they could crack a brick at five paces by merely clenching their jaws.

Squirrel whistled and clapped when he saw Andy. He was closest to the aisle, probably because he couldn't stop grooving along with his own silent opening credit TV theme. Everybody wanted to give him space. Next to him was Magnus, then Ramirez, happy to slink back into a position so relaxed he was nearly horizontal, with the half-lidded eyes and easy smile that didn't sit right. It was neither sly fox nor dullard, but rather an attempt at one from the other extreme. Which one, though? Lunatic or half-wit? He seemed a little too sharp, too quick for Andy to believe the man was a simple idiot. A scowling little Filipino guy named Ocampo was next. House finished out the pew; the wood creaked and threatened to crack every time he crossed his arms.

Carver, however, was three pews back, chained up all by himself. He gave Andy a wink.

The medics parked Andy next to the first pew and without any introduction or explanation of any kind, a screen descended from the ceiling up front above the expansive altar. A paused image from Miami's WTVJ popped up. Someone hit play. Unlike Channel 4, WTVJ still had a chopper in one piece and it was keeping an eye on the spiky rubble of the BB&T Center, using an overabundance of caution to maintain a safe distance. Black smoke seethed, rolling and folding into itself as crosswinds blew through suddenly empty space.

The bland blond anchor nodded somberly as she listened to a live, on-scene report from Hank Ferguson. Ferguson was WTVJ's fearless location reporter; he was the guy they'd send out to the shoreline to cover hurricanes. He was now reporting from the newly expanded demarcation zone. The wasp territory continued to grow, slowly and steadily each day, forcing the evacuations of more areas surrounding Sunrise.

Every once in a while, the director would cut to a *Hollywood Squares* of four experts. Two were mayoral hacks, demanding loudly for the federal government's assistance. The third was an urban disaster expert who seemed a little too excited with all the death and destruction and kept shifting in his chair like his pants were too tight.

The fourth expert was Dr. Fletcher. A few of the convicts hooted and hollered upon recognizing the hipster glasses, the high forehead, and the limp ponytail. He kept shaking his head in disagreement to most everything.

Ferguson was shouting over the rumbling activity in the background. "—lot more movement, and we're getting word that something is about to happen, and very soon."

"And that will be… when, exactly?" the anchor asked.

"Uh, details are still being sketched out, as safety is everyone's first priority. You, you can almost feel the tension all along West Broward and—"

One of the mayor's sycophants interrupted Ferguson. "While I can certainly appreciate the tension on the ground, I'd like to remind everyone to calm down. We have the largest military power in the civilized world and let's face it, folks: We won't have any further trouble with a bunch of angry bees."

Dr. Fletcher broke in to say, "No, you're a moron. Bees? These are not bees."

Both hacks tried to break in, but Dr. Fletcher got louder and angrier, shouting over their platitudes. "No, I repeat, *no* species of Hymenoptera have ever, ever, behaved such as these." He threw out an open palm, indicating the bank of television feeds in the studio. "And make no mistake, thousands, *thousands*, of new species are discovered every year. *Every year*, we've been lucky never to have found something like this."

The anchor tried to settle everybody down. "Well, it would appear that we have much to learn with the emergence of these very dangerous murder hornets." She kept her expression concerned and empathetic, something she tried to save for special occasions, like Amber Alerts and mass shootings.

"Wasps! They're wasps!" Dr. Fletcher shouted.

The director cut to a full shot of Ferguson, who stood in the midst of a line of reporters from other networks. They had been positioned at least twenty or thirty yards back from another line, this one of fire trucks and 18-wheelers packed so tightly it may as well have been a fence strung along a suburban highway. The harsh Florida morning revealed bags under the reporters' eyes so dark no amount of pancake makeup could help. "—quite insistent that not only is there no timetable yet, discussions have yet to begin. There's simply too much happening; the numbers… the numbers, frankly, are horrifying." The studio switched to shots of clogged expressways as hundreds of thousands of refugees, if not millions, fled north. Other shots featured the Miami International Airport, where crowds overwhelmed security checkpoints and surged onto the concourses and gates in total, abject panic.

The anchor shook her hair-sprayed wig. "I'm sorry, Hank, I have to interrupt. We are receiving new information to pass on, more reports of survivors still trapped. This is coming across the wire… live, ladies and gentlemen," and she began to read. "Local officials confirmed that perhaps as many as twenty-five survivors have found refuge within the fast-food establishment Chick-fil-A near the Jacaranda Golf Club after this morning's surge of murder hornets into areas of the city of Plantation. Several survivors were able to use their phones to send photographs, videos, and texts to loved ones and various law enforcement and emergency agencies."

The anchor read slowly and carefully, but it was unclear if she understood the words. "Using shared data and time codes, tireless technicians and editors working cooperatively between various networks have pieced together a rough chronological record of the event. This footage comes with the strongest warning for sensitive viewers and it is highly recommended for parents to escort children from the room."

The beginning of the footage was nearly incomprehensible. Images often blurred into enigmatic tiny pixel squares when people were unable to hold their phone level and motionless. Andy didn't blame them. He didn't know if he'd be brave enough to keep recording with eight or nine wasps loose in the restaurant. He'd be getting the hell out. Especially with everybody screaming and running. Unless maybe Jen was in there.

"Too bad it wasn't a Sunday," Carver said, just loud enough to be heard over the recorded screaming. "That place would've been closed and the true believers would have been safe."

A single soldier stepped forward to him. "You are in a house of God. Speak again, and I will personally nail your tongue to the nearest cross." It was impossible to read his eyes behind the unnecessary sunglasses. The only light came from the flickering screen.

A voice, taut as plucked piano wire, spoke from the back of the room. The cadence sounded familiar to Andy. "At ease, Staff Sergeant Miller. You and the rest of the Christian soldiers will be marching onward soon enough."

Onscreen, wasps flitted over the surging crowd, often coordinating attacks with four or five other wasps. The majority of the customers appeared to flee into the restrooms. Those that had followed the only employee left alive into the women's bathroom were lucky. She could lock the door from the inside.

Those in the men's room weren't as fortunate. Wasps battered the door, driving it open an inch at a time until a few slipped inside, and then it was all over. The humans had no hope of defending themselves. Without tools, their soft, fragile flesh could not withstand the impossibly sharp, impossibly strong stingers that were more fossilized bone than anything alive. When punctured, the two millimeters of human skin stretched tight over mounds of fat would literally pop. The wasps struck, over and over in a frenzy of stabbing, impaling, and injecting both venom and offspring into the shrieking hosts.

WTVJ's anchor reappeared. The footage had been far, far more graphic than she had expected and had to swallow a few times before she could speak. "I—I—again, I can only reiterate the strongest warning that these images are not appropriate for all audiences. " She gathered herself, nodded at some off-screen signal and straightened. "We have an update." She pursed her lips at the seriousness of everything. "A rescue mission is happening as we speak."

Now footage showed six BearCats hauling ass east along Highway 838. Andy squinted; the rising sun threw the four or five bulky figures clinging to the side of each Ballistic Engineered Armored Response Counter Attack Truck into sharp relief, sending their shadows far ahead on the asphalt. They weren't wearing the usual combat vest and fatigues. This was far bulkier, almost like flexible armor.

The armored trucks hit the careful, temporary break in the line of 18-wheelers, and pierced the demarcation zone. The highway was full of the dead, stuffed into cars and strewn across the blacktop. The BearCats swerved around vehicles, but not bodies. There wasn't any space. Sometimes the dead filled the highway, stretching across the pavement from one curb to another. The trucks kept rolling, pulverizing the already bloated corpses, causing bloody clouds of gore to erupt from whatever orifice was farthest from the tires.

The video lost focus for a second, then snapped back as the camera found the tanks, which had stopped in the center of the highway. The smoking remains of the mall could be seen in the background. The bulky figures climbed awkwardly off the vehicles and unslung rifle-like appendages off their backpacks. "I am being told that these brave soldiers have been equipped with a form of napalm and are wearing protective armor used primarily by IED technicians in Iraq." The rest of the tanks pulled up and stopped. The anchor gave a reassuring smile. "I am happy to repeat, a rescue mission is underway."

Soldiers lumbered across the pavement and crossed under the trees that lined the boulevard. The heavy protective suits were stiff and difficult to move. The soldiers stomped out of the shade and took up positions around the restaurant as inquisitive clusters of wasps rose into the heat of the day in reaction to the possible threat. One by one, the soldiers opened up, spraying streams of fire at the building and the clumps of furious wasps. For a few moments, wasps crisscrossed the lot in confusion and burning agony.

It almost looked like the rescue mission would succeed.

Until the wasps learned.

They followed the streams of fire back to their sources and attacked. No bigger than hummingbirds, they wriggled and slipped their way between the overlapping armor that had been designed for a single blast from one direction. The soldiers flailed and dropped their flamethrowers. Some tried to run, but didn't get far. Most stumbled into parked cars and fell out of sight. The wasps descended without mercy.

The last man standing saw his compadres fall and was able to keep moving while setting incoming wasps on fire. And while the flames scorched the exoskeletons and wings, a single-minded will inside the wasps refused to die and hungered for vengeance. The soldier suddenly found himself the target of kamikaze wasps. They knocked him off his feet and cooked him alive inside his bomb armor.

Those left in the BearCats saw the score and took off before the wasps targeted them.

The news anchor abruptly filled the screens. She swallowed any deer-in-the-headlights giveaways of panic and managed to say, "This, this emergency rescue has been, will be... we will be rejoining the effort to rescue the Chick-fil-A survivors any moment now." She paused, hoping the producer would have someone, anyone—an expert, a scientist, a government official who wasn't afraid of possible retribution.

Squirrel observed, "They fucked up right thoroughly."

The anchor looked at her desk and made sure that everyone knew she was tapping her earpiece. "Mark, Mark? Is the feed gone?"

The video feed died and the lights came up.

Haaga stepped forward and tossed the TV remote onto the pew. He didn't look like he'd slept in a couple years, his eyes and suit so dark they swallowed light. He slapped a stack of files on the altar. "Needless to say, the entire world is watching." He tilted his head, indicating the news. "And given this nation's... unprecedented levels of partisanship infighting, the mood on Main Street is that the US government is useless. Left and right alike. My job is to remind John Q. Public that we are a country of rugged individualism and ingenuity. The US still carries a big fucking stick and we aren't afraid to use it."

Carver gave a slow, sarcastic clap.

Haaga ignored him. "I have been authorized to offer clemency to every single one of you." He tapped the files.

"What's that mean?" Squirrel demanded.

"It means that you will receive a full pardon from the president of the United States for any and all crimes you may have committed while under employment of the US Army if you provide assistance to those unfortunate souls."

He gave everybody a moment to digest the news. "Right now, the prevailing winds in Washington are all about bombing these five square miles back to the stone age. You might be able to get people out before bad things happen. It's a simple proposition. You smarter fellows can explain it to the morons."

"Why us?" Carver asked. "You can order any poor bastard to go die instead, like your pets here." He indicated the soldiers against the wall.

"It's not entirely a rescue mission. It's a PR move. The footage has gone viral, as the kids say. According to the marketing experts, you all are diverse enough to not only have penetrated the mass eighteen to thirty-five market, but displayed four-quadrant appeal. Your brand is… viable."

Carver said, "Modern problems require modern solutions."

Haaga said, "Exactly."

"And how, exactly, does that work?" Ramirez asked.

Haaga tilted his head and turned to the prisoners. "That's your job. You figure it out. Bring them back alive. You do that, you get walking papers."

"Who?" Carver asked.

"Anyone who participates in the rescue."

"Anybody?"

"Anybody who participates in the rescue."

"Everybody?"

"Everybody."

"How many?"

"I told you. Everybody."

"No. How many people are we required to retrieve?"

Pause. "Well, most. There's a dozen, fifteen people in there at least. You bring ten back, you get to disappear."

"Five."

"No."

"Seven then, including any kids and their MILFs."

Another pause. "Fine."

"We're not going in there holding our dicks, I'll tell you that much." Carver spoke for the convicts. "We want to be able to do more than just cum with napalm."

Haaga nodded. "Figured as much. Your finesse with the shotguns was impressive. Exceptional, even. Considering you were not only working with three or four twelve-gauges firing double-aught pellets, number two if you were lucky." He gave what might have passed for a smile. "I, for one, am very curious what you gentlemen could accomplish utilizing this particular firearm, primarily supplied with a somewhat specialized load."

He reached behind the altar and held up a very heavy, very black shotgun that looked like a snake that had eaten a hubcap and it was going down sideways. "I took the liberty of locating a number of Atchissons. Some of you have heard of these; fully automatic shotguns with thirty-two–round drum magazines. I need video of you boys out there slaughtering murder hornets by the hundreds." He hefted the firearm like some kind of god of guns, good ol' Saint Shotgun.

"You'll be wearing body cameras. You rescue those in the restaurant, we all win. The wasps get you, we'll livestream it. If nothing else, it'll give the illusion we tried. Still a win," Haaga said, producing five more automatic shotguns from behind the altar. He laid them out butt-first, in a show of respect to the convicts.

The spec-op soldiers from the far side of the room unlocked the bike cables and allowed the five men to approach the altar and firearms. As they reached for the guns, someone spoke. "I, for one, would feel better with a bit of signed paperwork behind all this." It was Carver, still locked up in the third row.

Haaga said, "We're burning daylight. Ammo's on the bus."

* * * *

Of course, they used the bus. What else would they use? It worked as protection against the wasps and they had a brand to promote, after all. The 18-wheelers split and before the bus had gone ten yards, the trucks slid smoothly back into place, keeping the barrier tight.

The bus, Ramirez at the wheel, followed the path of the BearCats.

Carver was up front with Ramirez, pointing out the best route. Everybody else was busy shoving shells into the big drum magazines. It took a while to load thirty-two rounds. While Atchissons primarily used double-aught shells, this ammo was different. Double-aught pellets are roughly the size of peas, and you can only fit eight or nine into each shell; these shells were filled with number-9 shot, small enough to cram nearly 300 tiny steel pellets in each plastic casing. Every fifth shell had a third less shot, replaced with balls of pyrotechnic flares. This way, everybody would have a better sense of where the shots were going. The chokes had even been bored out even wider, so the shot would spread into a bigger blast diameter.

At least half the seats were full of canisters of shells and more shotguns. Carver knew Haaga had a hell of a lot more Atchissons stashed somewhere and refused to leave without more firepower. Haaga didn't even bother to argue.

He'd brought generic fatigues that more or less fit the convicts, even House, who wore size XXXL. Everybody except Andy. Carver refused to change until Haaga found another uniform for his pal. Haaga shrugged and pulled out his phone, ordered another one. "Extra- small." While they waited, Haaga leaned against the altar and lit a cigarette, blowing the smoke at the detector on the ceiling. "Can you even walk, son?"

"He'll do just fine," Carver said and stood behind Andy's wheelchair, hands on his shoulders. "He's our totem, our mascot." He slipped a pill under Andy's collar. "Our good luck charm."

Andy felt it and knew to keep quiet. He drew his shoulder blades together and guided the pill to his lower back. He pretended to scratch an itch and palmed it. If Haaga saw him dry swallow the pill, Haaga never said anything. Andy doubted he really gave a damn either way.

* * * *

Twenty minutes later he was feeling fucking awesome again. Standing and walking wasn't an issue. Granted, he couldn't load the drum magazines for shit with only one hand, but he'd worked out a system by linking the shotgun's sling to his own sling for his left arm. The support and tension of the slings allowed him to hold that sucker in the crook of his arm and by simply standing sideways to the target, he could effortlessly swing the whole thing back and forth, up and down.

He practiced along the bus aisle. The gun was a little large, like an assault rifle's chubbier cousin, and Andy wasn't sure how well he'd be able to control an automatic .12-gauge recoil. He looped a loose canvas strap over the barrel and tied it down. He was busy working his way backwards when a bemused Carver snatched the shotgun away and detached the magazine, ejected the live shell in the breech, and then handed the unloaded firearm back before Andy blew a big hole in the bus or someone.

Beyond the firepower and fatigues, Haaga had also supplied enough personal gear for a platoon. They all wore tactical vests, kneepads, black boots. Gloves. Canvas ammo bags that carried up to a dozen drums, worn as a backpack. Haaga wanted to obscure their identities as much as possible, so he'd included helmets, dark shooting glasses, and bandannas to tie around their faces.

As Ramirez turned north on Flamingo Road, Carver addressed the rest of the bus. "Two-minute warning, sports fans. This is nothing more than

an extermination, remember that. We're going to drive right up to the front
doors. Me and House will clear anything in the immediate area. Ocampo,
you and Clarence run for the restroom. Ramirez keeps the engine running.
Squirrel and Andy hang back and blast any that get close. Keep everything
clear when we come back.

"These bad boys"—he patted his own shotgun—"are famous for the
supposedly reduced kick. Let's hope they've earned it. Make sure your
field of fire is clear and use short bursts." He tossed the magazine back to
Andy. "Ready to rock?"

"Bring it," Andy yelled and slammed the drum home, racked the bolt
back to slam a live round back into the breech.

Rather than slow enough to make the sharp left turn into the Chick-fil-A
parking lot, Ramirez just bounced the bus over the curb through the trees
and across a narrow grass median.

They hit the corner of an orange Kia and sent it spinning away. If anything,
the bus picked up speed until Ramirez stomped on the brakes, but it was
too late to avoid smashing to a sudden halt, about five yards from the doors
when the bus hit an SUV.

All around them, agitated wasps rose to meet the threat.

Carver was first out of the door. His AA-12 erupted into a thunderous
barrage, flinging a gossamer strand of red stars at the nearest wasp. The
entire head, thorax, and most of the left wing instantly exploded into a
pus-colored mist. Empty black shotgun shells spun into the air. He eased
off the trigger, waited until settling on the next one before squeezing off
a second blast.

House was next, and went for the doors. A few wasps crawled out of
the baseball-sized holes, aware of the commotion. He opened up, but had
a hard time staying off the trigger. It wasn't long before he had to drop the
empty drum and lock a new one into place. By then, there was nothing left
of the doors except battered metal. He kicked the empty frames open and
immediately began firing at the lobby's ceiling.

Carver joined him and they lit the inside up with glowing red death.

Andy had seen House damn near hold onto the shotgun with one hand,
so Andy figured the big guy might as well have two, especially if he was
going to go through rounds that fast. He slung a second shotgun over his
right shoulder. He knew his job was to hang back outside, but it couldn't hurt
to deliver another shotgun to House. By this point, Magnus and Ocampo
had cleared the doors and ran through the lobby for the restrooms.

Squirrel head-butted the stiff wire cage near the stairs to psych himself
up and jumped out the door. Andy was right behind him and they spun,

shotguns up, ready for any wasps over the bus. "Oh fuckin' lordy," Squirrel breathed and Andy had to agree. Wasps, more than they could count, filled the smoky sky. Most were around thirty yards out, but they were coming fast.

Andy ran for the restaurant doors. The gunfire had stopped. Sweet gray smoke filled the lobby, obscuring details. Something seemed to be all over the floor, covering the lobby and blocking the aisles between tables in the dining area. House stood alone by the registers in the mist and yelled, "How bad is it out there?"

"We gotta go," Andy said.

They heard shooting from the back, somewhere beyond the kitchen.

"No shit," House said.

Andy had only taken three steps before his ankle rolled as his foot came down on someone's outstretched arm. Bodies blanketed the floor; they filled the area in front of the registers and blocked aisles in the dining room. As the gunpowder smoke dissipated, their faces grew clearer, and he saw that all were splayed out in frozen expressions of hideous agony. The medicine made him see things as a sort of miniature golf course, and so he was able to pretend he was just clambering over low hills and sand traps, small ponds even.

Andy tossed House the second shotgun. "Thought this might make you feel better."

House hoisted both shotguns. "Goddamn, you're right." He turned to the narrow hallway to the restrooms. His voice boomed down the hall, almost as loud as his shotgun. "Okay, motherfuckers, bus is leaving."

More shooting up ahead. Then a door banged open and Ocampo practically fell into the hallway. House jumped and almost blew him away with two .12-gauges. It was a good thing he missed. There wouldn't have been enough left of Ocampo to put in a gallon freezer bag.

Distant gunfire. Squirrel must have started shooting out by the bus.

People began tumbling out of the women's restroom after Ocampo, faces full of panic. They kept streaming out, at least a dozen and counting. They ran through the front, but could only stumble across a soft, bumpy surface that rolled and gave and shifted unpredictably.

Andy and House heard a fluttering from the kitchen and spun to find several wasps crawling through the drive-through window and lightly bouncing along the cutting boards and sinks. House gave both triggers a quick squeeze. Most of the wasps simply evaporated as microwaves exploded and the rest of the pieces were blown to the back of the kitchen, smeared across steel counters and the deep fryer.

The survivors slipped and struggled through the main dining area. For the most part, everybody was quiet, too busy sucking oxygen to shout or say anything. Until a woman in heavy makeup and an expensive haircut accidentally put her high heel through an eye socket, snapping the heel clean off. Her foot slipped off the skull, twisting her ankle so badly she went down like someone had upended her table centerpiece. One of her teenage boys was close enough to try and grab her, but too late. She fell headfirst into an obese man in a plum-colored tracksuit; her face plunged into the bulging belly as easily as poking the skin of pudding left out too long.

People pushed past, running over her for the bus. Andy knew he should be outside too, but wanted to keep an eye on the ruptured stomach of the man in the sweat suit. The impact had drawn the top away from his waist, revealing pale, stretch-marked skin. It rippled and pulsed as movement underneath grew more and more frantic until the inevitable. The flesh split, cracking open along the spiderweb of veins and slimy wasps clawed their way out. The stench of human excrement was strong enough to make everyone's eyes water.

The size of the wasps was disturbing. A dim part of Andy's mind wondered if the meds were screwing with his vision, but everything else appeared real and so he had to acknowledge that he wasn't imagining things. Because if anything, these wasps were even bigger than the ones outside. Their bodies alone were longer than a paperback book.

The boys finally got their screaming mother under each arm and were dragging her away, when House saw the giant baby wasps squirming out of the fat man. "Oh, good god," he blurted, deep voice wavering. As the first of the wasps rose tentatively into the air, House opened up with both shotguns. Wasps and humans alike exploded in an orgiastic eruption of blood and meat.

Ears ringing, Andy didn't hear Carver come up behind them until Carver slapped him on the back and said, "Go!" By then, most of the fifteen or sixteen survivors had cleared the dining room and were scrabbling through the doors. Andy joined them, and although he tried to tread carefully, it was still like running on wet pillows. He almost fell himself when he tried to overcorrect and stepped right on a little girl's chest. The ribs cracked and collapsed, and tight clumps of premature wasps burst out of her mouth. His center of gravity tipped precariously and he pinwheeled his right arm until finding his balance.

Outside, hunting season had opened. The convicts blasted at a sky full of gathering wasps as the survivors ran to the bus. Andy joined the party, pulling the trigger for the first time. The gun kicked and jumped like a rodeo bull thrashing around in a chute. Still, he managed to bring down at least four or five wasps before he had to reload. And once he learned how to ride the jumping shotgun, his angle of fire smoothed out, providing a virtual wall of steel shot that laid waste to the horde.

They had almost everyone on the bus when the wasps got Magnus. Too focused on the sky, he didn't see two that floated out from under the bus. One went for his Achilles tendon while the second latched onto his chest and thrust its ovipositor into his torso, just under the sternum. He spasmed, jerking the trigger. Steel shot and tracers sprayed along the bus's siding and bulletproof glass and blew through most of a young man's head. Everybody else hit the ground as Magnus spun, falling sideways into a palm tree and slumping into the wood chips at the bottom.

Carver and Andy were the last to board. Ramirez hit the gas, reversing away from the SUV. The bumper caught on the SUV's wheel well and tore the aluminum away as the bus hurtled backwards. Ramirez kept his foot on the floor until the bus slammed into a row of cars.

Wasps attacked from all sides, splattering themselves against the cracked glass and wire mesh.

Ramirez jerked the gearshift into *drive* and they got the hell out of there.

* * * *

"Doubt I'll keep a straight face. Might even puke," Carver said as he squinted dubiously at a sheet of paper. "'We're proud we could help.' Nobody's gonna buy it. It's no secret we're convicts. Says right there on the side of the bus."

Haaga lit a new cigarette. "People believe what they want. If you want your paperwork signed, you'll read that statement live, on camera."

One of the FEMA officials held a finger to his lips. "Ten minutes," he whispered. He frowned at the cigarette, but didn't say anything.

They stood in a wide hallway in the upper floor of the country club, just outside a door to the boardroom. Inside, a large news conference was in progress. Dozens of reporters, videographers, and photographers were gathered around the long table, while various state and federal officials, along with scientists and other experts, stood up front behind the podium.

The rest of the convicts had been requested to wait down at the end of the hall, still in all their gear. They'd been instructed not to take anything off. Nobody else got too close, not even guards. Not obviously, anyway. Andy spotted a few of the soldiers hanging in the background, keeping a general eye on the chaos.

He was getting irritated.

He'd taken Carver's pill over five hours ago; the pain was coming back and exhaustion was starting to creep into the edges of his vision. Plus, he was bored. They'd been standing around for over an hour, waiting for the first presser to finish so Miami's mayor could trot the heroes out like some dog and pony show. Every once in a while, when an aide would come out one of the doors, he caught snatches of the speeches and questions.

A few snippets of actual news slipped out between declaring a tearful victory and congratulating everybody above them on the political food chain. In addition to the FEMA camp updates for the evacuees and all the new safety protocols they had established, they were also planning an expedition to Central America. Apparently, they'd found the passenger on flight 87 who had brought the wasps aboard, and had been able to pinpoint the exact location, deep in the jungle wilderness of Honduras, where the passenger had been staying. No, they preferred not to identify the person and wouldn't give the nationality either.

Andy drifted away from the group and wandered down the busy hall. He stopped at the intersection, unsure of where he wanted to go. Nearby, banks of monitors had been set up for news producers, but Andy wasn't interested in watching politicians slap each other on the back.

Maybe he could find somewhere nice and dim and cool and quiet.

A soldier appeared out of nowhere, saying, "Hey, bro. Need some help?"

"I'm not your bro."

"Just trying to help, dawg."

Andy glared at the soldier and held up his stump. "I'm looking for some fucking Advil."

"Yeah, sure, we'll get you some. In the meantime, I'm gonna need you to wait down there, okay, bro?" He indicated the group of convicts; most were sitting on the floor.

Andy was about to light into the guy when the face he'd been dreaming about, her face, appeared briefly on one of the monitors. "Jen," he whispered and got closer, ignoring the soldier completely. Feeds from four different cameras inside the presser lit up the monitors. One of them was panning along the dozens of experts who would be joining the expedition, and must have already passed Jen. He recognized Dr. Fletcher and checked the other monitors for a wide shot.

Maybe he could spot her there.

"C'mon, bro. Let's get you back to your pals. You guys are up next." He put his hand on Andy's shoulder.

"Don't touch me, motherfucker," Andy said, shrugging him off, voice raising in volume until he almost shouted the last word. Several people turned and shushed him.

"Are we gonna have a problem here, bro?"

"You tell me. I ain't hurting anybody."

"Let's go," the soldier said, fake friendliness and patience all gone, gesturing quickly to get moving.

Andy turned back around to the monitors.

Again, the soldier gripped his shoulder, harder. But this time, Andy was waiting. He spun and popped the surprised soldier right in the nose. The guy didn't go down, but starbursts of pain exploded behind his eyes. He coughed out, "—dirty—fuck—sneaky bullshit," so Andy kicked him in the balls as a kind of public service, just to educate the man in *genuine* sneaky bullshit. That put the soldier on his knees. Andy turned back to search the monitors.

Seven or eight more soldiers materialized around Andy. He never took his eyes off the video feeds.

The sergeant said, "Look, Private. You might be a big internet star and all that, but you still have a contract with Uncle Sam. Don't make this hard." He waited a moment, then nodded to the rest of them. "Okay, then."

Andy thought he may have spotted her again when hands grabbed his arms and legs and head and jerked him completely off the floor. He reacted by kicking and shouting,

"Cocksuckers!" The soldiers held on, but the commotion was loud enough to catch the attention of everyone inside the press conference. It even got the mayor to stop speaking for a moment as he looked to the doorway at the back of the room in puzzlement.

Things got louder. Andy realized his right leg was free for some reason, but didn't waste any time and started kicking the two soldiers who had hold of his left as hard as he could.

Eventually, someone dropped his right side completely and Andy crashed to the floor as soldiers tumbled around him. Sounds of fists hitting flesh and curses and grunts filled the hallway.

It was Carver. A tornado of fists, legs, and long hair, he struck without mercy, cracking knees and gouging eyes. Eventually, reinforcements arrived and got things under control. Andy was gassed by that point anyway. As they were escorted back to the end of the hall, Carver palmed another pill and passed it to Andy, then popped one into his own mouth. "Let's get this over with."

* * * *

Haaga stood in the open doorway. In the room behind him, the mayor spoke into a very loud microphone, spouting banal platitudes that drew fresh rounds of applause. Haaga dropped his cigarette and ground it into the carpet with his shoe. He fixed his dead eyes fully on the cons. Most couldn't meet the intense stare. Haaga took his time pulling out a fresh pack of smokes and slit the plastic with his thumbnail. He told all of them, "It's so simple you might be able to manage it. Go in there, stand still, and keep your goddamn mouth shut. And when he's finished—" he nodded to Carver at the front of the line—"file out."

He watched them for a moment, then opened the door and stood aside, keeping well out of the reach of any cameras. Carver marched in, followed by Ramirez and Ocampo and House, like good little boys all dressed up in their matching Halloween costumes and a round of applause and cheering went up. As Andy got close to the door, Haaga put the unlit cigarette in his mouth and said, "Hold up." He took a medical gun-looking thing, some kind of heavy-duty syringe, and held it up. "Doc's orders. Antibiotic booster."

Andy blinked. "Now?"

Haaga shrugged. "Don't ask me. They don't tell me shit." Haaga took Andy's left arm, settled the barrel of the gun against the stump, and hit the button. There was a solid *chunk*, like a goddamn industrial stapler, and Andy jerked, damn near cried out in pain. "Holy fuck, man."

Haaga gave him a thin, humorless smile. "All set." He pushed Andy through the door.

Out in the big room, none of them quite knew how to react as they walked into the bright lights and looked to each other for understanding. Nobody knew what to do with their hands.

Carver stepped up to the podium and the room hushed. He unfolded the paper, leaned in accidentally on purpose too close to the mike, and started to read, making it quite clear these were not his words. "I will be making a brief statement and will take no questions."

Andy didn't give a shit what Carver had to say. He scanned the audience for Jen. The lights made it hard to see the back of the room, He cupped his eyes against the glare and squinted. She had been wearing a top the color of a sunflower, so he looked for that particular yellow shade.

Curiously, the lights also appeared to be slowly growing into a field of flowers; they glowed and glittered and were astonishingly beautiful and everything got groovy, baby as Carver's pill hit Andy's happy spots.

"We are the Exterminators," Carver said, popping his Ts. "We are volunteers, comprised of active-duty military personnel on both sides of the law." Squirrel snorted. Carver continued: "We are proud and honored to provide assistance to Dade County and the citizens of Sunshine, Florida, as well as many other federal teams, as I'm sure you've all heard plenty about today." It was clearly written to be a light joke, but Carver read it in such a halting rhythm nobody in the room dared to do anything.

Andy heard Carver's voice loud and clear, booming even, but he didn't bother attaching any meaning associated to the words at that particular moment. It was a trick he'd learned as a kid, to dissociate when his mom and her boyfriends got to fighting. He'd had a lot of chances to practice. Besides, right now he was too busy trying to see past the flowers in front of his face for Jen.

Carver kept going in the same dead, flat voice. "We offer our thoughts and prayers for all who have suffered during this tragedy."

There. That shade of yellow. Jen. And she was coming closer.

Jen raised her forearm and wiggled her fingers in a quiet hello. Andy tore off his helmet, then his bandanna, and shouted, "Hey! Jen! It's me! Andy!" Aware of little else, he stumbled down the steps and ran to her. "Jen!"

They crashed together and he hugged her as hard as he could with one arm. She threw her arms around his neck. They clung fiercely together for a moment, then stepped apart. He said, "I didn't know if I'd ever see you again."

"Of course you would," she said, and became aware of the rest of the room, watching. She saw in his eyes that he was high as a kite. "Um, I think it would be best if you went back up there," she said, as flashes went off and phones came out.

Andy turned to look at the rest of room. "Oh. Oh yeah."

"I'll be waiting for you, outside, after..." She gave him another quick hug, gently pushing him along. Light laughter and a smattering of applause spread as he stood next to the rest of the heroes.

Carver flashed him a huge grin. "Fun comes later, big fella, after we take care of business, baby." He went back to reading. "We are just *so* proud we could help and will continue to fight for your safety. Our next mission is tomorrow. Stay tuned."

"Say what?" House said.

"Yeah, what the fuck, man?" Ocampo asked.

Carver walked off, crumpling the paper as he went.

* * * *

Haaga was waiting for them in the empty employee cafeteria. He clapped, enthusiastically. "Well done, gents. Sincerely. You all performed admirably. Just what we needed. A bunch of rough-and-tumble tough guys with a soft side."

"What the fuck you trying to pull?" House roared.

"This wasn't our agreement." The edge in Carver's voice could singe the ears of small woodland creatures.

Haaga said, "I took the liberty of volunteering your services. Again."

Ramirez brandished a slim filet knife he'd stolen from the kitchen. "Let's just cut this *pendejo*'s dick off and leave."

"Why don't you try it?" Haaga said with a hint of a ghastly grin. "See what happens."

Even Ramirez was smart enough to know that when potential prey invites you to attack, it might be a good time to swallow your pride. He couldn't bring himself to step back or even return the knife to its hiding place; that would be too much. Instead, he straightened, releasing the tension from his muscles.

"Why don't we get down to it instead?" Carver said.

"All the necessary signed paperwork is being processed in Washington as we speak and should be here in a few hours."

"Not good enough. And we sure as hell won't be going back out there. We're not your puppets anymore."

"Perhaps you should hear the terms of the new offer before making a decision."

"Perhaps you should pull your head out of your goddamn ass and smell what you been shoveling," House said. He still hadn't released his clenched fists.

"You mistake me for some soulless bureaucrat. I would not ask you to risk your lives for nothing but fame. Fortune, though? You haven't been online lately, I suppose."

"We been busy." House was still ready to tear someone's head from his shoulders.

"You're all over it. People love you. People hate you. Memes out your ass. Twelve hours ago, bobbleheads of you dumb fucks went up for sale on something called Etsy. That alone has raised over ten thousand dollars so far for the evacuees. You're a PR flack's wet dream. Therefore, the Exterminators will earn twenty-five thousand dollars for their next mission."

"Tax-free?" Squirrel said. Haaga nodded. Squirrel looked around, trying to figure out the math, unconsciously moving his fingers as he counted. "That's...uh, that's how much apiece?"

Haaga shook his head again. "Each."

Most of the collective breath went out of the room. Guys glanced sideways at each other; that was a hell of a lot of money to all of them. Carver didn't like it. "Seems light, us risking our lives and all. This is the federal government we're talking about."

"You're right. And that's why you'll each receive one hundred thousand for every mission after. But the clock is ticking, boys."

"Is that US dollars?" Squirrel demanded.

"Would you prefer it in a different currency?"

"Nah. Making sure you ain't pulling a fast one. Hundred thousand pesos, some bullshit like that."

House crossed his arms. "Still smells like bullshit. What if I decide to decline?"

"It's entirely up to you, obviously," Haaga said. "Of course, we will have to replace you, making you redundant. This is why we haven't officially released your names yet. In the unlikely case we may have to... subtract anyone."

The room was silent until Carver said, "We're not going anywhere until we see the money."

Haaga pulled a briefcase from under the table and opened it, tossed tight rolls of cash to each of them. "Half now. Half after."

Andy eyeballed the money. As far as he could tell, it was all hundred-dollar bills. It was the most money he'd ever held at one time. A giddy joy rose inside of him and if there'd been music, he would have started dancing. All the cash, plus Jen waiting for him? "This is the best day of my life," he said.

* * * *

And it may have been, until Jen told him later that evening that she was leaving for Honduras in the morning to search for the origin of the wasps.

CHAPTER 16

Jen hadn't expected a Sea Knight.

When she'd first heard they would be taking a real-life helicopter for the last leg of their journey, Jen couldn't wait. She kept thinking of all those movies with beautiful shots from a helicopter gliding effortlessly over a lake or ocean and soaring up to a sparkling city. After learning nearly everything about aircraft from the movies, she had a vision in her head that was something cute, something from *The Jetsons*. It would putter daintily along over the jungle, giving her a breathtaking view of the flora and fauna.

She should have looked closer before boarding and kicked herself for not asking questions. Like, Can't they take a Jeep instead? Maybe donkeys? However, the sheer size of the helicopter, plus the fact that it had not one, but two of those spinning-blade-rotor-things, intimidated her into silence. Sure, it looked a little old and rusty, and those round windows were maybe kinda small, but she had no doubt it was perfectly safe.

The expedition had been arranged very, very quickly and she still felt a flush of pride over being chosen to participate. Dr. Fletcher had gotten the initial call, inviting them both. He kept pestering her as he tried on different combinations of clothing and jungle gear, wanting her opinion on his outfits. Finally, for fun, she gave him the worst advice she could, and in the end he looked a little like Crocodile Dundee in a hat a couple sizes too large and a T-shirt a size too small.

Then the pilots started the engine.

And Jen realized she knew nothing at all about helicopters. The sound was incredible. Everything shook, rattled, and rolled. This was a machine that appeared to have been designed to attack the air, to pulverize it, dragging the reluctant humans along to experience the warfare firsthand. The pilots had helpfully explained they were flying a Boeing Vertol CH-46 Sea Knight and Jen just hoped that didn't mean it had been built in 1946. They guessed the journey would take five, five and a half hours, depending on how much the weather wanted to cooperate.

Work was impossible. At least during the two plane rides they'd been able to debate various theories and gather evidence. Now, she couldn't even write legible notes, let alone focus on her laptop. Nine out of the fourteen various researchers and specialists were currently dry-heaving into plastic bags and the rest weren't far behind. It didn't help that the grinning pilots were making the helicopter sway on purpose. They kept looking back at Dr. Fletcher and cackling. He'd been rude to everybody ever since he'd found out he wasn't in charge of the expedition, especially the pilots with this ancient helicopter waiting at the airport in Honduras. He'd already filled one bag with half-digested *plato tipico*, his breakfast of fried eggs, refried beans, corn tortillas, cheese, and plantains and was working on his second.

Jen struggled to keep her own breakfast down as well. To keep nausea at bay, she played a game with herself, mentally cataloging every object on her cluttered desk back at the University of Chicago. This soothed her, as home felt very, very far away all of a sudden. First off, of course, would have to be the photo of the entire family gathered around the grand matriarch, Jen's great-grandmother. She thought about naming each face, but that was over thirty people, so she guided her gaze over the frame that had been decorated by her niece and nephew. Then there was the hilariously suggestive statuette she won during a bachelorette party in Vegas. And before she knew it, she was thinking of Andy.

* * * *

When she told him she was joining the expedition, his immediate reaction had been concern for her well-being in the jungle. Apart from her family, she'd never experienced this kind of instinctive love, without thought of himself. That led to hushed declarations, promises, and admitting they couldn't stop thinking of each other. She felt a sliver of guilt when she'd found herself relieved that he wasn't feeling any pain and then realized she might be taking advantage of him while he was on some mind-altering substance. For his part, Andy certainly didn't need any encouragement. Apart from closing his eyes when they kissed, he could barely look anywhere but at her.

Jen decided it would be best not to mix alcohol with whatever meds were in Andy's system, so instead of heading to the bar, they found a quiet bench outside. When the sun finally dropped beneath the horizon, after seemingly arcing across the sky and hanging up there forever, it went fast. Lights erected by FEMA flickered to life across the golf course. They talked. Traded childhood stories. Realized they were born on different planets. But… All masks, all walls had fallen away, and all the shapes and colors of their souls interlocked, like atoms smashing into each other in the depths of a black hole, fusing into singularity.

He told her why he'd been on the bus. "I killed a man. Never meant to. It was an accident. But it was a fight, so…" He shrugged. It had been a fair fight, no weapons, in a crowded public bar, and the dead man had asked for it. Like too many before him, the asshole had only seen Andy's short stature, had seen how the military buzz cut only made his ears stand away from his skull and how he looked kind of goofy, thought he was an easy target. Easy to ridicule. Easy to push around. But like the rest, the dumb sonofabitch had either been too drunk or too stupid or both to see the flat, unflinching rage burning just below the surface of Andy's dull gray eyes.

Andy sure as hell hadn't tried to kill the asshole. But sometimes, when his hands curled into concrete fists, the rest of the world, the bar patrons, the asshole's friends, the stupid goddamn country music, the neon beer lights—all of it would fall into nothing but a red haze. He managed to hit the asshole in precisely the wrong spot, with just the wrong amount of force.

The pathetic defense based their argument on Andy's anger management problems, pointing to the short string of assault charges on his arrest record that led to his semi-voluntary enlistment, and how the military had actually made controlling his temper worse.

That legal strategy backfired. Spectacularly.

Because when the dead man was the son of a local politician with his hand deep in the base's endless pockets, payback was an honored tradition. "But, I'm told the paperwork is in the mail, as we speak, wiping it all clean. Just wanted you to know, you know, why I was on the bus."

She kissed him, long and slow and deep and hard. "It's okay," she said, cradling his face. "It doesn't matter." She noticed Andy rolling his left shoulder and adjusting the sling. "Let's change those bandages."

He nodded and took another pill. Carver had given him a whole bottle, but said only two a day. This would be the third one today.

"Do you know the name of those? What's in them?" Jen asked.

He shook his head. "Nah. And right now, can't say I care a whole lot. Not yet, anyway." Jen couldn't argue.

The first aid tent was empty except for a mechanic getting a few stitches in his scalp. While the nurse cut away the old bandages, Andy looked away. His pill hadn't had a chance to take effect. Jen squeezed his right hand with both of hers and forced herself to look at the stump.

The amputation had been done about a third of the way up his forearm and a flap of thick skin had been stitched almost completely around the tip. The nurse was pleased with the lack of redness and heat. Jen pinched her lips together so tears wouldn't spill out of her eyes. She watched intently as the nurse rebandaged Andy's arm, memorizing it so she could take care of him later. As all her attention was focused on his arm, he surprised her by leaning close and giving her a soft kiss on her ear; breathed, "It's all good."

They found a quiet, dark garage full of golf carts. She was on him before he twisted the lock behind them. She had no idea where this hunger came from, as if a succubus had taken possession of her soul. His scruffy, defiant look; his voice, his smell, his touch, everything about him filled her entire universe. They spent the night on the front seat of a golf cart and never let go of each other.

* * * *

On the helicopter she felt very hot and hoped none of the experts or soldiers could see her blush. The passengers sat with their backs along both sides of the cargo bay, with the scientific equipment strapped down between them. She looked to her guardian angel in the expedition, directly across from her. Dr. Ross, who insisted everyone call her Araminta, was an entomologist from the University of California, Davis, with a specialization in aberrations caused by pesticides. She'd been published everywhere from the *Journal of Agricultural and Food Chemistry* to *The New Yorker*. Dr. Fletcher was fiercely resentful of the attention.

Araminta had decided to take Jen under her wing after seeing Jen and Andy embrace at the press conference. She was a stunning black woman who had found her calling as a teenager in the peace and love generation of the late sixties and had spent the following decades as a crusader for environmental rights and pioneering research into organic food, although she told anyone who would listen that the current regulations of "organic" food were 90 percent rubbish. She took great pride in being a right-wing radio host's worst commie nightmare. After one of the other scientists expressed doubt about her age, she just laughed and said, "Black don't crack, baby." At the moment, she was weaving an elegant, impromptu wreath or crown of flowers and strands of long grass from the edge of the airfield.

Next to her was Dr. Patel. A small man with round glasses, he was the leader of the scientific arm of the expedition. Currently, he was a professor emeritus with the entomology and nematology department at the University of Florida, and was considered one of the world's foremost authorities of Central American Hymenoptera. He studied one of two satellite phones on board and recorded information in a waterproof journal in tight, precise movements.

The other phone was carried by Staff Sergeant Fisher, sitting down near the back of the cargo bay. He appeared to be asleep. Although you never could quite tell, as his eyes remained hidden in a perpetual squint, face dominated by thick black eyebrows and a gigantic gray mustache. He commanded the military arm, a squad of a dozen Special Forces soldiers who rode in the back half of the helicopter with the rest of the gear, including a locked case the size of a child's coffin.

It held their primary tool for investigation, including, if at all possible, extermination. The large drone had been modified with a muted engine and carried a small tank full of napalm attached to a robotic nozzle. Dr. Fletcher had given them the idea, after watching a video of how a Chinese search and rescue group had started destroying wasp nests near the city of Chongqing.

If nothing else, it could provide useful aerial surveillance inaccessible to the Sea Knight. Everybody had their fingers crossed it was small and quiet enough to escape detection from the wasps, so it wouldn't end up like the news choppers back in Florida.

* * * *

As they banked over the landing zone, Jen twisted in her seat and risked a peek out of the round window behind her. Between raindrops on the glass, she saw nothing but featureless, dark mist, but then the helicopter broke through the clouds and she sucked in her breath without realizing it. The sun blasted through a clear sky behind them, painting the jungle a billion shades of green, while the sky ahead was the color of the inside of a gun barrel. The unnatural contrast gave the ridges and deep valleys a brilliantly sharp glow. She forgot her fear until the chopper began to wobble in a new, exciting manner as the pilots fought the unpredictable air currents and prepared to land.

They settled the helicopter on a massive slab of rock in the fork of a sluggish river. During the rainy season, this would be underwater.

Jen stepped out. The air felt and smelled like she'd descended into a particularly hellish high school locker room with the showers on full blast. Black gnats immediately found her eyes and nose. She wasn't the only victim either; everybody grabbed their bug spray.

A man in a boat was waiting for them. He could have been in his late forties or early nineties. He was so lean his muscles looked like ropy vines stretched along branches. He did not smile, wave, or react in any way. His boat was about thirty feet long, powered by a mud-spattered outboard and covered under a canopy of wood and leaves. The flat hull may have been aluminum, but it was hard to tell because it had been painted a dull green. Unless it was out in the open, like now, Jen thought it would be very difficult to see from a distance, especially if it was nestled under the thick foliage that drooped over the creek.

One of the soldiers, Private Vergara, greeted him in Spanish and they examined a map. Other soldiers quickly transferred the equipment and it wasn't long before Staff Sergeant Fisher was asking the scientists to find a spot on the boat. Five minutes later, they set off. The man, who only had been introduced as Miguel and nothing more, steered them slowly upstream to the steady drone of the outboard. The pilots remained behind; the valley's air currents had torqued the chopper beyond typical ranges and adjustments needed to be made.

The creek grew narrower as they made their way upstream, until the treetops from both sides nearly touched, blocking the brunt of the midday sun as they chugged through a vast, primordial cathedral. Perversely, the heat was even more oppressive under the trees. Sudden bursts of pounding rain didn't help. Jen wiped her face, then immediately applied more of the bug lotion that the soldiers had passed out: 98 percent DEET. Jen knew it was terribly toxic to aquatic creatures, but the unrelenting tenacity of the mosquitoes had put her in a murderous mood.

The comm tech, Specialist Belter, announced to Staff Sergeant Fisher that he'd received an update.

"Let's hear it."

Specialist Belter summarized: "Reports of increasing numbers of wasps have been confirmed. Most conservative counts are looking at estimates climbing to at least five times the population of the initial attack."

This news was greeted by a murmuring of concern among the entomologists. "That reproduction rate's not possible," Dr. Patel stated. "I'm wondering if perhaps a miscalculation has occurred." Others nodded.

Specialist Belter said, "Also, footage of the reproduction method has leaked online. Someone carried an infected family member into an emergency room and a nurse livestreamed the emergence from the host. Most of Florida is headed for the ocean or Alabama or Georgia."

"I'm sure that's going well," Dr. Fletcher said.

They watched the predictably horrifying video where a sobbing man hovered over his apparent wife in the ER. While doctors frantically grappled with the rapidly expanding stomach of the already obese woman, the nurse stood at the foot of the gurney, capturing the images clearly and calmly with her phone. Until the wasps burst through flesh. Shouts. Screams. The shot grew more erratic until the nurse fled the room with everyone else.

"They sealed off the entire wing of the hospital and sent in those Exterminator guys," Specialist Belter said, clicking to a new video.

"What?" Jen nearly shouted.

He turned his bulky laptop to her, where a news chopper watched as the bus, now reinforced with armor plating over the windows, smashed an ambulance out of the emergency room entrance. The boys had graduated to a new strategy and now tossed concussion grenades into the triage area, rushing inside immediately after detonation. It wasn't long before they ran back out to the bus, blasting a path with their automatic shotguns. Seven or eight survivors made it to the bus.

Jen thought, *That's my man*, with a quietly proud smile and a flush wholly independent from the rain forest heat.

Meanwhile, the humidity and eventual monotony were making some of the passengers irritable and a discussion over the size of the wasps that had started out relatively objective was growing louder. Dr. Hill, an entomologist from the University of South Florida, who had been grumpy and snide for most of the trip anyway, was insisting a five-inch body was ridiculous and even contemplating the supposed size was a waste of time. "We would have seen something by now. The Asian giant hornet has a maximum wing span of five inches, and that's a provable fact. A body that size would require wings at least eight inches in length. Structurally impossible."

"Come now," Dr. Chow, the paleontologist, said. "I published a paper nine years ago on Arthropleura, an invertebrate two meters long, most likely a meter and a half wide. That's six feet for you Americans." A low chuckle.

Dr. Hill shook his head. Popped up one finger. "One. Extinct." And another. "Two. Did not fly."

Dr. Hill's skepticism notwithstanding, the very real possibility of giant wasps lurking in the depths of the jungle ahead gave Jen a flutter in her stomach.

"You are casually ignoring that dozens of new species are discovered every year," Dr. Fletcher pointed out.

Always the peacemaker, Araminta tried to diffuse the tension by looking at another factor. "We haven't considered the hosts yet."

"Go on," Dr. Patel said.

"This, of course, is not entirely my field. But part of our work overlaps many studies of the modern American diet. Given what I've witnessed and the information we've been given, we can, for the sake of argument, assume that in the wild, this species would not rely on human hosts."

"Unless we're talking human sacrifice." Dr. Fletcher shrugged. "Devil's advocate."

"For a population to be able to sustain... anonymity"—she nodded to Dr. Hill—"Let us assume for the moment they do not, and utilize a different source of nutrition. Then it may follow, with these invaders, I wonder if their larvae are reacting not only to a different... birthing environment, but the rest of the flotsam and jetsam inside the modern American as well."

Jen thought of the fast-food place where Andy and his team had rescued the people trapped in the restroom.

"Given the obesity rates in the US, could something in us contribute to the increased reproductive rate, as well as the size?" Araminta ticked off possible suspects with her fingers. "Large amounts of progesterone or even testosterone, not to mention rBGH, could have significant effects on unknown invertebrates."

"Junk science," Dr. Hill huffed and watched the vegetation slide past.

"Perhaps. Nevertheless, one thing we can all agree on is that your knowledge is only exceeded by your charm, Dr. Hill."

CHAPTER 17

Andy stopped counting after the sixth or seventh run. It was too easy to get caught up thinking about the cash stacking up in their new bank accounts and not enough attention to the fact that wasps could come from anywhere. Last run, it happened to Ocampo. They'd been evacuating an elementary school; teachers had corralled most of the kids in the cafeteria or nearby classrooms. Ocampo and Andy had been sent up to the second floor to make sure that no kids were hiding. The job had been smooth. The school itself was fairly sealed, and they didn't have many wasps to worry about. Ocampo had been talking about buying a fishing boat and must have missed an open window or vent. The wasp came out of nowhere and nailed the bottom of his spine. Ocampo fell to his knees, then went face down. Andy filled the air over him with steel shot and glowing red tracers, disintegrating the wasp. He dragged Ocampo downstairs and they'd gotten him back to the medical tent, but his central nervous system had already begun to shut down.

Besides, Carver took a screwdriver and scratched a big X into the side of the bus after each return, so everybody knew the score, knew exactly how many runs had been made. They were making more money than any of them had ever seen in their lives and wanted to keep going, but Carver knew they were exhausted.

After Ocampo died, he ordered a mandatory six-hour rest back at the club.

But two hours in, Haaga summoned them to the garage where they parked the bus between runs. If they were lucky, they could call in a mechanic to keep an eye on the engine every few times while they banged out the dents, especially around the wheels. Everybody stood around, yawning and rubbing their eyes.

"This is bullshit," Carver said. "There's gonna be more mistakes out there. We need some shut-eye."

"Undoubtedly. However, when these people call, it's generally the best option to respond immediately."

"Fucking VIPs, man."

"In a way. This is..." Haaga checked his phone. "A medical rehabilitation retirement center."

Carver nodded in understanding. "It *is* Florida. Where else would the elite stash their parents?" He chewed it over in his head for a while. "Fine. As if we have a choice. We're charging double. Call it a bonus or emergency after-hours fee or whatever you want. Whoever they are, they can afford it."

As everyone gathered the gear, Carver eyed the bus critically. "And why do we still have to take the bus? You're not telling me that this piece of shit is stronger than a tank?"

"Yeah, I want a tank," Squirrel chimed in.

"Let's paint *Exterminators* on the side of the tank," Ramirez said.

"We should name ourselves the 'Motherfucking Exterminators,'" Andy said.

House agreed. "Hell, yes."

"Admirable suggestions, gentlemen," Haaga said. "Nevertheless, this"— he gestured at the bus—"like it or not, is an integral part of your brand. Think of this as your meal ticket."

Carver held Haaga's eyes for a moment, then dug into his kit bag, fished out an unmarked bottle of pills. He popped the lid, passed them out, and glanced at Haaga. "Any problems? This a drug-free workplace we got here?"

Haaga checked his watch. "The center stopped answering the phone half an hour ago."

* * * *

Ramirez hit the horn and the gas at the same time. People were quick to clear a path and the bus roared out onto streets flooded with soldiers and Humvees. The National Guard were more than happy to get out of the way for someone going into the zone. Nobody else was heading in that direction.

The edge of the wasps' territory had grown closer and closer to the club by the hour.

Jeeps and yellow school buses drove up and down the residential streets, endlessly broadcasting the same emotionless message from the EBS. Teams ran along, pounding doors, helping stragglers to the buses that joined the massive migration north as millions of refugees fled southern Florida.

Soon, the only vehicles they saw on the streets were either abandoned or full of the dead. Some intersections they found inaccessible, stuffed with smashed cars where panicked and dying drivers sparked a chain reaction of wreckage, effectively trapping or outright killing everyone.

Ramirez would have to pull a U and they'd go a few blocks back to search for a detour.

Too many vehicles held the husk of a child still locked into their car seat, denied a chance to even run. Andy couldn't help but imagine what that must have been like, to be pinned down and all you could do was kick and swat and scream while wasps crawled over you with impunity until a lone wasp would thrust what looked like an extra-long stinger into your belly, pumping you full of already wriggling eggs. Later, you'd feel movement in your guts, like cramping from food poisoning as the larvae ate around your vital organs to keep you alive and fresh as long as possible.

Andy decided right there and then that he'd put a bullet through his head before he'd let that happen. He'd stared down death by his own hand once already, so maybe the second time wouldn't be so bad. The speed and painkiller cocktail that had been simmering under the surface came to a full boil and he forgot where he was for a while until he saw another child seat and the medication went charging through his head in an odd mix of brute strength enveloped in Bubble Wrap, like a chain saw killer in a fuzzy Easter Bunny outfit.

He kept spinning one of the shotgun's steel ring attachments between his thumb and forefinger, rolling it in an endless circle like a Saint Shotgun rosary bead for the God of Thunder and Warfare and Heavy Metal. Andy and his Atchisson were lifelong friends now and took care of each other with a deep mutual respect and admiration. His sling, upgraded to allow ease of motion, was an intricate webbing of canvas straps, paracord, and a few heavy-duty bungee cords that supported and stabilized both his wounded arm and his shotgun. At first, he couldn't get his tactical vest tight enough to be able to lock his shoulders enough to absorb the recoil until they dug up a woman's-size small Kevlar vest for underneath the tactical vest. That extra bulk stretched the nylon fabric just tight enough that he could swing the barrel as if it rested on a gyroscope.

Snapping the butt to his right shoulder only took an instant. His speed rivaled Carver's.

Once in a while shooting made pain explode up his arm, as if he was getting buzzed with a giant tattoo needle in the heel of his phantom left hand. It was short, intense, and manageable. The rest of the time he felt nothing but the satisfying eruption, the feeling of unleashing a seismic chain of thunder and lighting, an act that demanded absolute devotion from his mind, his body, his entire being. He'd found his balance, both carrying and firing. Knew when to let his left arm go dead to ride the hyena cackles of recoil. Understood exactly the nine pounds of weight it took to ease the trigger across the event horizon.

Sometimes, though, especially when the blood roared after a run, he felt as if he'd traded his hand for an upgrade. That was depressing, made him feel guilty, as if he'd betrayed himself somehow. Either way, it wasn't the AA-12's fault. Amphetamines and opioids helped him to see the glass half full. He was now officially a genuine badass, a master of implementing instant death that stalked a wasp-ravaged Earth.

* * * *

It was best to keep as quiet as possible in the zone until you absolutely had no choice. There was no traffic in the wasp territory, no sirens, no kids yelling, no dogs barking, no lawn mowers, no birds. Not even electronic sound pollution, except for sports radio from a car whose battery refused to die. So the sound waves of automatic .12-gauges tended to carry.

And shooting always brought more wasps.

They learned it was better to get into buildings through the back door. Sometimes a side door, if Ramirez could get the bus close enough. Go through the employee entrance, the kitchens, maintenance corridors, bland offices. The public front of most places always had too many windows. If the wasps saw any kind of movement inside, the males would smash themselves against the glass until it shattered. Sometimes they would even chew at a crack in the glass, chiseling it into tiny splinters with their powerful mandibles, creating a hole large enough for the females.

More and more, they'd come running out and find the wasps still hadn't left the bus.

They were used to the attention when driving, because of the obvious sound and movement. Everywhere else, they'd witnessed wasps spend no more than a few minutes with some piece of inaccessible metal before flying off for something that took less effort, even if prey was inside. But even when the bus engine was off and had been sitting an hour for that exact reason, waiting for the wasps to grow frustrated, they stuck around, waiting. "I think they recognize it," Carver said. "And they're pissed."

"When aren't they pissed," Andy said. It wasn't really a question.

"I don't know about that. I do know this, though. They're getting bigger, man," Ramirez said. "You see that? Every goddamn day. That shit is real, man. They're getting bigger."

The others nodded in agreement. So far, there'd been no official statement from FEMA or the military or the scientists or anybody else. But there was no denying the average wasp, despite floating like a hummingbird, was now the size of a pigeon. Their dangling legs, those horrible thin bones longer than most fingers—they were wrong somehow, as if they mocked the laws of evolution and gravity like absurdly long crab legs with too many knuckles.

"Easier to hit." Squirrel patted his shotgun.

"Amen," House said.

The nursing home or senior center or hospice or whatever it was looked like another goddamn country club. Landscape lines led your eye through luscious parks and towering trees, concealing the true nature of the property, as if the whole place had been designed by Disney Imagineers. Naturally, the delivery and staff entrance was an entirely different driveway that used to be guarded, but the little house was now empty. Wasps were already following the bus, so it didn't matter if breaking through the barrier gate arm set off alarms or not.

Ramirez coaxed the bus up a short concrete drive so smooth it might have been marble, to a loading dock tastefully shrouded in a solid line of trees of varying heights. The trees grew dense enough that it might help screen some of the full onslaught if every wasp within a mile descended on the building. The bodies of those who had fled the building littered the cement and grass, somewhat spoiling the effect, but that was okay. Nobody worried about avoiding the corpses anymore and Ramirez simply plowed through them.

They'd learned to tape alternating rows of stun and smoke grenades along the top of the bus and run fifty-pound test fishing line though the pull rings so they could release the pins while still inside, eyes closed and wearing ear protection. They'd pull the stun grenades when everybody was good and lined up and raring to go. Then a couple seconds later, Carver would pull the second cord. He'd toss a few smoke grenades out the front door to mask their path to the door and they'd get down to it.

Don't move fast. Move steady. Be deliberate with each heartbeat. *Boom boom boom.* Out the bus door, take the time to clear the immediate area. Don't blow a hole in the damn door just so you can rush inside like a little girl. Have one guy pick the lock while the rest encircle him and blast away at everything that gets within twenty yards. Think ahead. Be cool. Leave the empty magazines on the ground. Grab 'em if you can on the way back. Once the door's open, shouldn't take more than five seconds, zip inside and shut and lock the motherfucker again. Keep the wasps out, see?

Everybody gave a deep sigh of contentment when they felt the air conditioning. First time they'd felt that outside the country club in two days. Too many downed power lines and no repairmen. "Generator," Carver said. An empty hallway two pallets wide connected the loading area to the receiving area. The main corridor continued for quite a ways, splitting off into other corridors or banks of elevators. No wasps in the immediate area. They spread out, slowly. Except Squirrel. His job was to find the fire-safety diagram federally mandated to be posted in every place of employment and he ran around like a chipmunk with bad eyesight until he found it. This would serve as a map for Carver. Squirrel liked his job. "Kinda like lookin' for that Waldo fuck." Carver and Ramirez determined this was the bottom level and it made sense to stick to the general plan of searching this floor, room by room. Once cleared, they'd head up to the next level. The first level turned out to be empty of both wasps and people, alive or dead. They found the stairs next to the industrial washing machines. The next floor, mostly offices and two giant kitchens, one kosher, was empty as well.

"Nobody's here, man," Ramirez said.

"That's not what the intel says," Carver said. "My bet is everybody's upstairs."

The third floor held more offices, and these were much, much more plush. They were no longer in the working-class areas of the business. Now they crept through the rarefied air of gleaming teak floors and hallways subtly widened just enough to allow ease of access for wheelchairs. Carver and Andy stayed on their hands and knees through the admin area and peeked over the sleek front desk.

The lobby was at least three floors high, with huge, built-in curving planters that hugged the walls full of colorful foliage, even trees. The front windows stretched from the ceiling to the goddamn dirt, creating a seamless feel with the outside, as if the forest stretched into the lobby and gently placed the patient in the organization's loving arms. Andy was glad they'd found the back door.

Crawling through reception, the lights were still on, and thanks to the generator, he hadn't thought about light. When he saw the windows, the first thing he thought was that they'd let the trees grow too tall in front or ivy grow unchecked, and it was cutting out most of that Florida sunshine, even if the sun was going down.

It wasn't trees. Or ivy.

Wasps crawled over every square foot of the windows. Hundreds. These were the big ones, some with their curved abdomens the size of gray squirrels' fluffy tails. They seemed to be congregating near the upper left side, but it was hard to tell with all the activity. Dozens flew away every second and even more landed in their cautious, hesitant way on legs that didn't look capable of supporting their body's bulk.

"Holy fuck," Andy said in one quick, quiet exhale, keeping close to the floor.

"You ain't wrong there, brother." Carver shook his head. "They should have been all over us at the back door. Something's more important than food or hosts or plain old assholery." They'd found some wasps lurking around bodies that had been freshly impregnated before, but never anything in these numbers.

"Think they found a way inside, or something else?" Andy took another peek. "I'd bet they're in the attic at least."

"Places like this don't have attics. They have maintenance areas. I don't think our friends are inside. Or they don't need to be yet. Either way, let's take this slow."

"Can't spend money if you're dead." Andy repeated House's favorite mantra.

"Amen," was the usual and appropriate response.

They crawled back and filled in the boys. Carver consulted his map and located the stairs. They eased through the next couple floors, nice and quiet. Then the plastic surgery wing. Same thing. Dark and empty, as if the employees had simply turned off the lights and left for the evening. They found a few corpses in some of the apartments upstairs that may have been nurses, judging from the shoes. These had not been hosts for the larvae. These had been lunch for the adults.

"Nobody's here," Ramirez said. "They're all dead."

"Not according to Haaga. Said the VIPs could see their parents' vitals online." Carver pointed at the assisted living wing on the map. "Everybody out back, that couldn't make it any farther than the backyard? I'm guessing they left those poor bastards still hooked up in bed upstairs."

* * * *

They found a dozen or so wasps feeding off a body in front of the nurses' station. Andy and Ramirez took them out with a few well-chosen bursts of gunfire.

"And there's our clock," Carver said. "Double-time, boys."

Andy and Ramirez went to the right while House and Squirrel went left, leapfrogging from door to door. They used their barrels to pop the doors open, and if no wasps emerged, they moved along, not worrying at first if anybody was in bed or not. Most of the rooms were dark anyway, as not only had the departing staff turned out the lights, they'd helpfully pulled the heavy drapes shut as well.

"Anybody left?" Carver called out.

Andy flipped the lights on and moved into the room. Out in the hall, he heard House and Ramirez yell affirmatives. An obese woman with very little hair left lay buried under blankets. Like many of the other patients, a clear ventilator mask covered the lower half of her face. Her eyes struggled to stay open. The eyelids were like crinkled paper and tinged brown, almost like nicotine-stained teeth.

Andy gave her an amphetamine-fueled grin and said, "Don't worry, ma'am. We're here to help. Gonna get you folks out." He let the shotgun sag in its sling and brought the wheelchair over to the bed. "Can you sit up, or can I help?" His words sounded from inside his head as if they were being filtered through a calliope, but he was sure the old lady understood.

Her hand moved under the blanket and fluttered at the side of the bed. She was trying to point at something.

Andy looked back and forth from her eyes to her hand. "You want help. You don't want help. The wheelchair. The light. You... want... to sit up. Pull up your blanket. Fluff your pillow. Find a wig." Every time he went to touch her, she stiffened in pain and uttered a keening sound.

"Sorry. Sorry. Shit, lady, I'm trying. Sorry."

He was hoping she didn't want him to redo her makeup or anything like that because he had no idea how to go about that, when he finally figured out she wanted him to move her ventilator mask aside.

She struggled to speak. Words came out like a slow leak. "It's... between my legs."

Andy took a step back.

"Take it away," she moaned. "Take it away."

He took a few steps down to the foot of the bed, gathered the corner in his right fist, and yanked. The first thing he noticed was just how much her distended stomach stretched, as if she was indeed pregnant. The second thing was the wasp nestled in the V of the woman's thighs, curled up like a sleeping kitten wearing fairy wings. Andy didn't have to poke it with the shotgun to know that it was dead. He called in Carver and they pondered it silently.

Ramirez joined them and said, "We got eight. Nine with this one."

"Squirrel, go check if the rest have their own pet."

The old woman started to say something, but Carver replaced her ventilator mask, soothing, "There, there dear." He kneeled, took her hand gently, and gave it a kiss. "You rest, love." He lifted a stray hair out of her face and cupped her jaw. "It's almost over now. You've done wonderful. Close your eyes and sleep. When you wake, you will be warm and with everyone you love. Good night." With the care of a new parent afraid to wake their infant, he pulled her hospital gown up and over the unnatural mound on her lower abdomen. Andy flinched and put up his hand to avoid looking at her soggy Depends.

Sure enough, they found a puncture wound a few inches left of her once wrinkled belly button. The edges were crusty with congealed blood while a rust-colored, viscous liquid seeped through the raw cracks. Carver applied slight pressure with his thumb under the hole. The woman gasped and they saw movement under the skin, wriggling away from the compression.

"Fuck a duck," Carver said. He drew her gown back down to be polite.

Squirrel stuck his head in, said, "Yeah, they each got one."

"Go back and look for a hole like this." Carver nodded at the bed. "They're all infected, is my guess. But let's make sure."

"Then let's get the fuck out." For reasons he couldn't quite explain, Andy seriously disliked the nursing home facility. Maybe it was the gaudiness, the astonishing eagerness to babysit the wealthiest clients as their bodies and minds slipped away and they spent their very expensive final years drooling into a silk bib. Or maybe it was the hypocrisy, this desperate need to avoid death, to treat dying as something to be ignored at all costs and secretly feared. The futile effort to cling to life, no matter how demeaning or artificial the attempts, hung heavy in the air and Andy wanted to burn it all away.

"I got no problem with that," Ramirez said.

"Me neither," House said.

Squirrel stuck his head back in the room and said, "Uh-huh. They're all…uh, expecting."

"So be it," Carver said. His features softened as everything kind of *drifted* inside. It was the first time Andy had ever seen the overwhelming energy that propelled the man forward like a locomotive; he slipped and faltered, as if the weight he pulled grew too much for a brief second. The moment passed and his eyes flared. "House, Squirrel, you guys grab every oxygen tank you can find. Dump 'em in the nurses' station. We'll send this place to the fucking moon."

* * * *

Carver kept Andy behind to watch his back in case any wasps found them. He said he didn't want anybody alive when the flames started, in case the initial blast didn't finish everyone off. "Seen it a few times. It can take a while." He glanced around the room, designed for long-term care. Half hospital, with the specialized bed and equipment, but surrounded with wood-paneled walls and thin, quiet carpet. A love seat along one wall for visitors, big TV on another. He picked up one of the decorative pillows from the love seat.

His phone rang. Carver met Andy's eyes and checked it. Hit *answer*. "We're busy.

Fuck do you want?"

"Stop what you are doing immediately." Haaga's voice had an edge that could leave a nasty emotional scar even over speakerphone. "Complete the mission or the consequences will be severe."

"The mission's dead," Carver said and glanced around the room. "Nobody's left."

"The other party disagrees."

"Who's the other party?" While he sounded sincere, he didn't look too interested, buying time so he could investigate the room further.

"I'm not at liberty to say exactly. Let's leave it at a very large, very powerful group of relatives, various consultants, and the patients themselves. And, of course, attorneys."

"I doubt anybody's last will and testament anticipated this."

"Every single advance directive specifically requires that any and all extreme measures are to be employed if any signs of life are present. Mr. Carver, I strongly suggest you continue the mission. Timing is critical, as you can imagine."

"Paperwork doesn't mean dick when monsters are chomping on your guts. This other party, they're watching, though, aren't they?" Carver folded his arms and watched his reflection in the TV's dark screen.

"Indeed."

Andy didn't get it. "What?"

Carver nodded at the TV. "People put their pets in places with webcams so they can watch 'em while they're on vacation or some shit. You don't think rich people wouldn't want to use the same tech to keep an eye on their own parents?"

"There's places you put your pet when you go on vacation?"

"They're watching you as we speak, Mr. Shaw," Haaga said with unusual patience. "As well as recording pulse and O-2 levels of their relatives, among other things. Take a look at the gold ring on her left hand. It measures all of it. The other party, they are monitoring every single thing and can control most functions from off-site. Understand the implications of this."

"You people want to watch Mom and Dad die?" Carver demanded, staring at the camera. "Eaten alive by bugs?"

"Of course not. You will take them to the closest rescue center."

"They won't make it. All we'd be doing is helping deliver more monsters into the world. Fuck that."

"I strongly suggest—"

"—that you tell your handlers there's nothing to be done. Let these people die in peace."

Haaga didn't answer right away. After a few seconds: "Again, the mission directives have not, and will not, be altered. If you continue to refuse to follow orders, your privileges will be revoked, including, but not limited to, your pardons and consulting fees."

Carver handed the phone to Andy and went to the woman. He continued to address the TV. "This is truly what you want?" He yanked the patient's gown up, revealing the distended stomach, then used both thumbs to squeeze the ovipositor wound. The crust split as most of one of the larvae popped out of the hole. The woman gasped and shrieked. The end of the larva remained in the fissure, squirming and flopping. It had come out backwards, the size of an adult thumb, mostly wrapped in an embryonic sheath, already knowing to thrust its stinger in fury. The wasp must have been nearing full development and it wouldn't have been long before it would have chewed its way out, looking for fresh air and flying away. Perhaps hours.

"I cannot stress how unhappy the other party is right now." Haaga's voice, so dry and detached at the best of times, now took on such measured tones that each syllable counted down a rocket launch. "This will not end well."

Carver ripped the squirming insect completely out of the woman and brought it over to the TV, where they could see it up close and personal. It dripped with blood and slime. "There's fifty more of these things inside of her. You tell the other party to go fuck themselves." He twisted it in half and tossed the pieces at the dark screen. One half splattered and bounced off, the second stuck and slid down, eventually falling to the pristine carpet. He wiped his hands on the pillow.

"Again, Mr. Carver, if you do not continue the rescue mission, your funds will be seized and pardons revoked. Final warning."

Andy felt the phone infect the air with electricity. The sound waves reverberated off the walls, made the threat real. The others had been lingering around the doorway and when they heard this, Ramirez stepped into the room. "Let's not get in a hurry about this, man."

Carver looked from the TV to Ramirez, then back to the TV. He twisted the pillow, seemingly unaware of how his fingers dug into the fabric so deep that the seams popped. At the noise, he spun so smooth his joints might as well have been pivoting on ball bearings soaking in olive oil. In a single, sustained motion he flung the stained pillow at Ramirez with his left hand, while drawing his pistol with his right and shot the old woman twice in the head in less time than it took to blink.

CHAPTER 18

Miguel steered the boat to the right bank in an area where the creek ran wide and shallow. Everybody piled out and gathered around Sergeant Fisher. He pointed and said they had three hours to reach a ridgeline before they lost the light. They'd camp there for the night and start out for the village in the morning. To distract herself from the hard, uphill hike ahead, Jen guessed he was pointing southwest, judging from the sun. She checked her compass to see if she was right and frowned. South*east*.

Miguel and Private Vergara took point, followed by four or five more soldiers. The scientists struggled into their packs and moved along in single file, doing their best to keep up. For a while, they made good progress, as the trail, though overgrown, was somewhat easy to follow. Jen felt a surge of confidence. This wasn't too bad; she wasn't in exactly bad shape, even though jogging along the lakefront in Chicago wasn't quite the same as fighting through thick vegetation. Especially while quietly praying that any spiders lurking within the cobwebs strung throughout the long leaves and vines weren't venomous.

Araminta had presented Jen with a wreath of flowers and grass, and Jen had placed it on the brim of her hat while the older woman grabbed a few quick photos with a disposable waterproof camera. Jen gave a mock high-fashion pose and Araminta laughed. "We'll get these to your boyfriend."

Dr. Fletcher discreetly pulled Jen aside and said quietly, "Humans aren't the only creatures that love flowers in the jungle. You may want to keep those in your pack, as your headdress here will attract every insect in a mile radius." Jen was disappointed, but took his advice and carefully folded the crown into her notebook, pressing the flowers flat.

The trail curled around the base of a steep hill, crossed over a jumble of moss-covered boulders, and continued along the bottom of the next bluff. Miguel stopped at the line of rocks and took a hard left, following a brackish stream uphill. He used the bank where he could and hopped from stone to stone only when necessary, as the moss was often treacherous. Sometimes it would be easier to work their way through the jungle instead, keeping the stream within earshot.

Sergeant Fisher tied off neon strips of polyethylene ribbon every so often to mark their trail. He didn't trust anything that was any more complicated than a basic watch, especially anything that ran off an electrical charge. The jungle had a knack for eating into their gear, and it seemed the higher the tech, the hungrier the jungle became. "Old school is the only school," he'd say.

Jen's world shrank to nothing more than mud, moss, and thick water the same temperature as the air. Breathing felt like struggling for oxygen through a moist paper towel. Black flies plagued her eyes. In some spots, she had to fight through tangled vegetation for every step forward. But at least she didn't have to join the pairs of soldiers who rotated in and out, carrying the heavy drone case.

Seven or eight hundred years later, the expedition reached a reasonably flat and open area and stopped as daylight climbed the trees and slunk away. If anything, the forest grew louder as darkness spread. They struck camp in the dying light. This meant the scientists stood around gasping while the soldiers did most of the work. Araminta, who still competed in half-triathlons well into her sixties, was the only one with any energy left. Dinner was quick and cheerless. Jen and everyone else retreated to their hammocks, zipped themselves into their bug nets, and collapsed into fitful sleep.

* * * *

Dawn came far too early.

Breakfast was lukewarm coffee and a protein bar. The drone pilot and comm tech set about assembling the drone while everyone else packed up. Essentially a square octocopter, it flew using blades at the four corners, above and below the central carriage. Four spindly, retractable legs radiated from the bottom of the five-gallon napalm tank. This morning, the tank was empty in order to extend the range for the initial reconnaissance. Harmon, the pilot, flicked a few switches on the remote control and the drone buzzed to life. The rotors began to spin, those on top clockwise, while those on the bottom spun counterclockwise, providing stability and additional lift. Foam sound dampeners created a thrum that put Jen's teeth on edge and she was glad when it lifted off and disappeared. Tiny cameras, mounted on all six sides, relayed their signals back to the comm tech's laptop. Everyone crowded around the operator, Private Harmon, and watched as the craft floated smoothly up the opening in the canopy. It hovered just above the treetops, getting a sense of the landscape. Low clouds obscured any features behind them. Ahead, a series of sheer cliffs and crags grew even more fearsome as the drone drifted closer. Belter translated directions from Miguel, who squatted nearby, watching the screens with an unreadable expression.

The drone drifted to the left, revealing a deep, thin crack that ran nearly parallel to the cliff face for at least fifty yards before curling away. Harmon gently coaxed the drone higher, following the fissure from above, as it was far too narrow to safely fly through. It kept rising, until they could see the entire mountain and realized the satellite images had been misleading. There was no typical peak; instead the cliffs formed a rough kind of hollow crown around a deep crater about a mile in diameter.

The images wobbled and spun. "Shit. Place has some screwy air currents." When he concentrated, Harmon had a habit of blowing small bubbles with his gum and popping them inside his mouth with a dull snap, then he'd chew aggressively until the next bubble. It allowed him to redirect nervous energy while his fingers performed the delicate task of riding out the currents.

Descending to the relative safety of the canopy, the drone eased over the steep slopes that sharply funneled to a small, greenish lake at the bottom. Slabs of sharp stone rose out of the center, creating a sliver of a spiky island. From the drone's vantage point, looking straight down directly over the lake, Jen thought it looked like a sick reptile's eye. Bare wisps of smoke on the opposite shore caught Private Harmon's eye and he brought the drone lower for a closer look.

It was a burned-out village. Narrow huts extended out from the steep bank, built ten feet above the water on what looked like bamboo posts. Most of the smoke came from the remains of a larger structure, set inland a ways, on one of the few reasonably flat spots. As the drone drew closer, they started seeing bodies floating face down along the shoreline.

One of the camera feeds blurred and the craft trembled.

Fisher asked, "Wind?"

Harmon held his head and fought for control. "I don't think…" The video smoothed out for a few seconds, just long enough for him to exhale and snap his gum again. Then it all went sideways as the drone sliced down through the air like a cleaver. "Fuck. Fuck. Fuck." Harmon overcorrected, and there was a flash of chopped leaves and a terrific shaking as it jolted to a stop, caught in the branch of a tree.

"I don't think that was wind," Harmon said.

"Mark it on the map. I don't trust the SATNAV," Sergeant Fisher said, then to everyone, "Ruck up. Let's get to the damn thing before anything else goes wrong."

* * * *

They followed the stream up to the narrow fissure in the cliff face, where the only path forward was trudging up the center of the slow-moving water. At least it was somewhat cooler, nestled deep between two sheer walls of solid rock. Vines and trees stretched across the ravine, creating even deeper shadows at the bottom. Dripping waterfalls appeared and some were tall enough to force the expedition to form human chains in order to hoist equipment along.

At the top of the third waterfall, Dr. Fletcher demanded a break. Jen was secretly relieved. Her legs and back hurt. Her arms were scraped and sliced. Most of the group was beginning to catch on to what Jen had known for a long time. That despite all the degrees and new species, all the work he put into being the smartest one in the room and a man of action, Dr. Fletcher's ego was rather fragile. The man was a pompous ass most of the time, but Jen couldn't deny that he knew his way around the jungle. She would be eternally, if begrudgingly, grateful, not only for Araminta's crown of flowers, but also that he taught her to tuck her pants into long, thick socks to help keep the leeches out.

The scientists were all happy to take a break, except for Araminta. She couldn't sit still. While everyone else found rocks to sit and rest and drink water, she climbed up to where the bare rock gave way to the lush foliage and plucked more flowers, some vines this time. She brought back a great looping fistful and went about arranging it. She held up a cluster of bell-shaped flowers that were a particularly vivid shade of bright purple and asked, "Can anyone identify this species?"

"My dear," Dr. Hill said, peering through smudged glasses, "have you not taken any precautions? Your fanciful bouquet may very well contain species that are quite poisonous to the touch."

"Your concern is touching, Dr. Hill," Araminta said, giving him a slow wave with her gloved hand. She looked to Dr. Patel. "May I borrow your phone for a moment, to look this up? It could be a new species, or at least a variation."

"No," Staff Sergeant Fisher said. "Emergencies only. You can come back Valentine's Day and pick all you want. Now it's time to go."

"Great," Dr. Fletcher muttered. "Now she gets to name a goddamn flower after herself too."

"What's that?" Dr. Patel asked sharply.

"I said you couldn't," Dr. Fletcher said, just as sharp. "Rainy season. All this will be underwater."

* * * *

The canyon fell away abruptly as the stream got lost in a marsh. Beyond that, the lake. The harsh, sudden sunlight left them blinking and sweating. Sergeant Fisher had a brief conference with Specialist Belter and Miguel, where it was decided the best path to the drone would be to follow the southern shore. This would take them through tall trees thick with hanging vines and meant slow going. Nobody complained. The northern side looked rocky and exposed and everyone was keeping one eye on the sky, listening for that telltale buzz.

The spiky little island in the middle gave Jen an uneasy feeling, like a thorn stuck in the bottom of a bare foot.

Once they entered the trees, Araminta's flowers were everywhere, hanging like bunches of grapes from the vines. It was impossible to tell if the vines themselves were part of the same plant or if the brilliant purple flowers were some kind of opportunistic parasite, only using the vines to cling to support the surprisingly hefty weight of the petals. They gave off a faintly sweet smell, almost like almond paste.

Everyone marveled at the shimmering tapestry of flowers that undulated gently in the soft, whispering wind that came off the lake. The fact that she could hear the wind made Jen realize just how quiet it was in this part of the jungle. No bird cries. No chattering warning from monkeys. No shrill insect calls. It was unsettling.

Sergeant Fisher made a short hissing sound to catch everyone's attention. He pointed up.

Everybody flinched and fearfully searched the canopy above.

Nothing. At least, not at first.

Then, a rustling up in the highest limbs. A shifting of something uncomfortably large. Dozens of large, dark shapes hung from the limbs. The canopy was teeming with them. Directly above, a single, immense brown wing extended in a languid stretch and Jen knew immediately this wasn't the wasps. It was bats. Hundreds of them. Maybe more.

And they were enormous. Like big house cats with four- or five-foot wingspans.

"Swell," Sergeant Fisher said. "This place is a regular fucking Skull Island."

"Golden-crowned flying foxes?" someone whispered.

"No. That's the Philippines."

"Fruit bats, at any rate."

"Probably... but where's the fruit?"

"Perfect. Of course. Great," Dr. Fletcher said under his breath, so low only Jen heard him this time. "Another new species. Araminta'll get credit. Probably get to name them too."

The rest of the group was already moving on, plunging deeper into a world of leaves and shadows and the shimmering clusters of purple jewels. Again, Jen's universe shrank to the soft earth under her feet, the cloying smell of rotting vegetation, the heat. Time ceased to matter. Progress was measured not in miles, but feet. There were no observations, no complaints, no idle chatter. Sergeant Fisher didn't have to remind anyone they were in wasp territory now.

Jen didn't know to stop until she bumped into Dr. Fletcher and found everyone gathering around a thick trunk and peering up at the drone caught in the branches. Private Harmon and a couple of soldiers unraveled their ropes and slipped spiky crampons over their boots. Sergeant Fisher and the group continued onward toward the village. Dr. Patel left his satellite phone with Private Harmon as the phones worked as short-range walkie-talkies as well.

* * * *

It was late afternoon when they smelled smoke and finally emerged from the jungle into a clearing. Well-worn paths ran from all directions through thick, waist-high grass to a large firepit in the center. The embers were cold and dead. The smoke came from beyond a narrow line of trees, from the remains of the building they'd seen earlier.

They found the first body near the row of huts on stilts. It might have been dead a week, maybe more. Putrefaction worked fast in the jungle. There wasn't much flesh left, anyway. The remaining meat had become a riot of maggots and worms and the rest of the scavengers of the dead.

More corpses were strewn in the grass and along the path that wound its way through the huts. Those on dry land were little more than skeletons, with most of the ligaments intact, and some of the flesh lingered, as if it had been hastily gnawed off. Even more floated face down in shallow water, lolling back and forth in the gentle waves. The meat that remained was bloated and doughy. Thick ropes coiled among the dead, still tied to a wide canoe that had come to rest within the bamboo stilts. Jen counted thirty-four of the dead in total.

"Remind you of anything?" Sergeant Fisher asked. He didn't expect an answer.

"Yes. But why now?" Dr. Patel asked. He didn't expect an answer either. "What changed?

Or, although unlikely, did the wasps simply appear? And if so, from where?"

The smoldering building turned out to be the remains of a church. The framework was charred, but still standing. At least half of the thin walls had been burned away. Smoke rose lazily from the still-glowing embers in the roof. It looked unfinished, as fires had been lit in several places, but the moist jungle air had stalled the job.

Unaware of the dismal state of the church, a sign out front proudly proclaimed this sacred building to be Cornerstones from Christ, a loving gift from the Kingdom of Faith Christian Center in Alabama, USA. A wide variety of objects had been laid out in a circle that surrounded the sign. Several backpacks. Plastic sandwich baggies full of what looked suspiciously like wet American money inside. Piles of waterlogged Bibles. A tent and two sleeping bags. Packages of freeze-dried food that reflected the sun. Western clothing. Plastic flip-flops. A tripod and sophisticated video camera with an attached shotgun mike.

"Don't know if that's good or bad," Sergeant Fisher said.

Specialist Belter examined the video camera. When he opened the side screen, water trickled out. "It's fried. But..." He withdrew the memory card and gave it to Sergeant Fisher.

He held it up to the light and squinted

"Dr. Hill?" Sergeant Fisher asked. "You mind getting your camera out? Let's see if we can't unlock this sonofabitch."

* * * *

John and Shelley Anderson had taken a lot of footage. A lot. They truly believed in their cause and the harder they worked, the happier they became. Little Matthew was along for the ride too, snug either in a sling at his mother's bosom or watching everything from his father's back.

Sergeant Fisher wasn't shy about fast-forwarding. Dr. Hill nearly had a heart attack when he saw the mud and grime smeared across the touch screen but kept his mouth shut. Everyone gathered behind the sergeant, who sat on the ground, effectively blocking the sun.

"Aww," Araminta said. She was leaning over Sergeant Fisher's left shoulder, who didn't mind at all. "That's a capybara." The largest rodent in the world, nearly the size of most pigs, a gentle and sweet herbivore that appeared to get along with most everybody else in the rain forest. The villagers were washing this one down in some kind of ritual. And it looked like everyone had shown up to watch the ceremony. After some initial protest from John, eventually the chief or shaman or whoever he was approached the animal. Araminta shielded her eyes and looked away.

"If they're gonna eat it, I don't need to watch."

It appeared that it was only some kind of blessing.

Shelley caught movement, back near the trees. She zoomed in and snatched a glimpse of a shrouded figure. Then, as if it sensed it was being watched, the figure vanished.

Back at the canoe, two men reverently placed the capybara inside. The animal remained at ease, blissfully accepting whatever fate awaited, even when the men started to slide it under a kind of netting hooked over the gunwales. At this, John went up to the chief, shaking his head and brandishing a Bible, holding it up so everyone could see. He kept shouting a few simple phrases, frantically begging them.

The villagers were uncertain. They looked to their chief, who remained stone-faced and silent. Eventually, John coaxed the two men to lift the capybara out of the canoe and set it back on the shoreline. The capybara didn't look like it gave a damn one way or another. John gently coaxed the animal back into the jungle, then gathered everyone in a large prayer circle and led them in the Lord's Prayer. Everybody joined in except the chief, who remained on the shoreline, back to his tribe. He stared at the tiny island instead.

After, John approached the camera and said, "There will be no sacrifice to a false god, thanks be to his Heavenly Grace." Pause.

"I think, you need to explain it again, you know? Just as backup, right?" Shelley's voice said, zooming in for a tight shot.

"Yeah, okay, good. Let's do the first part at the—the bone thing."

Cut. John is now in front of a strange white structure that seemingly grows out of the forest floor like giant fungus. When Shelley gets settled and zooms back, everyone can now see that it is built of bones, deliberately and even artfully stacked tight. "Dark legends tell us that in the old days, well over five generations ago, the Cáceres people engaged in human sacrifice." John runs his hands over the bleached bones. "But the light of our Lord shone even on those savage pagans, and now, each year the village sacrifices the gentle capybara instead, as a kind of substitution, like how those of the Catholic faith foolishly believe that simple crackers and wine become Christ's actual flesh and blood."

"We might have to edit that part out later," Shelley said.

"Okay, yeah. Fine." John got back into character of earnest missionary. "The bones in this monstrosity, this monument of false idolatry? Not human, praise Jesus. All capybara, as far as I can tell."

Cut. Back to the canoe. John is holding a long, coiled rope, connected to the bow. "The Cáceres people have worshipped a wicked lie. Somewhere around the end of rainy season each year, they place one of God's most innocent creatures, the capybara, into this very vessel, and ferry the poor animal to a cave in that island, where, I have no doubt, this unfortunate, doomed, pitiful creature dies a long, painful death of starvation." He nodded in satisfaction. "I am told that the island is the source of the spring, and as our drinking water comes from the lake, I will be taking the canoe out in the next few days to make certain the water is clean." He bowed his head in a quick prayer. "I'm honored and proud and filled up with his holy grace now that we have put an end to this barbaric sacrifice and given these poor people the gift of eternal life." A pause. "How was that?"

"Great, hon. It—" *Cut.* Next morning? Blurred images. Someone is running with the camera. Panting. Then screaming. A whip pan over a body. Then another. The village is in chaos. People running, screaming. But no wasps are visible.

Until they spot one. Just the one. It's floating through the huts, seemingly directionless, pushed by the wind like a dandelion, until it zips down and attacks, driving its stinger or ovipositor into flesh. Whoever was filming forgets the camera is on and Jen and the others can only see the ground in jerky, swinging movements as the person flees the village to a tent near the edge of the large clearing. The tent is apparently empty.

A shout. "Shelley! Shelley!" John spins, crying out louder, "Where is Matthew? Oh God, where is Matthew?" The horror in his voice hits Jen like a knee in her gut.

Then, as if realizing he still carried the damn camera, it dropped, and all of a sudden there was nothing but a nice static close-up of grass stalks. Distant screaming. Sergeant Fisher smeared mud around on the screen.

"There's... twenty-seven more minutes of this. Then I'm guessing the batteries died."

"Along with everybody else," Araminta said.

"Not the goddamn missionaries," Dr. Fletcher said.

CHAPTER 19

Nothing moved in the hospital room but the bone chips, brains, and blood dripping down the wall.

"Ah fuck," Ramirez said, hands on his head.

House and Squirrel found something interesting out in the hall and stayed out there. Andy had gone frozen, like a field mouse who knew there was a hawk out in the darkness somewhere.

Carver holstered his Glock. He stared at the TV. "You're welcome."

On the bed, the woman's distended stomach gurgled. It made disturbing, high-pitched squeals. Sometimes the pitch dropped and moaned. Long and loud. Despite being quite dead, she lolled from side to side as the larvae inside sensed the clock was ticking on fresh food and burst into ravenous movement.

Carver used his two fingers both to point at his eyes, then at the old woman's lively corpse. His meaning was clear: Watch her. He waved goodbye and pushed Andy out of the room, leaving the viewers to watch the feast.

"Hang up," he told Andy in the hall.

Before he could, Haaga spoke. "They've opened the front doors."

Everybody froze.

Haaga's voice continued. "Air vents are fully open. Back doors are locked. It appears... Blueprints would suggest that there may be a side door, some exit point disconnected from the main system. West side of the building. Good luck." The phone went dead.

"Piss up a rope," Squirrel said.

"Only if we have to," Carver said. "Gimme the fire map."

"They're not gonna just let it go, man. They're gonna toss us all in a cell and throw away the key," Ramirez said as he took his time driving to the country club FEMA base. They hadn't had to kill very many wasps on the way back to the bus, as most of the horde clustered around the lobby before venturing deeper into the halls. If nothing else, Haaga had been right about the side doors. Yet once aboard, nobody was in any hurry to get back and find out if his other threats were real.

"I don't give a shit if their feelings got hurt," Carver said. "They owe us money." He pulled out his phone and dialed. Listened to it ring. Nobody picked up.

"And we're fucking stars!" Squirrel blurted.

"Don't swallow your own bullshit," House said. "Them VIPs, they gonna be looking for payback." He looked out the window, avoiding Carver's eyes. "Since you went ahead and made the decision to shoot everybody."

Andy agreed with House, but kept quiet because he didn't know what to say. The whole thing had him spooked and his meds weren't helping. The speed from his last cocktail had him near obsessively shoving .12-gauge rounds into the magazine drums. He'd learned how to pin the magazine between his knees so he could use his right thumb to shove the ridged shells into the metal mouth of the drum, thirty-two rounds in each. He stacked them on the seat and folded each empty ammo box flat, tucking it neatly away. He'd never been that fastidious about anything in his life until it came to reloading and cleaning the firearm. It occupied his conscious mind, freeing up some other part of his mind to step back and really take a good, long look at the situation.

"They're gonna have bigger problems than the fucking wasps if they don't uphold their end of the bargain," Carver said. He hung up and dialed again. Still no one answered. "And if anybody on this bus has any qualms about that, they are free to step off the bus and untwist their panties."

Where Andy sat, Carver had most definitely made shit worse. Carver had refused to let anyone leave until he'd gone down one side of the hall, reloaded, and came back up the other, stopping in each doorway long enough to put two bullets into each patient's skull. For some strange reason, this led to a forbidden thought of Jen, forbidden because he could get lost in an ocean of thoughts of her and lose his focus like Ocampo. Except that had been daydreams of cash, and thoughts of Jen were worse—they were something far too close to the feeling of hope. If you wanted any chance at all of survival out here, beyond sheer good and bad luck, you stripped all that away, all thoughts of literally anyone else outside the bus. And hope, that bastard didn't have the decency to go away on its own. Andy'd thrown anything beyond five minutes in his immediate future in a deep well and nailed that door shut a long time ago, long before the wasps showed up. He suddenly knew what to say. "Anybody gets between me and my girl, I'll blow 'em apart."

Carver pointed at him. "One hand. And bigger *cojones* than anybody on this bus. Man can't even clap, for fuck's sake. Let him be a lesson, gentlemen."

"He's so goddamn high he don't know his own name," House pointed out.

"True. But little dude's got heart."

"No doubt."

Andy ignored them. The links were getting to within five minutes' distance and he still hadn't made up his mind whether to get off the bus or not. Carver had misunderstood. Andy hadn't been just talking about any lawmen that got between him and Jen, he'd included the outlaws as well. The bus slowed before he could decide.

* * * *

Dozens of Humvees, Jeeps, and police SUVs blocked West Broward Boulevard. When the bus slowed and stopped a block away, the place exploded with light; brilliant large arc lights, as well as the red and blues of law enforcement. Behind them, more vehicles rolled out and blocked the boulevard. More waited on the side streets. Trapping the bus had been easy as slamming a dumpster lid on a baby possum.

"It would appear that I have gravely underestimated our hosts' generosity, boys." Carver tried again. Hit speaker and they all listened to it ring. He studied the blockade. "Keep your eyes peeled for any fifty-cals; that'll take out our tires if nothing else. Heads down. No telling about the windows either." No answer on the phone.

A bullhorn hailed from the blockade. "Attention. This is Federal Agent Clay. Hoping we can talk it over without any shots fired in anger."

The phone kept ringing.

"Your service and sacrifice have not gone unnoticed." Agent Clay stepped into the open. "So tell you what, I'll come over and we can talk about it, face-to-face. Just me. No weapons, nothing. Flash your headlights if this is acceptable."

"Don't do it," Carver told Ramirez, who was already reaching for the lights.

Andy started filling a duffel bag with fully loaded magazines. The phone clicked. "No," Haaga's voice answered.

"Wow. Right out of the gate. Haven't even tried bargaining yet."

"Your only choice is to step off the bus with or without firearms. Wasps don't have RPGs."

As if he was listening, Agent Clay was on the bullhorn again. "You got about ten more seconds to make a decision."

"No cameras this time," Carver said. "Wouldn't be good for the fans."

"It's out of my hands. The vice president is one vindictive sonofabitch who doesn't give two shits about five convicts, even as expendable PR tools. You are no longer useful. South Florida is about as empty as it's gonna get. He watched you shoot his mother in the head in real time. That was your call, cowboy."

"That'll learn me to ever be a Good Samaritan ever again."

"See your doctor if you think Cialis might be right for you."

"Couldn't you have mentioned that at the time?"

"Under specific orders not to reveal her identity."

"Followed that one right down to the letter, didn't ya? Kinda surprised you didn't try harder there, eh, Willy Wonka?"

Haaga gave a dry and dark little laugh, the kind of bitter, defiant joy from a drunk at a hated relative's funeral. "Worth it, knowing that motherfucker was watching."

"You owe us."

"Already paid it. Got you out of the building. You—"

"Time's up," Agent Clay said in a squeal of electronic feedback. A warhead came whistling out of the darkness behind the blockade and an abandoned Dodge Caravan up the street exploded. It came down sideways and slid into the sidewalk. A burning tire bounced up the lawn and through a house's front windows.

Carver looked at the phone. It had gone dead. He looked back up at Ramirez. "Do it. Let'em know they've made their point. Buy us some time to figure something out."

Ramirez exhaled in relief and flicked the headlights, then left them on. After a few seconds, Agent Clay came out, hands held wide, and started walking to the bus.

Andy stood up and slid the duffel bag's strap over his shoulder. It weighed damn near as much as he did. He slapped a fresh magazine into his AA-12. "When he gets here, I'm going for it."

Carver shook his head. "That's when they'll expect us to make a move. They'll cut you down where you stand. Won't be nothing left to bury except your boots. And guaranteed this POS is carrying a piece. He'll put two in you faster'n you can say 'due process.' No. The only smart thing we got right now is to give ourselves up."

"You sure?" Ramirez asked.

"I ain't looking to be bar-b-que," House said.

Agent Clay was halfway to the bus now.

"Anybody has a better plan, or a hidden jet pack, then I'm all ears. If not, the only play that makes any sense is to live to fight another day. We get ourselves a good lawyer, we can use the public for help," Carver argued.

"We'll never make it to court," Andy pointed out. "VP wants us dead. They'll line us up somewhere against a wall and that's it. I'd rather go out with my shotgun in the only hand I got left." He started down the aisle to the door.

"You won't make it three feet." Carver put his hands on Andy's shoulders. "Think about your girl. If you're in jail, you can still see her. Can't if you're dead."

Agent Clay was nearly to the bus.

The mournful howl of tornado sirens rose above everything.

The urge to flee, to fight, to explode reached a full boil between Andy's ears and surged through his body. He felt the fingers on his left hand curl and squeeze into a tight fist. Every muscle in his body tensed, even his heart.

Ramirez opened the door for Agent Clay. The sound of distant shooting rose above the tornado sirens. The man put one hand on the safety bar and was about to take the first step aboard when he looked into the sky. His mouth dropped open. He fumbled for the radio at his hip.

An impossibly huge wasp knocked the man off his feet. The radio and his pistol clattered away. The wasp rode his head all the way down, its tarsal claws catching his lips and an eyelid.

It was bigger than any wasps anyone had ever encountered; it was the size of a goddamn seagull. Wings longer than his forearms. The stinger alone was thicker than a ballpoint pen and nearly the same length. It thrust its mercilessly designed slender spike into the soft spot just under the man's ear and he made a sound like he'd just slammed his dick in the dishwasher door.

Swarms of massive wasps, most of them larger than ferrets with wings, descended on the street, drawn by the flames of the Caravan. The effect was immediate and savage. More RPGs bloomed in the sky. Gunfire everywhere.

Ramirez jerked the bus into gear and stomped on the gas.

"No! Stop!" Carver yelled. "Everything off! Quiet!"

As Ramirez killed the engine, Andy glanced out the window and realized he couldn't see the stars anymore. They'd been blotted out by wasps. "Holy fuck," he murmured, instantly catching Carver's wavelength. He sat back down. This wasn't just a new ballgame, this was another sport entirely, the way hunting with high-capacity magazine is a sport.

"Think happy thoughts, boys. If they think we're a threat..." Carver whispered.

They sat in the dark, staring in horrified awe at the fresh new generation, not only watching but hearing the scratches and clicks from their legs for the first time as the gigantic insects crawled over the bus and windows. Andy felt like a mouse in a plastic cup surrounded by barn cats. Not all of the windows had been rendered completely opaque through wasps or gunfire and some details could be made out through the unbroken glass. Andy put his eye up to the window.

The wasps looked to have been sadistically engineered to be hunting machines by a hideous soul who took pleasure in the simplicity of death. They seemed constructed of some kind of biomechanical hybrid of organic matter and unbreakable plastic, as each red and black curving part slid with supernatural precision over the next, the entire being apparently having been born for the sole purpose of causing pain and was a living embodiment of the god of elegant genocide.

If he'd known, Andy would have agreed with the missionary. These things were fucking unholy.

Gunfire thundered up and down West Broward Boulevard. When the shooting and explosions slowed, they could also hear the wasps' wings even over the wailing sirens, zipping through the air like tinny two-stroke engines.

"I strongly suggest no one makes a goddamn sound," Carver said, barely breathing the words. "But every single one of you is to put both hands together and bow your head to give thanks for these little beauties. Andy, it's cool if you just bow your head."

* * * *

They waited until near dawn.

The wasps had flown on earlier in the night, leaving the bus alone with the smoking wreckage of several police cruisers and the Dodge Caravan. When faint blue light appeared to the east, Carver had Ramirez quietly steer the bus onto a side street and head south until they pulled over and stopped under an Interstate 595 overpass to hide from helicopters and satellites.

Carver motioned them all to the front. Cracked the seal on a bottle of Don Julio. Leaned back against the windshield. Took a long, long drink. Passed it around. "I'd say our mission objective has been somewhat altered."

"I didn't think they came out at night," Squirrel said, taking a hefty pull. He gagged, nearly vomiting on himself, and handed it blindly to House.

House spent a while wiping off the mouth of the bottle with his shirt. "I didn't think they'd get big enough to carry off a goddamn rat, either." He took a drink, handed it to Ramirez.

Ramirez didn't say anything, just took a few swallows, as much as he could handle. He seemed spooked.

Andy was next. The tequila was almost sweet. He enjoyed the burn down the inside of his chest. "They're big fuckers, all right. But they're gonna kill you if they're this big." He spread his hands out a few feet. "Or this big." He held his thumb and forefinger a few inches apart. "I'll take 'em as big as I can get. Like Squirrel said. Bigger they are, the easier to shoot." He patted his AA-12 like it was his favorite dog.

Carver took the bottle. "We have around thirty to forty minutes to sunrise. It's time to go. Thing is, our former employers know our location. Been tracking us, listening to us, watching, everything, since they first sent us out. Found this under the dash." He held up a piece of black plastic the size of a fly. Flicked it away like a cigarette butt. "Zero point in looking for all the cameras, mikes, whatevers. I figure they would've been on us a long time ago, but they got their hands full with them big boys. Eventually, though, they'll start looking for us. Time to hang up on their ass. Get the guns outside. I've been over them already. Same with the ammo and bags. Those are good. And Andy, your sling is good. But everything else stays on board. That goes for your clothes, boots, Underoos, everything. Hope y'all aren't shy."

* * * *

They piled their clothes along the bus aisle, siphoned gas out of the tank and soaked everything inside. Carver lit the match.

Andy hadn't had any meds in four or five hours and he was fading. He sat a safe distance away on the duffel bags full of magazines, each coiled with thirty-two .12-gauge buckshot shells. He hurt, but the early-morning air felt good and cool on his skin. The lumpy canvas and unyielding metal gave him comfort. The weapons and ammo were tangible tools and it had become second nature to wield them. They made him feel safe, made him feel like home.

He watched the men, only silhouettes from his vantage point, as they hooted and hollered and danced naked around the burning bus. The celebration seemed only natural, and a perfectly understandable reaction, given the circumstances. Their shadows danced wild and savage among the cement beams of the overpass.

As the sunrise grew closer, Andy looked to the south. Half a mile away, he saw a red-and-blue logo bathed in heavenly sodium vapor lights on a big square beige building and damn near laughed. He'd spotted a safe haven, an oasis of R and R in an unforgiving wasteland, straight back in the direction of the country club.

Costco. God bless.

CHAPTER 20

Getting into Costco was so easy everybody expected a trap. They popped the back door inside of three seconds and stood around in the receiving department, listening for a sound, a signal, something to suggest that someone was in the warehouse with them. The power was out, so there were no alarms. Carver upped the ante. He fired a round into the high ceiling. "Hey! Anybody here? We're here to help."

Utter silence.

They moved out through the large building, easing down aisles stacked with pallets of Keurig cups, inoffensive clothes, three-gallon jugs of detergent. In less than two minutes, they determined it was clear. No people. No wasps.

The whole goddamn place belonged to them.

First things first. Clothing. Soon, everybody found a few things in their size. It could have been worse, Andy thought, even if they did look like a crew of bland henchmen for an especially unimaginative bad guy from the sixties *Batman* TV show.

Carver disappeared inside the pharmacy for a while.

House and Squirrel grabbed a flat cart and pushed it past the electronic toothbrushes and Dyson Purple vacuums and genuine German and Japanese steel chef knives and cordless shop lights and batteries until they hit the alcohol.

"What should we get?" House asked.

Squirrel's answer was simple. "As much of everything as we can stack on here."

* * * *

The rules were simple.

Each forklift had a certain payload to deliver beyond the opponent's borderline. It soon became apparent that actual delivery was pointless. The only real power lay in blocking the opponent's ability to deliver their own payload and probably should have been clear from the beginning that the game was really just jousting with high-powered forklifts, punctuated with shots of expensive Kentucky bourbon. The only other rule was that the arms had to be extended as high as possible, and a pallet of sixty-five-inch OLED televisions was balanced at the top as each lift's payload. They'd shoved all the peanuts and candy and clothes and moldy baked goods out of the way, clearing out a long field of battle that stretched from the meat department all the way to the registers, at least thirty yards.

"Two men enter, one man leaves," announced Squirrel.

They'd gotten the idea after Carver tested one of his chemical cocktails and decided to play with one of the forklifts in receiving. He'd learned how to spin the forklift, throwing pallets of electronics, pet food, and bags of pasta at the wall. Plastic shards flew. Kibbles 'n Bits skittered under the steel racks. Raw vermicelli bounced across polished concrete.

It didn't take long before they were using all three battery-powered lifts and one double- pallet jack called a rabbit to trash the living shit out of receiving. Andy couldn't drive worth a damn with only one hand, but that didn't slow him down much.

Then they held races around the perimeter of the place, until Squirrel got too drunk and hit a girder hard enough it tore the bolts clean out of the concrete. The entire coffee aisle crashed into the first of two freezer units. It shattered a few of the glass doors and the smell from the rotting fish was nearly unbearable. Carver hosed the whole area down with fire extinguisher foam and they decided to clear the runway in the middle and steer clear of the freezer.

The lifts' batteries lasted about two hours. Rather, the battery of the last machine running was still a quarter charged when Carver accidentally hooked one of the hydraulic hoses on the wreckage of House's forklift and when it ripped free, his engine gave up.

They snuck back outside and siphoned gas from one of the Swift trucks and used it to fire up a generator. They set it up in the rancid meat department cooler and ran a series of extension cords out to the front end and kept that door firmly shut. While House and Squirrel pushed a few couches around the biggest TV they could find, Carver hooked it up to the satellite dish on the roof. Everybody grabbed drinks and snacks and settled in to watch the news.

* * * *

South Florida belonged to the murder hornets.

And that was about as much as anybody could agree on.

Initially, every channel was nothing but chaotic, late-breaking reports about how vast swarms of murder hornets had overtaken security forces and spread throughout the Miami metro area. Local stations had a scrolling list of rescue stations and evacuation centers further north, but nothing else. The cable news networks replayed endless loops of distant shots from their helicopters intercut with jumpy, amateur phone footage of murder hornet attacks. A few times, the Exterminators even saw themselves, blowing the shit out wasps and property. Everybody cheered. Andy, who had just snorted a bump of some fun new mix from Carver thanks to the Costco pharmacy, unloaded a magazine into the line of registers in triumph. None of the registers held any cash.

On MSNBC, a bunch of politicians and university professors pleaded with each other about the inequality of the evacuation. The poor were nearly always the last to go, except for photo ops with a few inner-city nursing homes and elementary schools.

FOX hosts seemed confused whether to criticize or agree with the federal and state response to the invasion. Messaging from the right had been sparse and erratic. Democrats were wringing their hands over the legalities of martial law in Florida with a GOP governor who had already started testing 2-4-5 Trioxin, a chemical agent banned by the UN, in Miami's more disadvantaged neighborhoods.

Everybody was an expert.

But nobody knew anything.

About the only thing that everyone knew without a doubt was that these invaders were murder hornets. Except one. A FOX personality chuckled at this. "And finally, a truly wacky theory out of Florida that proves a hotshot science degree doesn't necessarily come with common sense," as FOX cut to a shot of Jen at the press conference, editing out her disclaimer and just showing, "...these are not Asian giant hornets—" A journalist interrupts. "Don't you mean *murder hornets*?" Jen said, "They are not... hornets. They're wasps."

The personality smirked and gathered his papers. "Higher education, folks. Your tax dollars at work."

"You cockfuck." Andy jumped to his feet. "I'll smash that grin so far down your throat you'll shit your own eyeballs."

"Keep him away from the guns," Carver said with the proud shamefaced grin of an asshole father when his asshole kid slides into third base spikes up. "I don't want to have to hook up a new TV. And take his meds away for a while."

They couldn't find anything else about the mission. On any channel.

The uncertainties of southern Florida had tanked markets across the globe.

Then there were the reports of all the people trying to get *into* wasp territory. Most, of course, were looters with no plan beyond smashing their vehicle through some store's plate glass front windows and taking everything they could carry. Others went looking for fame and fortune. TMZ had enough material to set up a whole new website dedicated solely to social media influencers and YouTube personalities inadvertently filming their own deaths.

The Exterminators found this hilarious. Carver spent a while in the office and eventually found some passwords. He hooked up a laptop to the TV and logged onto the net. The first thing they discovered was a thriving black market for various products that claimed to make you "invisible" to the murder hornets. Far too many chuckleheads doused themselves with bleach. A few learned the hard way that most anything halfway flammable was a bad idea. Industrial-sized containers of coyote urine were surprisingly popular. Plenty figured a tactical assault vest, sunglasses, and a Punisher logo black handkerchief tied around their face were more than enough protection when you carried a God-given, genuine AR-15 with the infrared scope and all the rest of the American Dream.

Big-game trophy hunters looking to kill without destroying the wasps' bodies too much so as not to ruin the taxidermy process didn't make it far. The wasps had a tendency to chew right through nets and other traps. A bunch of animal rights activists chained themselves to the front doors of a pest control office for some reason. They had a banner, but it blew out of their grasp once they were locked up. Wasps found them about fifteen minutes later. Hours later, the activists were just shapeless sacks squirming with larvae. A unanimous decision from the rest of the internet rose up to bestow a groundbreaking, first-ever *group* Darwin award.

The origins of the murder hornet invasion proved to be the most popular source of conversation. A few connected the doomed jetliner, but those were called kooks. To be fair, most fans of the aircraft conspiracy also included monsoons in Taiwan as the primary reason the original swarm had been blown into a collision course with the aircraft. Some mused they were a result of some kind of fusing of advanced scout alien and murder hornet DNA. Genetic tampering by the Chinese lurking around Cuba was also a prime suspect. So was Bill Gates's experimental agricultural labs out in the Everglades. More that should know better claimed it was that other billionaire, Bezos, who had been testing out ecological-based package delivery organisms that could also be adapted for security and/or warfare details. Others insisted the insects were a hoax, and proved it by going through each frame of video footage in exhaustive detail and circling all the CGI flaws. Obviously, this elaborate cover-up was designed to draw attention away from the possibility that the evacuation of Florida was for another, probably more nefarious reason.

And then, in the middle of all the breaking news about the murder hornets swarming through the lines and rampaging through what was left of southern Florida, reports of the attempted arrest and subsequent escape became public knowledge. "In a shocking turn of events, authorities discovered the special rescue unit, also known as the Exterminators, who have been praised for their daring search and rescue missions such as those shown here, have actually been using these missions to conceal breaking into bank vaults and stealing untold millions. They've even been accused of letting civilians die while instead robbing a nearby Western Union."

"They can't say that!" Squirrel protested.

"The Exterminators, of course, are a joint task force of military police officers and inmates whose identities were kept secret until last night." The PR machine had turned, eagerly feeding the public everything it knew about the convicts. Every sordid detail. Andy: Manslaughter. House: Armed robbery. Ramirez: Attempted rape and murder. Squirrel: Public indecency. Carver. Well, Carver's past was a bit murkier, but those quoted in the segment seemed happy to somberly speculate that he may have been present at several terrorist bombings in the Middle East. The anchor ended the report musing that the convicts had intentionally let the law enforcement members of the team get killed by murder hornets.

Everybody yelled at the TV except Carver. He concentrated on the laptop and found a lively debate exploding across social media. The Exterminators had plenty of detractors, those that insisted they be rearrested, locked back up, and either spend the rest of their life in prison without parole or staked out in the middle of the street and left for the murder hornets. However, an equal number challenged the official version of the story, claiming betrayal by the government. Fans pointed out inconsistencies in the suspiciously brief statement from the Department of Homeland Security, such as how, when the Exterminators were supposed to be robbing said Western Union, they were actually recorded entering an upscale nursing home three miles away. Later, the nursing home conveniently exploded, erasing all evidence.

The others followed along, yelling responses and threatening any posts that claimed they were guilty. Ramirez turned to Carver, pointing at the laptop. "Shit man, can't you get on there, tell all these *pendejos* the truth?"

"Yeah," Squirrel agreed. "Set these fuckers straight."

"I got a better idea." Carver snapped the laptop shut. "What kind of video cameras they got?"

* * * *

Carver outlined his vision.

He sent House to go find rope and cables and any other hardware they might need. Squirrel went to the back to get the scissor-lift. Ramirez was in charge of running the video cameras. Andy was the smallest, and therefore got to be the star since he was the only one who would fit into the newly arrived children's Halloween costumes. The costumes ran the gamut of all the Marvel and DC characters, including stock heroes like cops, soldiers, firefighters. Andy and Carver gathered up anything they thought they could use and stopped off for duct tape and batteries and bungee cords before laying it out on the tables in the break room.

Preproduction took a couple hours, but the actual shooting, in both senses of the word, only took a few minutes. Then Carver dumped the footage that they'd all taken, including the GoPro Andy had been wearing, into the laptop and chopped it all together. After a quick search to prod his memory, he added some narration.

Showtime. They all sat back to watch with snacks and warm beer.

It opened with Squirrel disguised as a soldier. They'd put reading glasses and a fake makeup brush mustache on him. He screamed and overacted shamelessly as an offscreen House lowered a menacing Elmo piñata spray-painted red and black to look like a wasp with fairy wings stapled to the top. A shot of Ramirez, this time as a female cop in a bad wig and worse makeup, threatened again by a similar piñata. There was supposed to be a third, but House was such a terrible actor his footage would have just confused everybody. You couldn't tell if he was scared or so furious he might cry or bust into laughter. Or maybe piss his Kirkland slacks.

Then a shot of three wasp piñatas, another Elmo and a SpongeBob, shaking and looking as terrifying as possible as they menaced the camera.

Meanwhile, Carver's best no-nonsense, Joe Friday narration came over the soundtrack. "Ten years ago a crack commando unit was sent to prison by a military court for a crime they didn't commit. These men promptly escaped from a maximum security stockade to the Los Angeles underground."

Zoom to the top of the steel shelves. Andy, in his full Florida Man costume, raised his arm in triumph.

Close-up. Batman's gray and black foam muscles ran from his ankles to his jawline, creating the base of the costume. He wore Captain America's blue helmet/mask thing he'd spray- painted a brighter shade of blue to cover the big A and taken a black marker to draw a halfway cool-looking F and M across the forehead. He ran out of room for the M and so it ended up looking like a big F and U. Bane's metal mouthpiece covered the rest of his face. They'd stapled four or five red Superman caps together to make one big-ass cape that dragged behind him.

He still wore his sling and carried his AA-12. He had Thor's hammer dangling from his carpenter's belt he'd found in the hardware aisle. They'd wrapped a string of battery powered purple fairy lights like a wreath of crowns around his head. Children's neon blue sunglasses. Bricklayer kneepads they'd spray-painted red. Sparkling white Adidas. Pretty cool fingerless weight lifting gloves that were kinda badass if everybody was being honest.

Carver used a Samuel Jackson clip, making Florida Man say, "Is that right, motherfucker?"

Then the money shot, so to speak.

Andy jumped off the steel.

They'd rigged two ropes to a harness under his sling and around Batman's codpiece and hooked them to the struts at the ceiling in the middle of the store. Andy swung through space in slow-motion like a five-year-old's mash-up of all his favorite superheroes and Tarzan, only with more firepower. And for a few artificially slow seconds, with the cape billowing out all huge behind him, he almost looked... heroic. Fearless, probably. Dumber than dogshit, certainly.

They'd cleared off the jousting battlefield and hung the three piñatas from fishing line between two posts, just off the path of the ropes. It was decided that killing just the wasp piñatas wasn't gonna be cinematic enough. So they went through the warehouse and gathered all the TVs and computers they could find, including the jewelry case, and stacked them around the piñatas.

The plan wasn't all that complicated. Florida Man was gonna come flying toward the wasp piñatas and blow the living shit out of them. The end. The papier-mâché animals had been stuffed with bags of ketchup and mayonnaise and mustard and relish. They'd even set up three different cameras just to make sure they caught it all.

Andy unfurled his AA-12 as he plummeted, but they didn't know the motion would spin him completely backwards and he sailed past the target in silence. Without missing a beat, though, he unloaded on the piñatas the second he had them in his sights. Condiments and soggy papier-mâché exploded into a Jackson Pollock painting.

Carver's narration continued: "Today, still wanted by the government, they survive as soldiers of fortune."

Andy reached the opposite apex just shy of the steel and dropped the magazine. Reloaded.

"If you have a problem, if no one else can help, and if you can find them, maybe you can hire the A-Team."

Andy unloaded that magazine, blasting away at the electronics and glass, even before reaching the nadir of the swing. Problem was, his cape had caught up in the two ropes and now he was more or less upside down. You could hear his faint cry of, "I'm coming for you, Jen," before the sound abruptly cut to a jaunty little number they later learned was called "The Gonk."

Then a shot of a whiteboard with big block letters in red Sharpie. *SKAMMELIGE GJERNINGER HEVNER SEG.*

"Fuck's that mean?" House asked.

"It's Norwegian. My grandpa was a Viking. Telling 'em they'd better watch their ass," Carver said. He hit *enter* and uploaded their visual and sonic message into the endless interwebs.

* * * *

Carver woke everybody by putting a few rounds through the roof. "Gather your shit. Time to head north for the summer." He pointed to the TV.

The president was reading from the teleprompter in a slow, precise tone. "—established above the twenty-eighth parallel. Again, emergency powers are being used to enforce a mandatory evacuation of southern Florida. I, along with the Joint Chiefs of Staff, and an emergency mandate from Congress, have authorized the use of multiple ordnances to eradicate the deadly infestation of murder hornets. This includes, among others, the GBU-forty-three-B."

"Daisy cutters?" House asked. "They talking about daisy cutters?"

"These devices, known as Massive Ordnance Air Blasts, will take decisive action against these illegal alien... insects. It is our duty, as Americans, as citizens of Mother Earth, to defend our homeland against any invaders, no matter how large or vicious or political affiliation. This is why we must stand united under God, to hold off this incursion. It is his will." The president's eyes left the teleprompter and he stared America in the face. "Stand tall. Stand strong. Stand with everyone else." He raised a fist. "God bless the United States of America... and may his mercy fall hard upon south Florida."

CHAPTER 21

The trees shielded the sight of the village and most of the stench from the rotting bodies was downwind, so most everybody decided sitting in the sun for a few minutes wasn't a bad idea.

Sergeant Fisher tucked the video card into his tactical vest pocket and handed Dr. Hill's camera back. Dr. Hill promptly sat in the grass at the edge of where the Andersons had been building a path to the church. He withdrew a microfiber cloth from its special waterproof pouch and began cleaning his camera.

Dr. Fletcher wandered over to the church and tested the front steps. Looked inside. He straightened and froze in the doorway. He said, "Holy shit. Oh. Hello there." He called back at the expedition. "Hey. You guys, you need to see this." He turned back to the darkness and attempted to say hello. *"Bwen-ose tar...daze."*

Sgt. Fisher went inside and everybody followed. The far end of the church was steeped in shadows. The bright holes in the roof made it difficult, if not damn near impossible, for Jen's eyes to adjust to the unknown gloom lurking in the deeper reaches of the sanctuary. They moved further into the church and details became visible. A wide aisle led up the middle, like a traditional church, with four rows of blackened short benches on both sides waiting for the next sermon. The floor was charred and crackled under their feet.

A small, quiet man sat on the remains of the altar.

His eyes were closed, chin resting on his chest, hands in his lap. Blue, squiggly lines had been tattooed across his face many years ago. Matted gray hair erupted in patches over his skull, less like male-pattern baldness and more like mange. A very old survival blanket was draped over his diminutive physique. It may have been reflective once, but now served as a mossy shroud, cloaking his body in darkness. Jen got the unmistakable vibe that this was the tribe's shaman, or even the local sorcerer, resting victorious in the ruins of his enemies' castle.

Nobody could quite tell if he was alive or dead.

Sergeant Fisher stepped forward and said, "*Hola*, amigo."

As if he was waiting for his cue, the shaman lifted his crinkled face and gave them a toothless smile. He had no pupils; his blank eyes were the color of soft-boiled eggs. A cold recognition squeezed Jen's heart. She saw now how the seemingly random tattooed lines radiated out from his mouth and nose in the unmistakable reproduction of the veins in wasp wings.

Sergeant Fisher repeated, "*Hola*." No response. "Anybody have any ideas?"

"Give him a candy bar," one of the soldiers suggested. "Everybody loves chocolate."

The survival blanket crinkled, but Jen didn't think the shaman had moved.

Sergeant Fisher turned to Miguel. "Jump in anytime. We need to talk to this old fart."

Miguel looked uneasy; he didn't want to get closer to the man. He hailed the shaman in one dialect, then another. Still no response. Third time was the charm.

The shaman turned to the sound of Miguel's voice. Still smiling, he opened his mouth and hissed air, then began to tremble. Everybody thought he was having some sort of seizure as his skull bounced like a bobblehead on a dirt road. Then they gradually began to hear it as laughter. Dry and mirthless, it shook out of him, making the clumps of his hair shiver.

His movements stuttered and slowed until he sat motionless as before.

"What'd you say to him?" Sergeant Fisher asked.

"We are here to help, or like that. We bring help," Miguel said.

"That's what made him laugh his ass off?"

Tips of the clumps of the shaman's hair trembled, although the man himself didn't seem to move a muscle. The hair shifted and whispered and a large wasp crawled out from behind one of the matted locks and fixed all five eyes on the intruders. Another crawled out from behind his neck and perched balefully on the shaman's chin.

Dr. Fletcher whispered a quick, "Oh, shit."

The scientists drew closer while the soldiers stepped forward, armed with their own Atchissons and smoke grenades. Jen wasn't the only one on the expedition who had been studying videos of the Exterminators.

The soldiers brought something new as well. Chalk bombs. The thinking went that the chalk would coat the wasps' wings and, with any luck, prohibit flight.

"Tell him we mean him no harm. We're friends."

When Miguel translated, the man laughed even harder. The wasps on his face rode it like rats clinging to a ship in high seas. His blanket billowed and settled, breathing seemingly of its own accord.

Sergeant Fisher said, "Okay, then. We're leaving. Back, slow. Dr. Hill, you're closest. Out. Dr. Singh, you're next. Easy, easy."

Everything slowed and stopped. Jen felt unable to move, as if time itself was trapped in the jungle's sap. She could only watch as the shaman threw his arms up in seeming slow motion and hundreds of suddenly angrily buzzing wasps boiled out from under his survival blanket.

Time caught up, now going faster and faster as panic spread through the scientists like wildfire, stripping everything except the desperate desire for survival. They clawed at one another to get through the door. Being smaller, Jen was knocked askew and slammed into the doorframe. She spun away and went down, still inside. Then Dr. Fletcher was crouching over her, using his own body as a shield.

Sergeant Fisher yelled, "Chalk!" Two hollow thumps and neon orange dust filled the back of the church. A wraith the color of brand-new safety cones jumped onto the altar and used his arms in all his power and fury to direct the wasps to attack. Wasps shook off chalk dust like dogs after an unwanted bath and kept coming.

Seregant Fisher said, "Fuck it," and put three red holes in the neon orange shaman. Before the dead man flopped onto the altar, the four soldiers opened up in staccato bursts, churning the air with thousands upon thousands of tiny steel balls. In thirty seconds their magazines were empty.

They popped fresh ones in and waited.

For a few moments, nothing. Not even the ghostly, whispering wind from the lake.

Then the buzz.

It wasn't just the remaining wasps that had survived that initial onslaught of automatic gunfire. Fuzzy shadows filled the shafts of sunlight, visible in the swirling orange dust and gunpowder smoke. More wasps had appeared outside, and were now pouring into the church through the holes in the roof. They targeted the soldiers, especially Sergeant Fisher, and swarmed over the men. The wasps crawled under clothes, down shirts, up pants legs, into mouths, eyes; biting and stabbing and chewing. The men went berserk, shrieking and thrashing.

Sergeant Fisher managed to get his sidearm under his chin and ended himself.

Wasps also pounced on the scientists that had thought they'd found safety outside. Jen was dimly aware of their screaming, but in the chaos inside, it didn't matter. Orange dust and gunpowder filled the church like fog, and that gave the remaining scientists and soldiers a few precious seconds to gather their wits.

Jen and Dr. Fletcher helped each other to their feet. He picked up one of the dead soldier's AA-12s. It still held a full magazine and he emptied it into the floor. Jen understood and they both jumped on the splintered floorboards. Dr. Fletcher's side gave first and he dropped through. Jen fell onto him and they landed on the dirt under the church, rolling away. The rest followed; only Araminta, Dr. Patel, and two soldiers were left.

"The lake!" Dr. Patel gasped. "It's our only chance."

"Unless the fuckers can swim too," Dr. Fletcher said.

* * * *

The last two soldiers fired off the remaining smoke bombs in the general direction of the lake. Everyone scrambled out from under the church and sprinted into the cover of the swirling gray fog. Jen grabbed Araminta's hand in her left and Dr. Fletcher's with her right. The lake was only a short dash down a rough slope, through a narrow tree line and across the rocky shoreline.

Dr. Patel was the first to fall. Then the soldier who stopped to grab him. Wasps swarmed.

Jen got one last glimpse of the other soldier firing wildly before all three were lost in the smoke. Araminta ran even faster, pulling Jen along, who in turn dragged Dr. Fletcher. In his fear, he couldn't let go of the empty shotgun.

They burst through the tree line and stumbled down the rocks, finding a path along the village. The wasps were close enough that Jen could hear their buzzing even over Dr. Fletcher's gasping and her own pounding heartbeat. She risked a single glance over her shoulder and saw the wasps were only feet away, zeroing in on them. Araminta was the first to let go as she brought her arms together over her head in a graceful swan dive into the shallow water.

Jen's ankle went one way, while her knee and hip went another. She fell, crashing into water only a foot deep. It wasn't enough. The wasps were within inches now. Dr. Fletcher hadn't let go and dragged her with

him, pushing her into deeper water, then released her hand. He grabbed
the AA-12 by the barrel and smacked the first wasp out of the air. The
momentum of his swing pulled him sideways and he deliberately plunged
toward the water.

But the wasps were faster than gravity.

They went after him with such fury it might have been personal.

Jen heard his screaming and felt him splash into the water, only feet
away. But then she was rolling and grabbing at weeds, at the gravel on
the bottom, anything to get into deeper water. Her mind roiled, skipping
through images of the last five or ten minutes. It felt like five or ten hours.
Her heartbeat grew faster. She knew her reptile brain was still kicking
out demands to run, run, run in abject panic like an excited chimp with a
hammer. This was using up valuable oxygen. Flashing back to yoga classes
in the cramped studio on the south side of Chicago, she found her center,
as they say, and swam on. She could grieve and process later.

The lake was murky, but the dazzling sunlight helped make out blurry
shapes. It was surprisingly cold and she wondered if there was a freshwater
spring somewhere under the rocky little island. She scrabbled deeper,
risking rolling back over to look straight up. Fragmented shadows fluttered
over the surface, crisscrossing the ripples. She pushed herself farther into
the lake. The wasps followed. They could see her underwater and would
simply wait until she ran out of air. She looked for Araminta.

There, off to the right. Araminta was using one of the hut's posts to
hold herself underwater. They needed air, and fast. Jen frantically spun
through possibilities and she patted herself down with one hand, frantically
searching for anything she could use as a snorkel. A pen. No, that would
take her too close to the surface.

She had nothing. Bubbles escaped her nose. When they broke at the
surface, it brought more wasps.

The boat.

They could turn it over and use it for cover. But it was too far away;
she couldn't even see it. She'd never make it, not with her air running out
this fast. Simply thinking it provoked more bubbles to spill out. She knew
she had maybe ten seconds left.

Dr. Fletcher might have something she could use in his pack and she
pulled herself back to him. He was face down, his skin a riot of deep
lacerations after the wasps had furiously chewed at the flesh. His mouth
was open and the tip of his tongue was attached by a thin strip of muscle;
he'd bitten nearly clear through it when the wasps attacked. They'd eaten
half of one eye. The other stared at Jen as she slid underneath and rolled

him over, only to find that he wasn't even wearing his backpack. Her lungs began to burn.

She bumped into the shotgun. It had fallen into a patch of weeds and she hadn't seen it. Now she pulled it close and numb fingers scrabbled at the bolt. Somehow, she released the magazine. It sank and Jen ignored it, thrusting the stock at the sky. She put her lips to the end of the barrel and used the dead air in her lungs, nothing but carbon dioxide left anyway, to blow water out of the open breech above the surface.

The air tasted metallic and burnt and perfect.

She took a few more deep breaths and kicked out for Araminta. The ten pounds of empty shotgun helped keep Jen near the bottom of the lake.

Araminta had been able to snatch a couple of quick breaths while Dr. Fletcher was attacked, but now had none left. Her eyes fluttered and her dead hands threatened to let go of the post, allowing her body to float to the surface. She'd fought her own body's survival instincts until the battle left her near unconsciousness.

Jen blew water out of the barrel and gave it to Araminta. She put it to her lips and inhaled, shaky at first, then settled into three even breaths. She closed her eyes and smiled, bowing her head slightly in thanks. Then motioned, pointing. They passed the shotgun back and forth, rolling over onto their backs and taking long breaths like a couple of lifelong stoners taking rips off a novelty bong. They swam through the skeletal posts of the village until they found the canoe wedged between several posts.

Using the shotgun, they managed to tip the canoe over and when Jen came up inside to breathe, something caught her and held her under. For a quick second, panic flared in her mind and she almost screamed. It was the net. She shot her arms out, desperate to find an opening. Luckily, the net was attached to the gunwales only about five feet. Both ends were open and she was able to emerge in the bow, gasping.

Araminta came up in the stern.

For a long time, all they could do was cough as their lungs burned and vomit lake water. The heaving and gagging tapered off into something that was neither keening nor hysterical, sobbing laughter but an amalgamation of both as shock seeped into their systems and their bodies shut down for a while.

Eventually, Jen said, "I—we need to—where is—Oh, for God's sake, I mean, what the actual fuck?"

"Seriously," Araminta answered. They both lost it and fell into another round of convulsing with half screaming, half laughter.

Inside, it smelled almost as bad as the bus. Blood, animal excrement, and an acidic tang cut into Jen's nose like a dull box cutter. They held onto the netting, keeping the gunwales submerged at least a few inches in the water so nothing could crawl under, and stared at each other. Light filtered through the lake gave their faces an unearthly glow. Jen trailed her fingers over the chiseled wood. It felt smooth, as if a layer of lacquer had been applied. It gave off its own unique odor as well, something tantalizingly familiar to Jen, but she could only guess that it was a distilled version of some plant within the vast jungle.

The wasps' buzzing rattled the canoe. At first, they'd been convinced the wasps would smash and burrow through wood inside of five minutes. Ten, if they were lucky. But it didn't sound like the wasps even landed on the hull, much less attacked it.

After a while, Araminta said, "Let's take this canoe for a walk."

* * * *

There was no other way to find out. One of them had to break the surface of the lake and see if the wasps were waiting.

They'd walked for several hours, so long that an irrational fear grew in Jen's mind, that they were simply walking all the way around the lake and wouldn't that be hilarious. It would be the perfect end to this clusterfuck of human arrogance and the military's unhealthy interest in the wasps. Araminta assured her that at best, they'd gone only two hundred, two hundred and fifty yards, which wasn't even a quarter of the lake's circumference. Jen still had her doubts.

Her ankle was still tender, so she'd used the AA-12 as a crutch. That and the cold water took the pressure off and allowed the pain to subside. Nothing was broken or sprained and Jen gave a silent thanks to anyone who might be listening. They'd also gathered the trailing ropes and dumped them inside on top of the netting. Didn't need to be dragging those behind, disturbing god knows what.

Somewhere around dusk, when Jen couldn't see the bottom anymore, they heard shooting. They froze, listening. A brief flare of automatic gunfire, then a distant shriek of such agony Jen shut her eyes and shuddered. It had to be Harmon and Belter, drawn to the shooting earlier at the church.

"Poor things," Araminta whispered.

They waited for a while, but heard nothing: no voices, no more shooting. Even the wasps were gone. They moved slowly, carefully along the shoreline for what felt like hours to Jen. The water was nothing but pure inky blackness and she literally could not see her hand in front of her face. A new terror bloomed within the absolute darkness. With every step Jen took through patches of gravel and long, slimy strands of lake grass that whirled around her legs, she couldn't shake the conviction they were about to stumble over some slumbering beast. A crocodile. An anaconda. Piranhas. Giant snapping turtles.

"Please," she said. "I need a minute. I can't... I don't know."

"I got no problem with that," Araminta said, her voice full of the same exhaustion and dread. The fight in them was faltering. The chill in the water, while an initial offering of a bracing and refreshing temporary refuge from the jungle's stifling heat, had crept into their very bones over the long hours, and now they couldn't stop their teeth from chattering.

Eventually, their legs and lower torsos became too numb to keep going. They decided it was time to try for the undergrowth, worried that if they continued, they may not be able to run once out of the water. The plan was to creep, slow and quiet.

But they had no way of knowing if wasps were still watching. Araminta reached out from under the boat and let her fingers float up to the surface. Neither of them breathed. She fluttered her fingers, not much more than a fish snatching a fly floating along, but to them it sounded like she'd slapped the water so hard the impact echoed around the crater. She might as well have set off a string of firecrackers.

Nothing happened.

It was decided they would duck out from under the canoe and rise to the surface together.

"One," Araminta said.

"Two," Jen said.

"Three," Araminta finished and they sank into the water, came together under the netting, and took each other's hands. The other held onto the gunwale, just in case. One step to the shore. Araminta's index finger tapped out another count on Jen's wrist. On *three*, they tilted their heads back and pushed their faces out just enough to keep their noses and mouths above the surface.

Jen saw nothing but a half-moon floating in an ocean of glittering stars. She let a trickle of air drift out of her lungs on its own. Then an inhale. A second breath. Another. They brought their heads forward so they could keep their eyes above the surface and turned back to the village.

There wasn't much to see. Mostly shadows on shadows under a black, jagged horizon that cut off the starry sky. They took it one hesitant movement at a time, feeling along with their feet. Each step exposed more of themselves until they left the water completely and cautiously crept up the rocky shoreline.

In the dim light of the half-moon and the stars, they saw they'd come out of the lake near the edge of the clearing. They stopped and shivered and listened to the wind skim across the water and rustle the grass. No hint of the wasps. It didn't take long to find a halfway smooth and quiet path that led to the center. When they reached the firepit, a dozen paths led off to the jungle.

"For crap's sake," Araminta said. "Do you remember which one?"

They chose one that seemed to lead in roughly the right direction and were halfway across when Jen tripped over something. She didn't know what it was at first. Soft. Wet. Sticky. It could have been a rotting log. But when her thumb slipped across the unmistakable feel of human teeth, she involuntarily uttered a short yelp. She clapped her other hand over her mouth and her wide eyes found Araminta's in the starlight. It was either Belter or Harmon.

For a few seconds, they could only hear the wind.

Then a faint buzz.

"Run," Araminta whispered.

Jen and Araminta moved as fast as they dared, bent over and shuffling, constantly touching each other to stay close, connected. The path was only an unbroken shadow through the waist-high grass. The tense droning of the wings grew louder, louder, hacking away at Jen's ears, like a live wire bouncing along a serrated knife. They were twenty yards from the jungle when the grass opened up unexpectedly and they crashed into the Andersons' empty tent.

The change in the buzz was instantaneous. The vibrations popped into a much higher frequency as wasps swarmed into the clearing.

It was over. Survival instinct kept them moving, but hope's pilot light was flickering out. Jen and Araminta disentangled themselves from the canvas tent and plunged into the grass, knowing there was no way they would ever make it to the trees. And even if they did, the wasps could slip through the dense foliage like hot water through a colander.

They were done.

Until something somehow even darker than the blackest shadows swooped into the clearing. Something silent. Something huge. Something that left no wasps in its wake. Then another shadow. And another. More. Dozens. Hundreds.

The bats.

They came hurtling out of the darkness, malevolent vacuums with sleek, furry bodies the size of small children and wings approximately the size of World War II bombers. Dry crackling joined the buzzing and it took Jen a few moments to realize it was the sound of wasps being eaten. The voracious bats snapped up wasps as they blasted through the swarm, gluttons with seemingly insatiable appetites.

Araminta and Jen kept running and didn't slow down even when they hit the edge of the trees, hurtling themselves into dense undergrowth as dark as the bottom of a well. They clawed through the dead leaves and black soil, using exposed roots to crawl along. "Go, go," Araminta urged. "We're not out of it yet. Those bats can't eat all of them."

* * * *

They fought for every inch.

It might have been ten minutes, it might have been hours, when Araminta stopped. "Wait," she said. "We're going uphill."

"Shit," Jen said between gasps.

"No, no, it's good. Now we won't go in circles. This is the edge of the crater, right? If we head to the left, keep this on our right, we'll find the marsh, then the stream." They kept going, and what was a gentle slope began to tilt dramatically. Here and there, starlit slabs of towering rock loomed over them. The stone was smooth and cool to the touch. As they climbed higher, the worst of the muck, leaves, and clinging vines wrapped in more strings of flowers were left below.

When the terrain grew too steep to keep climbing, they turned left and worked their way along the incline. At times, the ground could be treacherous, not soil at all, but dips and sudden cracks in the hill, disguised with a thin covering of branches and broad leaves. Moonlight only reached the ground once in a while and this helped to camouflage these traps. And sometimes the soil itself would give way without warning. Still, they moved easier and faster than before, and while Jen fought it, an ember of hope refused to die inside.

Then they heard the wasps, filling the jungle behind them.

Far, far back in the detached, yet eternally curious academic halls in Jen's mind, a hypothesis unfolded on instinct. The wasps' first line of defense against the bats would be to disappear into the impenetrable tangle of the rain forest, especially near the ground. It was probably highly unusual behavior of the wasps to enter the open air of the clearing at night and had only been drawn there by the presence of tasty intruders. She was most certainly not surprised that once the wasps had reached relative safety of the undergrowth, the wasps had locked onto their alien scent and were tracking them through the darkness. And without something like the immediate safety of the lake, or even the dubious comfort of being out in the open with the bats, she and Araminta were doomed.

She tried to blurt out the necessary information, but her foot broke through thin branches and leaves that hid another shadowed crevice. In the flare of panic, she reached out and grabbed Araminta before she could stop herself. They plunged into the thick vegetation, rolling and tumbling down the steep hill. Jen's world spun and rolled crazily. All she could manage was to cling to Araminta, who clung right back.

Their bouncing, flailing bodies generated a hurricane of leaves, vines, flowers, and branches that enveloped and followed them down the slope. When they crashed awkwardly through some kind of huge, prehistoric fern, the strong vines caught up. Everything cinched tight around them, halting their descent with a jolt that mercilessly squeezed the air out of Jen's lungs. She couldn't move. Neither could Araminta.

As the din of their tumbling descent faded away, that vicious purr filled the jungle.

They'd been hung up on the side of the fern; Araminta was almost upside down, her hip squeezed tight against Jen's shoulder blades. A vine full of the purple flowers had been drawn tight against Jen's face and she had to twist her head to get them out of her eyes and mouth. She reached back, squeezing Araminta's hand with the last shreds of strength left in her arm. In about three seconds, it would be done. Her heart raced as a tidal wave of thoughts burst through her consciousness like a sledgehammer between the eyes.

Araminta breathed the words, "The Lord is my shepherd…The Lord is…"

Wasps burst through the trees all around them. They swirled in the speckled bands of moonlight and the sound of their wings was louder than the heartbeat in Jen's ears. Another tidal wave of images and memories and empty hopes followed the first, this one of deep sadness as she stared down her own annihilation. Her last thought was of Andy. She closed her eyes.

The wasps continued to boil through the jungle. They were everywhere.

Jen realized she was holding her breath. Araminta had stopped praying and was holding her own breath, waiting for the end. Both closed their eyes. It was time.

Nothing happened.

Jen's abject terror and fear curdled to an almost sweet fury. How dare the universe draw out their deaths like this? It was beyond cruel. She wanted to scream in frustration. Araminta sucked in a breath, convinced she had taken her last.

The wasps continued to cruise overhead. Jen inhaled sharply through her nose, jaws still clenched. The scent of the flowers snapped another piece of the puzzle into her hypothesis. The canoe. It smelled of these flowers. Therefore... Bats eat wasps. Bats pollinate flowers. Wasps link flower with bats? She worked her right arm free, reached up and crushed several of the flowers in her fist. She rubbed the sickly sweet-and-sour pulped petals over her face. Her hair. Her shoulders. It left purple stains on her skin. She worked herself free, moving slowly, methodically, quietly.

She kept grabbing flowers, rubbing them across her, pulling some of the broken vines free and wrapping them over her shoulders, and before she could stop herself, she rose slowly to her knees. Araminta grabbed her wrist, but Jen pulled free.

Wasps cruised down to investigate the movement. As they grew nearer, something made them veer away. None got within a couple yards. Jen stood up, moving ever so slowly. She took one decisive step forward. The wasps erupted in a great fury and the swarm circled around her naked, vulnerable flesh.

None got close enough to touch her.

She decided to push it. She took three steps in the center of the clearing, straightening her back, squaring her shoulders, and throwing her head back and arms out in a supplicating pose, like some kind of religious icon, a Virgin Mary enshrouded in vivid purple blossoms, a saint reborn as a beacon of hope within a green hell.

CHAPTER 22

Squirrel wanted to steal five Harleys and use the Second Amendment to blast their way to freedom in some red state that had decided it didn't have to answer to any federal statutes in this new world.

They stood in the Costco loading dock deciding whether they should head north or west. Carver asked, "Why?"

Squirrel was confused by the question. He had Carver repeat it a few times to get his head wrapped around the implications. "Because... how much more badass can you get in this life, brother?" He appealed to the others. "Think about it. Black leather, badass boots, Harleys coming on like a hurricane! We'll bolt a couple shotguns to a sidecar, put Andy in there, let him blow the shit out of anything he wants! People won't know whether to shit or piss when they see us coming." It was obvious that joining a motorcycle club, especially something like the Hells Angels or the *Sons of Anarchy* family, had been a lifelong dream of Squirrel's.

"That's awesome," Carver agreed in a gentle tone. He didn't want to shit on any of Squirrel's few life ambitions. "But right now, I'm not sure if going after the loudest, most exposed transportation we can find and shoot our way... to freedom... is the best way to sneak past the hornets and Johnny Law. Maybe we should go for something, you know, quieter."

In the end, it was a unanimous decision. Squirrel's idea was cool. But dying old and loved was better. So they moved out and found a charged Tesla. They spray-painted it nonreflective black before slipping into the migration with the last of Florida's weird and maligned and bruised and uncertain communities that had been forced from their homes into the streets.

It's easy to hide when you're surrounded by panic.

BUZZ KILL 187

* * * *

They hit the chaos of I-75 and folded into the migration heading west, then north.

A whisper past three AM EST, a whole eleven hours after the deadline, the United States Air Force dropped the most metric tons of explosive yield in recorded history. What made the whole situation especially galling to the generals at the top was that they were being forced to bomb their own country. The series of massive blasts leveled the entire metro Miami area and a chunk of the Everglades for good measure. The shock waves sent ash beyond the ozone layer and left the skies overcast worldwide for weeks.

The official data was laughably short, as most armchair talking heads vehemently agreed. Most insisted that the concussions, a series of blasts that could be seen from the space station even though it was over Paris at the time, had been a coordinated attack that utilized both an unheard number of American MOAB and Russian ATBIP thermobaric weapons. Then the Chinese president got angry that they hadn't been given proper credit for China's own contributions to the assault, which flummoxed PR departments in every country, from capitalist to communist to socialist and back again.

In the end, about the only thing that anyone could agree was that a series of massive explosions had blasted Florida's southern Atlantic coast, from West Palm Beach down to the Keys, all the way back to the Paleozoic Era.

Two hundred miles away, Andy felt the ground itself shake in surprise. They'd been stalling, pretending to have a flat tire in a strip mall parking lot, but brought no electronics with them from Costco so they couldn't be traced and didn't know the extent of the damage at first. A half hour later, a caravan of families pulled into the small parking lot. The kids flocked to the convenience store while most of the adults caught up with each other and stretched. Carver struck up a conversation and learned how much of southern Florida was gone when someone opened their laptop and pulled up the staggering footage.

"Holy hot dogs," Squirrel said. "They just blew the tip of America's dick off."

* * * *

"We go much farther north, we're fucked," Carver said the next morning. "Too many eyes looking for bad hombres such as ourselves, not enough making sure their own ass don't get stung." They'd waited out the night in the same strip mall, recharging while tucked mostly out of sight between a Dunkin' Donuts and a dry cleaner. Smoke filled the sky, horizon to horizon, like an endless fog out of a video game that needed to save money on graphics. The sunlight that managed to filter through was flat and dead. He rubbed his finger along his teeth, scraping them clean. "We need to stay off the radar for a few weeks. Then maybe we'll head west, stick to the coast. We'll find a boat and head for Mexico. Say *adios* to this fucking country for good."

They watched from behind darkened windows as refugees straggled along Highway 27, heading to a FEMA intake center in Lake Wales five or six miles north up the road. A large collection of National Guard vehicles and soldiers marched slowly a few miles south, slowly expanding the no-go zone. News radio had been thick with reports of strict quarantine rules being enforced with lethal results. The messaging had been clear across the board. If you were caught inside the no-go zone, it was assumed you were a looter, and looters were being shot on sight.

More vehicles appeared out of the surrounding counties, until movement along Highway 27 grew so slow it was easier to simply turn off the cars and wait it out. People got out and stretched. Kids ran amuck. Folks dug into their coolers and ice chests. Some shared. Some didn't. Quick-thinking, entrepreneurial residents that lived and worked along the route came out from the used car dealerships and two-star quaintly named inns and lodges to sell fruit and cold water out of wagons and shopping carts. Frisbees hummed overhead. A few folks flinched, then got mad, saying that shit was in bad taste and to knock it the fuck off. An improvised market sprang up between the vehicles, where folks traded and haggled over obviously looted goods such as socks, windshield wiper blades, brand-new phones without SIM cards, and toasters. Andy saw one guy trade his iWatch for a dozen rolls of toilet paper.

Then everything hushed while the president came out of the White House, planted his feet in a classic fighting stance on the Rose Garden lawn, held up his fists, and declared, "We got 'em," shaking his right like he'd personally punched the shit out of the murder hornet queen. The entire country went wild. For a few moments, Andy heard some of the loudest sounds he'd heard in a week of creeping around in a fragile quiet, outside of ammo of course, all vehicle horns and screaming and cheering and sweet release. Onscreen, the press secretary seemed to be trying to lead journalists in a chant, *"Vic-tor-eeee! Vic-tor-eeee!"*

"However," the president's tone grew grave as he cautioned, "it will be years before the cleanup will be finished. Victory always demands sacrifice. We are wasting no time to bring back Florida as a rightful player in the world's agricultural markets and therefore, starting right now, Florida's farms, orchards, and ranches are OPEN. FOR. BUSINESS!"

He led the applause, saying, "You all know me and my love for Florida. That's no secret. So we're throwing the biggest fundraiser of all time in two days! A Concert for Florida Hornet Relief! Right on NBC! Folks, you wouldn't believe who we've got lined up. Toby Keith! Jimmy Buffett! Pitbull! Kid Rock! And that's just the beginning!" He finished like the consummate showman, "Florida is *back*!"

"And Bingo was his name-o," Carver sang in a happy little falsetto. He turned the radio down and twisted the driver's seat to face the rest. "No way we're making it through that." He tilted his head north to indicate the FEMA camp. "So let's go the other way." He let his head fall back southward. "Let's find us a local, some good ole boy in a four-wheel-drive. Something's that got flags, gun racks, you know the drill. Most important, Florida plates. Ramirez, Squirrel, you take the east side of this highway. I'll take the west. You see anybody that fits that description, you let me know. Andy, House, you guys are too conspicuous, even for this crowd.

You hang back here and keep your eyes open."

As the implications of the president's announcement sank in around the world, a celebration erupted among the thousands of refugees along Highway 27. After over a week of growing terror and confusing, sometimes conflicting orders from the government, it was over.

The bugs were dead.

And Floridians were ready to party. Dancing on and around the vehicles. Illegal fireworks, even though they were mostly invisible in the sunlight. Music, everywhere. Biker drag races. Fistfights. Dogs shitting anywhere and everywhere. A pet alligator got loose. One ambitious thief decided to steal a motorcycle despite never having ridden before. He popped it into second and promptly veered into the fiberglass siding of a mobile home's porch, where the inhabitants came out and beat him savagely.

House said, "When these people sober up, they ain't gonna be so happy when they remember they homeless." He'd been drifting in and out of light sleep, rising to the surface whenever another firework went off.

"They'll have to get some money, won't they? A place to stay, right?" Andy tried not to scratch the itching around his stump. He knew it was good, that it meant he was healing, but there was nothing phantom about the sensation and it was driving him nuts. He eyed the clock. Still had two more hours before his next pill. "You can't just let all these people go homeless or starve."

"Brother, where you been? Government's gonna dump a shitload of cash and some of it might even filter down to these people. They'll get enough for rent for a year and a new TV. And when they get it, it'll be more than any paycheck they've ever seen, and most of 'em will party like this." House spread his hands at the windshield. "It'll never occur to 'em they got less than dust."

Carver and Squirrel appeared out of the crowd and climbed into the Tesla. Carver said, "We found our coyote."

* * * *

The coyote's name was Joe. Joe was big guy, built mostly of cheeseburgers and MoonPies. He wore a Lynyrd Skynyrd cowboy hat, a denim vest with an American flag stitched across the back, and a belt buckle big and heavy enough to use as a weapon. He had a Fu Manchu–style mustache, but the effect wasn't so much Lemmy from Motörhead as the biker from the Village People. Andy wasn't sure if Joe's mouth hung halfway open like that all the time or if he was excited to meet the Exterminators. He couldn't wait to shake everybody's hands, except for a brief moment of hesitation to take House's hand. Andy noticed, so he fist-bumped him instead, popping Joe's knuckles at the last second like an asshole because Andy wanted the guy to know he'd already had enough of his shit.

Joe eyed Andy like a rabid dog he wasn't allowed to put down and kept his distance.

To compensate, Carver became Joe's new BFF. Hung his arm around the guy's shoulders, laughed at everybody's dumb jokes and generally made Joe feel like an honorary member of the Exterminators. They grabbed the carry-on luggage to haul whatever they'd pillaged from Costco, left the Tesla's windows down and the keys on the driver's seat, and let the party carry them along, until eventually easing their way through the crowds to Joe's truck, parked behind a gas station.

Joe took empty back roads for half an hour before pulling over next to an orange grove so his new pals could all hide in the pickup bed under a tarp. He claimed to know a couple of the guys manning the roadblock ahead. Said they'd be caught if any of the Exterminators were obvious and out in the open, but Joe had played football with a few of the weekend warriors at this particular roadblock, and they wouldn't go to the trouble to search the vehicle. After ten minutes of stiff shocks and dust, they felt the pickup slow and stop. Joe didn't turn the engine off. They heard him hail someone, someone he apparently knew well enough that he could complain about the carnal performance of the guy's mother's the night before.

"If they pull off the tarp," Carver breathed into Andy's ear, "kill 'em all."

After some laughter, Joe was waved through. He went a mile or two down the road and stopped to let the guys out of the back, but said, "I… uh, I gotta ask everybody to put on blindfolds. That okay? I ain't supposed to bring outsiders in at all; compound's supposed to be all secret like."

"Ah, hell, that's the least we can do," Carver said. "Get to it, gentlemen. Find yourself something to cover those peepers." He winked and turned back to Joe. "Fact is, I got myself a souvenir from my previous career as an inmate." He whipped out the black hood that he'd been wearing when he stepped off the helicopter.

"That'll do it, I guess." Joe was way, way over his pay grade here, and he knew it. He had no idea what he'd do if they'd refused. Ramirez had a silk black tie in his luggage for some reason. House used a new pair of sweatpants. Andy used his Captain America helmet and goggles and pretended he couldn't see shit. Besides Carver, Squirrel was the only one who went ahead and truly covered his eyes completely with a towel.

When they were on their way again, Carver said, "Tell me about this militia of yours."

"It's a good group; guys and their families. Got a place, ways back up behind a pig farm, back in a swamp that's got access to fresh water from a little lake. Place to lay low, plan, train."

"Their name?"

"Oh, they've got something formal, but I can't remember." Joe looked uncomfortable.

"Affiliations?"

"What?"

"Are they part of a national chapter?"

"Oh. Um, I dunno."

"Electricity?" Carver asked.

"No. But that's intentional. Generators instead. Staying off the grid, you know."

"Smart."

"My brother, he's second-in-charge. That's how I'm involved. The commander there, him and his wife, they're in charge. I went to high school with their girls. All I can say is, they may not be much to look at, but they'll kick your ass. They're liable to jam a screwdriver in your eye, they get a bad vibe off you or something."

"Do tell." You could hear Carver's grin. "How many?"

"Three. And I wouldn't get any ideas. Oldest is—well, she ran off, got herself into all kinds of trouble. She's... ah, not around anymore. Second sister, Bridget, she's married to my brother. The women in that family, whoo-boy. They're more committed to the cause than their men. 'Specially Sigrid."

"And what's the cause, exactly?"

"Worshipping Jesus, way the Constitution wants us to." Beyond that, Joe was unsure. "Outwit the government? Overthrow the Florida state government? Live free and die 'stead of on your knees. Something like that. All that and Jesus. Honestly, for me, it's just a place to hang and shoot with my brother. He's more into it. And, and well..." He got a little bashful. "I kinda got a thing for the youngest, Hilda."

"Yeah?" Ramirez asked, eager and grinning at the thought. "How's she like it?"

"Like... huh?"

"From behind? On top? Or maybe a little more freaky-deaky?"

Joe physically flinched when he realized what Ramirez meant. Blood drained from his face and he brought his front teeth together on his lips hard enough to draw blood. His mouth turned the color of a frozen creek. "That's my girl. I'd appreciate you not speaking of her like that. That's not... appreciated." Pure, uncut hatred seeped from the pores in his livid skin and filled the cab.

"Ah. Okay." Ramirez looked out his window and tried not to smile. "No offense."

Joe kept his eyes on the road and didn't say anything. The route curled through orchards and farmland and swamps for a few miles. Eventually he asked, "Hey, you boys like country music?" Without waiting for an answer, as if the alternative was unthinkable, he turned up the radio.

Andy, who didn't like anything except his older brothers' Tupac and Eminem and Ice-T, found that this current pop music pretending to be country irritated the living shit out of him. Made him realize here he was yet again, stuck in a vehicle with crap AC, waiting to get somewhere he didn't want to go. He lasted four and a half songs. "Either find some other goddamn fucking station or turn that shit off."

That cracked everybody but Joe up, although he joined in when he realized he was the only one not laughing. "Okay, okay," Carver said, reaching out and fumbling blind with the dashboard controls. The station changed to an evangelical sermon.

"Fuck, no. I'd rather listen to static," Andy said.

This time, Joe was the only one laughing until he figured out it wasn't a joke.

"I'll kick the living shit out your little backseat here, Joe Bob Billy Bubba or whoever the fuck you are," Andy whispered from the back seat into his ear. "I'll take these goggles off and pop your goddamn eardrum before those girls get a chance."

More laughter from everybody else.

Joe figured out which side of the bread was buttered and turned off the radio.

"Oh yeah," Carver said like it had just occurred to him. "How many guys you got there in this militia?"

"Twenty-five or thirty regulars. These days, maybe forty or so folks came out here when this shit hit. Not just men. Women too. Don't be fooled. It's a new world, boys. Women're shooting just as good as us, and I had to learn it the hard way. Wouldn't tease 'em, if I was you. Made me look like I couldn't shoot my way out of a paper bag. Some friendly advice there, no charge."

Carver barked out a "Hah!" and a big smile.

Joe's brain caught up with his mouth and he said, "Of course, you all being soldiers shooting at murder hornets and all, I suppose..." He let that hang and die in the stale air.

Everybody was quiet for a while.

Until Andy leaned forward and yelled, "You suppose what, asshole!"

Joe jumped and blurted, "You guys gotta be the best shots I've ever seen. Was just talking is all. You guys, your shooting, holy shit. I never, I mean. Just making conversation is all. Didn't mean nothing."

"It's okay, Joseph." Carver reached out and patted Joe's shoulder with unnerving precision for a blind man. "You relax. Don't take Andrew back there personally. He's a fucking asshole, especially ever since he said goodbye to his girl. We keep him tranquilized and we're good as gold."

"Oh—okay?" Joe said in a high, shaky voice.

"What else can you tell me about this place? There's fresh water, you said?"

* * * *

The overwhelming smell of pig shit made the blindfolds more or less unnecessary.

Joe had turned down a rutted, chalky white road that trundled between an overgrown lemon grove and a long line of aluminum barns cooking in the late-afternoon sun. The guys all pulled their blindfolds off and tried to breathe through them, promising to put them back on when they got to the compound.

"It does have a bite," Joe agreed, pulling his T-shirt over his nose. He stopped the pickup before a sagging gate. It was unlocked, but Joe didn't get out. Beyond the gate, the land grew wild, wooded and swampy. He turned to them and said, "I wouldn't go wandering around, 'cause they got traps all over the place. Liable to lose yourself a—" He faltered, then gave Andy a terrified look in the rearview mirror. "Life," he finished.

"They're probably watching us right now, aren't they?" Carver said.

"You bet your ass they are," Joe said. "I woulda called ahead, but they don't answer any phones out here."

"Then why don't we let 'em know this ain't some kind of hostage situation or what have you. Everybody, raise your hands. Andy, you know what I mean. Let 'em know we're friendly, once you get to know us."

Joe guffawed at that and sure enough, after a few seconds, somebody in a ghillie suit rose out of a hidey-hole in the scrub ahead. They didn't move, just stood and watched the pickup through a scope attached to an assault rifle. At least, Andy hoped whoever it was, was just watching, not actually aiming the rifle. A few minutes later, a couple of guys on four-wheeled ATVs came bouncing up a trail. The one in front was a tall guy in a floppy boonie hat. He walked like a duck, stoop-shouldered and splayed feet. He spent a minute unhooking a thin wire hidden among the weeds at the bottom of the post.

"Claymore," the second guy said with a cheerful smile.

The first one finally opened the gate and came around to the driver's side. "What's the score here, Joe?"

"These are the Exterminators, Thomas. You've seen 'em. They rescued all them folk from the murder hornets."

"Holy smokes, yes I have."

"They need a place to lay low for a bit. Got the government after 'em."

"Do they now? Saw something about that. Damn shame." He considered for a moment. "Well, I'm sure Sigrid'll understand why things had to go this way." He hurried around the pickup and came up on the passenger side, yelling as he went. "Go ahead, take those blindfolds off. I know it ain't very Christian of us to have you put 'em on in the first place, but you boys being soldiers'll understand." When they had everything off their heads, he saluted. "Thomas Hunt, president and commander in chief of the um, central Florida three percenters, the Guardian Eagles. That's

Scotty, over there." He pointed to the guy on the ATV. "And that's my daughter, Bridget."

The figure in the ghillie suit pulled off the hood, revealing a woman in her late twenties who looked like she could hunt and catch and skin and cook her dinner in less time it took anyone else to go through a McDonald's drive-through.

"Carver, Exterminators." Carver shook Thomas's hand.

"Well, I gotta say, we'd be proud to help you boys out. Let's head down on foot. We got food and shelter for you. Joe, why don't you come with us too. Scotty'll bring your truck down in a while." Scotty got off his ATV and headed to the gate. Thomas hitched his jeans up, tried to be both casual and tough. "And, uh, no disrespect here, but I think we'd all be more relaxed if y'all left your firearms behind as well." He failed at both, which made things more awkward.

He planted both hands on his hips so he would stop wringing them. "Just until we get to know each other a while better. You can understand."

"Well. I hope this won't be an issue," Carver said. "Trust me." He stared Thomas full in the face. "It will go bad for you and your family if you think you just scored yourself a bunch of automatic shotguns."

Thomas chuckled. "I bet it would." His grim assessment was genuine, and therefore, tickled him. "Hell, I ain't after your guns. If'n I wanted automatic shotguns, I'd goddamn *have* automatic shotguns. We got plenty of firepower. Well, no such thing, but you know what I mean. Nah, got no eyes on your guns. Just a chance to size y'all up without anybody waving 'em around. This ain't some piss-brained biker club."

"Language," Bridget said, sharpish.

"Well, then. All right," Carver said. "Andy, that means you too."

"Hope you didn't bring any alcohol. Pornography neither." Bridget didn't look in the mood to argue.

"Yes, yes." Thomas waved everybody through the gate and set the trap behind them.

"Again, we all appreciate it." He didn't have to say it out in the open, but it was understood that Scotty would search everything. Andy wished he'd left a few open blades or something else unexpectedly sharp in his bag. As it was, he didn't have much. Some underwear and socks, a couple different T-shirts, his costume 'cause Carver had wanted to make a sequel when they got a chance, some toilet paper, a toothbrush and toothpaste, soap, and a nearly full bottle of pills. He carried everything else on him, like the sling. That was more important than his boots. Or his underwear. He slept in his Kirkland T-shirt and sling most of the time. He unhooked

his AA-12 and left it on the seat, but kept the sling and tactical vest on and
followed everyone down the slight hill.

* * * *

Thomas waved a fly away. "Don't mind the smell. You get used to it."
He led the way down through a thin line of trees into a small clearing.

A collection of vehicles, mostly pickups, had been squeezed under
trees around the clearing and covered in camouflage netting. A group of
children worked with papers and crayons inside a minivan, watched over
by a young blond woman sitting sideways in the driver's seat. She held
a big flash card, *F is for FLOOD*, and watched the strangers out of the
corner of slitted eyes. She popped the flash card with her middle finger
to get the kids' attention and pointed at the newcomers. She shouted the
verse from memory, allowing the fury to gather within each increasing
pause between lines. Her righteous anger and rhythm reminded Andy of
a poet who had come to his high school, although that particular black girl
had been trying her damndest to get the students to think for themselves.

This was more of a threat. "Isaiah thirteen-nine! Behold, the day of
the *Lord* cometh. *Cruel*, with *fury* and *burning anger*! To make the *land*
a *desolation*! *And he will exterminate its sinners from it*!" Her voice rose
to a shriek.

"Shitfire," Squirrel said.

"You think she means us or the wasps?" House whispered to Andy.

"My youngest, Hilda." Thomas gestured at the Sunday school teacher.
"A good Christian woman. Just like her mom."

"You must be very proud," Carver said.

"You're damn right," Thomas said.

They followed him deeper into the trees where the ground grew soft.
A series of wooden walkways of various degrees of age and expertise had
been built through the swamp, leading to a large central deck, surrounded
by a dozen or so shacks on stilts and even more hanging tents. He marched
them through tables long enough to sit at least fifty to an industrial-sized
stove and butcher's block that dominated the far end of the uneven deck.

Behind the block, a tall, frowning woman in a rubber apron sliced raw
pork belly into long strips. Her hair was so pale it may have been spider's
silk. She used a butcher knife that had been sharpened too many times
and was now more of a fillet knife. Her eyes never left the newcomers.
A large, red flag with a white cross in the center hung a few yards over
her head. A red comma had been placed in the middle of the cross. To the

left, slightly lower, an American flag with thirteen stars in a circle. To the right of the cross, still lower, was a yellow Gadsden flag. A camouflage tarp above funneled and filtered the cooking smoke.

A dozen standing people watched them with assault rifles either in their hands or in full view on the tables. All white, primarily men. Camouflage was yet again the dominant fashion print, with variants such as autumn shades or pixelated desert sprinkled throughout.

A number of shallow boxes with glass faces had been attached to various trees around the eating area. Each held a single wasp husk of varying sizes. Some were smaller, from the beginning of the invasion, still only the size of a sparrow. Others must have been hatched more recently, for they were nearly as large as seagulls. Andy couldn't see any reason for the boxes, unless they were trophies of some kind or another.

The woman behind the chopping block had brittle eyes and frown lines that cut to the bone, pulling her mouth into a permanent grimace. Her hands continued with their tasks, wholly separate from her unwavering gaze; gnarled, spindly creatures that scrambled about the stove and block of their volition. She probably didn't look very happy most of the time, but when she saw the Exterminators her expression hardened into something especially unpleasant.

Her husband had taken a breath and half-turned, preparing to introduce the new men, but she interrupted, saying, "Thomas." Somehow, she managed to inject that single word with not only a demand for explanation, but also a touch of loathing, permanent impatience, and enough bitterness you could taste from thirty feet.

Thomas deflated as soon as she spoke with the weary surrender of a puffer fish who'd swallowed the hook a long time ago and knew that it would rip his guts apart if he ever tried to get it out. "Sigrid, I'd like to introduce to you the Exterminators."

"And you thought you'd bring them down here, into our sanctum?" Propane hissed and ignited with a soft *pop*.

"They're... famous."

"Are they now?"

Giving up, he said, "Gents, my wife. Sigrid. She's the real backbone of the camp."

"Oh, I can't claim to be important around here," she said with a smile that made Andy's balls run screaming in horror and curl up somewhere north of his heart. Her gums were black from what appeared to be chewing tobacco. "Especially not when the security protocols I wrote— unanimously approved, I might add—are simply... ignored."

The grease started to crackle.

"Oh hon, I—I—we—they're unarmed," Thomas said. "Scotty's searching their gear now."

"Well, that makes it all okay then, doesn't it?" She folded a dishrag, embroidered with roses, in precise thirds. "Might as well give them the keys to the gun safe, since we're all such close friends."

"Dear—" Thomas tried.

"We can talk about this later. You—" she pointed to Carver with the knife. "Could be that the Lord sent you to join in our holy war. That said, I'd sooner trust a cottonmouth than anybody that's worked for the federal government."

"As a God-fearing man myself, I certainly understand your concerns, Mrs. Hunt," Carver said. His voice had grown richer, more expansive. Andy thought it sounded like Carver was having fun, acting like a mercenary Foghorn Leghorn. Any minute now, he was gonna erupt with, "I *say*, I *say*, I say, Mrs. Hunt…" Instead: "We have a checkered past, this is true. But with the grace of God, He has chosen to lift us out of the darkness and temptation, setting us on a new path that has brought us to your doorstep. There is no such thing as coincidence, ma'am. We await Jesus's orders."

Hilda joined her mother, whispered something in her ear, looked back at the newcomers. Sigrid said, "Good. Scotty know?" Hilda nodded. "Bring 'em down then." It didn't appear that Carver's new Southern accent and religious conviction swayed Sigrid's attitude one way or another. She kept moving, now laying out limp lettuce and sliced sallow tomatoes, along with loaves of Wonder Bread. A tub of mayonnaise was laid out next to more tubs of homemade potato salad and BBQ potato chips.

House observed, "I've never seen so much fucking mayonnaise in my life."

As if she heard, Sigrid said, "These are dangerous times, Mr. Carver. I'm sure you can understand. We will fight to the death to protect our family. Our way of life. Our faith."

"I expect nothing less."

Four militia members stepped onto the big deck and everything stopped. The rest of the militia jerked upright, and a few even started to raise their right arms before they were slapped down by their neighbors. The four men came over to the stove and stood off to the side, stiff, like they were at attention. None wore any kind of uniform. Instead, they were all dressed in basic jeans, T-shirts, Oakleys. Baseball caps, which were removed. Andy couldn't shake the feeling that Sigrid's chopping block was some unofficial altar. They pointedly ignored the new guys after she said, "Don't pay our guests any no mind."

She dipped her hands in steaming water in a pot on the stove and washed them with a chunk of lye soap. She deliberately let them air-dry instead of wiping them on her bloodstained apron. "We'll dispense with some of the unnecessary elements of our... older traditions, given the circumstances." She traced a cross across each of their foreheads, then pulled four keys out of her pocket. She passed them out, pressing the metal into their hands with significance while they bowed for another quick kiss on the forehead.

"Carry his light into their world," she said, and they nodded. Marched out.

The Exterminators exchanged a look. Carver rolled his eyes.

Sigrid went back to slicing pork belly. When she finished, she seemed to take pleasure in laying the cold slabs of pork belly out on the sizzling griddle, enjoying the sting of boiling grease. It looked like she'd forgotten about the Exterminators.

"It should go without saying, madam, that we offer our services," Carver spoke up. "Anything you may require. No freeloaders here. Strong backs, clean hearts."

Sigrid cackled at that. "You're one smooth talker, ain't ya? Seen a few boys like you up in the pulpit in my day. Voices sweeter'n honey. Talk an angel out of their own wings. Least they went to the trouble of being clean-shaven. Maybe you are who you say, maybe you ain't. We'll see, 'cause the Devil can't help himself. Truth always gets out. It's the natural order."

"I face my day of judgement with a clear soul, Mrs. Hunt."

"Ain't none of us can say that. Especially any of the likes of you." She included the rest of the Exterminators with a short, vicious slice of her knife.

"You are, of course, correct. We are all stained with sin." Carver paused for a mournful sigh, then asked, "Would you happen to have any kind of smartphone, laptop, or tablet? I could show you. We are who we say we are." He chose not to mention the collection of mounted and preserved wasps scattered around the deck.

"You should know better, Mr. Carver. We're out here to escape the pernicious reach of technology that spreads lies and demands the worship of false gods."

"There's no signal all the way out here neither," Thomas offered.

"Ah. Television then?"

"Up at the house," Thomas began, then snapped his mouth shut after a searing glance from his wife.

"Newspaper?"

Silence.

"Telegraph? Carrier pigeon?"

Nobody outside of the Exterminators found that funny.

Sigrid came around to their side, using a greasy towel to wipe away most of the juice off her hands. "Line up. Let's see what you're made of. Might have a use for you yet."

More glances between the Exterminators. Carver shrugged.

They stood, shoulder to shoulder, in front of the massive stove while Sigrid tossed her towel aside and walked through them, peering at the outsiders like a sergeant inspecting a pitiful new squad. She wasn't shy about poking and prodding, opening pockets, or sliding her hands up into anybody's special areas. She pulled a sheathed knife from Ramirez's crotch, another knife from the inside of Andy's left ankle, and a petite .22 handgun from the small of Carver's back.

She spit and smiled. "Believe y'all were asked politely to give up any and all firearms."

"No, ma'am." Andy shook his head. "We were asked to give up our shotguns. You got those. What else you want?"

"Anything you got that might harm my family."

"Far as I can tell, we got no cause to harm your family," Carver said.

"Not yet, anyways," Sigrid said. She'd stopped at House. "Jonny, get over here," she called out. "Find out if this guest is carrying a weapon." Jonny stepped forward. He was a big guy, a damn big guy bigger than House, even. Big like Bigfoot. Jonny had a Viking hammer symbol tattooed on his forehead and maybe another on his throat, but it was of such terrible quality it was impossible to tell what it was supposed to represent. He gave House a rough, impersonal search, purposefully avoiding House's crotch.

"Nothing to be afraid of." House grinned at everyone. "Only a genuine black anaconda. You can touch it if y'all want. He's sleeping right now." He eyeballed the red flag with the white cross. "Dumbass crackers."

Jonny spit and stepped back. Shook his head.

"Good. Makes things easier," Sigrid said.

Carver cocked his head.

Andy wondered where Joe was.

Sigrid cackled again and said, *"Now!"*

The edge of the deck erupted in ribbons of electricity. The Exterminators caught the Taser's vicious hooks in their backs and asses. Barbed darts from three separate Tasers alone struck Carver in the back. One got Andy in his neck.

Throughout the exchange between Sigrid and Carver, men had slowly collected behind them, each armed with Tasers. And now, at her order, it was time. The Exterminators went down.

"Praise Jesus," Sigrid said.

CHAPTER 23

When the advance team's radio went silent, the two pilots, Huss and Swelm, who'd stayed behind to repair the Sikorsky, let home base know that they'd lost contact with Fisher and the rest. They requested backup. It would still take close to twelve hours before anyone could reach the landing spot at the river, so they packed up and started out, following Fisher's ribbons, chuckling at the CO's lack of trust in any kind of high tech. Of course, they couldn't ignore that the lack of a radio signal only confirmed Fisher's bias.

They found Jen and Araminta halfway up the mountain. The women appeared above the rocks along the stream, materializing out of the fog like two forest spirits. They were covered in leaves and striking purple flowers. Mud and twigs filled their hair and their faces and hands—any skin, really—had been stained purple for some reason. They trailed vines full of more purple flowers. Their eyes were wide and haunted. They couldn't, or wouldn't, speak above a whisper.

It took a while to get the whole story out of them.

Huss and Swelm wanted to keep going. They argued that there still could be survivors. "I mean—" Huss stammered, "no offense—but a couple of women. No guns. If you made it out, the other soldiers could very well be pinned down, waiting for backup."

"We gotta make sure," Swelm added.

Araminta closed her eyes and lifted her face to the sun, summoning enough patience to zen out a meth head. "Boys, boys. You've got friends back there. So do we. However, they are dead. All of them. I understand the need to confirm this. We both do. But you are the only ones who can fly that damn contraption. You are going to take us far, far away from here. After that, I don't care."

"Listen, we get it," Huss tried to explain again. "You ladies don't want to be out here in the jungle alone. I promise, you follow these—" he pointed to the neon ribbons—"back to the river. Turn left, follow it downstream and you'll hit the chopper by nightfall tomorrow."

Jen shook her fists. "Are. You. FUCKING. KIDDING?" She jabbed her finger into Huss's face, less than an inch from his nose. His eyes crossed, trying to follow it. Her voice dropped to a harsh whisper. "Are you hearing anything that we say? Do I need to remind you that your mission is to support the scientists in any way, shape, or form? We have urgent, lifesaving information and samples that must reach home as soon as possible. It is vital we get this into a lab where it can be synthesized and massed-produced or those people, everybody back up there, your friends and ours, all of them will have died for nothing. Now, if you don't shut your flippin' trap and help us out, I will have you brought up on court-martial charges and if my boyfriend ever finds you, he will beat the absolute living shit out of both of you stupid motherfuckers." She finished, taking great gulps of air through gritted teeth.

Huss and Swelm glanced at each other.

"You got one of those satellite phones? Use it. You call whoever you need," Araminta said, taking Jen's hand and continuing down the hill. "Tell them what happened. Then get us to that air base. We truly do have an answer for the wasps."

* * * *

They used Manuel's boat on the way back and reached the Sikorsky the next day, even before the support helicopter arrived. There was no place to land another giant chopper, so a dozen soldiers descended thick ropes and encircled Jen and Araminta. Introductions were made. The new batch of soldiers didn't listen a whole lot better than the two original pilots, but they had a new, different objective.

Get the scientists and samples back ASAP.

This suited Jen and Araminta, but they decided to pack up the samples in the relative calm air of the rock slab rather than the shaking nightmare of being up in the chopper. They didn't know what might be necessary, so in addition to drying and pressing without any additional preparation, some of the flowers and vines were washed clear in the river and left to dry on the rocks. Some were packed on dry ice and some dropped in preservatives to isolate whatever properties affected the wasps.

Jen and Araminta were given new clothes, and their old, soiled clothing went into triple-sealed plastic bags. Even their underwear. She couldn't believe this was the second time this had happened to her in less than a week. "You sure?" Jen asked. "We can, you know, just bury it. Or burn it?" A medic had descended with the rest of the soldiers, and she went over Jen and Araminta as best she could with a first aid kit. Twenty minutes later, they were in the air.

They were connected to authorities back in Florida through a laptop, where they had to each give separate statements. Then the debriefing began in earnest. Jen and Araminta answered a slew of questions, most detailing what exactly happened back at the village. Many of the questions were rephrased differently, yet asked again and again, so they ended up answering the same questions four or five times. Jen knew this was standard, and allowed those in charge to capture an accurate account of what actually transpired. Still, she was exhausted, possibly still in shock, and knew the images and sensations of the village and lake would haunt her forever. Her patience was gone.

"Listen," she finally said. "We're going in circles. We've given our statements. We've told you everything. This isn't—"

"I sympathize," one official on the laptop screen said. He reminded Jen of the man she'd talked to on the phone a lifetime ago who called her office back in Chicago. He did not sound sympathetic. He sounded as if all his emotions had been programmed right out of him. After guessing at the appropriate time for sympathy to unfold or transpire or whatever was supposed to happen, he continued. "However, we still need to go over—"

"Uh-oh,"Araminta broke in, shouting, "turbulence!" She shook the laptop and then just shut the damn thing. The soldiers that could see what had happened pretended they hadn't and kept busy cleaning weapons or playing cards or reading. Jen curled up in her seat and wrapped her arms around her knees, trying to pull herself into something small. Something insignificant. Something that could disappear. She shivered and someone put a survival blanket on her. She yearned to be in Andy's arms. The heat of the jungle felt very far away; her bones seemed to have remained at the bottom of the lake.

* * * *

It wasn't as easy to hang up on Sheila, who was a relentlessly cheerful representative of the president. She was blond and pretty and did not register the word *no*. She kept calling them, using the video on her phone so they could see her on the laptop. She was desperate to discuss plans about some concert fundraiser that didn't have anything to do with them, as far as Jen and Araminta were concerned. Araminta tried the turbulence excuse and bumped the laptop a couple times until Sheila'd had enough and went to her boss.

Less than thirty seconds later, the pilots got on the intercom and said, "Uh, folks, I need everyone's attention immediately. We've got the commander in chief on the line. He'd like to speak with our two scientists, Jen Huang and Araminta Ross."

Jen and Araminta exchanged *oh shit* glances. Love him or loathe him, the president wasn't someone they could simply ignore, despite the circumstances. Jen opened the laptop and they saw the Man.

"Mr. President?" Araminta asked.

"Ah, there you are." The big man himself was holding the phone as he and his entourage moved through corridors of golden light. Sheila darted in and out of others' paths as she trailed him. "Sheila here says you were having technical issues. Glad to see that's all cleared up. Can't tell you how excited we all are to show you our appreciation for your bravery and fortitude. From what I'm hearing, your story is astonishing and inspiring."

"A lot of people died," Jen said and didn't know why she said it out loud.

Her statement caused a flinch in those listening, a slight blink, a near hiccup. Except the president, who never stopped moving. It didn't faze him. "The nation appreciates their sacrifice, of course. And that's exactly the reason I need you two to talk to Sheila. We're gonna bring this story to the rest of the nation in the big show tomorrow. We'll give you ladies a chance to clean up and see you then!" Ever the showman, he actually winked and handed the phone back to Sheila.

Sheila grabbed it, talking the whole time. "We can't wait to finally meet you! At the Concert to Restore Florida!"

"The what?" Araminta said.

"The president will be honoring you… and the memories of the rest of those poor souls who didn't make it back. We're going to be presenting your findings to the world, and gosh, won't that be exciting?"

"Wait, what? Presenting?" Jen and Araminta said at the same time.

"*Yes!* Yes! I know! Isn't that fantastic?"

"Slow down. We're presenting… what now?" Jen asked.

"The cure! The antidote. The solution! The... the thing that's going to kill the rest of the hornets!"

Jen was already shaking her head. "It's wasps, not hornets. And this isn't a cure. It's maybe a deterrent, at best. It won't kill anything."

Araminta asked, "Why on earth would you wait to tell people?"

For the first time, Sheila looked a little flustered. "Well, I ...uh, believe the overall thinking seemed to be that it would be for the best not to announce your findings quite so soon after... uh, other such extreme measures had been taken."

"Other measures?" Jen didn't like the sound of that.

"Oh. You haven't heard about it yet."

"Heard what?"

"Well, I have no doubt that once you approach the Orlando airport, it will be obvious. Actually, no, you won't see anything. The smoke is currently blanketing the entire eastern seaboard."

"Smoke?"

"Oh, yes. From the detonations."

"Detonations. You mean, bombs?" Araminta asked. "Bombs. You bombed Miami?"

Sheila didn't want to get into it, but finally gave a half nod and a shrug. As Araminta closed her eyes and rubbed her temples, Jen stared out the window as the undersecretary explained how several large nations had cooperated and eradicated the murder hornet threat.

Jen shook her head. "That sounds... All you did was spread them out."

Sheila shook her head. "Oh, no. Our approval ratings went through the roof! Americans love decisive action. And besides, now with your *cure*, we don't have anything to worry about! So, as for your itinerary, you'll be immediately flown back to the States and because of our extremely limited time window—no one knew you would be coming back out of the jungle." She gave a light laugh as if Jen and Araminta had been caught up in traffic for some silly reason, like a family of ducks crossing the road. "So I'm afraid there won't have time for a hospital visit—"

"Hold up," Araminta said. "Hold... on... up. You're talking to two people who have been through an extremely traumatic event. We are dehydrated, exhausted, and in dire need of proper medical attention and rest."

"I'm afraid, in order to keep things on time, we have no choice. Kid Rock is right after you and he's got such a tight schedule. We can't change that now, can we?"

Araminta and Jen glanced at each again, both equally confused. Araminta said, "I guess... not?"

"I'm sure they've given you plenty to drink. You know, to help with any dehydration. Have you tried Gatorade? Soak up those electrolytes. You raided the first aid kit, right? Great! We'll get you into makeup and wardrobe." She drew back, making a big show out of looking at her phone. "I'm so, so sorry. I have to take this. I've been trying to get in touch with this agent all day!" The screen went black.

Araminta said, "Well, then. It's decided. When we get there, I'm going to make sure they put us in the most expensive suite and we will have no choice but to order every single thing room service offers. Food. Drink. Baths for days. A deep-tissue massage from large men who have muscles on muscles and only speak French. Two, for each of us." She waggled her eyebrows and gave Jen a smirk. "And it's all going on Sheila's expense account."

CHAPTER 24

Next thing Andy knew, he was on his back and three or four defensive tackles from the White Power Dumbfucks stood on his arms while more of them wrapped duct tape around his ankles. One guy, somehow even bigger than anybody, went around and held them down like a silent Florida Sasquatch. His name was Jonny. They bound the Exterminators' wrists with the tape, but with Andy they'd been confused about how to go about it and got carried away and ended up using a whole roll to strap both arms to his chest. Jonny put his boot on Andy's jaw, just under the ear, and pushed down. Andy's mouth popped open like a goddamn trash can, and somebody else shoved a stainless steel scouring pad inside. Another roll of duct tape was used to make sure the scouring pads weren't going anywhere.

The defensive tackles carried them away from the main deck, stepping off onto wooden planks hidden by the swampy water. Jonny carried Andy by himself. They followed an unmarked path for a while and when everybody stopped, Jonny dropped Andy into the twelve inches of swamp water.

He immediately lifted his head out of the shallow swamp and snorted water out of his nose, making sure he could breathe. In his Taser-induced hazy vision, it almost looked as if he was looking at a large square out in the swamp, even lengths on all sides, with the water at the bottom. Eventually, he made out the two large trees, each about fifteen feet apart. They both forked at the same height, and a length of railroad tie had been settled in the branches, connecting the two trees. It appeared to have been there a long time, as the trees had grown around the moss-covered tie.

Five nooses hung from it.

A cheap folding chair waited in a few inches of water under each noose.

In the end, there were too many of the militiamen and no amount of twisting or kicking made much difference. Jonny stayed out of it, watching quietly and hanging back with Thomas, Sigrid, and Joe.

The Exterminators went up on the chairs and the nooses went around their necks. The hands vanished and the ropes drew tight and everyone backed away at the same time, leaving them to stand on the warped, rusty chairs, acutely aware of how unbalanced all four legs rested on more wooden planks under all the brown water.

Sigrid stepped forward in rubber boots, arms outspread and looking skyward. "I offer praise unto thee, who delivered our prayers. Even if I was a mite unsure how we'd manage things when said prayers marched right into camp." She cast a glance at Thomas, who was smart enough to keep his mouth shut. "Our Lord's loving grace carried us to this point. So that means—" she glared at her men in the dying light. "That means, from here on out, it's our responsibility. Understand? Mistakes will not be tolerated. Got no problem adding as many meat necklaces as I need. Find yourself up there with these boys so fast it'll make your head spin."

She looked up at the men on the chairs. "Y'all sleep tight. Tomorrow you're gonna run a few errands for us. Nothin' to it." She turned to go, then stopped. Drew herself upright, turned her head, all sly and snapped her fingers, like a sociopath who'd learned to imitate the timing for a joke. "Oh, yes. That's right." She turned and looked back at all of them. "We only got four more trucks."

Someone splashed in the water behind the Exterminators. Andy's chair gave a sudden surge and his sense of balance tipped back into nothingness. He went up on his tiptoes and arched his back, heart slamming against his ribs. Blood surged in his ears. He heard Joe's voice. "Real tough now, ain't ya, fuckface?"

"Language!" Sigrid said. Her heart wasn't in it, though. "And you know better. Not him."

"Fine." Joe kept his foot on Andy's chair, gave it a shake every so often. "Wanted these old boys, this sonofabitch especially, to know that me, that I—me, me. That me, me... y'all thought I was some dumbass backwoods peckerhead, and I outsmarted all y'all Army pussies." Looking back, Andy wished he could have stopped himself. Maybe things would have worked out different. Maybe not. Probably not. He tried to tell himself it didn't matter. Still felt like it was all his fault. Because when Joe had to brag about how smart he was and all that, Andy couldn't help it. This was an automatic reaction, ingrained after years of being helpless and abused;

the only power he had left was to let the bastard know how little he cared. How he found the whole thing funny as hell. He started to laugh.

And even though he couldn't speak because of the steel wool in his mouth, laughter was, as they say, universal.

Joe said, "Fine. Fine! Keep laughing, asswipe," and a half second later Jonny kicked House's chair clear off the platform. The railroad tie barked with the sudden weight. The drop wasn't fast enough to snap his neck, though, and strangulation took a long, long time. He bucked and he thrashed and he kicked while the men stood around and watched and sniggered.

Sigrid clasped her hands and watched like she was observing something as natural as a picturesque sunset.

And throughout the entire ordeal, every single awful second, Andy vowed that he would kill them all with an intensity that matched only his love for Jen. He wouldn't just kill them. He would make them scream and beg. He thought of hammers. Of pliers. Of scissors. Of railroad spikes. Of chain saws. Flashes of torture, threats of horrible violence sparked through his head as he screamed in impotent rage.

They left House there to hang with them all night.

* * * *

Next morning, Sigrid was back with over a dozen men.

Andy growled around the steel wool.

"Mornin' yourself, sunshine," Sigrid said while the men unhooked the ropes and sent the Exterminators tumbling into the mud. They cut the duct tape around their ankles and kicked them until they were up and moving. Sigrid led the way through the swamp, the meadow, and up the hill to the pig farm.

They left House behind, still dangling from the railroad tie. A few of the militiamen stuck around and set up a folding ladder so they could drape something that looked like a fishing vest over House's shoulders. Then they got the hell out of there and didn't waste time catching up with the rest of the group.

Andy recognized the place as a large-scale hog farm. Where he grew up, hog farms were common and plenty of work was to be found, as long as you didn't mind a job that was essentially moving pig shit from one place to another. The barns closest to the retention pond and stabilization lagoon were for mating and gestating; each barn successively closer to the other end focused on a particular stage of life, like farrowing, weaning, and fattening. Andy noticed the doors had been barred shut. Scraps from broken pallets covered any windows. The buildings had been sealed. And while the smell remained, the whole place, the whole goddamn operation, was quiet, as if all the hogs were asleep or dead. Andy suspected that something worse was happening.

As she marched them up through the middle of the farm, Sigrid confirmed it. "Lotta folks think these murder hornets are hell-spawn, sent from the Devil himself. And fake news is only happy to report it. 'Course, Lord helps those that help themselves, and what we have here is a giant, gift-wrapped opportunity to demonstrate our God-given superiority over the mud people."

They reached a large, gravel-covered lot. Four semis hooked to livestock trailers waited for them. The fourth trailer's back doors stood open. One of the militia boys drove a forklift up to the truck, carrying four gestation crates atop a pallet. Two side by side, then two more on top. Each steel gestation cage held two fat hogs, dead or unconscious. Wasp husks peppered the crates, pinned between metal and unconscious pigskin. The forklift settled the pallet on top of another four crates upon a pallet inside the trailer.

Andy figured they'd set out caged pigs as bait downstate. Could have been something as simple as bringing back one infected hog. That's all it would have taken. Just one animal. They'd planned ahead and when they brought it back, they had a sealed barn full of ripe pigs ready go. When it came to calculating how many of the wasps they might have bred, he stumbled and went around in circles. Math had never come easy. Numbers had a tendency to get slippery and refused to stick where they were supposed to stay on the page. He tried tapping out the possible numbers in each crate, counting silently in his head. It had to be in the hundreds. Each truck could transport forty, fifty crates at least.

Sigrid said, "Some folks will insist on calling it bioterrorism or some such nonsense. For those of us in the light, we can see that it is nothing more than our Lord's will at work. Joe figured out a way to further our cause without undue risk, and his plan has true value. Truth be told, I'd bet our boys would be more nervous about the neighborhoods you'll be parking in rather than the cargo." The militia guys thought that was pretty funny. "Therefore, let our Lord's will be done."

Knives came out and sliced through the duct tape around their jaws. The same guys who laughed earlier thought it was hilarious when the tape ripped away plenty of Exterminator hair. They used pliers when ripping the scouring pads out and left them where they fell. A few well- placed kicks in the backs of knees put the Exterminators on their forearms and knees.

"Speak out of turn, or ill of us or the Lord God, and you will be silenced again," Sigrid said. She placed a phone next to each of the scouring pads. "I really am proud of that nephew of mine. Of course, it's my side of the family," she said, giving her husband the side-eye. "He's got himself a special request." She stopped in front of Andy. "Believe this boy has hisself a comic-book alter ego."

Four of them came for him. Cut away the tape. Stripped him naked. Then put him in his Florida Man costume. First the tights, then the fake muscles, the cape. The shoes. The cowl. The kneepads. The gloves. Then the suicide bomber vest.

More of the militia moved on Carver, Ramirez, and Squirrel. Cut the tape around their wrists. Gave each of them a fishing vest crisscrossed with wires. Wrapped a bicycle chain up under their crotch and locked it with three padlocks up the center, and another at the throat for the hell of it. The vests were heavy as fuck, like they had been filled with lead fishing weights.

Jonny shook each of the Exterminators like they were starved dogs and made sure the suicide-bomb vests were locked nice and tight. Joe strutted around, took a few pictures of Andy in his Florida Man costume, then fiddled with his smartphone, supervising everything, until he was finally satisfied and said, "Okay. That's enough." He took a deep breath and opened his mouth.

Sigrid caught his eye and said, "No big speeches. Just do it."

Joe closed his mouth. Looked to his smartphone. Typed in a number. Hit send.

Back down in the swamp, there was a *bang*. Nothing outrageous, but there was some heft to it. The sound hung in the air long enough to qualify itself as a genuine explosion. Not huge. It was enough to get everybody's attention. Ramirez crossed himself.

"There went yer buddy," Sigrid said. "Mess with these vests, or do any damn thing I dislike and the same thing happens to you. Nothing too big, so forget any ideas you've got about rushing any of us. Also, I'd hang on to those phones, I was y'all," she added, casual as ordering breakfast. "You get more'n five, six feet away from your phone and all those plastic explosives in your vests there go boom and bang and make a hell of a mess."

She waited until they had each picked up their own phone. "Good, *good* boys." As if they were being praised for not shitting on the carpet. "Each of those phones has an address ready to go. A trained monkey can follow the directions, obeying all laws and such, and when you get close enough to park these trucks where we want, you get to walk away. You'll be watched some of the time. 'Course, you won't know when or where. But you get to where we want, the phone'll go dead, and you're free to walk away. Go see a locksmith or whoever you want. Can't imagine you'll be in a hurry to turn yourselves in."

She turned to the rest of the militia. "And y'all thought it was a joke. That Joe wasn't gonna amount to anything. It was a waste of a hunnert dollars for them credit hours at a community college. Well. Y'all take a good look. Coulda' been you driving these rigs this morning instead."

"Is this what your fuck toys were doing last night?" Carver asked.

Sigrid cocked her head. "I'll let you get away with that one stupid question. Seems only right. You boys don't seem awfully bright. Ask another dumb question, and Joe'll be happy to cut out your tongue."

"I got a fucking question," Andy announced.

"Ignore him," Carver said. "I got a question about the cargo. A serious question."

"I got a serious fucking question too," Andy said. Louder.

"The cargo doesn't concern you," Sigrid told Carver.

"Only if it becomes a concern on my way to the destination." Carver looked at everyone. "We all know what's in those trucks. How do I know I'll make it to the destination before I get an assload of murder hornets in my back seat?"

"You don't." Sigrid gave another black-gummed smile. "They been timed out, more or less. Got yourself an hour or two. Them hell-spawn, they grow fast. Maybe less than an hour. Guess you'd best be on your way then and stop all this dillydallying."

"Got me all dressed up," Andy said before anybody forgot him, "least you could do is answer a question before fucking me."

Jonny picked up Andy with the chain under his crotch and dropped him on his head a few times. Picked him up again and this time held him aloft. Joe knelt next to Andy's upside-down head and said, "I don't know, Grandma. This one's more dark than white, got no sense. Let Jonny crack his skull. Let in the light."

"Nah, you just need a soft touch. Not everything requires a hammer. Sometimes you just need something sharp." She unfolded a straight razor from her dress and turned to Andy. "You had something to say."

Jonny dropped Andy and stepped back as if he didn't want any blood on his clothes. Andy took a while sitting up. He managed to sit back on his haunches, swaying and drooling blood. "I have a question. Serious. A serious question," he said, all quiet and courteous around the blood.

Everybody thought that his sudden transformation into meek and trembling
choirboy after his beating was hilarious.

"Ignore him," Carver said. "He's not right in the head."

More laughter. "Ain't it the truth," Sigrid said. "But I told you to shut
your mouth."

They swept Carver's legs out from under him and flattened him. One
put his cowboy boot on the back of Carver's head and pushed his face
into the gravel. Ramirez and Squirrel decided to get back down on their
forearms and knees before somebody else got pissed and slammed them
into the ground.

Andy, on the other hand, found his feet and managed to stand without
assistance. He faced Sigrid, arms up, eyes downcast in respect. Or fear.
His face was a mass of contusions. One eye was swollen nearly shut, his
lips were split in several places, and fresh blood leaked out of his right
ear. He spit out a tooth. "Question."

"Are you absolutely sure?" Sigrid asked. She smiled at her straight razor.
"I helped castrate more'n my share of bucks with this. You thought last
night was so funny, you wanna keep laughing, then me'n the boys here'll
fry us up some Rocky Mountain oysters. Make you watch us eat 'em with
scrambled eggs. So. You certain you want to keep going?"

"Yes, ma'am," Andy said. He weaved back and forth. The silence
stretched and humidity under the rising sun grew heavier. Somewhere a
dog barked, then grew quiet. The birds had all gone clammed up, as if they
had gone into hiding. The distant chattering of a helicopter could be heard.

Sigrid grew impatient. "Well?"

Andy ceased swaying and finally met her eyes. She saw neither respect
nor fear in his eyes. Only hate, spiraling deeper and deeper. It caught her
off guard, for just an instant. He grinned at her, a wild, lunatic smile. "I
don't know who put the sand in your cunt. Well, that's not the question—"
That's as far as he got before they kicked his legs out from under him like
Carver and he went down like a sack of potatoes.

Sigrid's lips were pressed so tight they'd lost all color, a furious reaction
that must run in the family's DNA. She yelled at her husband, "Get over
here."

Thomas had been hanging back near the edge of the group. Violence
seemed to make him queasy and want to stay out of the way, under the
radar. She knew this and seemed determined to satiate her wrath using
both her husband and Andy as cannon fodder. "Shoot this disrespectful
pile of excrement in the balls immediately. Give him a few moments to
appreciate the mistakes he's made in life. Then two in his head."

Thomas knew better than to argue. He already had his pistol out and was moving toward Andy. This act would give him nightmares for the rest of his life, but the fear of his wife eclipsed anything and everything else. And any hesitation would be punished. He cocked the pistol and crossed the last ten feet, finger tightening on the trigger.

Carver started to yell, "You fuck—"

Andy was a half-second away from getting his balls blasted across the gravel when the world above exploded and the sky turned to night.

CHAPTER 25

"If she's waiting for us," Araminta said as the stretch SUV limo pulled into a line of vehicles along the inner drive of Gaylord Palms Resort & Convention Center, "I won't be held responsible if I slap those little chipmunk cheeks." The two of them got out, and even though the screaming and cheering crowd was disappointed they weren't celebrities, a small army of assistants armed with signs and tablets besieged the two women like a flock of nervous vultures. They knew what the two of them looked like and weren't about to let their quarry out of their sights. The path of least resistance seemed to be the best option, so Jen and Araminta allowed themselves to be marched through the elaborate convention center.

The center was dominated by a glass atrium well over an acre in size, serving as the hub that connected the outer rings of the hotel circle, creating a vast, open space patterned after an idyllic version of old Florida. The place gave the impression, reinforced by the real trees and foliage, that you were outside, traversing through the streets and across wooden bridges, despite the artificially cool climate, with entire buildings and pirate ships and plenty of bars and shopping, all connected by walkways curving over and around lush lagoons.

While waiting in security, Jen and Araminta watched the videos of the botched arrest and "commercial" of the Exterminators. They watched them in the wrong order, and Jen thought that Andy had been arrested or was dead when Araminta pointed out the time stamps and that made them watch the short video about the adventures of Florida Man again and laugh their asses off.

The aftereffects of all the adrenaline were kicking in.

Word was, the president of the United States had wanted the Disney Corporation to bow and offer to host the inevitable fundraiser and broadcast it on their own channel, ABC. However, Disney, for reasons known only to them, had remained silent. Perhaps it was a long-standing grudge. Perhaps it was a misunderstanding. Either way, with bitterness soaked into every detail, the federal government essentially launched its own GoFundMe and held a celebrity fundraiser for the project to rebuild southeast Florida in the nearby Gaylord Palms Resort & Convention Center. With NBC.

The assistants assigned to Jen and Araminta whisked them through the crowds and more security checkpoints until they reached backstage. Someone handed Jen a test tube full of a bright purple liquid. It looked like some kind of glass cleaner. "What's this?"

"It's the cure!" Sheila said, swooping between them. "Thank God you are here." She pulled a mock-worry face. "I don't mind telling you, I was worried. My God."

"What is this again?" Jen sloshed the test tube.

"Careful!" Sheila laughed, then dismissed it with, "I had my assistant whip that up. I think it's some kind of cleaner, so don't drink it, or spill any on your clothes." She looked them up and down. "Well... later, when you have your gowns on. You'll be giving that to the president."

"Why?"

"It's the cure! The medicine, poison, whatever! Of course you have to be seen giving it to the president."

"But that's all been taken to a lab," Jen said.

"What difference does it make?" Sheila said. "You must be seen giving him something! What else would you do? Go out and wave at people?" Her phone buzzed. "I have to take this." She looked to the handlers with venom. "Make sure these two get into makeup. Now." Her voice went saccharine as she turned to her phone. "Thank God you called."

The handlers steered Jen and Araminta through the backstage chaos until plopping them into makeup chairs, where the women faced ultrabright, zero-forgiveness lighting. They looked at themselves in the mirrors and saw visions of themselves from a bad future.

Everything came crashing down inside Jen's head. Staring at herself was the last straw. Too much, too fast. They'd been jerked around, dismissed, and ignored ever since they came upon the two pilots on the side of the mountain. Since then, every person she'd had to talk to had given her the same vague buzzwords and useless advice. The overwhelming sweetness that oozed around the razor-bladed patronizing was giving her diabetes. The next man who tried explaining literally anything about insects in general was in serious danger of being punched in the nose. She gave considerable weight to the option of finding a surreptitious way to trigger the fire alarm before realizing with a physical start that maybe she didn't have to go quite that nuclear and disrupt everybody and all their big plans. Nonetheless… this was unsustainable. She needed a break.

Jen caught Araminta's eyes in the mirror and gave her head a tiny shake.

Araminta, tuned to Jen's wavelength as usual, was way ahead. She stood and eased around the chair and leaned in for a confidential chat with the four or five makeup artists and assistants hovering around, saying, "I'm so sorry, but… can you give us a chance to freshen up? My girl here… her cycle… I just noticed…"

Jen picked up what Araminta was laying down and jerked upright, covering both her crotch and chest, acting all modest. "It's that time…I forgot." She pretended to remember and covered her crotch with both hands.

Everybody caught on right away and rushed around while looking everywhere and anywhere except in Jen's direction. Somebody gave her an old towel for some reason. The whole time, they could only focus on Jen's shoes; she wore her creased and stained boots, leather still moist with blood and jungle.

An escape path opened up and gave Jen and Araminta a wide berth to the hall. Once out of makeup, they slipped into the crowd of hundreds of people backstage. With such a large show about to happen, it was easy to force their way backwards through a security line that determined who got backstage and who didn't. Araminta danced through, pulling a starstruck Jen along, disappearing into the thousands who thronged through the rest of the hotel.

From there, they kept to the fringes, and Jen soon found an unobtrusive map that directed them to an elevator bank. Inside, she hit the highest button. She wanted a little peace and quiet, a chance to steady herself, a moment to breathe on her own.

The top floor, while much quieter than all the activity below, was far from deserted. VIPs strolled among frantic housekeeping staff. Araminta stopped by one of the suites, and made a big show of looking for her room key. She held up one particularly frazzled-looking cleaning woman and explained that her friend was very sick. "I'm so sorry… I don't know what I did with my key," she said in Spanish, lowering her voice and flickering her eyes to a nearby, pale Jen. "Pregnant.

Morning sickness," Araminta whispered.

The woman let them inside without a word.

Jen went in first and wandered around the opulence with a dazed grin. Araminta bowed to the housekeeper and deftly hung the *DO NOT DISTURB* sign outside the door before shutting and locking it behind her.

Floor-to-ceiling windows overlooked the exuberant activity of the elaborate water park. There was a balcony with several lounge chairs and a table if you felt like getting out of the air-conditioning and watching the families and kids scampering around the pools. And that was just the front room. Bedrooms and bathrooms flanked the living room. Abstract art. Ornate furniture.

Araminta checked out the extensive bar. The selection was bigger than most pubs or dive lounges she'd ever been. This place had everything she'd ever heard of and a few things that surprised her. Including fresh fruit. She found that she also had crushed ice at the press of a button and crushed iced made damn near anything possible. She set about making the most complicated cocktails she could remember, taking full advantage of the well-equipped bar.

She froze for a moment and left it all out on the counter. First things first. Ambience. She turned on the TV and found nothing but wall-to-wall coverage of the big concert fundraiser on nearly every channel. Absolutely not. Eventually, she found a show that always made her laugh, where Americans went looking for houses or flats in European countries and never failed to flinch when they realized their king-sized beds wouldn't fit in the bedrooms.

Jen, meanwhile, was making very slow and graceful snow angels on a bed roughly the size of a small country. Andy was still alive. Or had been, as of the time of the last video. She watched the flickering lights on the ceiling, absently wondering if they were reflections from the pools. The lower bedspread had been put on tight enough that even Jen's weight couldn't break the seal, yet under that, the mattress felt quite soft and welcoming. This gentle dichotomy, the yin and yang of hotel beds, brought Jen some peace. It settled her.

Until there was a knock at the door.

* * * *

Somebody, mostly likely Joe with his new electrical engineering classes, had been smart enough to pack concentrated amounts of ammonium nitrate fuel oil stolen from a highway development under the livestock trailers, just enough to blast relatively small holes in the front corners and the back gates. Not only would these controlled blasts kill minimal numbers of the wasps inside and piss off the rest, they would rupture the weak spots in the livestock trailers, creating holes large enough so the wasps could escape.

Team White Power Dumbfucks had gotten lucky with the timing. The light show signaling the launch of the concert started a half-second before the explosions and when the audience went berserk, the tidal wave of cheering drowned out the rest of the commotion outside.

Beyond that, Team White Power Dumbfucks' plan lacked anything resembling finesse.

Then again, it didn't need much.

Their four trucks rolled up I-4, each a Russian doll where things got worse the deeper you dug. Two peeled off on 192 and approached the complex from the south. They slowed way down, waiting for their own signal. The second pair coasted past the target and got off on Osceola Parkway, hauling ass around the retention pond from the north. The plan then was merely that the lead truck on Osceola would provide both entry and diversion for the north pair, smashing through the temporary concrete barriers and unleashing hell on the parking lot as the detonations unleashed the wasps.

Taking advantage of the chaos, the second truck would blast through the new hole, pass the first truck, and jump onto one of the inner drives around the convention center. Later, security footage made it more than clear that this second driver not only made it past his pal, he floored it and gained considerable ground. The driver triggered the trailer explosions an instant before plowing into the security vehicles. He'd deliberately left his seat belt off and disabled the airbag; no way he wanted to be still alive when the wasps got loose. The impact killed him instantly. The momentum of the collision drove the wreckage into the far northeast corner building of the property.

Thirty seconds later, giving everyone enough time to react to the news about the northern assault, but hopefully not enough time for anybody to suspect a second surprise attack from the south, the second pair of trucks used the same tactic to get as close as possible to the main entrance.

The idea, of course, was never to get inside. Close was fine.

The wasps were more than capable of hunting on their own.

Hog blood dribbled from the lowest air vents in the crumpled livestock trailers. Security unloaded on the cab, thumping bullets into the windows, seats, and the already dead flesh of the driver. People ran, ducked behind cars.

Inside, sounds of wet movement.

* * * *

Sigrid had noted the importance of size from the beginning. So when they'd brought back the dying, infected pigs she'd had the waiting hogs already on a steady diet of every steroid and growth hormone, legal and otherwise, they could find. The eggs grew to the size of footballs; the bloated, splayed five-hundred-pound hogs could hold up to forty or fifty. Each. And so Team White Power Dumbfucks had managed to breed wasps bigger than had ever flown on Earth.

These weren't the size of sparrows. Or pigeons. Or even seagulls.

The wasps that crawled from the smoking rubble, still coated in slime and hog blood, had wingspans that rivaled Canada geese. Four goddamn feet. Their bodies bulged like balloon animals, heads larger than softballs. Ovipositors over eight inches. Stingers longer than a cell phone. They'd already eaten their way out of their hosts, spawned, and were now looking to feast and deposit fertilized eggs.

They boiled out of the crumpled livestock trailers and swarmed over the screaming, running crowd. They swirled for just a moment, as if selecting prey, then pounced.

The cheering inside the ballroom continued to drown out anything from outside. These people were here to party and Praise Jesus that America had, yet again, triumphed over a monumental threat. The show had just opened. The latest country ingenue had given her version of the national anthem and someone else led the crowd through "America the Beautiful."

Lee Greenwood had just started the second verse of his signature hit, "God Bless the U.S.A.," the one where he wanted to make damn sure everybody knew he was proud to be an American, when the first wasp floated into the ballroom.

CHAPTER 26

In the liquid silence inside Andy's mind, there was a moment where everything above Thomas's nose seemed to say *see everybody later* and hitched a ride on a truck door flying through his head. Even in death and missing both eyes, lingering fear of his wife still managed to compel the muscles in his hand to pull the trigger. The bullet popped into the dirt a few inches away from Andy's hip. The rest of Thomas got tired and sat down. He folded into himself and what was left of his brains slid into his lap.

That didn't seem quite real.

More darkness. Paralysis. Maybe a nap. Maybe a blink.

He decided he was dreaming. He wasn't actually sure about this.

Light again. The sky? Something huge passed overheard. A storm or something like it; a hurricane of scrap metal. The lines and corners of steel or aluminum, perfect and ordered at first, unfurling as it flew through the sky, twisting and cracking into splintered chaos. And naturally, from within the ruptured metal, the gestation cages came apart like wet cardboard, blending with the rest of the trailer wreckage. Then the hogs.

Hogs flew. Hogs exploded.

A silent monsoon flooded Andy's world, punctuated by jagged bolts of straining steel, blood and ichor coming down like acid rain. At first, the only thing he knew was that his face felt flushed from something warm and wet above him. Other than that, he was stunned and couldn't move.

Consciousness and abilities came crawling back, one at a time, like ashamed and bashful alcoholics after a truly spectacular bender. First, he realized he was breathing. Fantastic. Pain, and plenty of it, somehow everywhere and nowhere all at once. He went to stand. A little movement—

what was that children's song, something about fingers and toes, fingers and toes.

Well, most of 'em, anyway.

He tried to sit up and it was a bad idea from the beginning. His world rolled and his head smacked the wet gravel. He pushed himself up to his knees and forehead, put his hand out to find balance. He figured out he was covered in hog blood, but not only that, something else, almost like wet, hard-boiled eggs. Something slapped his cheek and the realization spun him in a new direction. The blood and pork was laced with the sluggish twitches of the bits of premature wasps, unable to fly.

Flashes of sight came faster now, like an older TV getting warmed up.

A high, distant whine throbbed in his ears. The silence had been less painful.

He raised his head higher and couldn't shake the feeling he'd woken up inside one of those UFO crop circles, out near the edge; everything seemed to radiate away from the center. Then he finally figured out there had been some kind of massive explosion. A mistake? An accident? Not unless the militia had something a hundred times bigger than what they'd used to blow up House.

Ramirez was dead. It looked to be instantaneous. Various pieces of metal had punctured his body in too many vital areas.

Squirrel was holding his head and kicking one of the militia men.

Sound faded in and out, like distant UHF signals.

Then he saw *her* and he didn't give a damn what had just happened.

Sigrid.

All he knew was that he had a promise to keep.

He had a vague awareness of a few other survivors struggling with consciousness all around, but they could wait. So could the tremendous size of the infant wasps. He had a feeling whatever the fuck these people had been injecting their hogs with, it wasn't Flintstones vitamins. There were a few fires burning here and there, and smoke everywhere. Carver was moving wraithlike through the militia members struggling to their feet and helping them back to sleep.

As he crawled toward Sigrid, Andy realized she might still have her razor and he didn't have anything, and only one hand at that. He found the bottom half of a wasp and twisted the three-inch stinger away from the abdomen, like plucking a stem from an underripe grape.

Sigrid had caught a lot of glass in the back of her head; it had cracked out of the truck door that peeled the top of Thomas's head from the rest of him. Some of it may have punctured her skull. She was having trouble

Jeff Jacobson

moving around. Her dress had been blown up, revealing two very pale, rather hairy legs that flopped and kicked. She kept trying to rise, to get to her hands and knees.

Andy watched her for a few seconds, then decided it was time to finish her off.

In the end, it wasn't a fair fight. At all.

Andy crawled over and drove his elbow into the small of her back. She made a sound like when you step on a cat. He flipped her over, kneeled on her throat and put one of her eyes out with the wasp stinger. She slapped at him and screamed soundlessly. The stinger was too slippery to pull free and was easier to just push it in further. She was still alive, and it seemed like she could still feel pain, so he jammed his thumb into the corner of her other eye to pop it out.

Before he could properly force the eyeball from its socket, huge hands encircled his neck and lifted him into the air.

He felt himself weightless for half a second, then more disorienting pain. Something beyond huge slammed into him. The ground. He rolled to his knees, shook his head. His bearings were coming back faster and faster now, and part of himself remembered Jonny.

Jonny was taller and heavier than House. Andy still could shop in the young men's section of the department store if he needed. A racist old bitch was one thing, this mountain of a man was something else.

It didn't matter much to Andy. It only meant he had to fight smarter.

He needed a weapon. Jonny was ten feet away and closing fast.

Carver came out of nowhere and jumped for the giant's back. He had a knife and was aiming for the neck. But the big man heard him and reacted. The knife hit bone and the blade skittered away through the thick shock of hair. Jonny roared and flung him away.

Something hot popped Andy's ear. He touched the superhero cowl and almost laughed. He'd forgotten he was still wearing his dumbass costume. His fingers came away bloody. He turned slowly, senses tingling, still trying to climb back to full strength. Something jerked at his cape.

He looked up and gaped at Joe, who was steadying a pistol in his direction with both hands. Another *pop*. Somewhere close to his face. Any tried to move and felt as if he was underwater. Time would not speed up. It was an awful dream, where a hateful man was taking soundless gunshots at him, and he could do nothing but shrink and try to wriggle away.

He threw himself sideways and found his old friend the ground again.

Joe took another shot, missed. This time, the slide stayed open. He was empty.

Carver kicked Jonny in the nuts. All that did was piss off Jonny even more. Blood ran freely from his skull, matting the hair and pooling around all the fat and curly hair down his back. He came up with a sneaky left hook that twisted Carver right off his feet. Spun him twice before he hit the ground.

Joe dropped the gun and went for the big survival knife in his belt.

Andy kept scrambling sideways until his elbow hit Sigrid's leg. She trembled a bit but that was the only reaction. He shoved himself backwards on his elbows and heels and held his right boot over Sigrid's head, staring Joe down. The threat was clear enough. Keep going and Andy would drive his heel into her face.

Joe didn't stop.

Andy understood that Joe had called his bluff and revealed to everybody that Andy was faking. It wasn't that Andy had any problems kicking Sigrid in the face, it was more the fact that it wouldn't make a damn bit of difference.

He rolled over to run and got caught up in his own goddamn cape. Went down on his stomach. He knew Joe was nearly on top of him and struggled to find his feet. Everything kept moving in slow-motion. He was finished. Joe would step on his back and saw his head off with that big knife. He hoped Carver would be able to kill one or the other before both militia members ganged up on him.

His fingers, scrabbling through the gravel, found something smooth.

Sigrid's straight razor handle.

He whipped it around, catching Joe across the wrist mid-strike. The slash surprised the hell out of Joe, who didn't look like he quite followed the cause-and-effect chain of events that led to his forearm being split open to the bone. The razor had severed several important tendons, and the survival knife clattered from Joe's suddenly unresponsive fingers.

Any hesitation would get Andy killed. So he whipped the razor back at Joe in an awkward uppercut. The swing passed by Joe's face so smoothly he was sure he'd missed the man completely. He'd felt no resistance, no tug at the blade. In the next instant, Joe would grab that big Rambo knife with his good hand and split him from waist to shoulder in less time than it took to blink.

But Joe only took a step back. He raised a hand. Maybe he wanted to wave a fly away.

Whether the fly was real or not, Andy never saw it. He'd been wrong about not making contact.

A good chunk of Joe's upper lip and most of his nose weren't attached to the rest of his skull anymore. Andy had no idea where the missing body parts had gone. Blood gushed over Joe's chin as if it couldn't wait to leave his poisoned head. The yellow hue of a few of his upper front teeth stood out among all the crimson. He took a blind swing.

Andy ducked it easily and followed by cracking his left elbow across Joe's jaw. The man went down and Andy followed like a tick on a hound. He shoved his stump, still wrapped in helpful duct tape, straight into Joe's gasping mouth as far as he could, crushing the man's tongue against the back of his throat. With his right, he covered Joe's fresh nose holes with his palm and put as much weight as he could into his shoulders. All the blood was slippery as hell, so Andy leaned in harder. Joe's arms and legs flailed in a hilarious minstrel show as Andy introduced him to Jesus.

Carver, as it turned out, was only keeping Jonny distracted until he found a working gun. At the end, Jonny had gotten his hands around Carver's throat and thought he was just about to finish this particular problem when Carver pushed the pistol up under his jaw. Didn't matter how big you were—four or five .45 slugs blown through your brain pan would at least get you to slow down and rethink your situation.

* * * *

Shadows overhead. Military choppers. They circled, making sure their .50-caliber automatics were noticed. A loudspeaker announced, "Get your hands up, dumbasses." Something about the voice sounded familiar.

Carver glared at the choppers and didn't move. Andy glanced at them, decided he didn't give a damn, and pulled his costume tights down far enough to take a piss on Joe's corpse. Squirrel didn't bother reacting at all. It didn't look he'd even heard the helicopters and he kept kicking a guy who given up and curled into a fetal ball.

The first three choppers settled, a couple troop transports and some sort of gunship, sending smoke and dust throughout the hog farm. Soldiers fanned out through the swirling debris. A couple got close, winced when they saw Joe. Even though Andy's urine had washed a lot of the blood on his face away, Joe was still probably the deadest guy they'd ever seen.

Sigrid, though, was moving a little, but nobody was sure if she was still alive or if it was just nerves, the way a snake might writhe when you chop its head off. Either way, nobody volunteered to give her CPR.

Thunder cracked and hurricane winds rose and dipped as a truly gargantuan helicopter settled at the edge of the blast crater. A Boeing

V-22 Osprey. This monstrosity had two open propellers on either side that could rotate up and forward, allowing the aircraft to both take off and land vertically, while also using the propellers for great speed. Stairs unfolded as the door swung open. A hazy figure descended in no particular hurry.

Erratic winds whipped the smoke back and forth, alternately revealing and obscuring a tall, thin apparition in a suit dark enough to make an undertaker worry if it was appropriate. The figure paused to light a cigarette after deciding there wasn't enough smoke in the air. Haaga's eyes were so sunken you couldn't tell the color if you got up close with a flashlight.

He took a few drags, filled his lungs with enough smoke to breathe properly. Spent some time looking things over. Finally got bored enough and spoke. "Honored to meet you, Captain Florida Man or whomever. Always happy to see the winds of justice blowing where needed."

"Go fuck yourself," Andy suggested. He was still getting used to hearing and his own words sounded booming and hollow.

Haaga didn't appear to take it personally. He peered down at Sigrid. "Good morning, madam. You appear to be in distress."

Sigrid gasped and shuddered like a fish too far from water.

Carver ignored her and asked, "How long? How long you been watching?"

"Haven't been watching. Not since that shit you pulled at the nursing home." He let smoke drift out of his mouth on its own. "But I have been following." Meanwhile, a soldier came up with a pair of bolt cutters and snapped the chains so they could slip out of the vests.

Haaga nodded at Andy. "Stapled a tracking device in your arm back at the club. After you fellas torched the bus, I had a separate department track you from the Costco all the way out here. And when other satellites picked up the detonation earlier, a decision was made half an hour ago to erase this particular bunch of pretend Nazi dipshits from the funny pages before they could do any damage."

"Tell that to House," Andy said.

Haaga gave the barest of nods. "That's why we're here now."

"No rush," Carver said.

"You're lucky the trucks were the primary target, not the militia. We wouldn't be having this discussion otherwise. Stop whining. You're still standing."

"Complicates things for you, don't it," Carver said. "Leaving us alive."

"True enough," Haaga said. "You have no fans among upper management."

"Except you."

Haaga gave an actual laugh and the sound gave Andy the same chills as Sigrid's smile. Haaga said, "I'm not your fan. I'm not your friend. *You are a means to an end for me*."

"Sir! Sir! You need to see this." A wide-eyed soldier ran up with a tablet. He caught Haaga's expression and said, "Right...now?"

Haaga started to wave him off, but seeing the soldier's face, he looked down to catch the images. He jerked his attention back to Carver. "Trucks left earlier? How many? More than four?" Neither Carver or Andy answered. "And you saw no reason to let me know?"

"You didn't ask."

Haaga almost laughed again. He couldn't deny Carver's answer. He looked back down at Sigrid. She was still alive. Or at least still twitching. "Clever, clever girl. Would've liked to have seen her face when she realized it didn't matter." He caught the puzzled looks from Carver and Andy. "Your girlfriend," he said, nodding at Andy, "Jen Huang and her friends found the... well, from what I've been told, I can't quite say it's a cure. Or an antidote. Not a magic bullet, exactly. But damned if she didn't discover a hell of an insect repellent back in the jungle. Guess the wasps can't stand it. They're announcing all this at the big event in Orlando." He reconsidered. "Of course, it's too late for anyone at the event, including the president."

"Get a new president," Carver suggested.

"She's alive?" Andy asked. He hadn't moved while Haaga spoke. The question was emotionless, damn near flippant. But only if you weren't paying attention and missed how the hair at the back of Andy's neck bristled.

"Alive? Don't see why not. She's delivering this to the president. On stage. Or would've. Now?" Haaga turned the tablet around for Andy.

More footage from cell phones. Mostly distant, from a nearby expressway. Some kind of big-ass hotel, a huge resort center dominated by a truly gigantic atrium. Wild, zooming shots of trucks on fire and people running. And of course, the wasps.

"Goddamn, they got big," Carver said.

"You said Jen is there, right now?" Andy asked.

"Supposed to be, yes."

Andy stared at Haaga. He held Sigrid's razor loose, but ready to use at any second. He readjusted his grip, putting the words together in his head, little by little. It had already been a long day and he'd lost track of the last time he'd taken one of Carver's pills. He felt as if he had glass dust under his eyelids. "Why'd you call 'em wasps? Everybody else calls 'em murder hornets."

Haaga shrugged. "That's the term your girlfriend used. I've read her work. She knows what she's talking about. She has clearly identified them as wasps."

That was enough for Andy. He threw the razor away. "Help me, then. Help me save her."

Carver relieved the soldier of his pistol and gave Haaga a glare that made it clear he wanted to put the barrel under Haaga's jaw, like he had with Jonny. "Tell you what," Carver said in a conversational tone, knowing damn well he had a better chance of teaching a grizzly to square dance than rattling a man like Haaga. "We're gonna borrow your chopper and pilot for a while if you don't mind."

Smoke eased on out of Haaga's mouth like it was liquid in slow motion and he appeared about as concerned as if he had a hangnail. "It's all yours. Actually…" Haaga almost smiled. "I insist. The president is under attack. Sounds like a job for the Exterminators." He used his cigarette to gesture at his helicopter. "Shouldn't take you more than twenty, twenty-five minutes to get there."

Andy was already picking his way through the dead, gathering shotguns, pistols, anything he thought he could use to pulverize the wasps. He missed his old buddy the AA-12 and the sling. No telling where the militia kept those and no time to look.

"And him?" Carver cocked his head at Squirrel. They'd gotten him out of his explosive vest and he was wandering around, giving every militia member he found a few solid kicks even though they were dead. It seemed to make him feel better.

"I'm fine letting him wander off. He's earned it." Haaga exhaled.

Carver vanished along with the cigarette smoke.

Haaga pulled out his phone. Dialed. Cut off whoever answered. "Yeah, I know. This has top priority. Triple the official count of the dead and call it an estimate. Remind them the president himself is trapped. The surviving Exterminators are on the way."

The big Osprey rose like a tired eagle, slow and caring little of grace, but when the rotors tipped forward, it swooped smoothly away, going faster and faster, as if it had only been pretending to be old and frail. Haaga continued. "There's just two left, but they are the tip of the spear that the American government has launched in an all-out effort to save the president." Sigrid groaned. Sounded like she tried to say the word *please*, but it came out as more of a keening noise instead. Haaga put his shoe on her neck to keep her quiet for a while.

"Yes, the Exterminators are back. You can't use the actual word, but I want to read and hear the term *hero*."

CHAPTER 27

Araminta opened the door for Sheila and said, "Hey girl, where you been? You need a drink."

Sheila most definitely was not in the mood for a drink. Her voice quivered with a thousand anxieties. "I can't believe you ran away! That, that was so—That has never, *never* happened before. You must be downstairs! Now! The president himself is waiting! The show has already started! Oh my God, we are so late!"

Araminta was having none of it and wouldn't let Sheila's frantic mood bring her down. "Chillax, girl. Take a sip of this pina colada. Heaven. Absolutely heaven. Careful, though. My goodness. Maybe shouldn't have used one-fifty-one rum."

Sheila resisted the urge to slap the glass out of Araminta's hand. She started to shout instead. "You can't—"

The first explosion jolted her into silence. It didn't shake the room or anything as drastic, but it was loud and unexpected enough to halt Sheila's diatribe. Then the second blast detonated somewhere beyond the wing of the hotel across the water park. The sound brought Jen out of the bedroom and drew them all to the balcony.

After the hours inside the hotel, the overwhelming Florida heat and humidity hit like a big, soft hammer. It was almost as bad as the jungle. Nothing could really be seen, not at first anyway. The blast caught folks' attention for just a moment, but it wasn't more than a few seconds before they turned back to their children, the water, the fun. Then a whisper of black smoke worked its way into the sky above the opposite wing.

The first wasps found the water park even before the women heard the sirens rise.

"Oh no," Jen whispered. Her mind reeled at the size of the wasps. It didn't seem possible. It felt as if prehistory was launching itself on modern civilization. She started screaming, "Get inside, get in the water! Hide!" But from the top floor, her voice couldn't compete with the splashing, children yelling, or reggae blasting from hidden speakers. None of those frolicking had noticed the threat yet, oblivious to death gathering in fury. Evolution seemed to have bred that sixth sense out of most humans.

In equal fury, Jen threw a chair off the balcony, just to get somebody's attention. Nobody noticed, because as it fell, a second set of explosions came from the front of the hotel.

The chair hit a palm tree, tumbled through some ferns, but now most everyone was glued to the hundreds of wasps flooding into the park. The first true screams of terror rose above the generic reggae. As awareness of the wasps spread, so did the realization it was far, far too late. There was nowhere to escape.

The wasps sensed the growing panic and shifted gears. They'd been floating nearly silent earlier, and now that the hunt had well and truly begun, they grew faster, darting through the water park with wings popping and growling like two-stroke lawn mower engines.

Children barreled down waterslides, emerging into sunlight after the enclosed circles, only to find dozens of wasps waiting. Some of the wasps attacked at the top of the stairs, chasing kids into the slides themselves, happy to clutch the slippery, soft skin and ride the plump bodies to the pool at the bottom. The wading areas became clogged with tiny corpses. Some teens jumped from the top, but found that the fall wasn't fatal and the impact snapped bones. That left them immobile, easy prey for the wasps.

The wasps zoomed in on their victims, understanding nothing of mercy, listening only to the overpowering instincts of feeding and growing the population. The special nonslip concrete chewed into human skin like a cheese grater on those poor souls who scrambled onto their backs to get under a plastic table, perversely clear for some reason, so you could see the face of the monstrosity trying to jab you full of squirming larva. Shrieking filled the park as entire families flailed through the blood and chlorine that washed across the rough concrete.

Panicked bodies piled against the doors to the hotel, unaware the same thing was happening on the other side as people inside fled from the wasps from the second pair of trucks. Seniors were stomped. Toddlers were crushed. Doorways became clogged with bodies. Climbing on top of those around wouldn't help. Wasps crawled across the shifting mass, picking off their prey easy as selecting their favorite brands at a supermarket.

Even those in the water had to breathe sometime and even though they'd fight off one wasp to snatch a gasp of air, another wasp would be waiting with cunning patience to lance any soft tissue, often an eye or plump lip. The stinger was the size of a rifle barrel, just as tough, only sharper.

* * * *

Jen and Araminta backed away from the railing. Prey was getting scarce downstairs and wasps continued to surge into the water park, leading to the inevitable invasion of the building. Sheila had vanished; the room door was open. Either panic or an unshakable loyalty in her employers had driven her back downstairs. "How'd she even find us?" Jen asked, shutting the sliding glass door behind them.

"I don't care. I just need to know the plan," Araminta said.

Jen shook her head as they moved to the front door. "Not many options. Get downstairs. One way or another. Get far away, right?" She clasped hands with her friend, who nodded back with an equally ferocious stare.

"We fight and keep going," Araminta said. It was more of a chant or prayer than a conscious thought, and Jen understood it meant much more. It meant they were ready to smash wasps. It was a confirmation that each one was prepared to die in the process of saving the other. It meant it was time to go.

Jen wedged a solid-wood suit jacket hanger in their door, keeping the lock from catching. The hall was a turmoil of blinking, buzzing chaos; someone had pulled the fire alarm. Luckily, the fire sprinklers had not been triggered, even though this was a hotel. Yet. A few people from rooms on the opposite side of the building stood around in confusion. The general sense, though, was to get down to the elevators and stairwell at the end of the wing.

Araminta and Jen tried to coax the stragglers to move faster as they hurried down the hall. "Folks, please," Araminta said, loud, but not quite loud enough to qualify as shouting so as to avoid a panic. "There's been a terrible accident in the water park, and we all have to get downstairs as soon as possible."

An older lady, her wig slightly askew, asked, "Is the building on fire?"

"I wish," Jen said.

The elevator gave a gentle, reassuring *ding*. The group turned to it.

"I'm not sure we should—" Jen started to say.

As the doors separated, a dying woman who'd been slumped against them fell out. A dozen more bodies covered the floor. Three wasps, each the size of a teenage golden retriever, rose into the air with the sound of revving chain saws.

Everyone shrieked and ran. Two weren't fast enough, and the wasps took them down.

The word *fire* stuck with Jen somehow, and as she ran for the southern far end of the hall, back toward the center of the hotel with everyone else, she zeroed in on a red box. It jutted out of the wall exactly halfway between each elevator bank. She skidded to a stop and used her elbow to break the glass. This triggered a fresh round of alarms. She grabbed the fire extinguisher inside and turned to the lone wasp following. The other two were still feeding back at the elevators.

She broke the seal and ripped the ring away, aiming the nozzle with her right hand, supporting the base with her left. She waited, allowing it to get closer. "Come on, you beautiful monster, you." It was true. In spite of the horrifying circumstances, part of Jen still admired the grace and elegance that Mother Nature had birthed. She managed to wait until it got within ten feet, then blasted it with chemicals designed to kill fire.

The foam blinded the wasp and it crashed into the wall. The tarsal claws left gouges in the tasteful wallpaper. It hung on and wiped at its face with its antennae, then looked at her.

Jen ran. Hung onto the extinguisher. The chemicals wouldn't kill the wasps, but it could slow them down. The weight gave her comfort as well, on some primitive level, as she could always use the tank itself as a club. She sprinted to catch up to the others.

The bigger group were nearly to the main bank of elevators when the stairwell doors a few rooms back burst open and a man staggered out, gasping and trembling. Jen stopped running to avoid crashing into him. A woman slammed into him from behind anyway. More followed. Jen backed away, back to the approaching wasp. She couldn't let herself get trapped under the growing pile of bodies from the mass of people now piling from the stairwell.

Screaming, from inside. Then the full-throated buzz of wings.

The wasps were on the way.

One of the south elevator doors opened. It was empty.

"Go!" Jen shouted at the people who had just come out of the stairs, pointing them to Araminta's group, now jumping inside the open elevator. As they broke into a shuffling run, legs numb from the unexpected climb for their lives, the first wasp emerged. They were so big, only one or two fit through a doorway at a time. Too late to close it now.

Jen backed away. The wasp she'd sprayed with the fire extinguisher was still coming, flying erratically, crashing into walls.

More wriggled their wings through the door and came for her.

She yelled, "Go!" again at Araminta, then turned to the nearest room. It was locked. So was the next. And the next. No choice now. She blasted the wasp still following again and ran back to their original bedroom that Araminta had sweet-talked their way into. Once inside, she jerked the hanger back and slammed the door. Locked it. She knew it was only a matter of time, though. If these wasps wanted her, and they would soon enough, as soon as the other prey was used up, they would be back, and they would smash the door to kindling.

A taste of an idea flared up inside of her for just an instant, that if she could only find somewhere to hide, somewhere she could ride out this initial onslaught, someone would eventually be along to rescue her and any others, since the authorities now had a repellent. Problem was, there was nowhere to hide. Nowhere in the room, anyway.

The bedrooms had no connecting doors to other rooms; it wasn't that kind of hotel, at least not this wing. The air vents were too small, both for her and the wasps. That only left the balcony.

The wasps in the water parks didn't seem to have risen to the fifth floor yet, but again, it was only a matter of time. She didn't open the sliding door, but put her face against it to see if she could see the balcony next door. No. Too far. Too far to jump. She thought about something she could use to bridge the gap, then thought better of it.

If she got over there and found the sliding glass door locked, she'd be in a worse situation. She would be in full view of any wasps below. Breaking the door with the chair or table would only bring more. She'd be stuck again, only worse this time with the windows shattered and wide open for the wasps. Not that glass was ever much of a problem for them anyway.

Something scratched at the room door. They'd come for her and it wasn't surprising. She'd read several verified, peer-review papers over the last five years that proved some species of wasps could not only recognize human faces, but remember them for up to four weeks at a time. She had maybe a few minutes at most. She couldn't stay here, hiding in a closet or under the bed; the wasps would sniff her out.

Jen dashed into the bedroom and ripped the bedsheets off. She carried the whole bundle into the main room and started twisting the top sheet. The scratching at the door became harsher until she heard something crack around the hinges. She tied the top sheet to the fitted sheet and dragged it to the sliding glass door. Grabbed the sculpture, some abstract thing supposed to evoke a coral reef, which adorned the dresser and tied the sheet around it.

She eased open the sliding glass door, being as silent as possible.

The attacks at the front door became more pronounced, more frequent.

She eyeballed the overhang above the balcony and gauged the weight of the sculpture. Still on her knees, she began to swing the sculpture back and forth until she let the sheet trail through her fingers as the sculpture sailed out and up and over the edge of the roof.

It landed with a crunch. She flinched.

Nothing rose to the balcony.

The front door split open, so Jen didn't waste time and shut the sliding glass door while giving the sheet a tug. She used more force than she intended with the sheet and she knew she would have deserved it if the sculpture had ripped free and tumbled to the cement awash with blood below.

The sculpture held.

Jen, barely a hundred pounds soaking wet, scrambled up the sheet, relying mostly on the strength from her shoulders. Once on the roof, she pulled up the sheet quickly, just in case any wasps saw her escape route blowing in the wind. She crouched for a minute, taking everything in, before deciding which direction to run. Smoke rose from at least four different sources, but up on the roof, it mingled and reduced visibility.

Even through the haze of smoke, she saw the massive glass atrium at the center of the complex glinting in the sun. A few maintenance stairwells were scattered around it and she knew this was her best shot. Some kind of heavy thumping rose above the sirens and alarms, but nothing caught her eye or suggested an imminent threat. It receded into the far distance, so she dismissed it. She started across the pebbled roof, keeping low in case any wasps had cruised up over the top of the hotel.

The thumping grew louder again and she flattened herself against the roof as a shadow the size of a full-grown dragon washed over her. She rolled. The helicopter, or whatever it was, was even bigger than the one she'd taken in Honduras; the propellers were so big they looked like wind turbines. It felt so close she could reach out and touch it if she wanted. The gigantic aircraft kept spiraling, fighting physics and gravity the whole way. Hundreds of wasps clung to it and black smoke unfurled from one of the engines.

It roared over her yet again, pilot fighting for control as the colossal machine spun in a tighter and tighter death spiral. The engine's whine rose and rose until it sounded more like some demented dentist's drill. A crash was inevitable.

A flash of blue in the chopper doorway. Blue and red.

It was Andy. Covered in dried blood, wearing his Florida Man costume, and wielding a shotgun.

Their eyes locked and they saw nothing but each other, as if only inches separated them, not thirty or forty yards with one of them in a moving chopper. She saw nothing but love in his eyes and knew without any doubt that he was her man and would be always and forever. She could tell he was shouting something, but heard nothing over the cacophony of the aircraft's desperate, straining engines.

The giant chopper wobbled, clotted with wasps. It spun away and she lost sight of him again. It circled, almost righted itself, but the wasps were too much, and it spiraled into the atrium, where the world exploded.

Jen dropped, covering her head with both arms. Shards of glass filled the air, sliding the very molecules apart. Another deep, ripping explosion erupted out of the crater as the chopper sank out of sight. Tidal waves of fire unfurled out of the terrible chasm, blasting Jen sideways. She felt weightless until gravity reached up and snatched her back, flinging her down into the sunbaked pebbles. She skidded and scraped and came up looking like she'd just rolled out of a motorcycle accident. She turned to what was left of the atrium.

It now looked like some kind of volcano. Smoke unfurled from within.

It was over.

It was done.

Her man was dead.

CHAPTER 28

Ten minutes earlier, the Osprey streaked across central Florida. Haaga relayed current events over the radio. "… the president is still in the greenroom. Secret Service have the backstage entrance barricaded… ah, scratch that. Big guy is on the move. Backstage has been breached."

Andy kept himself focused by loading all the firearms, holding the weapon or magazine between his knees, feeding it rounds with his right hand. He had five shotguns, two pumps, and three semiautos. A few handguns. He'd come across a couple of old SIG Sauer P210s that fit snugly inside his costume. True, he could only hold one at a time, but it was always good to have a backup in case a round jammed the first pistol, and since they were classics, he'd found four magazines. Still, the shotguns were his most potent tool. He searched through the Osprey for anything he could use to carry them: a backpack, nylon straps, a goddamn quiver.

Carver noticed Andy's movements were getting a bit more impatient, a bit more frantic. He got Andy's attention, settled him into one of the bench seats along the hull, knelt in front of him. "Thinking about her will get you killed," he said. "I know you think she's there and she's alive, but this time doesn't sound good. That hope, that can hurt. Sometimes, things don't work out how we want. Are you prepared for what you might find, soldier?" Carver asked.

"No," Andy answered. Truth.

Carver held out four pills. Two for Andy, two for himself. "Swallow one. Snort the other soon as we get there."

Haaga cut into their headsets. "Mass production of repellent has commenced, but delivery is at least four to seven hours away."

They dry-swallowed the pills. "How much longer?" Carver asked the pilot.

"ETA... little less than ten minutes."

Haaga said, "He's on the move again. Be advised all external entrances and exits have been compromised. Local ground forces have been totally overwhelmed."

"Tell your boys to find somewhere to hide," Carver said. "We'll be there lickety-split and hole up until the eggheads work their magic."

"Coming into view," the pilot said. The great machine slowed and descended through thick tropical air while they got their first real look at the Gaylord Palms Resort & Convention Center. Andy didn't know resorts like this even existed. He'd never seen anything like the atrium that dominated the rest of the buildings. The wreckage of the trucks was easily visible. So were the bodies. And the wasps.

"Holy shit," the pilot said. "This is as far as we go. I'll drop you boys off on the expressway there."

"Fuck that," Andy said. He put the barrel of one of the pump shotguns against the pilot's neck. "You can drop us off on the roof."

"Are you crazy? Shoot me and we all die."

"Yeah, he's crazy," Carver said. "He's in love and will gladly kill us all to save his girl. So I'd listen to him."

The pilot shuddered. "You just be ready. I'm not gonna land or anything. For all I know, the weight'll collapse the roof. I'll get close. From there, you jump."

Haaga cut into the headsets again. "Signals are getting glitchy. Sounds like they're retreating deeper into the resort. Last I heard, they'd just entered the eastern edge of the lower levels, the big exhibition hall."

The Osprey zoomed past the news choppers, all keeping a safe distance and relying on their long-range cameras. Then the military choppers, maintaining a security ring several thousand feet out from the smoking complex. The pilot started sweating, cursing under his breath, and eased the Osprey into a sweet spot. Then in a casual tone but with no small amount of satisfaction, said, "I'd hold on about now."

The aircraft dropped like a stone.

Andy's stomach hit the back of his throat and he damn near spewed bile all over the cockpit. Kept it down. Good thing too, as the only thing in his stomach was Carver's magic pill. It hadn't really kicked in yet, but if he threw it up, he'd never feel any effects, and with this rescue, he'd take all the help he could get.

They streaked down, close enough to see the glass in the atrium was still intact. Close enough to see the bodies choking the lazy river. The Osprey banked and the rotors swung heavenward. It rode the wash like a rowboat in a tsunami, the pilot slamming on the big machine's version of brakes. Andy's stomach flopped again.

The sound was incredible, and it caught the wasps' attention.

A swarm shot toward the Osprey as it settled over the southern wing. "Get ready, get—shit, shit!" The wasps hit the chopper and they all felt the impact inside, like getting caught in a rip current. The pilot jerked at the controls, swinging away from the resort, but it was too late. The giant bird couldn't outmaneuver the wasps. They swarmed over the hull and hurtled themselves into the massive turbines. One engine erupted in black smoke and the craft started to spin.

"I'd say that's our sign." Carver grinned. He popped his capsule open, stuck both ends into his nostrils and snorted. "Rock 'n' roll, brother."

Andy imitated him and everything smoothed right the fuck out. He flicked the empty pill halves away and matched Carver's grin. "Rock and *roll*!"

Their sudden euphoria made them feel better, but had no effect on the Osprey's situation, as wasps crawled over it worse than ever, but the sudden attitude adjustment got Andy and Carver thinking proactively, as they say. The V-22 swung in tighter and tighter death spirals while Carver fought his way over to the door and ripped the upper hatch open. Andy hooked his feet under the seat struts, leaned out, and started blasting away.

As soon as he ran out of ammo, he traded Carver for a fresh semiauto. He unloaded that one as well, but it had no effect. More wasps kept coming. Andy had to wedge himself against exposed pipes and wiring as g-forces threatened to suck him to the back of the Osprey.

He continued shooting, even though it had become clearly pointless. Too many wasps.

He froze when he saw Jen, alone, on the hotel roof. The shock lasted only an instant, but even as he screamed he was coming for her, the spinning V-22 swept him away. Carver shook his shoulder. He'd seen Jen too. "We're done. This thing is going down and none of us are gonna make it. You got one chance. You ready?"

"What?"

"Hang on until I tell ya. Then go limp. Got it?"

"What?"

The Osprey swung back to the hotel, drawing even more wasps. "Ready?"

Andy had just begun to turn, the hotel sliding past underneath, when Carver yelled, "Now!"

And kicked him out of the Osprey.

* * * *

Andy missed the edge of the roof at least by ten feet. As he fell, he saw the V-22 spin overhead for the last time. He thought he was supposed to land somewhere on the eastern roof, the parking lot if he was really unlucky. Instead, Andy found himself in midair, plummeting past the wrong rooftop and heading for the water park. He felt warm. He decided he was still dreaming and everything was downright groovy.

The last he saw of Carver was right before the massive Osprey hit the atrium sideways, and apart from the surprised initial burst of glass, the rest of the atrium folded around the V-22 like an eager shroud welcoming the aircraft into its bosom for eternity. The props went off in twin explosions when they hit the walls and the whole mess erupted in a mechanical, volcanic fury as it slammed into the center of the complex.

Andy hit the center of the pool sideways, and maybe that had been the plan all along. It still felt as if he had been slapped into a brick wall. Water and bodies erupted, splashed in all directions as he plummeted through artificially blue water and crunched into the tiles at the bottom. He barely felt the impact. Carver's chemicals still gushed through his bloodstream.

As he floated back up, he had a chance to grab his thoughts. He'd lost all the shotguns. The only weapons he had left were the two SIG Sauers still nestled in the costume's foam rubber six-pack. He hoped they worked while wet. The next step was to find a way out of the pool and head for the roof. He'd figure things out from there once he found Jen.

He rose among the bodies, using a corpse's armpit as cover to snatch a breath.

He was just inches from the surface when he realized the wasps were waiting, using the bodies as rafts, either drinking from the pool or watching his movements. He ducked back down and maneuvered himself under a bigger pile of corpses. Came up directly under a wasp, put the barrel at the surface, and found out if it worked underwater.

It worked just fine, although the nine-millimeter bullets had no immediate effect. The rounds punctured the exoskeleton, singed through the pulpy insides, and popped out the other side, leaving little visible damage. Andy's lungs were starting to burn, so he said to hell with it, aimed at the cluster of what he thought might be the wasp's eyes, and emptied the clip.

Over a dozen bullets pulverized the skull, but that only slowed the wasp down a little.

Andy slammed a new magazine into the pistol, pushed his way up through bodies already swelling with fresh larva and started blasting. He flopped out of the shallow end of the pool, rolled under a bench, dodging swooping wasps and firing at any that got too close. The bullets slowed the wasps down, but only for a second or two.

Behind him, a tornado of fire filled the atrium.

Wasps were everywhere. He had to hide, find someplace to reload. Getting inside the hotel itself would be impossible with only a single pistol. The dead had piled up inside the doorways, making the doors impassable anyway. He'd have to find some other way. Maybe he could sneak through one of the bars that connected the water park to the rest of the hotel.

The resort had other, temporary bars all over the place, tucked among the palm trees and exquisitely trimmed shrubs and hedges, taking full advantage of the star-studded fundraiser. Most of those were too exposed, and the nearby bodies of the bartenders proved there was nowhere to hide.

As he scanned the park, Andy nearly missed the maintenance shed, as it was intended to blend in with the foliage. He dashed across the park, shooting only if the wasps got within five feet. Too often he had to leap over jumbled clumps of a dozen people and all the scattered lounge chairs. Sometimes, there was nothing he could do, and he had to step on the bodies themselves. He apologized the whole way, wheezing out a "Sorry!" with each exhale.

He only found the door when he got close, and the cold realization washed over him that if the door was locked, he was finished. It wasn't. He fell inside and kicked the door shut. Now at least, he had a chance to reload without getting a stinger in his spine. After the brightness of the morning behind him, he couldn't see a damn thing and had to reach out to find the workbench. He knew there might be something useful hanging on the wall, but his eyes were adjusting to the gloom with agonizing slowness. Carver's pills may not have been helping either.

Andy closed his eyes, forced himself to count to ten. Then, just in case, fifteen. When he reopened them, he found that God had smiled upon him. Among the rakes and shovels and safety vests, he found his very own Excalibur. A DeWalt twenty-two-inch cordless hedge trimmer, fully charged. When the trigger was depressed, the eager, thick teeth slid back and forth so fast human eyes could only comprehend it as a blur.

Still, he couldn't hold it and the pistol at the same time. Looking at the ragged remains of the militia duct tape still wrapped around his stump gave him an idea. And like any maintenance shed worth its salt, this particular shed had a fresh roll of gray duct tape. He used his teeth to tear off two fifteen-inch lengths and laid them out on the workbench in an X shape. The DeWalt went in the middle of that, and then his arm on top of the trimmer. The four ends of the tape came over and fastened themselves to his skin.

He thumbed out the air pockets and wrinkles, slapped his forearm, and figured the tape would just about tear his skin off before it gave way. The blade stuck out almost two feet from the end of his stump.

He heard the wasps attacking the door and knew he was out of time. He wound the rest of the roll around his arm, anchoring the trimmer. It wasn't pretty, but it worked. The wasps tore at the door and the lock shook, the hinges moaned.

Lastly, he fit a length of rolled-up tape to depress the trigger. The powerful battery hummed a happy little tune as a vicious whine rose from the shivering steel teeth.

The door split in half, and the first wasp was in his face before he could even yell. Without thinking, he slashed down with his left arm and split the wasp's head wide open. It went berserk, spasming and driving itself up into the dusty two-by-fours on the ceiling. Without time to take a breath, another took its place and headed straight for Andy. He brought the trimmers upwards this time, and sliced the wasp's head right off.

That didn't slow it down much. Momentum kept it buzzing past him until it crashed into the wall. He launched himself at the door and had to slice open another wasp before he pushed through. Once outside, he sprinted around the South Beach pool, heading for one of the bigger bars, something called Wreckers Sports Bar. It seemed to be closer to the center of the resort. He still had to find a way around the inferno at the center of the resort hotel, but again, he'd cross that bridge when he got to it.

It got dark. At first he thought clouds had covered the sun. Then he realized he'd been stupidly optimistic. Hordes of wasps swarmed overhead; so many they dimmed the Florida sunshine.

If any got close, they lost wings, legs, and even their heads sometimes, depending on the angle. He ran, ducked, spun, rolled, weaved, and bobbed his way across the water park, leaving twitching wasp bodies in his wake.

The western doors to the sports bar were wide open, propped open by a couple of dead men who lay face down. Andy kept his speed up and leaped over the bodies in the doorway. He figured the best chance he had was to keep the element of surprise on his side. He burst on top of any wasps in the place and chopped them in half before they had a chance to get turned around and come after him. He used the trimmer as much as possible, saving the pistol for emergencies. Once he was out of ammo, that was it. He had no way to get any more, and the DeWalt battery would last at least thirty to forty minutes on full power.

After that, he had no idea.

He only hoped he could find Jen in that time.

Andy pumped and faked his way through the sports bar in a manner that would make the running backs on the big-screen TVs proud. The kitchen itself in the back wasn't a proper kitchen; it was only a prep area for warming food that had been cooked somewhere else on the property. But there was a back door.

It led to a bland, industrial corridor. It was empty. A thick layer of gray smoke clung to the pipes that ran along the ceiling. A disconcerting rumble from somewhere deeper in the resort made the walls tremble. He knew that meant that time was running out even faster. Another explosion might bring the walls down around them.

He froze, unsure of which way to turn. Left would be north, while right led south, deeper into the resort. He figured there'd be more stairwells to the roof if he plunged farther into the hotel, so he turned right and headed down the corridor. He was so anxious, he damn near opened the first set of double doors he came upon, but after burning his palm on the door handle, figured it might be smarter to come around and approach the burning center from a better angle, instead of jumping right into the goddamn fire.

He ignored the next five or six doorways, noting the skein of smoke seeping through the cracks, and kept going. The hallway ended in a wide stairwell headed up to the next level, and equally wide stairs leading down. He chose to go down, guessing he'd have better luck going down and under the burning chaos the Osprey had wrought. And he hoped he'd find more stairwells that led to the roof down in the basement, emergency stairs that only needed a single door, not this wide-open path for employees heading to their various departments.

The stairs ended at the exhibition level, a huge space where hundreds of booths could be set up, showcasing the extreme niches of a new industry every damn week. He cracked one of the doors, putting his eye up to the sliver of light. It appeared that the wasps had interrupted the latest convention, some kind of dentist thing, judging from all the advertising that featured unnatural photoshopped pictures of human teeth and gums, incredibly specialized equipment, the latest X-ray technology, and all the other uncomfortable-looking sharp tools on display.

The wasps had left the usual evidence of an attack. Still-living bodies lay scattered across the shining concrete, unable to move as the huge larvae chewed into their fatty tissues and noncritical organs like the spleen or appendix and the stomach. A few children had been left semiconscious, as they could only be filled up with one or two wasp larvae. Most of the children inside had been eaten.

A few of the booth walls had been knocked down in the panic. Reflective streamers hanging from a table fluttered from the air-conditioning, but that was the only movement.

At least, as far as Andy could tell. Nothing rose over the fabric and plastic booth walls.

Above, muted explosions triggered by the Osprey's death spasms rippled and echoed through the walls, reminding him he was running out of time. He unwrapped the twisted length of tape that held the trimmer trigger down and let the DeWalt rest for a second. The sudden silence in such a vast hall made him nervous, a feeling that had to fight to rise above the fear-deadening effects of Carver's pill.

He thought he heard shooting, but it stopped and remained quiet. He waited, counting again. It wasn't so much that the counting gave him a measurement of some sort to follow, but that it forced him to calm down and slow his racing heart. He held his breath and pushed through the door.

The endless convention center remained silent. No wasps flew at him. He slid to the right, sticking to the perimeter of the hall. No way did he want to get turned around and lose his sense of direction in all those dentist booths. More shooting. This time, the sound was clearer and he could follow the direction.

He jogged toward the far end, still unsure exactly of where he could find whoever was firing weapons. It was more than one, he was sure of it. He came upon a wide set of swinging doors with narrow portholes set in them. Kitchen doors.

Shooting exploded at the end. Tight bursts of gunfire that refused to quit.

Andy dropped low, pushed inside the doors, found the wide hallway empty. The absence of wasps made him nervous, but he followed the shooting all the way to another set of swinging doors.

Andy pulled his trigger tape tight and revved the DeWalt. Settled himself into a battle stance and anchored the tape. The steel teeth got loud. Wasps pushed through the swinging kitchen doors and zoomed toward him. He sliced through the first wasp, turned gracefully to let the next one miss him until he brought his left arm down in a devastating blow that left it in three pieces before it had even thought about starting an attack.

He tore through the next few before the wasps figured out he was dangerous. Beyond the trimmer, he still had a full magazine in the SIG Sauer in his right hand, and a second SIG Sauer twin waiting in the left folds of the foam rubber abdomen of the costume. He kicked open the kitchen doors.

He looked out over one of the resort's anchor kitchens, endless rows of counters, burners, and stoves. Hundreds of wasps were hunting the president's group, thinning the herd each time an opportunity presented itself. There were only five Secret Service people left, and they hustled the president through the room, doing their absolute damnedest to kill every single wasp that got within ten yards, using fire axes on the wasps. They used their firearms as little as possible, because they knew that sooner or later, they would run out of ammunition, and they would find themselves as hosts to squirming larvae and beg their living colleagues for the sweet release of death.

A couple dozen wasps started for him.

He waited for them, knowing using the trimmer was his only chance as well.

Jen burst through the doors to the right, putting herself right between the president and his Secret Service detail and Andy. She'd found another fire extinguisher. They only had an instant to register that it was actually each other before the wasps attacked.

Andy brought the trimmer up, down, across, and used his pistol if any got too close. The Secret Service got picked off, one by one, until there was only three of them left, two sandwiching the president, using their fallen colleagues' pistols in both hands, the third firing almost blindly. Jen used the foam to keep her attackers at bay.

The wasps would not stop.

Especially not for someone with only a fire extinguisher. Twenty or thirty massed and came after her. She ran toward him, but Andy knew he was too far away to reach her in time. He dropped his empty SIG Sauer, grabbed the second one, and without thinking emptied the entire clip into the cloud of wasps following Jen.

It worked. Slowed the wasps down just enough for her to give them another blast of foam to further disorient them. The ones that had been struck by Andy's bullets would eventually die; it would just take a while.

What he didn't know, or anybody really, was that one particular nine-millimeter round, the third shell down in the magazine, to be specific, punched through a wasp's abdomen and exited the other side, having lost just enough velocity so that when it hit the president right in his forehead above his left eye and tore through his brain, popping out the back of his skull and burying itself in drywall, at least it wasn't going as fast as normal.

He dropped like a rock.

One of the Secret Service reacted immediately and slapped gel pads across the holes in the president's head and pulled him into a walk-in freezer while the two others covered them and kept firing at wasps.

Andy and Jen were now close enough to touch. Jen stayed low and out of the way while Andy swung the trimmer with precision, but he was losing strength in his bad arm. Wasps filled the room; their angry buzzing echoed off the stainless steel and vibrated right into their souls. They were finished. But at least they would die together. She took his right hand.

Andy knew it was over as well. The DeWalt battery was steadily dropping in pitch and starting to hiccup. He kept slashing, and while the pile of dead wasp parts littering the tiles around them grew and grew, more filled the air, swarming into the kitchen to finish the humans and eat in peace.

Then Jen saw the cooler, next to the freezer where at least one of the Secret Service men had dragged the president. She pulled Andy toward it. The door would be heavy, thick enough to keep the cold inside. It might buy them time. Perhaps just a few minutes.

Better than nothing.

But then the last remaining Secret Service agent was shouting incoherently at the wasps, holding aloft some kind of black cylinder about five inches long. Jen didn't know what it was until she watched him pull the ring out and shut his eyes.

She jerked the cooler door open, fell backwards, with Andy landing on top of her.

The explosion blew the heavy door shut.

For a long time, there was only darkness and silence.

Then hands, feeling her, making sure she wasn't broken or bleeding. She was doing the same to Andy, but touching both fresh and dried blood and wounds everywhere. He flinched and grunted in pain, but then chuckled. "I'll live. You?"

She listened to the silence outside the door, felt the chill in the air. The power was still on. She tested the door. It wouldn't move. Something had fallen against it. She hoped it wasn't the roof. Still, they had enough air to breath and no wasps. And with the president so close, she knew the authorities wouldn't stop looking until they found him, dead or alive. The last time she'd seen him, he'd been shot in the head, so who knew.

She realized that Andy couldn't see her smile, but it didn't matter. She didn't stop. Couldn't. They were safe. "I'm good. Shouldn't take long for them to evacuate the resort with the repellent. Maybe within hours."

She reached up and touched his face. Andy was smiling as well. He said, "Well, we better get busy, then."

Editor's Note:

The author conducted hundreds of interviews and spent countless, exhaustive hours researching this definitive record of the tragic events of South Florida, and as of publication, would like to update the public on a few key events.

The few surviving wasps are now property of the Department of Homeland Security and after a strong campaign by Ms. Huang, have been officially named *Fletcherson Hymenoptae*.

Araminta Ross managed to find shelter for over thirty-seven survivors of the Gaylord Palms Resort & Convention Center, and all were rescued eleven hours after the initial breach of the property.

Unidentified bone and tooth fragments are all that apparently remain of William Alexander Carver, yet rumors of sightings persist, primarily in southern India and Western Australia.

Andrew Shaw is set to be released from a rehabilitation facility in several months. Jennifer Huang has stated she will be waiting for him.

And the president, as everyone knows, is doing just fine. Despite the controversy, medical experts marvel that he continues to perform his duties consistently in more or less the same way as the previous two years, despite missing a third of his brain.

SLEEP TIGHT

By Jeff Jacobson

They hide in mattresses. They wait till you're asleep. They rise in the dead of night to feast on your blood. They can multiply by the hundreds in less than a week. They are one of the most loathsome, hellish species to ever grace God's green earth. Thought to be eradicated decades ago, thanks to global travel they're back. And with them comes a nightmare beyond imagining.

Bedbugs. Infected with a plague virus so deadly it makes Ebola look like a summer cold. One bite turns people into homicidal maniacs.

Now they're in Chicago. And migrating to all points north, south, east, and west. The rest of the world is already itching. The US government and the CDC are helpless to stop it. Only one man knows what's causing the epidemic. And the powers that be want him dead.

Look for *Sleep Tight*, on sale now!

Printed in the United States
by Baker & Taylor Publisher Services